Counting Chimneys

Also by Sandy Taylor:

Brighton Girls Trilogy
The Girls from See Saw Lane (Book 1)

Counting Chimneys

SANDY TAYLOR

bookouture

Published by Bookouture

An imprint of StoryFire Ltd.
23 Sussex Road, Ickenham, UB10 8PN
United Kingdom

www.bookouture.com

ISBN: 978-1-78681-016-8
eBook ISBN: 978-1-78681-017-5

This book is a work of fiction. Names, characters, businesses,
organizations, places and events other than those clearly in
the public domain, are either the product of the author's
imagination or are used fictitiously. Any resemblance to actual
persons, living or dead, events or locales is entirely coincidental.

To my children Kate and Bo.
Love you all the world and tuppence on Sundays.

CHAPTER ONE

London
1969

It was one of those lovely days that sometimes happen in March when the air is warm and people have left their coats at home, the daffodils are bobbing in the plastic buckets outside flower shops and you know that spring is just around the corner.

I decided to walk back to my flat after work, rather than catching the bus as usual. The North London streets were busy with commuters, and I wove in and out of them, smiling at everyone and feeling so happy to be part of the city, a single girl with a career, living my life just how I wanted. I stopped at the corner shop to buy bread, milk, cheese and tomatoes and treated myself to a magazine.

'You're looking cheerful,' said Mrs Spatchcock, the owner, suspiciously. She was suspicious of everyone because everyone, she said, was a potential shoplifter – even regulars like me.

'I am cheerful,' I replied, adding a tube of peppermints.

'Huh,' said Mrs Spatchcock. 'Well you want to be careful going around smiling like that. The day's not over yet. There's still plenty of time for things to go wrong.'

'Good day to you too,' I said. She wasn't going to bring me down, not that day.

I cut through the park, smiling at the familiar characters that always seemed to be there: the man who hugged trees, the dog walker who must have had half the dogs in Islington running round her heels, young mothers with prams and the joggers who circled the park in a never-ending production line. If someone had told me four years ago that I could feel this happy I would have laughed at them, but I *was* happy. I had good friends, a great job on a music magazine and the nicest and kindest, not to mention sexiest, boyfriend in the whole world. I knew I was lucky, but now and again a niggling thought would nudge at my brain. I was happy, but did I deserve to be? Time for a Scarlett O'Hara moment: 'I would think about that tomorrow.' For now I was going to enjoy this beautiful day.

I almost skipped along Victoria Terrace, past the tall Victorian houses with their long windows and their steps. I avoided the children playing marbles on the pavement and listened to 'Hey Jude' coming out of an open window. The cherry trees were just coming into blossom, and the grey paving slabs were already dotted with pink petals, like confetti. I said 'hello' to a couple of neighbours, trotted up the steps to the front door of number 59 and opened it with my key. I was met with the familiar mixture of smells: Mr Sheen furniture polish, bleach, Rive Gauche – the perfume that my friend Polly wore all the time – and cats.

The two of us rented rooms in 59 Victoria Terrace. Our landlady, Evelyn Pierce, lived on the ground floor, and we had to go through her hall to reach the stairs. The telephone was mounted on the wall just outside her front room. This was a constant source of irritation, partly because it meant going up or down stairs every time we wanted to make a call or answer the phone, and partly because its location made it impossible to have a private conversation. Mrs P did not even bother trying to pretend she didn't eavesdrop. It was her favourite pastime. She called it 'taking an interest', because she saw it as her duty to look after the moral well-being of Polly and me.

There was a long wooden table against the wall beneath the telephone where the phone directories were stacked. This was where our post was laid out in the morning and where we left messages for one another.

I stopped and picked up a letter addressed to me. There were also two yellow slips of paper, the kind reserved for telephone messages, with my name on: Dottie.

Without looking at them, I went up two flights of stairs and into my room. It was not a large room, but it wasn't small either, and although I had no say in the decor, which was entirely to Mrs P's pink and peachy floral taste, I had added my own touches: posters and a couple of nice lamps from Habitat and throws over the furniture to tone it down a bit. I switched on the kettle to make tea then went over to the window, slid open the sash to let in the fresh air and the traffic noises and sat down to read my messages.

The first made my stomach flutter with pleasure. It was written in Polly's scrawled writing and said:

Message for Dottie

Time 5:15 pm

From Polly, your attractive housemate

Message Joe called (!!!) wants to meet you tonight he has a surprise for you am not supposed to say but it's TICKETS TO SEE 'THE WHO' on April 23rd!!!!!!

Action required Call him back ASAP or I will

Any other information Knock on my door when you're back I have BUNS!!!!

I leaned my head back, letting my hair fall over the back of the chair. The sunlight was warm on my face. Could the day get any better? I wondered. I could have tea and buns and a good gossip with Polly and then, if the bathroom was free and there was still some hot water left, I'd have a bath and wash my hair, put on the amazing new maxi dress I'd bought in C&A earlier that week and then I'd go out and meet Joe – probably the most perfect boyfriend in the world – and he could surprise me with tickets to see one of my favourite bands in the whole world EVER, although I still remained loyal to Paul McCartney and… Who knows after that?

I looked at the second message. This was in Mrs Pierce's handwriting and was as curly and fussy as her wallpaper.

It said:

Message for: Miss D Perks, lodger

Time: 10 a.m.

From: Mrs E Pierce, landlady

Message: Your sister Rita called to let you know the baby's christening will be at 3 p.m. on April 23rd followed by a reception at her house. As the chief godmother your presence is required all weekend.

Action required: None. Await official invitation

Any other information: Your sister sounds a dear. Why don't you ever call her?

CHAPTER TWO

Joe and I were snuggled up together half watching *Peyton Place*. The little television took pride of place in the living room. Mrs P was always telling us how lucky we were to have access to a television, and we knew she was right. It was very small and you needed a reasonable amount of imagination to work out what the picture on the flickering screen was supposed to be. Right now Mia Farrow appeared to be walking through a white field at night, in the middle of a heavy snowstorm.

We were the only two people in the living room, because it was our night for the couch. Polly and I had a rota pinned to the wall in the kitchen with our names on and our allocated nights. Mrs P allowed gentlemen callers, as she liked to call them, as long as they were gone by 10.30 p.m. sharp and they didn't go within a mile of a bedroom.

Joe nuzzled his face into my neck. 'You smell nice,' he said. 'What is it?'

'Polly's Rive Gauche,' I said.

'Strange name for a perfume.'

'No, I mean the name of the perfume is Rive Gauche, but it belongs to Polly. She let me borrow a couple of squirts earlier.'

'Well it's nice, whoever it belongs to.'

'Thanks.'

'And you look nice tonight.'

'C&A bargain rail.'

'You're funny, do you know that?'

'Yes, I rather think I do.' The credits for Peyton Place rolled down the screen. 'Fancy a coffee?' I said.

'Sounds good.'

I stood up and stretched then walked into the little kitchen and filled the kettle. The water did its usual spitting as it came out of the tap. It used to make me jump in the beginning, but now I was so used to it that I thought something was wrong if it didn't spit. Darkness was falling beyond the window; London was quietening down, settling in for the night. I lit the only gas ring on the cooker and waited for the kettle to boil. There was a film of grease half-way up the washing-up bowl, and the kitchen window needed a clean. Stockings hung over the drying rack overhead. Neither of us were very good at cleaning up – we were too busy being young and having fun to worry about that. Now and then Mrs P would come upstairs and have a grumble, and then we'd have a frantic clean up for fear she would chuck us out, but apart from those occasions, we were a bit lazy about the domestic arrangements.

I thought about the nice things that Joe had just said about me. Now I was able to accept a compliment without making some smart-alec comment. If someone told me I looked nice, I believed them, which hadn't always been the case. Polly said I still thought of myself as the fat girl, and she was probably right. I always made sure I laughed at myself before anyone else had a chance to. I wasn't fat any more – I wasn't exactly thin either – but I had accepted that the fat girl would always be a part of me. Life had taught me that there were more important things than how I looked.

The kettle began to jump about and whistle. I sniffed the contents of the bottle of milk we kept in the cupboard under the sink, which was the coolest place in the flat.

'Black all right?' I shouted to Joe.

'Milk gone off again?' he said as I brought the two cups in and put them on the coffee table.

'Fraid so.'

'It's okay, I'm getting a taste for black coffee, definitely more sophisticated.'

'Oh definitely.'

Joe put his arm around me. 'I wish you weren't going away this weekend.'

'I have to. I'm the godmother. I would never be forgiven if I didn't go.'

'I can't believe I'm going to see The Who with my brother and not you.'

'Don't talk about it. I'm beginning to think my darling sister practises witchcraft on the side and deliberately picked the day of the concert for the christening.'

'I'll miss you.'

'I'll miss you too,' I said, snuggling into him, and I would. We saw each other practically every evening, and it had been like that almost from the start.

We had met a year ago at a promotional night for the magazine *Trend* I worked for. Joe had come along with a friend, and I had been passing round plates of food. He'd stared suspiciously at the canapés and said, 'Is that fish or meat?'

I'd looked down at the food. 'I haven't a clue,' I'd said, laughing. 'But it smells okay.' Then he'd taken the tray from me and put it down on a nearby table. 'Fancy a dance?' he'd asked, and before I'd had a chance to respond, he'd led me onto the small dance floor and taken me into his arms. I remember thinking how well our bodies fitted, the gentle pressure of his hand on my back, and how smooth his face felt against mine. After the dance I'd gone back to passing out food and drinks and making sure that all our guests were happy. Every now and then I would catch his eye, and we would smile at each other. At the end of the evening I wasn't surprised to find him waiting for me. We'd walked hand in hand through the dark streets of North London to his flat in Holloway Road. I wasn't in the habit of going home with strange men but Joe hadn't felt strange. There'd been something about him that I liked. I'd felt safe with this boy.

We'd lain on his bed listening to his *Revolver* LP, he'd lit a candle that was wedged into the top of a rosé wine bottle and then he'd turned off the light. We hadn't spoken at first – we'd just lain there listening to the Beatles singing 'Doctor Robert'. I'd closed my eyes as he'd run his hand gently up and down my arm. Then we'd spoken about our pasts. I'd told him about my funny, bonkers family. He'd told me about his rather normal one. I'd told him about my friend Mary Pickles. I hadn't realised I was crying till I felt Joe gently wiping away the tears that were running down my face. It was in that moment that I knew this was something special. I'd turned my body into his and we'd made love, gently at first and then with a passion I hadn't known existed, and then I'd cried again and felt stupid for crying, but it was okay – Joe had let me cry until I fell asleep in his arms.

'Penny for them,' he whispered into my hair now.

'Oh they're worth more than a penny,' I said. 'I was remembering the first time we made love.'

Joe stood up. 'Fancy a rerun?' he said, smiling down at me and holding out his hand.

'Not unless you want to get me chucked out of the flat.'

Joe sat down again and put his arm around me. 'You could always move in with me.'

'Now there's a thought,' I said smiling at him.

CHAPTER THREE

As soon as I walked out of Brighton station I could smell the sea, that particular smell that goes with seaside towns, a mixture of seaweed and orange peel and fish and chips. The air was filled with the taste of salt, a sharp tang that stuck to my tongue and coated my lips. The wind blowing up West Street from the promenade carried memories that settled on my shoulders like an old overcoat. I walked down towards the seafront. So much had changed since I was a girl but not the sea or the beach. This place was the keeper of all my dearest memories. They were there amongst the pebbles and the rock pools. They ran along the beach, splashing and laughing as they plunged into the icy cold water. No one else saw what I saw when they leaned on these old green railings. Only I could see those moments caught in time – those precious memories with my best friend Mary Pickles. Wherever I went in my life I knew that this was where I would always find her.

I caught a bus back to the estate and walked the last few hundred yards from the bus stop to the house where I'd spent my childhood. During the course of the journey I had somehow gone from being a young, free, fashionable young woman into an awkward ugly duckling. As soon as Mum opened the front door to the house wearing the same pinny she always wore and drying her hands on the same dishcloth she always used to dry up, I felt the transformation was complete.

'Look at you! You're a sight for sore eyes!' Mum said, hugging me close. Her wiry hair was rough against my cheek. She let me go and stepped back, holding onto the tops of my arms with her hands. 'I swear you get more sophisticated every time we see you! I hate to say it but London seems to suit you.'

'It's good to see you, Mum,' I said, kissing her cheek.

'Why don't you go up and unpack and freshen up, and I'll put the kettle on,' said Mum. 'I made you some jam tarts specially.'

I put my head round the living-room door. My sister Rita was sitting on the sofa next to her husband Nigel, baby Miranda was sitting on the floor and Dad was in his usual chair by the fire. He winked at me and grinned. I said hello to everyone then hauled my case up the narrow stairs and into my old bedroom, the one I used to share with Rita. All the old furniture was still there: the two single beds, the wardrobe and the chest of drawers. It was all crammed together, nothing matched anything else, and it all seemed a bit dowdy and old-fashioned. But it was home.

I took everything out of my case, hung the dress and coat I'd bought specially for the christening in the wardrobe, and laid my cosmetics and washing stuff on the top of the drawers. Then I sat down on the bed. The room looked just the same as it always did; it was as if I had never gone away. I remembered counting the days until Rita got married and I would have the room to myself. I had imagined Mary and I spending hours in this room trying out new make-up, fiddling with our hair and listening to our favourite records. I picked up the framed photo of us that stood on the cabinet next to my bed and even though it had been taken eight years ago, I remembered the moment as if it was yesterday. Mary had been given a brownie camera for her fifteenth birthday and we had gone down to Brighton seafront. We'd asked an elderly couple who were walking along the prom to take our picture. We'd sat on the railings, and I had my arm around Mary's shoulder. It was windy that day and the breeze was ruffling our skirts and Mary's hair had blown across her face. We were both laughing into the camera.

I dusted the glass with the sleeve of my cardigan, then I traced the outline of Mary's face with my finger. I still missed her.

I could hear the baby crying downstairs and Rita's voice rising above everyone else's. I knew they were all waiting for me, but I didn't want to move. I knew Mum was worried about me. For all she said about me being sophisticated, I could see the way she looked at me sometimes, as if she were trying to read my mind. I had to try and look happy all the time, which was wearing. In London I could be myself, but here I felt suffocated. I loved my family but there were too many memories in this house, in this town.

'What are you doing up there, Dottie?' Mum shouted.

'I'm coming,' I shouted back and headed downstairs.

It was very warm in the living room. Everyone except Dad was staring at the baby, who had stopped crying and was on Mum's lap, holding onto her fingers with her fat little hands and trying to stand up on two stiff little legs. Her eyes were red and her nose was running. The last time I'd seen her she'd still been a little baby, but she was growing up, she was changing, and I hadn't been here to see it. I told myself it was because of work and Joe, but it was more than that. I loved my family, but being back in Brighton unsettled me. It was easier in London. I had my work, and I had Joe and Polly. In London I could convince myself that the past was behind me, but that was just geography wasn't it? Every time I returned home, the past was there to meet me as soon as I stepped off the train.

'Her nose is running,' I said, gesturing in the general direction of the baby.

'What do you mean... *her?* She *has* got a name, you know. It's Miranda Louise, which is a very pretty name, and I'd be obliged if you used it,' said Rita. She had gone all red in the face.

'Sorry,' I said. 'Miranda's nose is running.'

'That's because she's off colour, Aunty Dottie,' said Mum. She smiled in a slightly scary way, put her face close to the baby's and said in a silly voice: 'Aren't you, my little precious? You're off colour, your little tummy wummy's poorly, isn't it?'

'I'd rather you didn't speak to her like a baby, Mother,' said Rita.

My dad, who had been sitting reading the paper, looked up and said: 'She *is* a baby. How's your mum supposed to speak to her? Like she's an old-age pensioner?'

'Now, Nelson,' said Mum. 'Our Rita's got a perfect right to say what she wants and what she doesn't want where her baby is concerned.'

'Thank you, Mother,' said Rita.

Dad looked up from his paper. 'And when did you start calling your mum 'Mother'? What's wrong with 'Mum' all of a sudden?'

'I think Mother's more polite. It's what I shall teach Miranda Louise to call me.'

'Stuff and nonsense,' said Dad. 'What does Nigel think about all this?'

Rita's husband, who had been sitting quietly, nearly jumped out of his skin. His ears went all red, and he was opening and closing his mouth like a fish.

'Well,' said Dad, 'haven't you got an opinion, Nigel? Or are you under our Rita's thumb already?'

Nigel seemed to have completely lost the ability to form a sentence, and a red rash was beginning to creep up his neck. He started pulling at his collar as if he was choking.

'Take no notice of him, Nigel,' said Mum. 'He had a port at lunchtime to wet the baby's head and port always makes him gobby.'

I thought I had better help Dad out and show some interest in my beloved sister and her offspring. I mean, I was glad Nigel and Rita had eventually managed to have a baby – they had waited a long time to get her – but, according to Rita, no one had had a labour like she had and no baby was as perfect as hers. I looked over at Miranda, who was trying to pull Mum's glasses off her nose. She was rather sweet, but I was pretty sure she had inherited Nigel's sticky-out ears. We stared at each other suspiciously then she sneezed and a load of snot shot out of her nose, which she then proceeded to rub all over her face with a tight little fist.

'Nelson get me some toilet paper quick,' said Mum, holding Miranda at arm's length.

Dad looked up from behind the paper. 'What do you want toilet paper for?'

'Are you blind as well as daft?' said Mum, rolling her eyes up to the ceiling. 'Miranda needs her face wiping.'

'Why can't Rita go?' said Dad.

'Because she's resting.'

'*I'm* resting.'

'Don't worry, Mother,' said Rita in a martyred kind of way. 'I'll get it.'

'You will *not,* our Rita, your father will. Nelson, get up out of that chair or I won't be responsible.'

'All right, all right, keep your hair on, Maureen, I'm going.'

'Well don't make such a meal of it.'

Dad got up from his chair, folded his paper very precisely and went to get the toilet paper, winking at me on his way out the door.

'You look tired, love,' said Mum to Rita. 'Did Miranda have trouble sleeping again last night?'

'She doesn't need much sleep,' said Rita. 'Does she, Nigel?'

Nigel, who looked as if he was about to nod off, nearly slid off the couch. 'Sorry, Rita, what?'

'I was just saying, Miranda doesn't need much sleep.'

'Erm no.'

'Well don't just sit there, tell them why?' said Rita, settling herself back in the chair and folding her arms, as if she was preparing to bask in whatever wonderful revelation Nigel was about to bestow on us about why Miranda Louise didn't need much sleep.

'Rita read in a book…' started Nigel.

'Oh for heaven's sake, I didn't read it in a book, I saw it on the television – we've got a coloured one now, Dottie.' As if we didn't know! 'Anyway this doctor said that bright children don't need much sleep. It's all to do with their brains being so active.'

'Dottie didn't need much sleep,' said Mum.

Rita chose to ignore that. 'So we don't mind, do we, Nigel?'

'No, no, we don't mind,' said Nigel, looking as if he'd willingly donate a kidney for a good kip.

Dad came back in with the toilet paper.

'Took long enough, didn't you?' said Mum, taking it from him and starting to wipe Miranda's face.

'I took the opportunity while I was in there.'

'You should have given me the paper first and took the opportunity afterwards. Look at the state of Miranda's face!'

'I need a fag,' said Dad.

'Well, make sure you go outside,' said Rita. 'I'm not having smoke in the house with Miranda Louise here.'

'I smoked in the house when you were young,' said Dad.

'Yes,' said Rita, 'and we went to school smelling like three packets of Woodbines.'

Rita came out with these really funny comments and what made them even funnier was that she was being deadly serious. Dad wasn't amused though.

'Bloody hell,' he said. 'It comes to something when I'm told what to do in my own house. Fine. I'll go outside.'

'I'll come with you,' I said and followed Dad through the kitchen and out the back door. We sat on the steps leading down to the garden.

'It'll get better, Dad,' I said, linking my arm through his.

'Will it?' he said gloomily.

'I bet all new mums are fussy in the beginning.'

'It's nice to have you home, love,' he said, smiling at me. 'We don't see nearly enough of you these days.'

'I'm sorry, Dad, it's work.'

'Is it, Dottie?'

I leaned over and kissed his stubbly cheek. 'It's other things as well, Dad.'

'I know it is, love'

'But I'm fine, really I am, and it's getting easier.'

'Your mum and I worry about you.'

'I know you do.'

We sat quietly together for a bit and I slipped my arm through his. 'I promise I will try to get home more often.'

'We'd all like that, love. You're missed.'

Dad took a last drag on his fag, tossed the end into the flower-bed and we went inside. As we went into the front room I heard Mary's name mentioned.

'What were you saying about Mary?' I asked.

Rita looked up. 'I was just telling Mother that Mary Pickles' husband Ralph is getting married to Nigel's cousin Fiona and we've invited them to the christening tomorrow.'

I felt in that moment that any moving on I'd done had been completely wiped out. It was as if I'd been punched in the stomach. Rita must have noticed.

'What?' she said.

I didn't know what to say, but Mum saved me from answering.

'Dottie finds it hard, Rita,' she said.

'Oh for heaven's sake,' said Rita. 'Mary has been dead for four years and you're all still talking about her in whispers. I'm surprised you haven't applied to Rome to have her canonized.'

'That's unkind, Rita,' said Mum. 'Mary was very important to Dottie. It takes a long time to get over a loss like that.'

'Well at least this time Ralph Bennett is marrying someone because he *wants* to, not because he *has* to. And I'd be obliged if you'd bear in mind that tomorrow is all about me and Nigel and Miranda Louise and not about Dottie and Mary Pickles.'

Dad winked at me. 'Don't worry, Rita. I don't think that's something we're likely to forget,' he said.

CHAPTER FOUR

I didn't sleep well that night. It might have been the lumpy old mattress on my bed, or the fact that the green and cream striped winceyette sheets were worn and slightly damp, or maybe it was the quiet of the estate after London. Perhaps I was missing the traffic noises and the hustle and bustle of the city. I'd grown up as part of a generation of children on the council estate, and now most of us had moved away or moved on, and it was mainly older people that lived in the houses surrounding Mum and Dad's. The gardens were better cared for, there were fewer toys and motor-bikes in the front yards and more net curtains up at the front windows, but everything was quieter.

Or maybe I didn't sleep because every time I closed my eyes all I saw was the face of Ralph Bennett. His lovely face, the face that I'd loved and lost and which, by the sounds of it, was about to marry somebody else. I wish I didn't feel like this every time I came home. It made coming home something to worry about rather than something to look forward to. I loved spending time with my family but Brighton was too full of memories. The sights, the smells, the sounds of my hometown pulled me back like a magnet to somewhere I didn't want to go. There were times when I wondered whether it would have been easier to have stayed, to have gone through the pain of losing my best friend and the boy I loved, but when Mary died my only thought was to get away from this place, to walk out of the door and never come back, but life's not that simple, is it? Coming home is like rubbing salt into a wound that is trying to heal, and so I walk the pavements I walked with Mary and Ralph, I go out of my way to pass the café that is haunted by the people we were. I walk beside the sea, and

I sit on our special bench by the lake. I open the door to the past and let it back into my heart, and tomorrow I will have to face Ralph and I am frightened that my heart is going to break all over again. What does all that say about my feelings for Joe?

Having given up on sleep I got dressed and went downstairs to make a cup of tea. Dad was already up, sitting in the kitchen in his vest and braces, polishing his best shoes on sheets of newspaper laid out on the table, his trademark cigarette burning on the rim of a metal ashtray beside him.

'Do you want a brew?' I asked.

'Go on then,' he said. 'Though I think it'll take more than tea to get us through today.'

'You could be right.'

'I've got a little something in my hip flask,' Dad said. 'For emergencies only.'

'Like when I feel like strangling our Rita?'

'Exactly.'

'Hope it's a big flask,' I said.

The morning passed far too quickly. I had a bath, a nice hot one with Mum's best bath salts, and then sat in the garden with a magazine until my younger brother Clark arrived with his new girlfriend. I hadn't seen Clark for a few months, and although I was prepared for the fact that he was about three inches taller each time I saw him, he had changed his appearance somewhat too. His hair was wavy and came all the way down to his shoulders, and he was wearing round, narrow-rimmed glasses like John Lennon and a long, bright blue coat with what looked like fur on the inside. His trousers were embarrassingly tight and his boots had pointed toes and heels.

'Bloody hell!' Dad said when he saw Clark.

'Hi,' I said, going over to hug my brother. He hugged me back.

'Good to see you sis,' he said. 'This is Emma.'

'Hello, nice to meet you,' I said. The girl was tiny, elfin, with a pale little face looking out from behind a huge pair of false eyelashes and lots of blue eyeshadow.

'What's going down?' Clark asked.

'My life,' said Dad. 'It's going down faster than the bloody Titanic.'

'Now, Nelson, don't go getting all in a lather,' said Mum, swooping into the kitchen.

'Have you seen what he looks like?' Dad asked, nodding his head in the general direction of Clark. 'People will wonder if he's our son or our daughter.'

'I think he looks very nice,' Mum said in a tone of voice that implied the exact opposite.

'But what's the point of us raising a lad if he insists on dressing like a girl? Our Dottie'll be turning up in a bloody jockstrap next!'

'Nelson, don't use words like that in front of Emma!'

'I'm sure that's not the first time she's heard someone say "bloody".'

'Not that, the "J" word!' Mum hissed under her breath.

Emma had gone very pink.

'Where's your boyfriend, Dottie? Joe, isn't it?' Clark asked, no doubt to change the subject. I felt an immediate, strong pang of guilt. It had never, not for one moment, occurred to me to invite Joe to the christening or to meet my family. The idea just hadn't crossed my mind. Even worse, now I was thinking of it, he'd dropped quite a few hints that he would have liked to be here with me. What was wrong with me? Joe was, everybody agreed, the best boyfriend ever, and I'd treated him like an afterthought.

'He couldn't come,' I muttered. 'He's busy.'

Aunty Brenda turned up just as we were about to go.

'No Carol?' said Mum, enquiring about her niece.

'She seems to be having trouble getting her body out of bed. She said she'd be round later.'

Mum clapped her hands. 'Now are we all ready? We want to get the 1.20 bus to be sure we're at the church in good time.'

I ran upstairs to fetch my coat and hat. I was pleased with them both. The coat was short, nipped in at the waist, with big buttons. It was a sherbet-orange colour. The hat was cream, with a wide, floppy rim and a ribbon that matched the coat. I put them on and checked my appearance in the mirror in the hall. I put on a little more make-up, hoping that the Dottie behind it would disappear, and I was ready – or as ready as I was ever going to be.

The christening was being held at St John's Church, where we had all been christened. It's a nice church, with a nice vicar. Luckily the bus was on time so our party arrived early. Dad stayed outside smoking, but the rest of us went in to find our seats. Rita and Nigel were already there, Rita looking glamorous and cross, Nigel looking red and sweaty. Baby Miranda was wrapped up in so much lace she was like a caterpillar in a doily. All you could see were her beady little eyes staring in a rather panicked way from deep inside her bonnet.

'Oh bless her little heart!' Mum said, going all teary-eyed and moving in to kiss Miranda's cheeks.

'Mum! You've got lipstick all over her now!' Rita cried. 'She looks like she's going down with some awful skin disease.'

'It's only a little smudge,' said Aunty Brenda. She took a hand-kerchief out of her sleeve, licked the corner and went to dab at Miranda's cheek.

'And that's unhygienic!' Rita squealed. 'Am I the only person round here who cares about anything?'

I wished Dad was beside me. I could have done with a nip from his flask already.

I sat down next to Nigel, in the very front row. I figured that this way I wouldn't have to see Ralph when he came in with his fiancée. And he would go out of the church before us, and I'd just hang around after the service until he'd left. Still I felt nervous. I would be in the same building as Ralph, breathing the same air, singing the same words to the same hymns. I would know that he was there. My heart would know that he was there.

Nigel's parents arrived next, and there was a lot of helloing and how-are-youing amongst the older generation. Rita always behaved a bit better in front of her in-laws – what with them living in a mock Tudor house and taking their annual holidays on the Costa del Sol – which meant the rest of us could relax a bit.

Only I couldn't relax. I had to keep fighting the urge to look back over my shoulder to see if Ralph had arrived.

In the end, the christening went very well. There was a hairy moment when I had to walk to the back of the church, down the centre aisle to the font, carrying Miranda in my arms, but I kept my eyes fixed on her face and didn't look to the left or the right, so if Ralph was there, there was no danger of inadvertently catching his eye. Miranda stared at me with the utmost fascination, as if she believed I was very wise. She was beginning to grow on me. She was good as gold and didn't cry, even when the vicar sprinkled the holy water on her forehead. Rita, Mum, Aunty Brenda and Nigel's mum were all dabbing at their eyes and even mine were misting over a little.

Once the christening was over, the family started making their way out of the church, but I hung back. I hadn't seen Ralph yet. I didn't even know whether he was there.

I walked across to the little side altar and lit a candle. I was all over the place. There was a part of me that longed to see Ralph and a part of me that dreaded it. I had managed to avoid seeing him since I'd left Brighton four years ago. Maybe today that was all going to change.

I said a little prayer and made my way outside.

Clark, who was working as a junior photographer on local paper *The Argus*, had brought his big work camera along and was jumping all over the place taking arty shots.

'We don't want "arty",' Dad grumbled. 'We just want something to put on the mantelpiece.'

'Shhh,' said Mum. 'Our Rita wants arty and that's what she's going to get. Now smile like you mean it!'

There was still no sign of Ralph. Perhaps he'd decided not to come. Part of me was relieved, but I knew in my heart that I wanted to see him, even if it was going to hurt me.

The photographs took so long that most of the other guests had wandered off by the time we were finished. Clark wanted to take one more close-up of Rita, Nigel and Miranda standing by the cherry tree in the church garden. It was full of pink blossom, and I could see Rita was really pleased Clark had noticed it, because the baby would look gorgeous with that in the background.

They went over to the tree. Mum and Emma had nipped over the road to use the public convenience. I couldn't see Dad, but pale grey smoke was drifting up from behind one of the larger gravestones. I stood at the entrance to the church with my eyes closed and my face turned to the sun. Suddenly I heard footsteps running along the path. I opened my eyes and looked down into the face of a child.

For a moment my heart stopped.

She had gorgeous red hair, a tiny little freckled face, and she was the spitting image of my friend Mary Pickles.

Peggy had been about a year old when I'd last seen her but I would have known her anywhere.

'Hello, Peggy,' I said.

She peered up at me.

I touched her cheek. 'My name's Dottie. I used to know your mummy.'

'My mummy's in heaven,' she said, running past me and into the church.

I walked down the aisle behind her. She crawled under a pew and came up holding a doll.

She held the doll up for me to see. 'Her name's Tina,' she said.

'She's lovely. Did someone knit her clothes for you?'

'Fiona did. She's going to be my new mummy soon.'

Just then the door opened and a pretty young woman came hurrying down the aisle towards us. She crouched down as Peggy launched herself into her arms.

'Peggy, you scared us!' she said. 'You mustn't run off like that! We didn't know where you were!'

'I forgot Tina!'

'You should have asked me or your dad. We would have come with you.'

'You were talking.'

The woman looked up at me, shaking her head.

'She's always running off,' she said. 'It doesn't seem to matter how often we tell her not to, she still does it. I've never known a child with such a mind of her own.'

'Just like her mother,' I said.

The woman stood up, keeping hold of Peggy's hand. She smiled at me warmly.

'I'm Fiona.'

'Hi,' I replied. 'I'm Dottie, Rita's sister.'

Fiona stroked Peggy's hair. 'I thought you must be,' she said. 'Ralph has told me all about you.'

I wondered just how much he had told her.

'You were Mary's friend, weren't you?'

I nodded. 'Since we were children.'

'Yes, Ralph said. Look I'd better go, he's running round the graveyard trying to find Peggy, he'll be worried sick.

I nodded. 'Yes, sure.'

I watched as they went back up the aisle, Peggy skipping along beside Fiona, the doll dangling by one arm. Peggy's red curls were bouncing off her shoulders, catching the rays of light that were streaming through the stained-glass window above the altar. When they were gone I sat down on the nearest pew. I had recognised the doll. Polly and I had found it in a little toyshop in Brick Lane. I had tried to keep in touch with Peggy over the years. I had sent birthday cards and Christmas cards. I had carefully chosen gifts that I thought she'd like. The doll was one of them. Ralph had sent cards back from Peggy with little scribbles on the bottom. As she got older she was able to write her name and to say thank you in her childish scrawly writing. I smiled at all the crossings out. I had kept every one of those cards; they were precious to me. It had been a connection, not only with Peggy but with Ralph. A few times over the years I had walked round to their flat and stood in the quadrangle looking up at the windows. Once I had even climbed the stone steps, but I just couldn't do it. The thought of stepping through the door and being back in those rooms where Mary had been so ill and so unhappy was more than I could bear. If I was going to make a life for myself in London then I had to try and detach myself from a past that only brought me pain. I know that I should have tried to see the little girl, but I just couldn't. Losing Peggy had been as painful as losing Ralph. I covered my face with my hands and cried.

CHAPTER FIVE

The christening party was being held at Rita and Nigel's house. They lived on a modern housing estate that had grown since they had first moved in. A row of shops had been added, and there was a petrol station at the end of the road. Rita said it wasn't as exclusive as it used to be and they might have to move. Compared to the council house we had grown up in, I thought it was the height of luxury. Dad didn't like going there, because Rita made you take your shoes off at the door.

I went through the side gate and into the garden. Dad was sat in a white plastic chair on the patio. He was smoking furiously and flicking the ash into a plant pot.

'Don't let Rita catch you doing that,' I said.

'Our Rita wants to cop on to herself.'

'Bit late for that,' I said smiling and carried on through the back door and into the kitchen.

Aunty Brenda was getting a tray of sausage rolls out of the oven. The smell hit me as I opened the door, making me feel a bit queasy.

'Can I help with anything?' I said.

'You can get the cups out if you like. I asked our Carol to do it half an hour ago, but she disappeared off somewhere. Now stand there and let me look at you,' she said, wiping her hands on a tea towel. My Aunty Brenda had been saying that to me for as long as I could remember. 'Your mum was right about all that fat dropping off. You look lovely, Dottie.'

'Thanks,' I said, reaching into the cupboard for the cups.

'Still happy in London are you?'

'I love it.'

'Your mum misses you. She doesn't say much, but I can tell.'

'I miss her too. I miss all of you. I'm just not ready to come home yet.'

'Maybe one day, eh?'

'Maybe,' I said.

Just then Carol came into the kitchen. I still couldn't get over how much she had changed. When she was younger I used to call her the barrel because she was short and fat, but the apparition draped over the kitchen cabinet was nearly six feet tall and as thin as a rake. She was my cousin but we had never got on. We still didn't. She picked up a sausage roll and immediately dropped it back on the tray.

'Bloody hell,' she screamed, 'why didn't you tell me it was hot?'

'You didn't ask,' said Aunty Brenda, putting another load into the oven. 'Don't you think Dottie looks lovely, Carol?'

Carol looked me up and down in a sneery sort of way then said, 'Your friend Ralph Bennett's just arrived with his new girl-friend. Aren't you going in?'

I felt sick. It hadn't occurred to me that they would be at the party.

'She's helping me, aren't you, Dottie love?

I smiled gratefully at Aunty Brenda. She knew how I must be feeling.

'Which is more than can be said for some.'

'I'm here, aren't I?' snapped Carol.

'Well make yourself useful and take those vol-au-vents into the front room.'

Carol picked up the plate, boredom oozing out of every pore, and turned just as she was going through the door. 'Rita says you're wanted, they're cutting the cake.'

'Come on, Dottie,' said Aunty Brenda, 'we can't miss that.'

I didn't want to go, but I knew I couldn't put it off forever, so very reluctantly I followed Aunty Brenda into the front room.

'Come on,' said Mum when she saw me, 'you're needed for the photo.'

I took a deep breath and walked into the front room. Ralph and Fiona were standing by the fireplace. My tummy was doing somersaults, and I could feel my face going red, but I managed to smile at them, and they smiled back.

Clark was busy setting up his camera. 'Okay, Dottie,' he said. 'You hold the baby.'

'*I'm* holding the baby if you don't mind!' said Rita.

'But Dottie's the godmother,' said Clark.

'And I'm the mother,' said Rita, getting all stroppy. 'This is all about me and Nigel and Miranda Louise.'

'Just for a change,' said Clark, winking at me.

Suddenly I felt a little hand slip into mine. I looked down at Peggy, who was smiling up at me.

'Do you want to hold my doll?'

'I'd love to,' I said, taking the doll she was offering up to me. I sensed, rather than knew, that Ralph was looking at us. I was starting to feel awkward. Even the outfit I had thought looked so sophisticated this morning now seemed brash and loud and not in the least bit trendy. I had noticed earlier that Fiona was wearing a simple pale grey dress in a kind of floaty material. I felt fat and ugly. I felt like the old Dottie. I knew exactly what Polly would be saying now. 'Cop onto yourself, girl, and stop playing the bloody victim. You look fab in that outfit. We don't do floaty in London, we do style.' Yes, that's what Polly would be saying. I smiled to myself and stood a bit taller.

'Come on everyone,' said Clark. 'All gather round behind Rita and Nigel for a family shot.'

'Shall I get Dad?' I said.

'If you must,' said Rita.' But he's not standing beside Miranda Louise reeking of Woodbines.'

'Perhaps we could put him under the coffee table,' said Clark.

I went into the garden. 'You're wanted by royal command,' I said. 'We're having our photo taken.'

Dad got up and started to walk towards the back door.

'Don't forget to take your shoes off.'

'For heaven's sake, hasn't she got a vacuum cleaner? She's got every other bloody gadget known to man.'

'Just take them off, Dad,' I said. 'It makes for an easier life.'

I helped him with the laces and we went inside to join the others.

They had grouped themselves round Rita and Nigel. The cake was on a little table in the middle, and Rita and Nigel were poised to slice into it. I took my place in the line-up. I was now facing Ralph and Fiona, who hadn't joined the rest of us. Peggy was standing between them and they each had a hand on her shoulder. They already looked like a family. There was a hot feeling in my stomach, and sweat was forming under my armpits. I wanted to march across the room and tear them apart. I was filled with jealousy. I hadn't felt this bad when he had married Mary, but I guess that was because I knew he still loved me and that it was just something he had to do.

'You've got to be in the picture too,' said Rita, beckoning them over.

'I just thought,' said Ralph, 'as I'm not family...'

'But you will be soon. Won't he, Nigel? Ralph will soon be family!'

'Of course,' said Nigel.

Ralph and Fiona joined the group and ended up standing right behind me.

'Move forward a bit, Fiona,' said Clark. 'We can hardly see you behind Dottie.'

My face was burning with embarrassment. If I'd a gun at that moment, I would have happily shot my little brother in the head.

Fiona moved forward until she was beside me. 'That's better, now everyone say cheese.'

Ralph was standing so close behind me that we were almost touching. How easy it would have been to lean into him, to feel his body, which had once been so familiar to me. I shuffled forward to put some space between us.

'Cheese!' shouted Peggy and everyone laughed. That was when Clark pressed the shutter. I hoped this wasn't the picture that was going to adorn the mantelpiece for all eternity.

Once the photos were over, I escaped back to the kitchen to make tea. I put the kettle on to boil and was looking through the cupboards for the teapot when Ralph and Peggy came into the kitchen. I looked behind him expecting to see Fiona, but she wasn't there.

'Hi,' I said. My voice sounded high and squeaky. 'Where's Fiona?'

'Rita's giving her a tour of the house.'

I smiled. 'Lucky Fiona!'

Ralph smiled then knelt down until he was at Peggy's level. 'This is Dottie, Peggy.'

Peggy lowered her eyes.' I know,' she said.

'Do you?' said Ralph.

Peggy nodded.

'Well this is the lady who sent you all those presents and cards for your birthday and Christmas.'

Peggy looked up at me and smiled.

'You can thank her now,' said Ralph.

'Thank you,' said Peggy.

Ralph stood up and ruffled her hair. 'Good girl,' he said.

'Daddy, can I go and find Fiona?'

'Of course you can, love.'

Peggy ran out of the kitchen leaving Ralph and me alone.

'Do you need a hand with the tea?'

'No, no. I can manage.'

'Okay.'

There was a long pause. I found the teapot and put it on the counter. Then I started to lay out cups and saucers. I could feel Ralph's eyes on the back of my head, and although there were a million things I wanted to say to him, I couldn't put a single one of them into words.

'You're looking well,' Ralph said after an interminable time. 'London obviously suits you.'

'Yes.'

Lord, I wished the kettle would hurry up and boil. I wished I hadn't filled it so full. I wished I was anywhere else in the world but there, and at the same time I was glad I wasn't.

Ralph cleared his throat. 'Can we talk, Dottie?'

'You're getting married. What is there to talk about?'

His eyes never left my face but he didn't answer.

I pulled open a drawer and took out the teaspoons.

'When are you going back to London?'

'Tomorrow.'

'Oh.'

I put the teaspoons out, one on each saucer. I found the milk in the fridge and poured a half inch into the bottom of each cup. The kettle was still rattling on the gas hob. Only a wispy thread of steam was coming from its spout.

'I've missed you,' Ralph said. He said it so quietly I could only just hear him.

That made me angry. It was as if we were sharing some big secret again. Hadn't we been through enough already?

'Don't, Ralph. Please don't say things like that.'

Ralph just stared at me, then very deliberately he said: 'Every day, Dottie. I missed you every day.'

I turned away. I knew that if I looked into his eyes I would be lost. So I didn't. I acted as if I hadn't heard him. I lifted the kettle off the hob and poured water into the teapot. I kept my back to him.

'Dottie?'

'Please Ralph,' I said. 'If you care about me one little bit, you'll stay out of my life.'

'I can't do that, not when there's so much we need to say.'

I turned then. I made myself look into his eyes.

'There's nothing to say,' I said. 'I'm happy now, Ralph. I'm with somebody else and it's uncomplicated, and it's easy, and he loves me, and I love him. So I'd really appreciate it if you'd stay away from me and get on with your own life.'

Ralph listened throughout this little speech. He didn't blink or take his eyes off mine for a moment. Afterwards he nodded.

'If that's what you want.'

'It is!' I said, but there was a fracture in my voice. 'It really, really is.'

CHAPTER SIX

I was so relieved to get back home that evening. Clark and Emma went to the chippie for our supper. Dad put the telly on while Mum laid the table in the kitchen and I walked to the phone box at the end of the street and called Joe. I really wanted to hear his voice and to be reassured by him. I knew he would make me feel normal again. But he wasn't in. The phone rang and rang but nobody picked up. So instead I called 59 Victoria Terrace and counted to thirty-five, which is the amount of time it takes Polly to get from her bedroom down the stairs to the phone in the hallway.

'Hello!' she answered breathlessly.

'It's me,' I said. 'I've had the most awful day, and I feel terrible, and Joe's not answering his phone, and I don't know what to do, and I wish I was back in London, and I've got a feeling Joe's upset because I didn't invite him to the christening, and I wish I had because then he could have had a really miserable day too, and then he'd understand what it's like for me, and I'd do anything in the world to talk to him, but he obviously doesn't want to talk to me because I've hurt his feelings and he's sulking and...'

'Joe's gone to see The Who,' Polly said. 'He's probably having the time of his life. I bet he hasn't thought about you once.'

I'd completely forgotten about the concert, and I know Polly was trying to make me feel better but knowing that Joe was doing something fun and exciting when I was about to eat fish and chips with my family while Mum conducted a post-mortem of the day's events didn't make me feel any better.

'Chin up,' said Polly brightly. I could tell by the tone of her voice that she was probably on her way out somewhere and didn't want to get into a long, involved conversation with me.

'Look, why don't I meet you off the train and we'll go to the pub and have a good old chat. Save up all the funny stories for me then, okay?'

'Okay,' I said. The prospect of Polly and me sitting in the pub, her with tears of laughter streaming down her face as I regaled her with the awfulness of my family, cheered me up considerably. She loved hearing about my dad and Rita, and now I had a whole new batch of material to entertain her with. I would have killed anyone else who made fun of my family, but it wasn't really wrong of me to do it with Polly, because she knew how much I loved them deep down.

'That's a date then,' said Polly. 'I've got to go, I've got henna on my hair, and it stinks and clumps of it are falling off all over Mrs P's carpet. See you tomorrow!'

I walked the long way home, round the block, past the house where Mary used to live with her parents and her six brothers. The house was in just as bad a state as ever. There was a car in the front garden held up by four stacks of bricks where the wheels used to be, and I could see the skinny legs of one of Mary's brothers sticking out from beneath it. A stack of tyres was heaped by the front door, along with several bags of cement and a scruffy old concrete mixer. I remembered, vaguely, Mum telling me that Mary's parents were planning to make a patio in their back garden. Mum had said patios were the epitome of poshness these days but that it took Mary's dad so long to get round to doing anything practical that they'd have gone out of fashion before the first slab was laid. I couldn't much see the point of patios myself, and neither could Mum, but I had a feeling Rita would be interested.

I smiled as I walked past Mary's house, remembering the fun we used to have when we were children. The estate hadn't felt small and claustrophobic then – it had been our whole world and had seemed full of excitement and opportunity. I remembered how Mary and I used to while away our weekends spying on her heart-throb, Elton Briggs. I was so lost in my thoughts that I didn't notice the man walking towards me until we almost bumped into one another.

I stepped to one side. He went the same way. We both stepped the other way. We both grinned.

'Sorry,' he said, stepping off the kerb into the road to allow me to pass. For the first time we looked at each other's face, and I recognised him. It was one of Mary's brothers.

He said: 'Dottie? Is that you?'

'Wayne? Oh gosh, I was just thinking about you and your family! How are you? How are your mum and dad?'

'They're fine. Only…' He reached out and took my elbow, gently turning me around and steering me back towards the alleyway that connected various roads on the estate. 'You need to get home quickly, Dottie,' he said. 'There's an ambulance outside your house.'

CHAPTER SEVEN

I ran all the way back down the twitten, round the corner and along the street. I could see two men lifting Mum into the back of the ambulance on a stretcher. I was terrified. This was my mum. What was wrong with her? She was pale as a ghost and had an oxygen mask over her face, and Dad was walking beside her in his socks, holding her hand and telling the ambulance men to be careful and stop bumping the stretcher. At exactly the same moment as I arrived on the scene, Clark and Emma arrived from the opposite direction, Emma sitting on the back of Clark's Lambretta. She was clutching a box full of fish and chips. Clark jumped off the bike and rushed over.

'What's happened Dottie?'

'I've just got here. I don't know anything yet.'

We both ran over to our parents. 'Mum, what's the matter?' I asked. 'What did you do?'

Mum mumbled something from behind the oxygen mask.

'Silly woman went and had one of her funny turns at the top of the stairs,' said Dad. 'I told her, if she's going to have funny turns to have them somewhere flat, but does she listen to me? No.'

'What funny turns?' I asked. 'How long has this been going on?'

'I kept telling her to go and see the doctor before something like this happened but she would insist that she was fine and dandy and…'

'Excuse me, Mr Perks, but we need to get your wife to the hospital,' said one of the ambulance men. 'Would you like to ride with us?'

Dad was not one for hospitals. I could see the colour drain from his face, but Mum looked at him rather desperately over the top of the mask. He tugged at his collar and said: 'Yes please.'

'We'll meet you at the hospital,' said Clark.

This was too much for Mum. She pulled off the mask and raised her head a little. 'You young ones eat your chips first. I'm not having good food go to waste.'

'We could take the chips with us!' Dad suggested.

'No food in the ambulance. Now *please*, Mr Perks…'

'I'm coming with you,' I said firmly. I climbed up into the back of the ambulance and sat down. Dad followed. Mum was tugging at the mask again to argue. I took hold of her hand in a way that I hoped would let her know I wasn't going to be bossed about.

'We can warm the chips up later,' I told her.

It was the first time in my life that I'd felt responsible for my mum. I was completely out of my depth. I didn't know what I would do if anything happened to her.

The ambulance raced through the streets. Mum lay on the bed, her hands worrying at the striped blanket. Dad didn't take his eyes off her. He looked pale and scared. I reached across and held his hand.

At the hospital there was nothing we could do but wait. Mum was sent off for 'tests' but we didn't know what they were testing for, and we didn't know who we ought to ask, so we just sat in a poky little room trying to think of things to say to one another.

Dad smoked one cigarette after another until the waiting room was so full of smoke that my eyes were stinging, and it was hard to see across the room, but there weren't any windows we could open, so we had to put up with it. Emma was very sweet. She kept asking me questions about London in her quiet little voice. She and Clark had spent a day there a few weeks back and they'd gone shopping in Carnaby Street and gone to a free gig in the park. Emma twirled a piece of her long hair around her delicate little finger.

'It was groovy,' she sighed.

Emma was a lovely girl, but I was finding it hard to have a conversation with her when all I could think about was my mum.

'We've rung Rita,' said Emma. 'She's coming straight here.'

I'd forgotten about Rita, and that made me feel bad. 'Thanks Emma,' I said.

Clark kept interrogating Dad about what was wrong with Mum.

'I don't know, son,' Dad said. 'She's just been coming over a bit unnecessary lately, every now and then.'

'And you didn't think to *make* her see a doctor.'

'Oh you know what your mother's like, stubborn as a mule.'

I didn't blame Dad. I knew that he'd have been worried, but Mum would have insisted she was all right. She hated going to the doctor or the dentist or anything like that, because she always thought she was wasting their time when they had better things to be getting on with. I don't think I'd ever heard her complain about her own health. She used to moan about my dad a lot, but that was more of a hobby than because she was actually unhappy.

I chewed at my cuticle. I had a particular horror of the hospital, because it was where Mary had died four years ago. Just being back there, smelling the same hospital smells, brought so many sad memories flooding back to me.

The second last time I saw Ralph had been there, at the hospital.

The last time had been at Mary's funeral.

I felt a hand on my shoulder. It was Emma.

'Shall we go and see if we can get a pot of tea anywhere?' she asked me.

I nodded gratefully and stood up when the door opened and a nurse came in.

'How is she?' Dad asked.

The nurse squinted and wafted her hand in front of her face to clear a gap in the smoke.

'She's fine. She's having a bit of a wobble with her blood pressure, so we need to keep an eye on her to be sure of what's going on, but apart from that she's all right. Would you like to go and see her? Just two of you at a time I'm afraid – hospital rules.'

Dad and I followed the nurse down the corridor to the women's ward, leaving Clark and Emma in the waiting room.

Mum was lying in bed, partially propped up by pillows. She was still a little pale but insisted she was perfectly all right and that it was ridiculous that she wasn't allowed to go home when there was nothing wrong with her. She gave Dad a right telling off over the fact that he was still in his socks and asked us to be sure to bring her handbag with us in the morning so she could put on some lipstick.

I pulled a chair up to the bed and leaned across to hold her hand. It seemed so small in mine. 'I wish you had let me know you were ill, Mum,' I said.

'I didn't want you worrying about that up in London, and anyway it's nothing, just one of my turns.'

I looked across at Dad, who was holding Mum's other hand. He looked almost grey with worry, and it suddenly occurred to me that for all their sniping and grumbling they would be lost without each other.

I leaned over and kissed her cheek.

'Now mind you go back to London tomorrow, Dottie. I'll be right as rain.'

I didn't answer her.

After a bit I went outside. Clark and Emma were leaning against a wall in the corridor.

'How is she?' Clark asked anxiously.

'She seems okay, a bit pale, but we'll have to wait for the results from the tests before we know what's wrong. Go on in.'

When I got back to the waiting room, Rita was there. She looked all puffy-eyed, as if she had been crying. I almost felt sorry for her till she opened her mouth.

'Oh, Dottie,' she said. 'I got such a fright when Clark phoned. I'd just started the tea. I dropped everything and came straight here. I had to get the bloody bus and there was all sorts of riff-raff on it. I'm still shaking.' Rita held her hand out in front of her as if to prove it.

'Couldn't Nigel drive you?' I said, sitting down next to her.

'Don't be stupid. I *have* got a baby, you know. What was I supposed to do, leave her on her own?'

'Sorry, I wasn't thinking.'

'You never do, that's half your problem.'

'Well it's a relief to know it's only half,' I said. Even at a time like this, I couldn't help winding Rita up.

'Well don't just sit there,' said Rita. 'Tell me what's wrong with Mum.'

I couldn't help noticing that she'd dropped the 'Mother' bit. 'I think she's okay,' I said. 'At least the doctor doesn't think it's anything too serious.'

'Well what happened? All Clark said was that she had a funny turn. He made it sound as if she was doing some sort of stand-up comedy routine.'

'From what Dad says, she's been having dizzy spells for a while now.'

'Well why didn't she tell me?' said Rita, her eyes filling with tears. 'I'm her daughter, I should have been told.'

I didn't like to remind her that I was also her daughter, and I hadn't known either.

'You can't go back to London now, you know,' she said, standing up as if to emphasise the importance of what she was saying.

I looked up at her.

'You can't. And don't look at me like that.'

'Like what?'

'You are so annoying, do you know that?'

'Am I?'

'You think just because I live around the corner that I should be the one to look after Dad. Well I can't – I've got Miranda Louise to look after. I can't be running round there every two minutes. You have to stay, Dottie, you just have to.'

She had said all this without seeming to take a breath. She went over to a machine that dealt out water in polystyrene cups, filled one and gulped it down in one go. Her face was red and sweaty, and there was a look of panic in her eyes.

'What about Clark?' I said. 'He's still at home.'

'Clark can't look after *himself* let alone anyone else – and anyway he's a boy.'

'Haven't you heard, Rita? We are living in an enlightened age. Sex doesn't come into it.'

'Who said anything about sex? If you ask me, Dottie, the sooner you leave London the better. You are getting a very smutty mouth on you.'

'Oh good,' I said. 'Smut's all the rage this year.' Why did my sister always bring out the worst in me?

'Well?' she said.

'Well what?'

'Well are you going back to London or not?'

'Of course I'm not.'

The relief on Rita's face was palpable. 'Well you could have said.'

'You didn't give me much of a chance.'

Rita then started pacing up and down the small room. 'And I don't know what Emma is doing in there, she's not even family.'

'I expect she wants to support Clark.'

'Well it's me that should be in there, not her.'

Just at that precise moment, Emma came into the room. I hoped she hadn't heard Rita.

'Your mum's been asking for you,' she said to Rita in her gentle little voice.

None of us wanted to leave Mum in the hospital, but she insisted, and the nurse said she needed to rest.

Clark and Emma went home on Clark's bike and Dad, Rita and I went back on the bus. I ran into the house to get Dad's shoes so that he could take Rita home. Now I knew Mum was all right I was suddenly starving, and because Mum wasn't there we ate our supper off our knees in the living room, in front of the telly.

I was washing up afterwards, stacking the sudsy crockery in the plastic tray at the side of the sink, when Dad came into the kitchen. He stood behind me and cleared his throat.

'Dottie, love,' he said. 'I don't like to ask but…'

I turned and smiled at him over my shoulder. 'It's all right, Dad, I'd already decided to stay. I'll stay until Mum feels better.'

'Thanks, love. You're a good girl.

'Try not to worry too much.'

'I'll stop worrying when she's back home.'

I kissed his cheek. 'Try and get some sleep, Dad.'

'I'll try. Put the lights out when you come up.'

CHAPTER EIGHT

I woke early the next morning. The sun was warm on my face as it filtered through the gap in the curtains and into the room. I could hear Dad moving about downstairs. I pushed back the covers and sat on the edge of the bed. I couldn't believe how well I had slept and then felt guilty when I remembered that Mum was in the hospital.

I stood up and looked out of the window. My bedroom was at the back of the house so I could look down on to the gardens on either side. An Indian family had moved in next door a couple of years ago, and there were two saris hanging on the line. The colours were so vibrant, reds and oranges and golds. They were flapping about like two exotic butterflies trying to make a bid for freedom. Mr and Mrs Baxter's oversized knickers and long johns on the other side looked dull in comparison.

I washed and dressed and went downstairs. There was no one about, but the back door was open. I put the kettle on and went outside. Dad was standing in the garden. There was a newspaper on the ground beside him, and he was cutting daffodils and laying them down on it.

'Morning, Dad,' I said.

'Thought I'd bring these in for your mum,' he said, turning round.

'She'll love them. Did you sleep all right?'

'Not really,' he said, laying another flower on the paper. 'Do you know, Dottie, apart from the war, this is the first time since we got married that we've been apart?'

'What about when us kids were born?'

'She only had Rita in the hospital, and I slept in the waiting room. Wasn't supposed to but I had been in the army with the porter who was on duty, and he sort of turned a blind eye. You and Clark were born at home.' He was staring down at the daffodils. I had never seen him look so lost and frightened.

'You never know, they might let her out today.'

'I only want her home if they think she's okay to come home,' he said, taking a hankie out of his pocket and dabbing at his forehead. It was already hot in the garden, even though it was early, and it held the promise of a beautiful day. I should have been looking forward to meeting up with Polly. We could have gone to the park and done some people watching, and later Joe and I could have gone to the little Italian café down at Camden Lock. London was so alive when the sun was shining, it was just about the best place to be, but there was no way I was leaving Brighton yet. My dad needed me and I needed to be close to Mum. I knew that she would worry less about Dad knowing that I was with him.

Dad finished picking the daffodils and wrapped them in the newspaper. As he stood up, he rubbed the small of his back 'No fun growing old, love,' he said, smiling at me.

'Wait while I get the violin tuned,' I said, linking arms with him and leading us inside. I was trying to be light-hearted, but there was a twinge of fear in my stomach at the thought of my mum and dad getting old.

My Aunty Brenda and Rita were visiting Mum this afternoon, and Dad and I were going up in the evening. I was on my way to Rita's to take Miranda out for a walk. She was in her pram when I got there, and Rita had her kitted out as if she was going on an expedition to the North Pole.

'Isn't she a bit overdressed?'

'No,' said Rita. 'She's still not right, and I don't want her catching a chill.'

I looked into the pram. Miranda's little face looked very pink. 'She looks hot.'

'What would you know?' said Rita, getting all huffy.

'It was just an observation. Excuse me for breathing.'

'Now there's a bag under the pram with a bottle in and some nappies. Make sure she's changed regularly. I don't want you leaving her in a wet nappy.'

'I've looked after a baby before, you know,' I said, remembering Peggy, who I'd taken care of when Mary was so ill.

Rita bent over the pram, adjusting the covers and touching Miranda's face. I could tell she didn't want me to take her out, but Nigel was at his mother's, and Rita didn't want to take Miranda to the hospital, because she said it was full of germs.

After a thousand more instructions, I was eventually allowed to wheel the pram down the garden path, leaving Rita gazing anxiously after us.

I walked down West Street towards the seafront. So much had changed since I was last here. The In a Spin record shop, where Mary and I had spent so much time choosing the latest records and where on that fateful day we had met up with Elton and Ralph, was now a hairdressers called Mary Eleanor and Bellman's the wool shop was a second-hand car dealers.

I walked further down the road till I came to the café. It looked exactly the same. I could even see the jukebox through the steamy window. How I wished I could just open the door and find Mary, Elton and Ralph sitting at one of the tables smiling at me. I felt a lump forming in my throat and hurried away.

I wanted to be back in London. I didn't want to be here – it hurt too much. I continued along the seafront, feeling sad and empty inside. Miranda started making little mewing noises like a kitten. Her face was pink, and she was fussing with the ribbon that was tied under her chin. 'What the eye doesn't see the heart won't grieve over,' I said, removing the bonnet and a couple of blankets. 'That's better, isn't it?' Miranda stared back at me. I wondered what she was thinking. 'You're a very wise little girl, aren't you?' I said, smoothing back the hair that was sticking to her forehead. 'I've got a feeling that you and I are going to get along fine. But don't let on to your mother.' All of a sudden she smiled at me as if she understood every word I was saying. 'Yep,' I said. 'I think we are going to get along fine.'

I walked all the way along the seafront, past the King Alfred swimming pool and the bowling green and turned in at the gates to the lagoon. Then I saw him. He was sitting on our bench overlooking the boating lake. He had his back to me; his body was bent forwards, his elbows resting on his knees. I stared at him for a long time, then I turned the pram around and walked away in the opposite direction, every footstep taking me further away from him, every breath taking me further away from where I wanted to be.

CHAPTER NINE

After Mary's death 'I went into myself'. At least that was how Aunty Brenda described it. Her remedy was to 'get out of myself'. Simple right? Wrong. I was like a lost soul. I had literally lost the other half of me. I should have been able to turn to Ralph, but I couldn't. Every time I thought about Ralph and Peggy I was reminded of Mary. Ralph had written to me during that time, but I had never opened even one of his letters. I eventually threw them away. Everything was too raw. I was dying inside, and no one could help me. I was making everyone around me miserable, so I'd walked a lot. The trouble was there was nowhere I could go that didn't remind me of Mary. The seafront, the beach, every street, every shop. It was my brother Clark who had come to my rescue.

Clark had always wanted to be a photographer, and as soon as he left school, he got a job on *The Argus*. My little brother was following his dream. He came home one day with a magazine. 'We get this every month, Dottie,' he'd said. 'It's got a job section, and there's one here that I think might interest you.'

I looked at the job he had circled.

'I can't do this. It's about working for a magazine. What do I know about magazines?'

'You read them, don't you?'

'I eat sausages, but I don't have a clue how to make them. They'd never hire me in a million years.'

Clark drew my attention to a line in the advert. 'Look – no experience necessary.'

'But surely you need to be able to type?'

'It's worth a shot.'

'And it's in London.'

'So?'

I shook my head. 'Thanks, Clark, but I'd just be making a fool of myself.'

'Do you fancy that sort of job?'

I'd never thought of any sort of job except Woolies. As far as I was concerned that was where I was going to work until I got married. But then I never knew that my life would turn out the way it did. How could I ever have imagined that my best friend would die and the love of my life would betray me in the worst possible way?

'Come on, Dottie. What is there to lose?'

'But London?'

'I'll come with you. Answer the ad. Just see what happens.'

It had been a Saturday when Clark and I had caught the train from Brighton station and travelled to London for my interview with *Trend* magazine. I had hardly slept the night before. I'd been convinced I was going to make a complete idiot of myself – I could just imagine the interview.

INTERVIEWER: 'Miss Perks, why do you want to work for this magazine?'

ME: 'I haven't got a clue.'

INTERVIEWER: 'What experience do you have in this field?'

ME: 'Umm, none?'

INTERVIWER: 'Typing speed?'

ME: 'Come again?'

INTERVIEWER: 'How fast do you type, Miss Perks?'

ME: 'Where's the toilet?'

If it hadn't been for Clark I wouldn't have gone at all. I'd thought the whole thing was a complete waste of time. Yet some-thing had made me get up early, wear my best clothes and catch the bus to the station with Clark. I'd realised I had to get away from Brighton. If I wanted to change my life then it was up to me to change it. No one was going to do it for me.

I'd sat opposite Clark staring out of the window as the train raced towards London. Clark had bought a copy of *Trend,* but I'd been too nervous to read it. Clark had been totally absorbed in it. 'I'd have given anything to have been there.'

'Where?'

'Woodstock,' he'd said, passing the magazine to me. 'It's like the biggest rock festival there has ever been.'

I'd looked at the pictures. 'They've hardly got any clothes on.'

'I know, isn't it brilliant?'

'Is it?'

'It's all about freedom, Dottie, being young, turning your back on the establishment, giving young people a voice. Imagine the photos I could have taken.'

I'd looked at the pictures again. Yes I had been able to see why Clark would have loved this, and he'd been right, there was a kind of abandonment in the young boys and girls with flowers in their hair, dancing with a sense of freedom that I had never known.

'And you'll never believe who performed there. Santana, Joan Baez, The Grateful Dead, Janis Joplin. And guess who the closing act was?'

'Surprise me.'

'Only Jimmy bloody Hendrix. It'll never happen again, you know. Those people have made history.'

'Why don't *you* apply for the job at *Trend?* You'd be more suited to it than me, and they're not going to give me a job anyway.'

'Just stay cool, Dottie – they might be desperate.'

'They'd *have* to be desperate to take me on.'

The train had pulled into Victoria station much sooner than I had wanted it to. We'd walked across the crowded platform and down the escalator. I'd never been to London before, let alone on the Tube. I'd been terrified. Clark had sensed how frightened I was and taken hold of my hand. I had smiled at him gratefully.

As the train had rattled its way beneath the streets of London, I'd tried to imagine doing this every day. I couldn't.

We'd come up into the sunshine of Sloane Square and for the first time since I'd left home that morning I'd felt a twinge of excitement. It had all looked so different to Brighton and I'd wanted different. I hadn't wanted memories of Mary and Ralph on every street corner.

I'd straightened my shoulders as we made our way up the King's Road.

The offices were above a tattoo parlour called Pierce on Earth.

'Cool,' Clark had said.

'Would you mind if I went in on my own?'

'You sure?'

I'd nodded. 'I think I'll be less panicked on my own.'

'I'll have a wander round and meet you back here.'

The reception area had been small and colourful, with loads of posters on the walls advertising concerts and festivals, and I'd started to feel excited.

Someone had given me a cup of coffee. I could hardly drink it, my hand had been shaking so much. There'd been another girl waiting as well. I'd smiled nervously at her, and she'd smiled back. It had been comforting that she'd looked just as terrified as I had.

After she had been called in I'd leaned back into the leather sofa and closed my eyes and asked myself if this was this really what I wanted. To live in this big city on my own, to leave my family, to leave everything that was familiar to me?

'Miss Perks?'

I'd opened my eyes. A young girl had been smiling at me. 'Late night?'

'Early morning,' I'd replied, smiling back and standing up.

'Don't look so worried,' she'd said.

I'd followed her along a corridor, then she'd opened a door and I'd been immediately hit by the noise. I had never seen so many people in one space before. Everyone had seemed to be talking at once, typewriters clicking away, people rushing around, everyone seeming to have a purpose. The place had been full of energy and life and excitement, and suddenly I'd wanted to be part of it. I'd wondered if I could. It had been a million miles away from Woolies, where you just stood behind a counter watching the clock.

People had smiled at me as I hurried after the girl, and one boy had given me the thumbs up.

At the end of the room we'd stopped outside a door. There'd been a sign on it that read 'PETER LESSING EDITOR'.

'Good luck,' the girl had said as she'd stood aside and motioned me in.

The guy sitting behind the desk had been surprisingly young. I had expected someone much older. He'd stood up and held out his hand. 'Peter,' he'd said, smiling.

'Dottie Perks,' I'd said, taking his hand.

'Coffee?'

'I just had one thanks.'

'Okay, tell me about yourself.'

I'd decided to be perfectly honest. 'I'm afraid that I have no experience of working for a magazine. I've worked on the cosmetics counter at Woolworths since I left school, and I can't type.'

Peter Lessing had laughed. 'Are you trying to talk yourself into the job or out of it?'

'I'm not sure.'

He'd leaned back in his chair and stared at me for what seemed forever, as if he was weighing me up. 'Well, I like a challenge, Dottie.'

I'd bitten my lip. 'That would be me then,' I'd said.

He'd stared a bit more. 'Would you be willing to start at the bottom?'

'I wouldn't mind starting in the car park.'

He'd laughed and stared at me some more.

Was he actually going to hire me? I'd wondered.

'You live in Brighton?' he'd asked.

'Yes.'

'Can I ask why you want to leave there and come to London?'

Well I'd been honest so far, so I'd thought I might as well continue being honest. 'Broken heart,' I'd said.

'Oh dear, I've had one of those myself, not good.'

'Not good,' I'd agreed.

'Have you thought about where you're going to live?'

'If you offer me the job, you mean?'

Peter Lessing had grinned. 'I rather think that I *am* offering you the job, Miss Dottie Perks.'

At the time, I couldn't believe it. He actually thought that I could do it.

'Really?' I'd asked, smiling.

'If you want it. The question is *do* you want it?'

I would have been leaving everything I knew for something I didn't have a clue about, but I had liked the man sitting smiling at me from across the desk instantly, and I'd known instinctively that I could trust him. If it didn't work out I could always go back home. I'd taken a deep breath. 'Yes, I do want it.'

'I'm pleased. We'll take a chance on each other, eh?'

I'd nodded.

'Did you come here on your own?'

'I came with my brother.'

'Then I suggest you buy a paper, go for a coffee and look for a flat. Welcome to *Trend*.'

Clark had been sitting in the reception area when I'd come out. I'd walked towards him with a big grin on my face.

'They were desperate then?'

'They were desperate.'

Clark had given me a big hug. 'Better find you somewhere to live then, girl.'

We'd done as Peter said and bought a newspaper and found a little café. Clark had bought a map of London so that we could pinpoint where I needed to live.

'Do you want to share with someone, or do you want to live on your own?'

'I think I'd rather share, just to start with anyway.'

Clark had spread the map out on the table and studied it. 'I think we should look at North London,' he'd said. 'There's good Tube links to here.'

We' found a couple in the right area, but only one where I would be sharing with a girl.

'Right,' Clark had said. 'Fifty-nine Victoria Terrace, landlady Mrs Evelyn Pierce, top-floor flat, sharing with one girl. Own bedroom, shared kitchen and bathroom. Sounds perfect. Let's find a phone box and give her a ring. It would be good if we could see it today.'

Luck had been on our side. Mrs Pierce had been in and said that we could come round and view the flat.

It turned out to be in Islington, a lovely red-brick house in the middle of a beautiful Victorian terrace.

'I shouldn't think it gets much better than this,' Clark had said, staring up at the house.

I'd looked around. We were standing on pretty tree lined street with a park opposite. I'd been able to see people walking their dogs, women pushing prams and kids running about. It had felt friendly and busy, and suddenly it became important that Mrs Pierce liked me, because I'd thought that perhaps, maybe, I could live in a place like this.

We'd gone up the steps leading to the front door and rung the bell. A small thin woman had opened it. My Aunty Brenda would have described her as wiry.

'You must be Miss Perks,' she'd said, holding out her hand. 'And this is?' she'd asked, looking at Clark.

'My brother,' I'd said.

She'd shown us into a large sunny living room at the front of the house. Everything about it was fussy, from the patterned wallpaper to the flowery curtains. Several small tables were dotted about the room and on top of each one was a china chamber pot holding a plant, whose leaves drooped over the sides and snaked across the table. The whole place had felt claustrophobic, and I'd hoped the flat wasn't going to be the same.

Mrs Pierce had small eyes that were too close together. 'Do sit down,' she'd said, motioning towards a peach sofa that had so many cushions on it that we'd had to perch on the edge. Mrs Pierce had settled herself opposite on a matching chair and peered at us over a pair of large tortoiseshell glasses.

'So, Miss Perks, you are interested in renting my flat?'

I'd smiled at her. 'Yes I am.'

She'd sat very precisely, with her hands on her lap and her legs close together. I'd found myself imitating her. I'd wanted her to like me.

'Do you have employment?'

'Yes, I've just been offered a position at a magazine.'

'May I ask what sort of magazine?'

'Music,' I'd said. 'Popular music.'

It had been hard to tell from her face whether this met with her approval or not.

'And where do you live at the moment?'

'I live with my parents, in Brighton.'

'And can I ask your age?'

'I'm nineteen.'

'Have you lived in London before?'

'No, never.'

'Well this a nice neighbourhood, and I have always felt very safe here. You will have your own bedroom, and you will share a kitchen and a lounge with Miss Renson. It's at the top of the house, and I have told Miss Renson to expect you. Tap on my door when you're done, and if you like the flat we will sort out the rent.'

'Oh, I'm sure that I'll like it. Thank you, Mrs Pierce.'

The young girl who'd greeted us at the top of the stairs was quite beautiful. She'd been wearing blue jeans and a long black baggy jumper. Her fair hair had been tied back in a ponytail, and she'd had these amazing blue eyes fringed with ridiculously long dark lashes. She'd looked like the models you see in a magazine. I hadn't been able to stop staring at her.

'Polly,' she'd said, holding out her hand.

'Dottie,' I'd said. 'And this is my brother Clark.'

Polly had smiled, revealing a set of perfectly straight white teeth 'Well at least you look normal,' she'd said.

'Don't be fooled,' Clark had said.

I'd made a face at him.

'Well you seemed to have passed the Mrs P test – otherwise she wouldn't have sent you upstairs to meet me. Want to look around?'

'Yes, please.'

We'd followed her as she'd led us into a small kitchen and a surprisingly large living room.

'And this is your bedroom,' she'd said, opening a door. 'The best room in the house if you ask me. I did think of moving into it myself after the last girl left, but I couldn't be bothered to lug all my stuff in here. So it's all yours.'

The room had been about twice the size of my bedroom at home with a large window that looked directly onto the park.

'Nice, isn't it?' Polly had said.

'It's lovely.'

'Very swanky,' Clark had said. 'I'm getting quite envious.'

'I'll tell you what,' Polly had said. 'I'll get us some coffee and leave you to think about it.'

After Polly left, Clark and I had sat on the bed.

'I think you should take it,' he'd said. 'And Polly seems lovely.'

'Not to mention drop dead gorgeous.'

Clark had grinned. 'I noticed that.'

'Thought you might.'

I'd stood up and walked across to the window. Was I really going to do this? I'd thought. Was I really going to live in this city, work in this city? Could I do it?

Clark had joined me and we'd stood side by side looking out over the park.

'You can always come home if it doesn't work out,' he'd said.

We'd joined Polly in the living room. There'd been mugs of steaming coffee waiting for us on the table and we'd sat side by side on the couch. Polly had sat on the floor leaning back against an armchair.

'What was your last flatmate like?' I'd asked.

Polly had screwed up her face. 'Ghastly. Absolutely bloody ghastly. I was glad to see the back of her.'

I'd loved the way Polly spoke, kind of posh but friendly.

I hadn't liked to ask in what way she was ghastly.

'You *will* take the flat won't you?' she'd asked.

I'd smiled at her. 'Yes, I'll take it.'

'Really?' Clark has said.

'Yes, really.'

Polly had smiled at me. 'We'll be best friends,' she'd said.

It had reminded me of the day I had met Mary. 'Wanna be best friends?' she'd said.

And so I met Polly, and we did indeed become friends, the very best of friends, and I don't think Mary would have minded one bit – in fact I think she would have approved.

I spent those first months at *Trend* making an awful lot of tea, and I learned two things. Firstly that I was not a writer, and secondly that I had an eye for detail, which led me to my perfect job as a proofreader. I learned to type at night school and became a valued member of that noisy exciting room full of young people. I had found a new life, and I loved it.

CHAPTER TEN

They had kept Mum in the hospital for two days. When she came home she seemed paler and thinner but absolutely refused to acknowledge that anything at all was the matter.

'It's all a big fuss about nothing,' she said, bustling into the kitchen as if she'd been away for a month. She unhooked her apron and tied it round her waist, put on her rubber gloves, picked up her cleaning brush, rinsed it under the hot tap – making the boiler roar – and retrieved a bottle of bleach from under the sink.

'Shouldn't you be resting, Mum?'

'I don't need to rest. There's nothing at all wrong with me. I just went and got myself a bit run-down is all.' She squeezed a blob of cleaning fluid onto the draining board and attacked it fiercely with the brush.

'Have they given you any tablets or anything?'

Mum had been distracted, temporarily, by the vegetable rack. She picked up a potato that had a slightly green tinge to it and held it to the light.

'What have you all been eating while I've been away?' she asked. 'Fresh air?'

'Fish and chips mostly,' I admitted.

'It's a good job I'm home then, isn't it?'

'Come and sit down, Mum, you really shouldn't be doing that. That's why I'm here.'

To my horror, Mum suddenly burst into tears. She grabbed a tea towel and held it to her face. Her shoulders hunched, and she began to cry as if her heart was breaking.

'Oh, Mum, what is it?' I cried, jumping up from the table and putting my arms around her. 'Please, tell me what's wrong! Are you really poorly? Is it something serious? Oh, Mum, what is it? What's the matter?'

She was crying so hard that she couldn't speak, so I just held her. It was then that I noticed how slight she was. Her shoulders were fragile, and I could feel the knobbles of her spine beneath the fabric of her dress and cardigan.

I helped her into a chair and stroked her hair until the kettle boiled, then I made her a very milky cup of tea, put four heaped spoons of sugar in it and sat beside her, waiting until her sobbing had reduced to a series of hiccups. Mum took a sip of her tea. She had taken off the gloves, and her hands were cold and trembling. Her skin felt dry, as soft and thin as tissue.

'I thought that I was going to die, Dottie, aren't I silly? A bit of low blood pressure and I thought that I was going to die.'

'Oh, Mum, you weren't being silly. You were scared, and it's perfectly normal to be scared.'

'I wasn't scared for me, love. It was your Dad, see. I couldn't bear the thought of leaving him alone. I owe him a lot, Dottie. I owe him a lot.'

I wanted her to explain what she meant, but she looked diminished, as if the soul had gone out of her. She sniffed and then blew her nose loudly on the hankie she always kept tucked up her sleeve.

'He wouldn't be alone, Mum, because he'd have us. He'd have all three of us and we'd make sure that he was okay. But we won't need to, will we? Because you're not going anywhere for a long, long time.'

Mum stared down at her hands and started fiddling with her wedding ring, twirling it round and round her finger. I'd never seen my mum like this, and I'd never heard her talk this way. She was the strongest person I knew. I guess you just took it for granted that your parents loved each other. I hadn't realised just how much. And what on earth did she owe my dad?

'Where is he now?'

'I've sent him off to get a few bits. He was making me feel nervous hovering around me all the time.'

'You've sent him to the shops? Does he even know where they are?'

Mum laughed. 'He doesn't need to love, he's got me to look after him.'

'And you've got *us* to look after *you*, so make the most of it.'

'I know I have, love, and I'm grateful to you for staying a bit longer. I hope you won't get into any trouble at work.'

'No, my boss is lovely.'

She turned her hand over and took hold of mine. 'Now that's enough about me, what about you, Dottie? How are you?'

'I'm fine.'

'I thought you might have been upset seeing Ralph and Fiona together.'

'I was a bit, but I'm okay now.'

'Have you still got feelings for him, love?'

I took a deep breath. I knew I could confide in Mum. She'd understand if I told her about Ralph, about how I felt when I saw him -- how all those old feelings rushed back and left me confused and angry and unsure of myself. But then how could I burden her with all that when she was feeling so low herself? It would be selfish and wrong and unfair. So I found a smile from somewhere and put it on my face.

'I'm absolutely fine, Mum. The truth is I've got a nice new boyfriend, and he's always taking me out places, which is why I haven't been back here as often as I should have been.'

'Maybe he could take you out down this way one weekend.'

I nodded. 'Yes, I'd like you to meet him. I'd like that very much. Now stop worrying about Dad and start getting well.'

CHAPTER ELEVEN

Polly and I were spending Saturday morning wandering round the stalls in Portobello Road. She picked up a purple velvet boa and slung it round her neck.

'Don't you think this is just so me, daaarling?' she drawled, draping herself across the table.

'Mind the goods, love,' shouted the fat little man who owned the stall. 'If you ain't buyin', I'd be obliged if you didn't handle the merchandise. That's very delicate fabric, that is.'

'Who says I'm not buying?' said Polly, grinning at him. 'How much is it?'

'17/6p,' said the man. 'Cheap at half the price.'

'No, I don't think so,' said Polly, winking at me and putting the boa back on the table.

'Fifteen bob then,' said the man. 'And that's takin' the bread out of me kids' mouths.'

'Ten bob,' said Polly.

'Twelve,' said the man.

'Done,' said Polly, 'and I'll wear it.'

Polly paid the man and we walked off arm in arm giggling. The purple velvet of the boa looked amazing against her fair hair. I noticed people staring as we walked through the market. People noticed Polly. People always noticed Polly, but she didn't seem to realise it.

I'd stayed in Brighton for a week, until I was absolutely sure that Mum was okay. I had hardly left the house. I was so afraid that I would bump into Ralph, even though that was the only thing that I wanted to do. I kept making up little scenarios where I would be coming out of a shop just as he was going in, or getting on the same bus he was on. I knew that I had to get back to London. Between worrying about Mum and worrying about Ralph, I was so stressed all the time that it was making me feel ill. Even darling Rita commented on it.

'I hope you're not going down with something,' she'd said, glaring at me as if I was about to get ill just to annoy her. 'You look peaky, so don't breathe all over Miranda Louise.'

'You can't wrap her in cotton wool, Rita.'

'I can wrap her in a dirty dishcloth if I decide to. I don't need you to tell me what I can and can't do with my own child.'

Yes, I was definitely glad to be back in London, especially on a beautiful morning like this with my best friend Polly. We walked around for another hour. I bought a set of coasters with Bob Dylan's face on for the flat, as Mrs P kept moaning about the coffee rings on the table. I also found a couple of Beatles tapes and Polly got some chunky plastic earrings and bracelets. We decided to stop for some lunch at an Italian restaurant that had a garden out the back.

'So,' said Polly sitting down at a table under some plastic hanging vines. 'Tell me exactly what happened when you were in the bosom of your family, because you've been like a cat on hot bricks since you got back.'

'Have I?'

'You know you have, and you also know you want to tell me, so spill.'

'I saw Ralph.'

'I thought he might figure in it somewhere. So was that good?'

'He's getting married.'

'Not so good.'

'I don't know, I don't know how I feel.'

'Do you still have feelings for him?'

'Yes, no, I don't know.'

'Well how did he make you feel?'

'Excited, scared, awkward, sick.'

'And how does Joe make you feel?'

I smiled. 'Safe, happy, loved.'

'And he's single and not engaged to someone else.'

'So why do I feel so confused?'

'Because you're only twenty-three, and maybe you're not ready for safe.'

'When did my cynical friend get so wise?'

'Don't be fooled by the cynical bit. I've succumbed to the odd broken heart.'

'I think mine's been broken for years.'

'Then isn't it time you did something about it?'

'There's more to it than that.'

'I know there is, kiddo, but until you tell me what it is, there's not much I can do.'

'I will one day.'

'Good.'

The evening was just as beautiful as the morning, maybe more beautiful. There's something about early evening in London in the spring. Maybe it's the light, or maybe it's just a feeling in the air, but it seems as if anything is possible. In Brighton, it feels like all my possibilities are behind me, like there's no future, but here in London, on an evening like this, my heart just feels lighter, and I gradually lose the old Dottie and find myself again.

It was too nice an evening to stay in and as neither Joe nor I had any money to go to the pub or the pictures, we went to Kensington Gardens, which is just about my favourite place in London. Ever since Joe had shown me the statue of Peter Pan, I had been fascinated by the story of the boy who never wanted to grow up. It reminded me of Mary.

It was very stuffy in the Underground, and we were glad to come above ground for some fresh air. It seemed as though the entire population of London was out on the streets. Some were dressed up to the nines, as if they were going to the theatre or out for dinner, others wore casual clothes just strolling around. I loved the buzz. When I was growing up, I never thought I would leave Brighton, and once I fell in love with Ralph, I thought my future was mapped out. A little house, kids, Mum round the corner and Mary down the road. But it wasn't to be, and now I was here in London, on a beautiful evening with a lovely man, and I loved it.

I put my arm through Joe's as we negotiated the busy road and went into the park. It was pretty crowded, but our bench by the statue was empty. There was a bunch of hippies sitting not far away strumming guitars; a few of them were handing out flowers. A beautiful young girl in a long flowy dress came across to us and handed us both a daffodil. 'Peace and love,' she said, smiling.

We sat on the bench holding hands and listening to the music. I stared at the statue.

'They didn't stay together, did they?' I said.

'Who didn't?'

'Peter and Wendy.'

'Well that's because Wendy wanted to grow up and Peter didn't,' said Joe.

'That's sad, isn't it?'

'I suppose it is,' said Joe, putting his arm around my shoulder.

'Do you think there are lots of people that are meant to be together, but it just never happens?'

'I'm sure of it,' said Joe.

'So what do they do?'

'I guess they get over it and find someone else. Blimey, I wouldn't have brought you here if I thought you were going to get all soppy on me,' he said, grinning.

'I thought you said you were a romantic.'

'I am over real things, but that's just a story.'

'Well I believe in Peter Pan. I believe in you, Peter,' I shouted across to the statue. One of the hippies looked across at us and said, 'So do we.'

'See, it's not just me,' I said, laughing.

'You're daft, do you know that?' he said, smoothing my hair away from my eyes and smiling.

'Endearing, isn't it?'

'Totally,' said Joe, kissing me gently. 'Now isn't it time I met the future in-laws?'

'I don't know about future in-laws, but I did tell Mum I would bring you down for a visit.'

'Well now that's a start, isn't it?'

CHAPTER TWELVE

The sunlight streaming through the net curtains in Joe's bedroom held the promise of another beautiful day. I had stayed the night, because today we were going down to Brighton. I hadn't been home for almost a month, and I wanted to check up on my mum. I raised myself onto one elbow and peered at the clock on the bedside cabinet. It said seven fifteen. We weren't getting the train from Victoria until eleven. I snuggled back down under the covers.

Joe was sleeping with his back to me, so I put my arms around him, inhaling the familiar smell of Hai Karate and the rather musty morning smell that for some odd reason was turning me on. 'Are you awake?' I asked hopefully.

'No, I'm asleep,' he mumbled.

'But you spoke,' I said, kissing his back.

'I was sleep talking.'

'I need a cuddle.'

'I need to sleep.'

'But I really, really need a cuddle.'

Joe turned over so that he was facing me. 'Happy now?'

'Better,' I said, smiling. I shifted down the bed so that I could put my head on his chest. On the wall opposite was a huge poster of Raquel Welch, dressed like a cavewoman. Was this the sort of woman that Joe liked? I certainly didn't look like that and it made me wonder about his past girlfriends. 'You've never talked about any of your old girlfriends,' I said.

'You've never asked.'

'Well I'm asking now.'

'Bit early for the Spanish Inquisition isn't it? Why do you want to know?'

'Just wondering whether some long lost love is going to suddenly turn up out of the blue and steal you away from me.'

'No chance.'

'I'd still like to know.'

Joe brushed the hair out of my face and kissed my forehead. 'Well I've only really had ten serious relationships.'

'Ten!' I said, sitting up and staring at him.

'Just kidding.'

I slid down the bed again. 'Well don't – I believed you.'

'Okay, if you really must know, I've had lots of flings, as you would expect of a rather handsome lad like myself,' he said, giving me a cheeky grin.

'Of course.'

'But serious ones? Three.'

'How long did they last?'

'The first one lasted four years.'

'But that's ages, why did you break up?'

'Because when she was eight her parents moved house.'

'Was it true love?' I said, twirling the hair on Joe's chest around my finger.

'Ouch,' he said, pushing my hand away.

'Well was it?'

'Absolutely. She even took her knickers off once and showed me her little pink bottom.'

'Sounds kinky.'

'It does, doesn't it?'

'And the second one?'

'That one lasted a year and then she stalked me for another two years. I thought she was cool and mysterious when in fact she was barking mad.'

'And number three?'

Joe didn't answer right away, and suddenly I wished I hadn't asked. I could feel my stomach tense. The bed that five minutes before had felt all cosy and comfy suddenly felt hot and sticky, and all thoughts of making love had gone completely out of my head.

'Penny,' he said eventually. 'Her name was Penny.'

'Why have you never mentioned her before?'

'Because I didn't think it was important. Is it important?'

'I don't know,' I said, moving away from him in search of a cool patch of sheet. 'I mean I've told you all about my limited love life, haven't I, but you haven't said a word about yours.'

'Are we having an argument?'

'I don't think so.'

'So why have you moved away from me?'

'Because I'm hot and sticky and probably smelly.'

'I love it when you talk dirty.'

'So what was she like? Did she look like the poster?'

'What poster?'

'The one on the wall.'

Joe looked at the poster of Raquel. 'No, Penny was very dark. Her parents were Italian.'

'I hate her already.'

'Silly girl,' he said, pulling me towards him and kissing me very gently on the lips.

'Was she thin? I bet she was thin. She *was* thin, wasn't she?'

'Does it matter? I'm with *you* now, and that is exactly where I want to be. Why are we wasting time talking about something that's ancient history when I could be ravaging your young nubile body.'

I knew I was being silly, and wished I hadn't mentioned his old girlfriends. He was with me now, and that was what mattered. I teased him. 'Why sir, what kind of girl do you think I am?'

'You're my kind of girl, Dottie Perks. Now stop wittering on and come here.'

Between spending far too long in bed and crawling round the floor trying to find one of my shoes, we very nearly missed the train, but now here we were, sitting opposite each other, with something that was passing itself off as a ham sandwich on the table between us. The further the train took us from London, the more nervous I felt, and I couldn't really put my finger on what it was that I was nervous about. Maybe I was afraid that Joe would see me in a different light, as I seemed to morph into a completely different person once I turned in at my front gate. I had also exaggerated the quirkiness of my family and maybe once Joe actually met them, he would find them rather dull. I'd met Joe's family once, and they were lovely, even though they were very different to mine. For a start they didn't live on a council estate – they lived in a proper house with a drive and a garage. I wasn't ashamed of where I'd come from, not one bit. In fact if I thought for one minute that Joe might look down on them I'd drop him like a hot brick.

'Are you feeling brave enough to try this sandwich?' asked Joe, staring suspiciously at the limp wet ham lying between two pieces of grey bread, which was already curling up at the edges. 'I'm not sure this ever had a face.'

'I think I'm going to have to, I'm starving.'

He passed me half of the sandwich, and I bit into it. 'Actually I think I've lost my appetite.'

'That bad, eh?'

'It tastes like something the cat brought in – in fact no cat would bother to bring it in.'

I put the sandwich back down on the table and stared out of the window at the passing fields and houses. A few more stops and we'd be home. And I knew in my heart that I wasn't worried about Joe meeting my family. I was worried about being in the same town as Ralph, especially with Joe.

CHAPTER THIRTEEN

I could see Mum looking out of the window as we got near the house, and she was at the front door as we walked up the path.

'I've been looking out for you,' she said.

I was pleased to see that she looked much better than the last time I'd seen her. 'You look better,' I said, kissing her cheek.

'I am better, love.'

'Really?'

'I keep telling everyone it was just one of my funny turns.'

'Well it wasn't very funny.'

Mum smiled at Joe. 'It's lovely to finally meet you, Joe,' she said.

'You too, Mrs Perks.'

'Your Aunty Brenda's here,' she said in a whisper. 'She wanted to meet Joe.'

That didn't surprise me at all. Aunty Brenda didn't like to be left out of things.

Joe and I followed Mum into the kitchen. Aunty Brenda was at the sink, filling the kettle. She lit the gas ring, placed the kettle on the flame and turned around.

'Let me look at you,' she said, smiling.

'I can't have changed that much,' I said, laughing. 'You only saw me a few weeks ago.'

'Well I like to make sure, and this must be your young man,' she said, smiling at Joe.

'Yes, this is Joe,' I said. 'Joe, this is my Aunty Brenda.'

Joe held out his hand. 'Pleased to meet you.'

Aunty Brenda went all coy. 'Lovely manners,' she said. 'I like to see that in a man.'

'I've put Joe in Clark's room,' said Mum. 'Clark's staying round at Emma's.'

Just then Dad walked into the kitchen. 'He's always staying round at Emma's,' he said. 'Young people today are very casual about sleeping arrangements.'

'Joe this is my dad.'

'Joe shook Dad's hand'

'Now I hope you don't think I'm rushing you,' said Mum, 'but…'

'She's rushing you' said Dad, lighting the end of a very thin roll-up.

Mum wrinkled her nose. 'What have I told you about smoking when we've got company.'

'Joe's not company, he's our Dottie's boyfriend, practically family. You don't mind do you, Joe?'

'Not a bit,' said Joe.

'Good lad.'

'Now what was I saying?'

'Something about not rushing us,' I said.

'Oh yes. Well we've all been invited round to Rita's for a barbeque. I hope that's all right with you, Joe.'

'It's fine with me, Mrs Perks.'

'Bloody barbeque,' said Dad. 'Who wants to eat burnt bloody sausages in the bloody garden when there's a perfectly good table in the dining room.'

'Rita says it's a special occasion,' said Mum. 'I can't for the life of me think what it can be.'

'Perhaps it's in honour of Joe,' said Aunty Brenda, smiling at him.

'And pigs might fly,' I said.

'Yes you're probably right, Dottie. That's not Rita's style, is it?'

'Perhaps they're having another baby,' I said.

'I shouldn't think so, love. She had a terrible time with Miranda Louise.'

'And don't we know it,' said Dad, relighting his roll-up.

'I don't know why you bother with those things, Nelson,' said Aunty Brenda. 'They go out more times than they stay alight.'

'Leave him, Brenda,' said Mum. 'Striking a match is the only exercise he gets.'

'Very funny, Maureen,' said Dad.

'Right then, Dottie, you take your bags upstairs and have a bit of a freshen up and then we'd better get going.'

Joe picked up the bags and followed me upstairs. I showed him Clark's room, and he put his bag on the bed.

'Your parents are lovely.'

'My parents are bonkers.'

'Nice bonkers though.'

Joe lay back on the bed and pulled me down beside him. 'What a waste of a perfectly good double bed.'

'Don't even think about it,' I said, grinning. 'Dad would have a fit.'

'So I get to meet the lovely Rita?'

'You don't mind, do you?'

'I'm intrigued. She sounds like quite a personality.'

'I suppose that's one way of putting it. We're just very different, that's all. There are times when I wonder if we actually come from the same family. We don't even look alike. Rita got all the looks, even down to the blonde hair.'

Joe twirled a lock of my hair around his finger. 'I love your hair,' he said.

'And I love *you*, but I have to get changed.' I kissed him on the lips and went into my bedroom. I brushed my hair and put on a bit more lippy, then Joe and I went back downstairs.

We all caught the bus round to Rita's. Joe and I ran up to the top deck while the rest of the family stayed downstairs. I pointed out all my special places: Mary's house, the park and the youth club.

When we got to Rita's house we went through the side gate and into the garden. Rita was coming out of the kitchen carrying a bowl of salad. Nigel was leaning over a very shiny red barbeque that was belching out thick white smoke.

'Bloody hell,' said Dad, coughing. 'What are you trying to do, kill us all?'

'That's rich coming from you,' said Rita. 'If fifty fags a day hasn't killed you off then nothing will.'

'Where's Miranda?' I said.

'It's Miranda Louise, if you don't mind. That is what she was christened before God and that's what we call her.'

Rita and I were already off to a bad start. We couldn't seem to help ourselves.

'Sorry. Where is she?'

'She takes her nap at this time.'

'I thought you said she doesn't sleep much.'

'That's why she needs a nap,' she snapped. 'Anyway I suppose this must be Joe.' She put the bowl of salad down on what looked like a trestle table, with a red and white and blue paper cloth on it, and held out her hand.

After the introductions were over, Joe and I walked down the garden.

'Mmm, I see what you mean about Rita,' said Joe, raising his eyebrows.

'Exactly,' I said.

We walked over to the barbeque and said hello to Nigel. Tiny beads of sweat were running down his face and disappearing into his collar.

'Do you want a hand?' said Joe, rolling up his sleeves.

'Thanks, mate,' said Nigel, almost crying with relief. 'I've never used one of these before. It took nearly an hour to read the instructions, and I still haven't got the hang of it.'

'My parents have got one,' said Joe. 'Once the coals are nice and red it's a breeze.'

I left them to it, Joe looked pleased to be doing something, and Nigel looked relieved. I wandered over to the family. They were all sitting in a circle on the white plastic chairs.

'Do we know what we're celebrating yet?' I asked.

'No, it's still a big surprise by the look of it.'

As if on cue the 'surprise' came through the side gate – Peggy ran into the garden, followed by Fiona and Ralph.

CHAPTER FOURTEEN

I felt sick and panicky and wrong-footed. Fiona looked just as lovely as the last time I'd seen her. She was wearing a white cotton shift dress with a pale pink cardigan around her shoulders. Her fair hair looked sleek and shiny. It caught the sun as she smiled up at Ralph. She looked about sixteen, young and fresh and happy. I felt grubby from the train journey. Why hadn't I spent more time getting ready? Why hadn't I washed my hair this morning instead of lying in bed till the last minute? But I knew why – because it was just the family, it was just Joe.

I wanted to run, but at that moment I couldn't have moved if my life had depended on it. Peggy spotted me and ran across the lawn.

'We're going to Stralia,' she said, looking up at me.

'Where?'

'Stralia, where the kangaroos live.'

I could see Ralph and Fiona watching us. I turned my attention back to Peggy and what she was saying. 'You're going to Australia?'

She frowned. 'That's what I said.'

'For a holiday?' My stomach was now in a tight knot, and my heart felt as if it was about to jump out of my chest. They weren't going to live there, were they?

'Did you know that mummy kangaroos keep their babies in their pockets?'

'For a holiday?' I asked again.

Peggy stared down at the ground then she looked up at me. 'I'm going with my daddy and my new mummy. We're going to Stralia. That's where we're going.' Then she ran off.

I seemed to have got the use of my legs back, and I made my way over to Joe and Nigel. I desperately needed to be near Joe.

Clark and Emma came into the garden just as I reached his side. They looked like a couple of exotic birds. Emma was wearing yellow flared trousers with flowers embroidered down the legs. She had a red bandanna tied around her head. Clark had on green velvet flares and a suede jacket edged with fur. They waved at us.

'That's my brother Clark,' I said to Joe. 'And his girlfriend Emma.'

'And I'm presuming that the chap with the pretty girl is Ralph?'

I didn't get the chance to answer, because just at that moment, Rita's voice soared across the garden. She was banging a wine glass with a spoon. 'Attention everyone. Nigel,' she shouted.

Nigel was taking his job as chef very seriously. His bottom lip was thrust out as he concentrated on the sausages and burgers. Joe nudged him. 'You're wanted, mate.'

'What?'

'You're wanted by your missus, and you might want to ditch the pinny.'

'Nigel,' shouted Rita, louder this time.

Nigel hurried across to where Rita was standing.

I stood as close to Joe as I could get. He smiled at me and draped his arm around my shoulder. I was beginning to feel calmer now that I was near him.

'Listen everyone,' said Rita. 'As you all know, Ralph and Fiona were going to be married in a few months' time, but all that has changed and they're now getting married in four weeks.' She looked across at Ralph and Fiona for confirmation. Ralph held up three fingers. 'Sorry,' said Rita, giggling. 'They are now getting married in three weeks,' she said. 'They are going to be Ten-Pound Poms and emigrating to Australia. So let's all raise our glasses to Ralph, Fiona and little Peggy.'

I guess I now knew why Ralph had wanted to talk to me. He had wanted to tell me this news himself so that it wouldn't come as such a shock, because it *was* a shock, a huge shock, and there was nothing that I could do about it. I was surrounded by people. I couldn't cry, I couldn't scream. I had to pretend that I was all right, but I wasn't.

Nobody had a drink so there was this silence.

'Nigel,' hissed Rita, 'why haven't they got drinks?'

'I was cooking the sausages.'

'Well they can't make a toast with a sausage, can they?' said Rita, glaring at him.

'Oh, I don't know,' said Clark, 'I'm starving.'

'You're always starving,' said Rita.

'Come on,' said Joe to me. 'Let's help the poor chap out and pour some drinks.'

I was glad to be busy. I couldn't look at Ralph. I had barely looked at him since he had arrived.

Joe and I poured the drinks and handed them round. Then Joe went back to the barbeque to help Nigel.

'I'd rather have a cup of tea and so would your dad,' said Mum.

'No, I wouldn't,' said Dad. 'I'd rather have a beer.'

'I'll get you one once we've done the toast, and I'll make you some tea, Mum.'

'Now that you've all got your drinks,' shouted Rita, 'let's raise our glasses to Fiona, Ralph and Peggy, and wish them health and happiness for their new life in Australia.'

I forced a smile on my face as I raised my glass, then looked across at Mum. She was looking at me in a way that only my mum can, as if she was looking into my very soul. She has always been able to do that. I have never been able to fool her.

'Come and sit next to me, love,' she said.

I sat down in one of the plastic chairs. Mum took my hand and held it in her lap.

'Are you all right?'

'I think so,' I said. 'At least I think I will be.'

'Well you don't have to keep it all inside. Sometimes it helps to get it out.'

'Listen to your mum, Dottie. She knows what she's talking about.'

'I know, Aunty Brenda, and I'll think about it.'

'Think about what?' said Clark.

'Life,' I said.

'Oh that old thing. Well as far as I can see, life just happens whether you want it to or not.'

'Thanks, Clark,' I said. 'That was very deep.'

The chair that I was sitting on was hard and unyielding, but the sun was warm on my face. I closed my eyes. I could hear snatches of conversation going on around me. I could hear Peggy's laughter. If I could have stayed like that all afternoon I would have. Why did I feel like this every time I saw Ralph? I loved Joe. I did, and as long as I didn't see Ralph I was fine. Well I wouldn't have to worry any more, because after today I wouldn't ever have to see him again. Ralph would marry the beautiful Fiona, and they would have a beautiful house in Australia, and that would be the end of it.

Suddenly I remembered a saying that some bright spark at the magazine wanted to use after Otis Redding died in a plane crash. 'Our crown of sorrows is remembering happier times.' We never used it, and I wasn't even sure that I understood it at the time, but I did now. I remembered another sunny day. Ralph and me up on the Sussex Downs, talking about our future together. How we would build a house on the hillside with a porch running round it. How we would sit together on two rocking chairs and watch the sun setting over the sea. I opened my eyes and looked straight into Ralph's. He was staring at me. I wanted to run over to him and say, 'Don't marry Fiona. Don't go to Australia.' Then I noticed that Joe was standing right behind him. He smiled at me, but it was a sad kind of a smile.

I somehow managed to get through the rest of the afternoon. Miranda Louise woke up and was passed around the family. She was overdressed as usual. Rita seemed to have an obsession with keeping her warm – the poor child was sweating under multiple layers of clothes. Then Peggy fell into a pile of nettles and screamed the place down. She looked just like Mary when she had a cob on. Rita blamed poor Nigel for the nettles.

The afternoon seemed endless. I was desperate to leave, but I couldn't. Rita would never forgive me. It crossed my mind to say that I was feeling ill, but I didn't want to draw attention to myself. I just wanted to be on my own, but I was with Joe, and I had a feeling that he would know why I wanted to go, and I couldn't hurt him like that. So I smiled, I managed to eat a sausage, I watched Peggy running around, I held Miranda and I avoided being alone with Ralph and Fiona. I did the best I could until eventually the party came to an end and I was able to leave.

We all piled back on the bus and went home. Joe was quiet but he held my hand, and I felt safe again.

Once we were back indoors, Mum put the kettle on, but Dad said he fancied a pint. 'Why don't we all go down the Queen's Head for a drink?' he said.

'Take Joe,' said Mum. 'I'd like to spend some time with my girl.'

'You up for it, Joe?'

'Absolutely,' said Joe.

Once they were gone I took cups and saucers out of the cupboard and put them on the table. Mum poured some hot water into the teapot, swished it round then poured it down the sink. She always warmed the pot before she put the tea leaves in. It was comforting watching the same routines that I'd seen all my life.

It was warm in the kitchen and even though it was late afternoon, the sun was streaming through the net curtains. I took off my cardigan and sat down.

'How are you, love, are you all right?'

I stared down at the tablecloth. I didn't want her worrying about me.

'I'm fine,' I said.

'I saw the look on your face today, Dottie, when you heard about Ralph and Fiona emigrating.'

'I wasn't expecting it. I wish I'd known what the barbeque was in aid of, then it wouldn't have come as such a shock. I can't get it out of my head.'

'I thought as much.'

'I've cared about Ralph for so long that I don't know how to stop caring for him. I don't know if it's love or habit. Knowing that he's with someone else, that he is going to marry her and go to Australia, scares me. It feels as if I'm losing a part of who I am. Does that make any sense?'

Mum put the tea on the table and sat down. 'You have some decisions to make, love.'

'Do I?'

'I think you know you do.'

'But what have I got to decide?'

'Whether you want to be with Ralph or whether you can let him go.'

'But that's just it, I don't know. I wish I did.'

'Well only you can decide that. Only you know the truth, Dottie, and you've got three weeks to work out what you want.'

'But what about Joe? And what about Fiona?'

'This isn't about Joe and Fiona. This is about you and Ralph.'

I took a mouthful of tea. It was too sweet. I made a face. Mum just couldn't accept that I'd given up sugar.

'Too much sugar?' she asked.

I nodded.

'I keep forgetting.'

'What am I going to do, Mum?'

She reached across the table and held my hand. 'The right thing,' she said. 'You must do what's right for you.'

CHAPTER FIFTEEN

I'd been back in London a week, and I was no nearer to making a decision. Polly and I were sitting in the kitchen of Victoria Terrace eating a Vesta beef curry. Last night over a couple of bottles of Blue Nun I had finally told Polly the whole story of me, Ralph and Mary.

'Bloody hell, Dottie,' she said. 'Sounds like a Mills & Boon novel.'

'Without the happy ending,' I said.

'You must miss her.'

'I do. It's easier here in London. It's when I go back to Brighton that it hits me the hardest.'

'You must have been mad at her when she got pregnant. How the hell did you cope with that?'

'I didn't, not really, and we didn't speak for months, but I missed her so much, maybe even more than I missed Ralph. I think it was the worst time of my life. I trusted them both. Mary was my best friend, and Ralph was the boy I loved, and between them they broke my heart.'

'How did you manage to forgive them? I'm not sure that I could have – in fact I'm sure I couldn't have. I mean, bloody hell, he was your boyfriend, and he got your best friend pregnant!'

'I was tired of carrying all that hate around with me, and in the end it all just sorted itself out. It was so hard to keep on hating them when I still loved them both so much.

As the evening wore on Polly and I got progressively more sozzled, and we came up with a very drunken solution to it all, which in the cold light of day neither of us had any recollection of.

'How long have you got?'

'Two weeks now.'

'What if you decide you want to be with him, and he decides that he doesn't want to be with you?'

'I guess that's just a risk I'll have to take.'

'Hell of a risk – you could end up with no one.'

'I guess I could.' I put my fork down on the table. 'Sorry, I can't eat this curry.'

'You've hardly eaten anything since you came back from Brighton.' Polly scooped the remains of the curry onto her plate. 'I'm going to be as fat as a house if I keep having to eat your leftovers.'

'You don't have to eat them.'

'Waste not want not,' she said. 'Besides, other people's problems always give me an appetite.'

The sun was streaming through the large Victorian windows and into the kitchen. I loved it here. I loved sharing this flat with Polly. I loved my job, and most of all I loved being with Joe. Why the hell was I even considering giving it all up to go back to Brighton to be with Ralph?

'I'd miss you if you went back,' said Polly, putting her fork down. 'I've lost *my* appetite now.'

'Sorry.'

'Why don't we do one of those brainstorming things that we had to do at school? You know, make a list of all their pros and cons.'

'I think we did that last night.'

'Did we?'

'I think we did. It should be around somewhere.'

Polly went into the front room and came back with a scrappy piece of paper with some scrawls on it. This was obviously the light-bulb moment that we were sure would be the solution to all my problems.

'What does it say?'

Polly, who is very short-sighted but won't give in and wear glasses, squinted at the piece of paper.

'I'm blowed if I know,' she said, passing it across the table.

I looked at it. 'I think that Joe won.'

'So?'

'We were pissed – it doesn't count.' I wasn't ready to make a decision based on drunken ramblings.

'I always think that everything's so much clearer when you're pissed,' said Polly.

Suddenly Mrs P shouted up the stairs. 'Are you cooking foreign food up there?'

Polly grinned at me. 'No, Mrs Pierce, it's English.'

'Well it doesn't smell English from down here.'

'It doesn't smell English from up here either,' I whispered.

We listened for her footsteps on the stairs, but all was quiet

I sat at the table with my head in my hands. Time was ticking by, and maybe I should just let it tick. For heaven's sake, I loved Joe, didn't I? And Ralph loved Fiona. I shook my head trying to clear it.

'Come on girl,' said Polly. 'I'm taking you out.'

I groaned.

'Well it's better than moping around here. Where do you fancy going?'

'To bed?' I said hopefully.

'Time to visit Mrs Dickens,' she said, smiling.

'Good idea,' I said. I could certainly do with a distraction and I loved visiting Mrs Dickens.

We took the bus up to Highgate. As we climbed up the steep hill I began to feel better. I was glad that Polly had made me come out. This was a part of London that we both loved. We jumped off the bus and walked through the big iron gates that led into the cemetery. It was like being in another world. It smelt of rotting vegetation and decay. We walked along pathways through overgrown shrubbery, past sleeping angels and crumbling tombstones, long abandoned and soon to be overtaken by nature. Gnarled roots of old trees snaked their way across graves so old that epitaphs that had once been chiselled into the stone were long gone.

Eventually we came to the grave of Charles Dickens's wife, Catherine. We sat down on the grass beside her. I loved this place; it was so peaceful. The only sounds were the gentle movement of the trees and the rustling of leaves, unseen creatures rummaging around in the undergrowth, the dull drone of the bees and the constant twittering of the birds.

I suppose it was a bit of a daft thing to do, visiting a dead poet's dead wife, but we'd been doing it on and off for about a year. Polly and I used to use the cemetery as a kind of cut through to the shops. We had stumbled across the grave purely by accident – we hadn't even known that she was buried there. Highgate Cemetery was popular with visitors who came to see the grave of Karl Marx. No one seemed to visit Mrs Dickens. I suppose she just wasn't that popular. Polly said that she felt sorry for her, all alone and forgotten, and that we should pop in and see her sometimes. So that's how it started. Then Polly took to telling her, her problems, and she swore blind that Mrs Dickens sorted them out.

I concentrated hard and told her what was worrying me. Nothing happened.

'Give her a minute,' said Polly. 'She's thinking.'

Just then a robin flew down and settled on the top of the old stone grave.

'If he was called Ralph or Joe instead of Robin, I would have taken that as a sign,' said Polly, grinning. 'Have either of them got a red breast?'

'Not that I've noticed,' I said, and we both fell about giggling. An elderly couple walking past smiled at us.

'Hang on,' said Polly, wiping her face on the sleeve of her cardigan. 'Ralph's got red hair, hasn't he?'

'Absolutely,' I said, still giggling.

'Well there's your sign. I knew Mrs Dickens wouldn't let us down.'

Polly took off her cardigan, made a pillow for her head and lay down on the grass.

'What is it with you and Ralph?'

'What do you mean?'

'Well, you say you're in love with Joe, and I really think you are, but one glimpse of this Ralph bloke and you go to pieces. It's almost as if he's got some sort of hold over you.'

'Don't be so dramatic.'

'Well, it *is* dramatic, isn't it? The whole thing's pretty dramatic. I mean you love it here, you love your job, your flatmate – obviously – and yet I bet if Ralph Bennett snapped his fingers you'd go running.'

'I wouldn't.'

'Are you sure?'

'I'm as sure as I can be.'

'Which isn't very.'

I lay down beside Polly and closed my eyes. Was she right? Would I go running if Ralph snapped his fingers and why now? I could have stayed in Brighton after Mary died. I'd known that Ralph still loved me. I could have given us another chance. But I didn't. I ran away, and now he had fallen in love with someone else. Is that why I wanted him? Because I was about to lose him?

'So what is it about him that keeps you dangling?'

I opened my eyes. Polly had propped herself up on one elbow and was staring down at me.

'I'm not dangling.'

'Well you're doing something.'

'It's hard to explain.'

'Try.'

How do you explain a lifetime of loving someone, and how do you know if what you are feeling is really love?

'Well?' said Polly, poking me.

'I can't explain something to you that I don't understand myself. Go and have a wander through the gravestones and stop nagging.'

'I'm not nagging, I'm just concerned.'

'Well go and be concerned somewhere else.'

After Polly had gone, I lay staring up at the sky, watching a cloud of midges floating in the rays of the sun that filtered through the tall trees. One day I would figure out what tied me to Ralph but it wasn't today.

CHAPTER SIXTEEN

Monday morning found me back at my desk, looking at a picture of Paul McCartney and Linda Eastman, standing outside Marylebone register office. It had been besieged by hundreds of distraught teenagers, weeping and wailing because their idol had got married. For heaven's sake what did they expect him to do? Stay celibate because some spotty little girl in Clapton-on-Turnip thought he should be marrying her? No one had loved Paul more that I had, but I was under no illusion that he would ever pick me out of a line-up to be the next Mrs McCartney.

I thought Linda looked lovely. She was wearing a bright yellow coat and Paul was wearing a matching tie. Maybe yellow was Linda's favourite colour, the same as Mary's.

I hoped Linda would take care of Paul. I don't know why, but I always had the feeling that he needed taking care of. Mary had been crazy mad about John Lennon, and while I thought of myself as Paul's counsellor and confidante, all Mary wanted to do was jump John's bones, which, looking back, seemed more natural somehow.

The pictures were good. I looked at the name of the photographer, but I didn't recognise it.

The piece was written by resident office creep and general pain in the neck Miles Denton. He was writing about how, in his opinion – which seemed to be the only opinion he cared about – their marriage would never last. My job was to go through the article with a fine toothcomb to make sure he hadn't written anything that would end up with the magazine being sued. Part of me was hoping that he had. I would love to be the one to wipe that smug look off his face. The annoying part of it was that he seemed to get the stories that no one else managed to get. At the weekends he would be propping up the bar down the Elephant and Castle picking up all the local gossip. He even said he had it on the best authority that John Lennon was about to marry Yoko Ono. I wondered what Mary's reaction would have been to that.

Mary had been dead for four years, but not a day went by without something reminding me of her and the friendship we shared. A song, a face in the crowd or passing a hospital. My life had changed beyond all recognition. Working on a trendy music magazine was a far cry from the cosmetics counter in Woolies. And yet there were times when I longed for those days, those summer days that seemed to go on forever. Sitting on the school field next to the boy with the ginger hair. Soaring high into the sky on the Ferris wheel, Mary in the car above us with Elton Briggs, the love of her life. Walking over the Sussex Downs, holding hands, planning a future. Was that what I wanted back? Those innocent days were gone. That boy was gone. Did I love Joe enough to give up the lovely life that I was now leading? The whole thing was giving me a headache.

Polly worked just round the corner from me in Boots. She stood behind the Elizabeth Arden stand selling perfume. She always smelt lovely and her make-up was always perfect. Today we were meeting for lunch.

By the time I got to the Bluebird café in the King's Road, Polly was already sitting down at a table.

'I've ordered egg and chips for both of us, is that okay?'

I wasn't really that hungry, and the thought of eating a plate of greasy egg and chips was making me feel a bit sick.

Polly noticed. 'Egg and chips are just what you need, girl, you're fading away.'

'Hardly.'

'You are. I'm pig sick.'

'You can have my problems any time you like. I'll give them to you gift wrapped.'

'Come to a decision yet?'

'I have actually.'

'Crikey, tell me all.'

'I've decided to stay with Joe.' Saying this out loud felt like someone had lifted a huge weight off my shoulders. I had been tormenting myself over something that was never going to happen. I knew that there would be times when I would be sad that Ralph was going to begin a new life in Australia, but the time had come to let him go – not just out of the country but out of my head.

'Really?'

'I think so.'

' *Think* isn't a decision, think is a maybe.'

'I'm going to stay with Joe.'

'Why am I not convinced?'

'You tell me.'

'You don't look that happy about it.'

'Give me a chance, I've only just decided – about ten minutes ago to be precise. I haven't had time for it to filter through yet.'

Just then the usual waitress that served us plonked rather than placed two plates of egg and chips on the table in front of us.

'Want any sauces?' she asked in a bored voice.

'Ketchup, if it's no bother,' said Polly.

The girl sighed as if we had just asked her to catch the next plane to Italy and pummel the tomatoes with her feet. She returned to the table with the tomato-shaped plastic bottle.

'Anything else?'

'No thanks,' I said, smiling at her.

'I don't know why you always smile at her, Dottie. She doesn't deserve to be smiled at – she's positively rude. I don't know why she works here if she hates it so much. If it wasn't for the fact that they do the best chips in London I wouldn't come here at all.'

'Yes, you would, Polly Renson. It's not the chips you fancy, it's the chef.'

Polly grinned at me. 'It's true. I can't deny it. I want to marry him immediately and bear his children.'

'You like him that much?'

Polly squeezed a great glob of ketchup over her chips and sighed. 'I'd just like to like *someone* that much.'

'I think you're better off as you are.'

'So speaks the voice of wisdom.'

'So speaks the voice of utter confusion.'

'That doesn't sound like someone who's just made a decision.'

'Doesn't it?'

'No, it doesn't.'

'Oh God.'

CHAPTER SEVENTEEN

I met Joe outside The Roundhouse. I'd been given two free tickets to a gig there. That was one of the perks of working at the magazine – we were given lots of freebies. It was a lovely soft summer evening. London was buzzing, as always, traffic on the roads and the Tube trains rattling in the distance. Already a crowd was gathering outside the venue, waiting for the doors to open. The crowd was mostly young men wearing jeans and leather jackets and Pink Floyd T-shirts, huddled together in their little groups, smoking and talking and miming strumming guitars. I smiled to myself, imagining my dad beside me snorting with indignation.

Joe was leaning against the wall. He looked… oh he looked beautiful. The light was behind him, and he was so relaxed, so natural. I slowed my footsteps. I thought how lucky I was to be going out with such a good-hearted, good-looking boy. Some people passed in front of me, and I lost sight of him for a moment, but they moved, and there he was, and he must have felt my eyes on him because he looked up and saw me. He smiled and wandered over. He took hold of my hand and put his face down to kiss me, but I turned at the last moment so his lips touched my cheek, not my mouth.

'Are you okay?' he asked.

'Yeah, fine,' I said. I tried to smile in a reassuring way, but even I could tell that it was unconvincing. 'I've got a bit of a headache,' I said.

'Well you've come to the right place then,' said Joe. 'A rock concert will soon sort that out.'

I smiled a little more enthusiastically and took my hand out of his. I pretended to look for something inside my handbag, found some lipgloss and put it on. I spent a long time doing it. Joe stood beside me. I couldn't look him in the eye.

The truth was I was angry with Joe. He hadn't done anything wrong; he hadn't said anything or stepped out of line at all. No, I was angry with him because I had decided to choose him over Ralph. It wasn't Joe's fault of course. He had had absolutely no say in the matter. It was all down to me. There was no point chasing might-have-been dreams. Ralph was a part of my past. Joe was my present – Joe was my future. But none of that stopped me resenting Joe for being Joe, not Ralph.

'We've got time for a drink,' he said.

'Hmm?'

'There's time for a drink, before the gig. We could find a pub. There's got to be one round here.'

'No,' I said. 'The pubs will be full of rockers. I don't want to be part of a crowd.'

'Okay,' said Joe, 'suit yourself. I just thought a glass of water might help your head.'

'Oh stop fussing, Joe,' I snapped. He took a step away from me. 'Sorry,' I said. 'I'm sorry.'

We walked, together but apart, closer to the building and joined the back of the queue.

I can't remember anything about the concert. I couldn't name a single song that was sung or anything that happened. It must have been hot and noisy. There must have been banter, the music must have been amazing, but I don't remember any of it. All I remember is standing stiff and awkward beside Joe, thinking about Ralph. I tried to snap myself out of my mood, but I just couldn't.

Afterwards we went back to Joe's flat. He opened a bottle of wine and poured me a glass. I drank it straight back, and then refilled the glass myself and drank that too. It wasn't like me, but I thought if I drank enough, then maybe, just maybe, I could stop counting off the minutes until Ralph and Peggy left England.

Joe was watching but pretending that he wasn't.

'How's your head?' he asked.

'What?'

'Your head. You had a headache.'

'Oh, it's better.' I held out my glass, and he topped it up again. The wine was sloshing about all sour in my stomach.

'Sit down,' said Joe. He pointed towards the couch with its cushions and blankets. I normally curled up on that sofa and tucked my legs underneath myself. But not that evening.

'Perhaps I'd better go,' I said.

'Don't be daft – you've only just got here. Stay the night.'

'Why? Because you don't feel like walking me home?'

'Dottie!'

'I'm sorry,' I said again. I sat down, not on the couch but on the little single chair. I put the glass on the floor and put my head in my hands.

'What's the matter? Are you worrying about your mum?'

I shook my head.

'What then?'

I didn't answer.

'You don't have to do this, you know.'

'Do what?'

'Oh, Dottie, you know what.'

I said nothing. Joe stood up again. He went over to the window. The curtains were open. Outside, night had fallen but the street lights glowed orange.

'You don't have to be with me,' he said.

And there it was, clear as anything – the light-bulb moment. The thought of losing Joe was like a knife going through my heart. All right, that was a bit dramatic, but I knew right then and there that it was Joe I wanted to be with. It was such a relief that I threw my arms around him and sobbed into his chest.

'Hey,' he said, holding me tightly, 'what's this all about?'

I could hardly speak. 'I love you, that's all.'

'Shouldn't that be making you happy?'

'I am happy.'

'Oh, so that's what happy looks like these days, is it?'

'I've been rotten to you all evening, haven't I?'

'I wouldn't go so far as to say rotten. A bit detached maybe.'

'I know and I'm sorry.'

'You've had a lot on your mind, haven't you?'

I let him speak.

'And I'd have to be pretty dumb not to know what it was.'

I didn't know what was coming, but I guessed it wasn't something that I wanted to hear.

'You see, I saw you. I saw the way you looked at Ralph, at the barbecue,' he said.

'I'm an idiot, aren't I?'

Joe took my face gently in his hands. 'Not an idiot, darling girl, just someone with a big heart. The thing is, I need to be the only one in it. I need to know that in a few years' time you won't be regretting anything.'

'I won't, I promise I won't.' And I wouldn't. Joe was good and kind, and I'd been pretty stupid – I realised that now. I had been struggling with the fact that Ralph was going far away. He wouldn't be in Brighton any more. My last links with him would be broken.

'Good, because I intend to keep you in my life for a long, long time.'

Joe knelt down in front of me. At first I wondered what he was doing, then he took a little box out of his pocket. I could feel my heart racing.

'Dottie Perks,' he said. 'Will you take a chance and muddle through this funny old life with me?'

It had been such a strange, barmy day, and my emotions were all over the place. I looked at Joe's dear face and started crying again.

'Do I take that as a yes,' said Joe smiling, 'or should I be worried?'

I took a deep breath and said, 'Yes, of course, yes.'

CHAPTER EIGHTEEN

I woke up the next morning feeling refreshed. I had slept the sleep of the dead. For the first time in ages I felt at peace, absolutely and totally at peace. I hadn't realised quite how heavy a burden I had been carrying round, but now it was gone. I could think of Ralph without feeling sick and anxious and worried. His imminent departure had been like a ticking clock that I couldn't get out of my head and Mum's words had kept coming back to me. 'You've got three weeks to work out what you want.' Well, I've worked it out, Mum, and I want Joe – and I didn't have to do anything. Ralph would marry Fiona, and I would marry Joe, and that's the way it was meant to be.

I lifted my hand and looked at the ring glittering away on my finger, and I was truly happy.

I looked at Joe. He was fast asleep, one of his legs hanging over the side of the bed. That's the way he always slept, as if he was perpetually ready for flight. I sat down on the bed and kissed his cheek. He murmured and turned over.

'I have to go,' I whispered.

Joe yawned and opened his eyes. 'What time is it?'

'Six o'clock.'

'Come back to bed. It's the middle of the night.'

'I wish I could, but I have to get home.'

'Why?'

'I can't wear these clothes to work.'

'I'll take you.'

'No point, I'll get a bus. Go back to sleep.'

I kissed him again, properly this time. He groaned.

'Throw a sickie.'

'You're leading me astray.'

'That's the idea.'

I stood up. 'Really, I have to go. I am a very busy and important person, and the office will fall apart without me.'

'You don't know what you're missing.'

'I think I probably do.'

I got to the door and turned around. 'Thank you for asking me to be your wife, Mr Austin.'

'You are very welcome, Miss Perks.'

Once back at Victoria Terrace I went straight into the kitchen and popped two pieces of toast under the grill, then I went into my bedroom to get ready for work. I had this bubbly, excited feeling in my tummy. I felt like singing or dancing or… oh I don't know, just something. I felt like a child on Christmas Eve. I hadn't felt like this for so long.

I opened the window to let in some air. A few early risers were making their way across the green towards the station. The sun was shining on this perfect of perfect days.

By the time I went into the kitchen, Polly was plastering the toast with butter. She handed me a slice and we ran down the stairs, eating the toast as we went. We walked across the park and headed towards Highbury & Islington Tube station. There were the usual million people waiting on the platform.

'How I love mornings,' said Polly, sighing.

'Cheer up,' I said, smiling at her. 'The sun is shining, and we are two fantastically successful girls about town with the world at our feet.'

'Bloody hell, Dottie. You hate mornings more than I do. You must have had one hell of a night with Joe.'

'I did actually.'

Just then the train pulled in, and we nudged and elbowed our way onto it. I ended up under some bloke's armpit and was separated from Polly by two nuns of all things.

'You've definitely made up your mind then?' she said, peering between two black and white wimples.

'Definitely,' I mouthed. Then I raised my hand and waved my finger around.

'Bloody hell!' she screamed. The two nuns glared at her. 'Sorry,' she said.

'He asked you to marry him?' she mouthed.

I wasn't going to have this conversation under a whiffy armpit, so I ignored her. She glared at me and I smiled sweetly back.

As the Tube rattled its way into Sloane Square Polly was almost overcome with curiosity. 'Tell me, tell me, tell me.'

'I *will*, just not now. I'll meet you in the café at lunchtime.'

'How am I going to get through the morning?'

'Think about the chef.'

At work, I managed to hug my secret to myself. For some reason I didn't feel like sharing it just yet. The creep kept coming across to my desk, reeking of Old Spice and bad breath.

'What did you think about the McCartney piece, eh? The editor thinks it's very cutting edge.'

'I'm very pleased for you, Miles,' I said between gritted teeth.

'It's all about keeping the customers satisfied.'

'What are you talking about?'

'No one wants that marriage to work, do they? Least of all the fans.'

'Why not?'

'Well who is this Linda Eastman anyway? No one's heard of her.'

'She's the woman that Paul loves. What more is there to know?'

'Mark my words, Dottie dear. It won't work.'

'Well I hope it does.'

'Fancy a bet on it?'

'I've got better things to do with my money, and as much as I'd love to spend my time talking to you, Miles, I have work to do.' Who did he think he was – the bloody oracle?

I left the office as soon as I could and started to make my way down the King's Road.

'Dottie.'

I turned around and saw Polly running towards me.

'I thought I'd never get away,' she said, catching up with me. She stopped to catch her breath. 'We should start running, Dottie, I'm so unfit.'

'*You're* unfit, so *we* should start running?'

'Okay, *I* should go running.'

We went into the Bluebird café and sat down at one of the tables. There weren't many people in there.

A waitress that we hadn't seen before came over. 'What can I get you?' she said, smiling.

'Where's Miss Happy?' asked Polly.

The girl looked confused. 'Miss who?'

'The girl that usually serves us.'

'She's left.'

'Well I shouldn't think she'll be any great loss,' said Polly.

'No, she won't, but the chef will.'

Polly frowned. 'What do you mean?'

'She's taken the chef with her.'

'*My* chef?'

'*Your* chef?'

'So who's doing the cooking?' I asked quickly.

'George the owner.'

'Is he any good at cooking chips?' said Polly, looking fed up.

'He isn't any good at cooking anything. I would have a sandwich if I were you.'

'Two cheese and tomato then,' I said. 'Is that okay for you, Polly?'

'I suppose so.'

'And two teas.'

Polly put a sugar cube into her mouth and crunched away furiously. 'What on earth does he see in that sour-faced cow?'

'Maybe she has hidden depths.'

'I'll never have his children.'

'I bet he's got a ton of them already.'

'Do you reckon?'

'And he was pretty spotty.'

'He was, wasn't he?'

'All that chip fat.'

Polly grinned. 'Let me see the ring again.'

I held out my hand towards her.

'You lucky cow,' she said. 'Tell me all.'

'You know we went to the concert?'

'Yes.'

'Well, I was awful to him all evening.'

'Why?'

'Because he wasn't Ralph. I was blaming him for not being Ralph.'

'I'm confused. Your love life never fails to confuse me.'

'It never fails to confuse me either.'

'Okay, to recap. All evening you wanted Joe to be Ralph, and then you decided that Joe was the one you wanted, then Joe proposed and you accepted.'

I nodded.

'So that's really it with you and Ralph?'

'I suppose you could say that I came to my senses.'

'Was it terribly romantic?'

'It was terribly unexpected.' I thought back to last night. 'And yes, it was romantic.'

The waitress came back with the sandwiches and put them down on the table. 'Can I get you anything else?' she asked.

'Just the tea,' I said.

'Did he go down on one knee?'

'I think he might have gone down on two knees. I remember thinking that he was about to start praying.'

Polly bit into her sandwich and screwed up her face. 'Too much butter. I hope George hasn't set his heart on a career in cooking. He can't even make a decent sandwich. I mean, even *I* can make a sandwich.'

'Perhaps you should apply for the job.'

'No point now the chef's gone. Anyway tell me – what made you choose Joe?'

'I just knew. All of a sudden, I just knew.'

'Was that before he proposed?'

'Luckily, yes.'

'And you still feel the same this morning.'

'I should jolly well hope so, I just agreed to marry the guy.'

'Thank God for that. Perhaps now we can concentrate on finding *me* a love life.'

'I'm all yours.'

Polly smiled. 'I really am glad for you, Dottie, not least because it means you won't be leaving me.'

'Thanks. I just suddenly feel so free.'

'Welcome to the club. In my experience freedom is overestimated.'

'I don't mean that sort of free. I mean I don't have to worry any more. I know what I want, and I finally know what I don't want.'

'And you want Joe?'

'I want Joe.'

CHAPTER NINETEEN

It was Saturday, the day that Ralph was marrying Fiona in Brighton. I knew it was early. The light beyond the thin curtains barely cast a glow into the room. I leaned over and picked up the white plastic alarm clock beside the bed. It read 5.30. I wanted to roll over, pull the blankets over my head and go back to sleep, but I knew that wasn't going to happen.

I remembered another morning just like this one, when all I had wanted to do was sleep the day away and shut out the world. It was the morning of Mary's wedding to Ralph. It had been Rita of all people that had dragged me out of bed and helped me to face the day. Well she wouldn't be helping me today, that was for sure. Last week Rita had sent me a letter.

As soon as I'd seen the pink envelope propped up on the hallstand, I knew it was from her. I wondered what on earth she could be writing to me about. I just hoped it wasn't bad news. I'd taken the letter upstairs. My room had been stuffy, so I'd gone across to the window and pulled up the sash. A cool breeze wafted into the room. Then I'd opened the letter.

Dear Dottie, it read.

I know this is short notice, but I bumped into Fiona at the weekend, and she has invited you to the evening reception. The wedding is at 2.30 p.m. and the evening do is from 7 onwards. I shouldn't think that you will want to be there, but I thought it was very nice of Fiona to ask you. She says you can bring your boyfriend. Like I said, I shouldn't think that you will want to go, but I said I would ask you.

From,

Rita

I wondered what Mary would have thought of today. During their short marriage she had grown to like Ralph, maybe even love him. I know she would have wanted him and Peggy to be happy, but she would have wanted *me* to be happy too.

I had answered Rita's letter and told her that I couldn't come to the reception but to thank Fiona for her kind invitation. Rita would have been relieved. She wouldn't have wanted me there, and I certainly didn't want to be there.

I stared up at the ceiling. There was a large water stain in the corner that had spread into the room. I tried conjuring up a picture, but I couldn't see anything. I used to have a similar stain on my bedroom ceiling when I was a child. It had looked like a rabbit. This one didn't look like anything. It could have been the perfect shape of a country I didn't recognise. Mary would have known. Mary knew all about the world. There was a map on her bedroom wall that she used to stick pins in.

'Those are all the places I'm going to visit when I grow up,' she'd said. 'You can come with me if you like. The world's your oyster, Dottie.'

'I don't like oysters,' I'd said.

I looked at the clock again. There was still eight and a half hours to go before Ralph and Fiona walked down the aisle. I imagined Fiona waking up this morning, happy and excited. She might be looking at her wedding dress, hanging on the wardrobe door. She would be thinking of her perfect wedding and her new life in Australia with Ralph and Peggy.

Joe was watching Arsenal playing away in Manchester this weekend, and I was glad now that he wasn't here. I needed to get through this day in my own way.

I twirled the pretty ring round my finger. I loved Joe, and I knew that he was the right man for me. I had no regrets about Ralph, but today would still be hard – letting go would be hard.

There was a tap on the door and Polly came in, looking bleary-eyed. She was wearing short pink baby-doll pyjamas.

'I thought you'd be awake. Do you want some company?'

'Yes, please.'

Polly got into bed beside me.

'We should go out today. We should definitely go out,' she said, plumping up the pillows and leaning back against the faded pink velour headboard. 'It's going to be a long day, and you need to take your mind off it. How about breakfast at the café?'

Thank God for Polly.

'What would I do without you?'

'You don't have to do without me.'

It was 11 a.m. when we eventually left the flat. We took the Tube to Sloane Square and walked to the café. There was a notice on the door saying 'Closed until further notice'.

'George must have given up on the cooking,' said Polly.

I hadn't expected to feel hungry, but I was suddenly starving. 'I need to eat.'

'Me too.'

'Let's just get a sandwich and go and talk to Mrs Dickens.'

I knew that we were killing time, but that's exactly what I needed to do.

We took a couple of Tubes and got off at Archway. Then we stopped at a grocer's just outside the station and bought fresh bread, cheese and a couple of apples. Polly bought a bunch of daffodils for Mrs Dickens. It was a beautiful day, so we decided to walk up the hill instead of getting the bus. We cut through Waterlow Park, past the lake and the squawking ducks and through the imposing iron gates that led into Highgate Cemetery.

As always, we were enveloped by the peace and utter tranquillity of the place.

There were a few people wandering around. You could tell the tourists visiting the grave of Karl Marx by the cameras slung around their necks.

Polly picked up an old stone urn that stood on Mrs Dickens's grave and filled it with water from the tap against the crumbling wall.

'This weighs a ton,' she said, struggling back with it.

I took the cellophane off the daffodils and arranged them in the urn. The bright yellow flowers were like a ray of golden light against the darkness of the place.

We sat on the grass.

'Aren't you going to ask her anything?' said Polly, biting into an apple.

I stared at the grave. 'No need.'

'So all your dreams have come true, eh?'

'Yes,' I said, looking down at the ring on my finger.

I was just about to bite into my apple when Polly said, 'There's Ralph.'

'Where?' I said, jumping up and letting the apple roll across the ground.

'Sorry,' she said. 'I meant Ralph the robin.'

'You nearly gave me a heart attack.'

'Sorry,' she said again.

'Anyway, how do you know it's *that* robin?'

'I just do. He's got that Ralph look about him.'

'You've never even met Ralph.' I looked at my watch. 'And you never will now,' I said. 'It's over.' It really was all over. Ralph belonged to Fiona now.

'I know,' said Polly, lying down beside me.

'Thank you for being with me today.'

'That's what friends are for, isn't it?'

The sunshine had made us both drowsy, so we decided to catch the bus home instead of walking. We didn't talk much on the way back, but that was okay. Polly seemed to realise that I wasn't up for much conversation. We got off the bus opposite the Tube station and walked across the park. As we turned into our road, Polly suddenly stopped and said, 'Bloody hell, there's Ralph.'

'For God's sake, Polly, stop freaking me out with the robin jokes.'

'I don't think it's a robin, Dottie.'

And that's when I saw him. He was sitting on the old stone steps leading up to the front door of 59 Victoria Terrace.

CHAPTER TWENTY

Neither of us had moved. 'It *is* him, isn't it?' asked Polly.

I nodded. I couldn't speak. I was numb with shock.

'Didn't he just get married?'

I had no answers for Polly. I just couldn't get my head round the fact that for whatever reason, Ralph was here, in London, and sitting on our front steps when he should be at his wedding.

Ralph saw us and stood up slowly, then sat down again as if standing was too much effort.

'You go on,' I said to Polly.

'Will you be okay?'

'Right now I haven't got a clue what I'm going to be.'

She squeezed my hand and ran up the steps. Ralph didn't even look up as she passed.

I walked across and sat down next to him. He looked ill. His face was an awful grey colour and he kept running his hands through his hair. I took hold of his hand and held it in mine. I suddenly felt very calm and I didn't know why.

'You didn't leave her standing at the altar, did you?' I asked gently.

When at last he spoke, his words were so quiet I could barely hear them. 'I might as well have.'

He hadn't married her. Every emotion I had gone through today had been for nothing. He hadn't married her at all, and I didn't know how I was supposed to feel.

He shook his head, as if he was trying to make sense of what he had done. 'I couldn't stay there. Everyone was putting their two pennerth in. Fiona's parents, her brother, Mary's mum. Elton was the only one I could talk to in the end.'

'How has this affected Peggy?'

'She's confused and angry and sad. She thought she was going to be a bridesmaid. She thought Fiona was going to be her new mummy. Fiona isn't the only one I've hurt.'

Ralph looked like a broken man, and I could understand that, I could, but why was he here? Did he just need a shoulder to cry on? Was that all he wanted?

We sat on those cold stone steps until the light had faded from the sky and the street lights were beginning to come on. He didn't say another word, not one. There were so many things I wanted to ask him but the main one was, 'What do you want from me, Ralph?'

Eventually the front door opened and Polly came down the steps carrying two steaming mugs of coffee. She slowly mouthed, 'What the hell is going on?'

I shook my head.

Then she mouthed, 'It's bloody dark.'

I mouthed back, 'I bloody know.'

She handed Ralph one of the coffees. 'I'm Polly.'

'My flatmate,' I said.

He looked at me as if he had just realised that I was there.

'I should get going,' he said, trying to stand up.

'Where?'

He put his head in his hands. He seemed so lost. 'I don't know.'

'We could try and sneak him past Mrs P,' said Polly.

'I can't stay here. I shouldn't have come,' he said.

'Do you have somewhere else to go?' I asked gently.

'No.'

Whatever I was feeling and no matter how confused I was, Ralph was my friend, and he had come to me because he needed to. I made a decision. 'Then you're staying here,' I said.

Ralph gave a deep sigh. 'Thanks.'

Polly picked up his bag, and I held onto him as we walked slowly up the steps and into the house.

Ralph sat at the kitchen table drinking his coffee, while Polly and I made a bed up for him on the couch.

'What about Mrs P?' said Polly, carrying an extra pillow in from her room.

'I'm going to tell her he's my brother.'

'Do you think she'll buy it?'

'I don't care whether she buys it or not, I can't have him wandering around London all night.'

'He must have left her standing at the altar. Imagine being left at the altar. I'd die.'

'I don't think he did. From what I could make out, there was no wedding today.'

'All that worrying we did and he never got married.'

'I know.'

'What are you going to do?'

'I'll speak to him tomorrow. There's no point in trying tonight, he's exhausted.'

I sounded in control, but I wasn't. I had yet to find out why Ralph had come to me, but at least I knew that it had nothing to do with anything that I'd said or done.

Ralph fell asleep as soon as his head hit the pillow, and I wondered when he had last slept. I, on the other hand, lay in the darkness trying to make sense of what had happened.

Having spent most of the night tossing and turning, I didn't wake until 8.30. When I opened my eyes, Ralph was standing by my bedroom window looking out onto the street. I shifted myself up the bed.

'Hi,' I said.

He turned round. 'Hi,' he said, giving me a weak smile.

'Sleep all right?'

He nodded. 'Thanks for letting me stay.'

'I was hardly going to let you walk off into the unknown.'

'I've made such a mess of things,' he said.

'Can you tell me what happened?'

Ralph turned away from the window and came and sat on the bed. He didn't speak for a while, and when he did I could tell that he was struggling not to cry. He cleared his throat. 'I've been on a kind of roller coaster for months. The wedding plans were going on around me. The banns were read out at the church. I'd given my notice in at the bakery. Fiona had done the same. She was so happy, and Peggy was so excited, and I just felt numb. My brain was wrecked trying to think of a way to let Fiona down gently, but I kept putting it off. I couldn't bear to hurt her.'

'But you must have cared for her enough to have asked her to marry you?'

'Of course I cared for her. There were times when I convinced myself that I loved her. She deserves to be loved, she's a great girl, and she loved me. I wanted it to work. I thought we could be a family. Peggy adores her.'

'But?'

'I saw you at the barbeque, and I knew that I was done with pretending. I should have told her then, but I was hoping that I would feel different. I left it till a week before the wedding, and then I told her that I couldn't marry her. Everyone was furious with me, and I didn't blame them. Like I said, Elton was the only one who didn't judge me, but then you know what Elton's like.'

I smiled when I thought about Elton. Cocky, devil-may-care Elton, the boy that Mary had loved. The boy who, in the end, found it in his heart to make Mary's last wish come true by taking her in his arms and dancing with her, just before she died.

'What was his advice?'

Ralph smiled. 'He said that marriage was bad enough without marrying the wrong girl.'

'Sounds like Elton.'

'He also said that I knew who the right girl was.'

That was when he took hold of my hand and noticed the ring. He swallowed.

'Joe?'

I nodded. I didn't want to talk to Ralph about Joe. I wore his ring on my finger. I had given him a promise. If Ralph had loved Fiona enough then he would have married her. I couldn't make this right for him, but I could be his friend. 'Come here,' I said, making room for him on the bed.

We lay on my little single bed with our arms around each other, both of us lost in our own thoughts. Ralph and I were just two pretty unremarkable kids who became friends then fell in love. The path ahead of us had been straight and clear – house, kids, normal things. We weren't reaching for the stars; we were content just to be together. Life, fate or whoever was in charge up there had other plans for us, and it was time that we both accepted it was over.

'Dottie?'

I put my finger against his lips.

'Hush now,' I said.

CHAPTER TWENTY-ONE

I walked with Ralph down to the Tube station. We didn't speak – there was nothing to say. We stood outside Mrs Spatchcock's shop and said our goodbyes. I could barely breathe. There had been so many goodbyes. Sometimes it felt as if my relationship with Ralph had been one long goodbye.

Ralph reached for my hand. I let my fingers close over his.

'Don't worry about me,' he said, kissing my cheek. 'I'll be okay.'

'I know you will.'

He started to walk away then turned around. 'Be happy, Dottie.'

I watched until he was out of sight, and it felt as though he was taking part of me with him.

I was meeting Joe in the afternoon. We had planned to have a picnic up on Hampstead Heath, so I bought some grapes and tomatoes and a loaf of crusty bread from Mrs Spatchcock's shop and started to walk home.

I knew that Polly would be dying to hear what had happened, but I wasn't ready for that yet.

I got as far as Highbury Fields and sat down on the nearest bench. A watery sun was breaking through the clouds and a cool breeze rustled the leaves on the trees. I shivered and drew my cardigan closer around my body. I pulled down the sleeves so that they covered my hands.

I was filled with an overwhelming sadness. For Ralph, for Fiona, for Peggy and for me. I wondered what Ralph was thinking about as he made his way home to Brighton. He'd more or less said that I was the reason that he couldn't marry Fiona, and yet he hadn't asked anything of me. Perhaps he would have done if he hadn't seen the ring. Perhaps he would have asked if there was still a chance for us, but he hadn't, and for that I was grateful. I was going to marry Joe, sweet uncomplicated Joe, and that was what I wanted.

I got up from the bench and walked home across the field.

I put the food in my room and tapped on Polly's door. She was playing 'Little Red Rooster' really loudly, so I knocked harder. She opened the door and almost dragged me inside.

'I've been on hot bricks all morning! Has he gone?'

'I just took him to the Tube.'

'What the heck happened? Did he leave her at the altar?'

I sat down on Polly's bed. 'No, thank God, he just couldn't go through with the wedding. He called it off a week ago.'

'Bloody hell, you can't help feeling sorry for the poor girl.'

'I can't even think about it.'

'Why did he come *here* though?'

'To tell me that he couldn't marry her knowing that he still loved me.'

'Bloody hell. Did you tell him that you're engaged to Joe?'

'I didn't have to – he saw the ring.'

'So what happens now?'

'Nothing. He's gone back to face the music.'

'Dottie, are you really sure that you want to marry Joe?'

'I'm positive.'

'Well, as long as you're sure.'

'Never been surer of anything in my life.'

'On a purely selfish level I thought you might be going back to Brighton with him. I'd really convinced myself that you weren't coming back.'

'You thought I'd just leave without saying anything?'

'I know, but I'd really wound myself up.'

'Well you can stop worrying, because the only place I'm going today is up on Hampstead Heath with Joe. And for heaven's sake turn that music down. We'll have Mrs P up here in a minute, and I haven't taken the bedding off the couch yet.'

Polly made a face. 'She's already been up. She asked who the man was that stayed overnight. I told her he was your brother.'

'What did she say?'

'She said she very much doubted that, on account of his ginger hair.'

I started to giggle 'And you said?'

'I said he was adopted.'

'You said what?'

'I couldn't think of anything else.'

By now we were both giggling.

'She said she hadn't arrived at 59 Victoria Terrace on a push-bike.'

I left her laughing and went into my bedroom to get ready for my picnic with Joe. I wanted to be with him. What Ralph had said was still whirling round my head, and I needed to touch Joe. I needed to feel his arms around me. Joe was real; Joe was the boy I was going to marry.

I heard the doorbell ring and I ran downstairs. I opened the door and Joe stood there grinning, carrying a bottle of wine. I threw my arms around him and gave him a hug.

'Well that's a nice welcome.'

I smiled and kissed his cheek. 'I won't be a minute,' I said. 'I just need to get the picnic.'

I ran up the stairs, grabbed the food and a blanket and shouted goodbye to Polly. I yelled down the stairs. 'Joe, have you brought a bottle opener?'

'Screw top,' he yelled back.

'Glasses?'

'Sorry.'

I grabbed two glasses and ran down the stairs.

I loved Hampstead Heath. It was an oasis of green in the very heart of the city, with its rolling hills and meadows, beautiful lakes and acres of woodland.

We walked past the magnificent Kenwood House and up towards Parliament Hill, one of the highest points in London. We found a shady spot and lay the blanket on the ground. I was here in this beautiful place, but today it wasn't working its usual magic. Ralph was in my head, and I couldn't get rid of him. I was here with Joe. I didn't want to think about Ralph.

We lay down on the blanket holding each other's hands.

'Hungry?' said Joe.

'Why, are you?'

'Always.'

I sat up and started unwrapping the food. Joe poured the warm wine into the glasses. The bread was soft and crispy and the cheese was delicious.

'To us,' said Joe, clinking his glass against mine.

'To us,' I said, smiling.

I could taste the fruity wine on Joe's lips as we kissed.

We lay there in the sun, listening to the voices of children running down the hill. Above us kites were bobbing about in the sky like gloriously coloured butterflies.

Soon Joe was snoring gently beside me. I got up and walked to the brow of the hill and looked out over London. When I had first arrived here, I had ached for the sea and the Sussex Downs. The sea and the beach would always remind me of Mary, but it was the Downs that held my memories of Ralph. It was Joe who had brought me up here to Parliament Hill. It couldn't match the Sussex Downs, but it was the closest thing I could find here in London. I could always think more clearly in the open air. I was remembering my answer to Polly's question when she'd asked me how Joe made me feel. 'Safe, happy, loved,' I had said.

I suppose that's what everyone wants to feel. It's what I always wanted – to feel safe. Mary had wanted more. She used to say, 'What's the point in doing something if you already know how it's going to end?' Mary taught me to be brave. She'd held my hand, and I'd walked down the slippery groyne towards the edge of the sea. She'd spun me around as we jumped down onto the pebbles, and she'd shouted up to the sky, 'You did it. You did it.' Maybe loving someone wasn't about feeling safe. Maybe loving someone was the most unsafe thing that you would ever do. Mary would know. I could almost hear her telling me what to do.

Below me were two paths, each going in different directions. I seemed to be standing at the very crossroads where they met. Two paths. Two destinations. I knew what I had to do.

I was going home.

CHAPTER TWENTY-TWO

Joe had been so angry. I had never seen him angry before, not with me anyway. When I'd stood on the Heath that day, everything had seemed so clear, and yet I was scared – petrified really. I wanted to run away and not have to face Joe. Rush home and write him a letter, anything not to have to see the hurt in his eyes when I told him that I was leaving him, that I couldn't marry him. He had shouted at me, when he'd never so much as raised his voice to me before. I noticed people looking at us, and I felt like a fool, but I didn't blame him. I couldn't. This was all my fault.

'I gave you the chance to tell me the truth about Ralph before I asked you to marry me. What were you doing, hedging your bets?'

'No, no I wasn't.'

'Really? Well I think you were. You couldn't have Ralph so you settled for me.'

Tears were streaming down my face. I could hardly speak. I had never been the cause of so much pain before. I didn't hurt people; I wasn't like that. 'I'm really sorry, Joe. You have to believe me.'

'Do I? Well, I'm sorry that I believed you when you said you loved me.'

'I did. I do.'

'Then you need to grow up, Dottie, if this is your idea of love.'

I didn't know if Joe would ever forgive me. I hoped he would. I really hoped he would, but I would understand if he couldn't.

My boss Peter was lovely, but I was so upset by what I'd done to Joe that I burst out crying as soon as I stepped into his office.

'My dear girl,' he'd said, guiding me towards a chair. 'What on earth's wrong?'

I could barely speak. I felt like an idiot. Peter gave me his handkerchief.

'Deep breaths, Dottie.'

I eventually calmed down and managed to hand in my notice.

'Am I that scary?'

'You're not scary at all, I just couldn't cope with anyone else being angry with me.'

'I'm sad to be losing you, but I'm not angry.'

'This is the best job I've ever had,' I'd said, gulping back more tears. 'I've loved it here.'

'And we've loved having you here, but I imagine you have your reasons.'

'I need to go back to Brighton. I need to go home.'

'Do you have a job to go to?'

'No. I suppose I can always go back to Woolworths until I find something better. I haven't really thought it through, Peter. I just know that I have to go home.'

'Now I don't want to raise your hopes, but I know a guy who runs a small literary agency in Brighton. We were at university together. He's a great chap. He hasn't been going long, but I've heard he's building a decent stable of writers. He might have something for you. If you're interested I'll give him a ring.'

'Oh I'm definitely interested.'

'Then I'll contact him and see if he's looking for someone. Are you on the phone at home?'

I felt the colour rush to my face. 'No, we use a phone box at the end of the road.'

'Can I give him your address then?'

'Of course.' I wrote the address down for him – 15 See-saw Lane. Now I really felt like I was going home.

Telling Polly was harder.

'You're the best flatmate I've ever had,' she said. 'The last two were bonkers. What am I going to do without you?'

'I have to go home.'

'Why?'

'I've been running away. I have to stop running away.'

'It's because of Ralph, isn't it?'

'It's because of a lot of things. I don't know what will happen with me and Ralph, but I do know that I have to find out.'

'Who's going to visit Mrs Dickens with me?' Then she burst out crying, which started me off again.

I had managed to hurt another person I loved.

Mrs P was surprisingly nice. She presented me with a box of Dairy Milk chocolates on the day I left the flat.

'You've been an exemplary tenant, Miss Perks. I have no objection to you staying with Miss Renson if you want to visit in the future.'

Polly was making faces behind Mrs P's back; it was difficult to keep it together.

'Like I said, Miss Renson, I didn't arrive here on a pushbike. Next time you want to make faces behind people's backs, make sure you are not facing a mirror.'

Polly looked mortified. 'Bloody hell. I mean sorry, Mrs Pierce.'

'Well good luck, Miss Perks.'

'Thank you,' I said.

Peter had let me get away with two weeks' notice instead of a month. I wrote to Mum to let her know that I was coming home. I had a letter back by return of post, saying how surprised and delighted she was and that her and my Aunty Brenda were going out that very afternoon to buy new sheets for my bed.

I intended leaving on the Friday, but Polly was having none of it. 'Don't think for one minute that I'm going to let you sneak off while I'm at work. You can bloody well wait till Saturday, when I'm here.'

Mary Pickles was the only real friend I had ever had growing up. I had thought that I would be friendless in London, but I'd met Polly, and now I was saying goodbye to her too.

As the train pulled out of Victoria station my mind was full of doubts. Was I making the right decision? These past few years had been happy ones with Joe, Polly, my job. They had all helped me grow in a way that I hadn't thought possible. This wonderful city had opened its arms and welcomed me in, and now I was leaving it and all that had become dear to me.

As the train raced towards Brighton I became more and more anxious. I'd written to Ralph and told him that I was coming home. I didn't say anything else except what time my train would be arriving at Brighton station. I knew there was a chance that he wouldn't show up, but I hoped that he would. I had no plan. I had taken a leap of faith -- everything was in the lap of the gods now.

As I lugged the case along the platform. I kept my head down. I didn't want to tempt fate by searching for him in the crowd. He probably wouldn't be there. He could be there. He might be there.

I got to the gate and handed my ticket to the man. It was the moment of truth. I couldn't avoid it any longer. I looked up and my heart sank. He wasn't there. I should have known that I'd left it too late – it was the story of my life with Ralph. But I'd made my decision, and I wasn't running back to London. I'd done enough running. I was home and whatever happened from now on I was going to stay here and make it work. This town might be filled with the saddest of times but it was also filled with the happiest.

Then out of the corner of my eye I saw a flash of red and he was running towards me. I dropped the case and fell into his arms. He kissed my lips, my face, my forehead. My face was wet with tears, and so was Ralph's. We were laughing and crying all at the same time.

'The bus didn't come, Dottie, I had to run.'

'You ran all the way from the estate?'

'I would have run all the way from Scotland.'

CHAPTER TWENTY-THREE

Being back home, London seemed a million miles away. Ralph was still living with Peggy in the flat that he had shared with Mary. I desperately wanted to be with them both, but I really hated going there. Ralph knew how I felt, so we took Peggy out as much as we could, and in the evenings we went for long walks, while either Ralph or Mary's mum looked after the little girl. I loved being with Ralph, There were times when it felt as if we had never been apart. I had no regrets about leaving London. I had no regrets about leaving Joe. I was where I was supposed to be. We had been given a second chance, and a lot of people don't have that. We had both hurt good people for it to happen, and now we had to make sure that only good came out of it.

It took a while before I realised that Peggy wasn't warming to me. I had never thought for one minute that she wouldn't. I had loved her so much when she was a baby. I couldn't have loved her more if she had been mine. But at five years old, Peggy wasn't that tiny baby any more, and she didn't remember a time when we had loved each other. Instead she was hurting, and I didn't know what to do to help.

I decided to talk it over with Mum.

'She's been through a lot, that little girl,' Mum said, sitting down at the kitchen table with me and pouring us each a cup of tea.

'I know she has, and I want to make it better, but I don't know how to.'

'They say children adapt to change easier that adults, but I'm not sure that's entirely true. Poor little thing never knew her mother, and she's been led to believe that Fiona would be her new mummy, and now it's all changed again. She must be very confused. Sometimes I think we expect too much of children. We expect them to just go along with what we want and when they don't, we get cross.'

'What should I do then?'

'Be patient, Dottie, and don't let it upset you. It's not fair on her. Just let her know that you love her, and she'll come round in the end – you'll see.

'I'll try.'

Just then Aunty Brenda burst through the back door as if there was someone after her.

'Get me a cup of tea quick,' she said, plonking herself down on a chair.

Mum got another cup out of the dresser and started pouring the tea. She added lots of sugar because Aunty Brenda was in such a flap.

'What's happened?' asked Mum, pushing the cup towards her.

'Oh my God, she's been spotted.'

'Calm down, Brenda. Who's been spotted?'

'Our Carol, who do you think?'

'Spotted doing what?'

It crossed my mind that she might have been caught shoplifting.

'She was in the butcher's getting me a bit of scrag-end for the stew when this scout approached her.'

'In the butcher's?'

'As true as I'm standing here. Our Carol was approached in the butcher's by a scout.'

'Why?' I said.

'To be a model. He wants to take pictures of her in his studio in London.'

'You're never going to let her go, are you?'

'I don't know what to do, Maureen. You know our Carol. If she wants to do something she won't take a blind bit of notice of me. Is there sugar in this tea?'

'Three.'

'Give me another couple, I'm in shock.'

Mum shovelled more sugar into the cup and stirred it. 'You can't just let her go to London to meet some strange bloke, Brenda. He could be a white slave trafficker.'

'That's exactly what I told Carol.'

'And what did she say?'

'She said I read too many Agatha Christie novels.'

'When has she got to go?'

'He gave her his card. He said he'll wait to hear from her.'

'I could go with her,' I said. 'If that would make you happier about it. I know London, and once I'm sure that everything's above board I could leave her and visit my friend Polly.'

'Would you really, Dottie? I'd feel so much better knowing you're with her. You've got more brains in your little finger than our Carol's got in the whole of her body.'

Carol might not have had much up top, but what she *had* got might just be about to make her a lot of money.

I was walking across the green towards Ralph's flat and thinking about what Mum had said about Peggy. She was wise my mum – she was the wisest person I knew. I just had to be patient. The truth was that whenever I thought about Ralph, I thought about the two of us together, the way it had always been. The way it had been in the beginning. No Mary to stand in our way and no little girl called Peggy. Just him and me. Walking on the Downs, strolling along the seafront, going to the youth club, sitting in our café listening to records on the jukebox. What I wanted was our young selves back, before life tore us apart. I hadn't considered Peggy. I felt ashamed. I'd been selfish.

Rita certainly thought I was. She'd gone ballistic when she'd heard about Ralph and me. I'd gone round to her house to get it out of the way.

She'd opened the door and glared at me.

'Hello, Rita.'

'Don't you 'hello, Rita' me. You've got some nerve coming round here, Dottie Perks. Luckily for you Nigel's not in, he's very upset.'

'I'm sorry he's upset.'

'Well, so you should be.'

'Can I come in then?'

'I suppose so,' she'd said, backing away from the door. 'Don't forget to take your shoes off. And don't make any noise, Miranda Louise is asleep.'

It had been on the tip of my tongue to mention that according to her bright babies didn't need much sleep, but I'd thought better of it.

I'd had a feeling that it wouldn't go well and I'd been right. She'd launched into an attack as soon as I'd walked into the front room.

'How could you? How could you do that? She'd bought her wedding dress and Peggy's bridesmaid dress. Can you imagine how she feels? Can you imagine how Nigel feels? How I feel? We're all heartbroken.'

I hadn't been able to see what Rita had to be heartbroken about. It wasn't Nigel that I was running off with.

'I didn't set out to hurt anyone.'

'You might not have set out to hurt anyone, Dottie, but you bloody well did. Fiona is Nigel's cousin. She's family. I'm ashamed, I really am. They had everything planned. Tickets bought, passports got.'

'I know.'

'Why couldn't you have just stayed in London? You are always banging on about how happy you were up there and what a great job you had. Well you won't be working on any trendy magazine here.'

'I'm not expecting to.'

'And where do you think you are going to live? Because Ralph has given the flat up.'

'The council are letting him stay there.'

'Well lucky old you.'

'I wouldn't live there anyway.'

'Too posh to live in a council place are you?'

'That's rich coming from you. You couldn't get away from the estate quick enough.'

Rita had chosen to ignore that.

'So why have you done it? Why have you spoiled everything?'

'Ralph came to *me*, Rita. I didn't go running after him. I didn't ask him to leave Fiona.'

'You might not have asked him to leave her, but *you're* the reason he did.'

Rita had sat down on the sofa and picked up a little pink teddy bear. I'd guessed it belonged to Miranda Louise. She'd held it up to her nose, breathing in the smell of her baby.

'I know that what Ralph did to Fiona was awful, but he didn't love her enough to marry her. Now if that's my fault then I'm sorry.'

'I'm still pissed off with you.'

So what's new, I'd thought. You're always pissed off with me.

I was just about to walk across the quadrangle to Ralph's, when I saw Fiona emerge from the block of flats. She was carrying a box, and she was crying. I ducked behind a wall until she had gone, then ran up the stone stairs.

Ralph opened the door. He didn't say anything. He just walked ahead of me into the front room and sat down. His face looked drawn. He leaned forward and rested his head in his hands.

'Fiona was here. She picked up her things.'

'I know. I saw her.'

He looked up at me. 'I've hurt a lot of people, Dottie.'

I wanted him to hold me. I wanted him to say that it was worth it, but he didn't.

CHAPTER TWENTY-FOUR

When I got back round to Mum's, she handed me a letter.

'It's got a London postmark on it, Dottie,' she said. 'Who can that be from?'

'It could be from Polly,' I said. I looked at the envelope. 'No, it's not Polly's writing.'

'Joe?'

'I hope not.' I wasn't ready for a letter from Joe.

'Have you heard from him?'

'I think he's too hurt and angry to ever get in touch again.'

'I suppose you can't blame him.'

I didn't want to talk about Joe. I didn't want to think about Joe. I felt sick at the thought of what I had done to him.

I went upstairs to my bedroom, sat on the bed and opened the letter. It was from Peter. I started reading.

Dear Dottie,

As promised, I contacted the friend I mentioned and he is happy to see you. They are a small but up-and-coming literary agency based in Kemp Town. He can't promise anything, but I have a feeling that if he likes you, he may take you on. I have of course praised you up to the nines, so don't let me down. We all miss you here at Trend, even Miles. The editor's name is Tom Brown. He's a nice guy. I think you'll like him, I know he'll like you. I've put his phone number on the top of this letter. He is expecting to hear from you.

Let me know how you get on and do pop in and see us if you are ever back in London.

All the best,

Peter

I read the letter again. Oh my God, the chance of a job with a literary agent and a local one at that! I had been so worried that I would end up in a factory or back at Woolies. I ran downstairs and told Mum.

'Ring him, Dottie, ring him now before he changes his mind.'

'He hasn't made his mind *up* yet, Mum. He hasn't even met me.'

'Well you know what I mean. Strike while the iron's hot.'

'Have you got any pennies?'

Mum rooted around in her old brown handbag and gave me a handful of coins.

'Off you go then,' she said.

The phone box was on the corner, opposite the park. I went inside and dialled the number on the top of the letter. After only two rings someone answered. I pressed button A, and the pennies clanged down into the box. There was a young girl on the end of the line.

'Tom Brown agency,' she said. 'How can I help you?'

'Could I speak to Mr Brown?' I said.

'May I ask who's calling?'

'Dottie Perks, he's expecting me to call.'

'Please hold while I put you through.'

I had butterflies in my tummy, which disappeared as soon as Tom Brown started to speak. His voice sounded warm and friendly on the other end of the line. 'Dottie, I'm so glad you called. Peter has spoken very highly of you.'

'That was kind of him.'

'So I think we should meet, that is if you're still interested, of course.'

'Oh I am.'

'Then shall we say… Hang on, let me just check the diary. Tomorrow?'

'Tomorrow would be fine,' I said. 'And thank you for seeing me.'

'You are more than welcome. About elevenish?'

'Eleven is fine. Where exactly are you?'

'Of course, sorry. Let me pass you back to Millie – she'll give you directions. Until tomorrow then.'

'We're over the top of the bookies, next to the bank,' said Millie. 'The stairs are around the back but be careful, they're a death trap.' I thanked her and put down the phone.

I liked the sound of Tom Brown. I wondered how many people had asked him what his school days had been like? I really hoped he liked me. I really hoped there was a job. I really hoped that this was the start of better things to come.

CHAPTER TWENTY-FIVE

We started off slowly, Ralph and I. We were both fragile, both still ashamed of the ways in which we'd treated the people who had loved us. It was worse for Ralph. He'd almost married Fiona. He'd let her dream of a future with him. And poor Fiona hadn't only lost Ralph but Peggy too. As for me, I couldn't even bear to think of Joe and what I'd done to him. I tried my best to put him out of my mind, to convince myself that he hadn't really loved me, and what I had done to him wasn't *that* bad, but I wasn't fooling anyone, least of all myself.

The only person who really understood what I was feeling was Ralph, and the only person who could completely empathise with him was me. Our guilt pushed us closer together. We didn't pick up where we had left off – it was completely different this time, more intense. It was so intense that I wanted nothing more than to be with him, to be close to him, touching him, feeling him close to me, holding his hand and listening to his voice, waiting for the next kiss, but at the same time using so much emotional energy was exhausting. I had to fill myself up with him so there was no room for doubt, no room for guilt, no room to think about Joe. And I know that it was the same for him.

'I still can't believe it,' he said to me over and over. 'It feels like a dream. It feels as though any minute I'll wake up and find that you're gone again.'

I'd have to reassure him and tell him that I was here to stay, and that I wasn't going anywhere unless he was beside me.

We were walking on the beach one day, the pebbles turning beneath our feet and the little frothy waves foaming where the sea met the shore. His arm was about my shoulder. I leaned into him and put my arms around his waist. I could hardly believe it either – that we were back together, that not everything was lost, that there was still the chance of a future, that the love between us had been strong enough to survive all the damage that had been done to it.

He turned to face me and we stood there, at the edge of the sea, with the gulls screaming overhead and the sound of the waves breaking and, more faintly, music from the pier, and we pressed our bodies together. My cheek was against his chest, his mouth was close to my ear, and I could feel his breath and his heartbeat, and honestly we were so close, it was difficult to know where I ended and he began.

'I have to go,' he said.

'Why?'

'To pick up Peggy. I promised my mum I'd be back in time for tea.'

'All right, I said.

'You could come with me.'

'No, I have to get back too. My mum's cooking for me.'

We drew apart and began to walk the other way, back down the beach.

'Dottie,' Ralph said, 'how we are now, it's lovely, but we need to talk about where we go from here. It's not like we're teenagers any more.'

'When?' I said.

'Meet me tomorrow, after work.'

'Okay, where?'

'How about the café?'

'Our café?' I nodded. 'Why not.'

I hadn't been to the café since Mary had died, and I was feeling anxious about it, but it was the only place I could think of where we could relax and be together, just the two of us.

Ralph was sitting at our table when I walked in. The place had hardly changed at all. The jukebox was still there in the corner. I guess the records we used to play were long gone. The football table still needed a paint job, and even the plastic tablecloths were as I remembered them. I wasn't sure whether the familiarity of the place was a good thing or not. I half expected the girls from the sack factory to waft in bringing their smell of fish with them. Or Mary fussing with her hair or her lipstick in case Elton walked in. Or Elton himself playing on the football table or leaning against the jukebox, slicking back his hair and looking slightly dangerous. The café was full of ghosts.

Ralph smiled at me as I sat down. 'Here we are again,' he said. 'Are you okay with this? We could go somewhere else.'

'No, it's fine. It hasn't changed much, has it?'

'I just wondered if it brought back too many memories for you.'

'I'm going to have to deal with them, so I might as well start here.'

'We'll make new memories, Dottie, happier ones.'

'That's the trouble. The memories I *have* are happy ones. It might be easier if they weren't.

'Where's Peggy?'

'She's at my mum's house.'

'I hope that she comes round soon, Ralph. I'm beginning to feel like the wicked stepmother.'

Ralph concentrated on stirring his coffee then said, 'How would you feel about moving in with us?'

I knew that this was going to come up – of course it was. I'd thought about it a lot. I had tried to imagine living in the flat with Ralph and Peggy, but every time I thought about it I saw Mary sitting on the couch, pale and sick and unhappy. I couldn't live there. I couldn't. It was hard enough just visiting.

'I want to be with you Ralph, and I want us all to be together but not there. It would be like going backwards, and I don't think it's what we should be doing. The flat holds bad memories for me. I could never be happy living there.'

'I thought that might be your answer,' he said. 'And I do understand. I suppose I was just thinking of the easiest option. I want us to be together. I want to see you every day. I want to wake up beside you every morning and go to sleep with you every night.'

'And that's what I want too, but I want it to be in a place that we choose together.'

Ralph held my hand and smiled. 'That's what we'll do then, Dottie Perks.'

'Really?'

'Absolutely. I shall set to work immediately and build us a nice little house up on the Downs.'

'Or a two-bedroomed flat?'

Ralph grinned. 'Okay, a two-bedroomed flat it is.'

'Coffee?' said Ralph, getting up.

'Please.'

I stared out of the window. There used to be a hairdresser's just across the road. It had a big mirror in the window, where we would all go to fix our make-up and do our hair. It was a bicycle shop now. I wished the hairdresser's was still there. I wished Mary was still here.

Ralph came back with two coffees and set them down on the table.

'So how's the job hunting going?' he asked, spooning sugar into his cup.

'I've got an interview.'

'Already? That's great! Where, when?'

'Tomorrow morning. It's at a literary agency in Kemp Town.'

'I'm really proud of you, Dottie Perks.'

'I haven't got it yet.'

'They'll love you.'

'You're prejudiced.'

'Guilty as charged, but I still think you'll get it. From now on, whatever lies ahead of us, we will deal with it together. We owe it to each other to make this work.'

'And we owe it to Peggy,' I said. 'I want her to like me.'

'She will, and once we're all together in a new place, things will be better.'

'I hope so, Ralph. I really hope so.'

The next morning I was up with the larks, trying to decide what to wear for the interview. I plumped for a pale blue shift dress that I had bought in Carnaby Street with Polly. I wondered what Polly's new flatmate would be like. Maybe they would become best friends and visit Mrs Dickens together. I wasn't sure that I wanted Polly to have a new best friend, but I didn't want her to be lonely either.

I could smell bacon frying as I went into the kitchen.

'I thought I'd make a good breakfast to set you up for the day,' said Mum, emptying a tin of beans into a saucepan.

I smiled at her. I'd been looking for signs of her being ill again ever since I'd come home, but she looked the picture of health, and that made me happy. Mum had a thing about setting us up for the day, which is probably why I had ended up being the fattest kid in the school.

'I'm not really that hungry, Mum.'

'Of course you are. You're a growing girl.'

'I hope not,' I said, grinning at her.

'Maybe not,' she said, smiling. 'It's just nice to be able to cook for you.'

Dad came flapping down the hallway in his slippers and came into the kitchen.

'Something smells good,' he said, smiling at Mum.

'Dottie's off for her interview this morning. I just wanted to make sure she had something in her stomach before she goes rushing off.'

'And what could be better than one of your Mum's fry-ups,' said Dad, smiling at me.

'I think you might have to eat mine, Dad. I've got an attack of nerves.'

'I think I can do that,' he said. 'And don't you be nervous, girl. They'll be lucky to get you.'

'Thanks, Dad.'

I managed to eat a piece of toast, kissed Mum and Dad goodbye and walked to the bus stop.

I took the bus into Kemp Town and followed Millie's directions to the agency. I was feeling pretty nervous as I climbed the steps at the back of the building. Millie was right – the steps were a death trap. I could feel the rickety wooden structure moving beneath me as I gingerly made my way up to the office. I pushed open the door. There was a young girl sitting behind a desk. She had blonde hair and a sweet face.

'You must be Dottie,' she said, grinning at me.

'You were right about the steps,' I said.

'I make the sign of the cross every morning before I go up them.'

'What about when you go down?'

'I hold my breath.'

I was going to like Millie. Perhaps we could be friends. I needed a friend right now.

'He won't be long,' she said. 'Do you want a coffee while you're waiting?'

'No thanks, I'm fine.'

'Nervous?'

'I feel like I'm about to throw up.'

'You'll be okay. Tom's a lovely guy.'

'He sounded nice on the phone.'

'He is, and he's got the patience of a saint. He's got an author with him at the minute who thinks she's Virginia Woolf. She's good, but she's a right pain in the butt.'

Yes, I was going to get on with this girl.

Just then the door opened and a woman swept out. Tom made a face at Millie.

'Don't worry about the cover, Celeste. I will get on to the publisher right away.'

'Well I sincerely hope you do, Tom. I am a serious literary writer. That cover looks as if it just fell off the front of the Beano.'

She nodded to Millie as she went out the door. 'Millie,' she said.

'Celeste,' said Millie.

Then in unison both Tom and Millie shouted, 'Mind the steps,' to her disappearing back.

'Don't worry,' said Tom, coming towards me with an outstretched hand. 'They're not all that bad. Most of our writers are lovely. I'd get rid of her, but the woman knows how to write. Should I be telling you that? Probably not. Come on into my office, and we can have a little chat. Coffee on the go, Millie?'

'Fancy one now?' said Millie, looking at me.

I nodded. My nerves were settling down. I followed Tom into his office.

'So Peter tells me you are relocating to Brighton?'

'It's my hometown; I've only been in London for four years.'

'And now you've come home.'

I nodded.

'For good?'

'Yes.'

'It's just that I don't want to train you up and have you running back to the bright lights.'

'I'm not going to be running anywhere. I'm here to stay.'

'Okay, so you'll want to know what this job entails?'

'Yes, please.'

'It will be up to you to find me the diamond in the rough. The little gem amongst all the rubbish. You will be reading the manuscripts that come in the post almost every day from writers who are looking for an agent. How does that sound?'

'Exciting.'

'Millie assures me that it can be mind-numbing.'

'So we'll both be doing the same job?'

'Not exactly. She is also my girl Friday. She answers the phone, she keeps me supplied with coffee, she chases up the publishers. She also protects me from the divas.'

'Divas?'

'Oh we get plenty of those. You've just seen one of them. I put up with that one because, as I said, the woman can tell a decent story. It's just a pity she's such a pain in the arse.'

I giggled.

'She really is. So Millie needs some help, and she's delighted that you have come along. Another part of the job, which would entail the odd evening, is the book launches. They're generally good fun – you just have to pass around the wine and look jolly.'

'I can do that, and I'm happy to work evenings.'

'Good. So shall we give it a whirl?'

'I'd love to give it a whirl.'

'When do you want to start?'

'I have to find a flat.'

'Shall we say four weeks then?'

'That will be perfect.'

Then he held out his hand. 'Welcome to our little agency, Dottie,' he said smiling.

CHAPTER TWENTY-SIX

That evening I went round to Ralph's flat. I ran up the concrete steps and rang the doorbell. Peggy opened the door and stared at me.

'Hello, Peggy,' I said. 'Is your daddy in?'

She didn't answer, she just continued staring. Oh, Peggy, why can't you like me, even a little bit? I thought. I smiled at her. 'Can I come in?'

Nothing.

Then I heard Ralph calling from inside the flat. 'Who is it, Peggy?'

Ralph came to the door, wiping his hands on a tea towel.

He smiled at me then looked down at Peggy. 'Well aren't you going to let Dottie in?'

Peggy gave me a sour look and pushed past Ralph and into the flat.

'What can I say?' he said, kissing me on the cheek. 'She's five going on fifteen.'

He was making it sound as if Peggy behaved like this with everyone, but we both knew that wasn't true. As far as she was concerned I'd taken her daddy away from Fiona, and she was angry with me. I wanted the three of us to be a family, and that wasn't going to happen while Peggy felt like this, so I had to find some way to get through to her.

Ralph took my hand as we walked into the front room.

'Where's Peggy gone?'

'To her room. This isn't her, you know. I've never known her to be rude like that. I don't know what I can do about it,' he said sadly.

'Maybe we can get her excited about moving to a new place. We all need to be together. She'll come round,' I said, but I think I was trying to convince Ralph of this more than myself.

'You're right – a new place, a new start. She can't stay cross forever... can she?'

'We have to make sure she doesn't.'

'So how did you get on?' he said, sitting me down on the couch. 'I want to know everything.'

'I got it.'

'I told you, you would, my clever girl.'

'It's nine to five and some evenings, but that's just for book launches. Tom says all I have to do is pour the wine and look jolly.'

'You can do jolly,' said Ralph, smiling.

'I really liked it there. My boss is called Tom Brown and he's lovely.'

'Not too lovely I hope.'

'Jealous?' I asked, teasing.

'Should I be?'

'Never.' I looked into his eyes. 'Never as long as you live.'

I snuggled into him. I loved the familiar smell of him and how safe I felt in his arms. I was where I belonged, and the road ahead of us was at last the road we were meant to be on. We were going to be a family, and I knew that Ralph was going to love and protect us forever.

I looked up at him. 'So where should we look for this flat then? Any preferences?'

'Well it needs to be round here, because Peggy will be starting school in September. I've got her name down for Whitehawk Juniors.'

'Our old school?'

'It's the closest one to the estate. So we need to find a flat nearby.'

I didn't want to live on the estate again. If we were going to start afresh then it had to be somewhere else, somewhere completely different.

'I'm sorry, Ralph, but I don't want to live back here.'

'We don't have to, just somewhere close to the school.'

'There must be other schools.'

'Of course there are, but Peggy's made friends round here and they will all be going together.'

I wanted Peggy to be happy, but Ralph wasn't considering what I might want.

'I'd like to be close to my new job,' I said. I knew that I was being awkward, but I didn't care. I wanted Ralph to consider my needs as well as Peggy's. 'I was thinking Perhaps Kemp Town.'

Ralph looked disappointed. 'I have to think of Peggy. There've been enough changes in her life lately. If a simple thing like going to school with her friends will make her happy, then that's what I must do for her. I know Peggy's not your child, Dottie, and I can't expect you to feel the same way about her that I do, but if we're going to be a family then you will have to accept that I must consider her needs.'

I stood up and walked across to the window and stared down at the quadrangle below. I felt angry suddenly, but I didn't know who I was angry with. Ralph? Peggy? Myself? We had gone through so much – it wasn't supposed to be like this.

I felt Ralph's arms around me. 'I'm sorry,' he whispered.

I leaned against him. 'So am I.'

He turned me round so that I was facing him. 'I'm asking too much of you, aren't I?'

'I just want you to consider what I want as well,' I said. 'I don't want Peggy to be unhappy, but we have to make decisions together. I feel as if you and Peggy are a team, and I've been left on the benches.'

'Is that what I'm doing?'

'Pretty much.'

'I'm sorry.'

'There are other schools, Ralph, and Peggy will make new friends. It's not the end of the world. She was going to have to make new friends in Australia, wasn't she? Why is this so different?'

'You're right – of course you're right. It's just that when Mary died, I got the feeling that no one thought that I could be a good father. I wasn't even sure myself that I was up to the job. For a long time I relied on my mum and Mary's mum, then I realised that *I* was Peggy's father and the responsibility of bringing her up was down to me and no one else. Okay, I've made mistakes along the way, but I've done the best I can, and now I've made her unhappy, but you're right, there are other schools, and she will make new friends. I promise that I won't make you feel like an outsider again. We'll find a flat. We'll make it work.'

'That's all I need to know.'

Ralph took my hand and led me into Peggy's bedroom. The cot was no longer there. In its place was a little bed, covered by a yellow candlewick bedspread. There was a shelf above it holding books and there was a doll's house on the floor.

'Time for bed, little lady,' said Ralph, smiling at the little girl.

Peggy hadn't even looked at me.

'Read me a story, Daddy,' she said, standing on the bed and taking a book from the shelf. She handed it to him. 'It's the one about the shoemaker and the little elves that come in the night and mend all the shoes.'

'Good choice,' said Ralph.

I loved how gentle he was with her. I loved that he was such a good dad.

'How about, as a very special treat, Dottie reads you a story?'

'No, I want you to read to me.'

'I'd love to read to you, Peggy,' I said gently.

She glared at me. 'Well I don't want you to.'

'Peggy,' said Ralph. 'That was very rude. Say sorry to Dottie.'

'Won't, won't, won't,' she screamed, and then threw the book across the room. Tears were streaming down her face. 'I don't like her,' she mumbled.

I could see that Ralph didn't know what to do.

'I'll go,' I said sadly.

'You don't have to go.'

'I know.'

Ralph walked me to the door and held me close. 'It will get better love.'

I nodded.

'She just needs time.'

I kissed him goodbye and walked down the steps. My legs felt shaky. I was shocked at how angry Peggy had become. If she got that upset at the thought of me reading to her, how was she going to feel about living with me?

I walked home slowly. There was a soft misty drizzle, the kind that soaks you to the skin, but it was just what I needed to cool me down.

When I'd left London, my job and Polly, it had seemed like I was the heroine in a Jane Austen novel, where the girl always gets the boy and they live happily ever after. Ralph would sweep me off my feet, which he sort of did on Brighton station, and then we would walk off into the sunset. The reality was that I went back home to Mum and Dad, and Ralph went home to Peggy. I had to gain Peggy's trust – it was the only way forward. I needed to do it for me, for Ralph and for Mary. I didn't want to let Mary down. Peggy had been her little girl. She had never asked me to look after her, but I guess that was because she had no doubt that I would. But I wasn't looking after her, was I? I couldn't – she wasn't letting me.

When I got back home Mum was in the front room with Aunty Brenda. They were listening to Nat King Cole singing 'A Certain Smile'. I'd always loved that song

'You're soaked,' said Aunty Brenda.

Mum went into the kitchen and came back with a towel. 'Dry your hair, love.'

'Thanks, Mum.'

'I thought you were spending the evening with Ralph.'

I sat down and started rubbing at my hair. 'So did I.'

Mum got up and turned down the volume on the radiogram. 'What happened?'

'Peggy happened.'

'Not getting any better then?' asked Mum.

'I'd say that it's probably getting worse, and I don't know what to do.'

'What does Ralph say?'

'He doesn't know what to do about it either.'

'That child's coming between you two,' said Aunty Brenda. 'And that's not right.'

I happened to agree with her, but I was trying to stay positive.

'We're going to find somewhere else to live. Somewhere we both like and hopefully Peggy likes as well.'

'That sounds like a good idea,' said Mum.

'Well, you'll have to get married first,' said Aunty Brenda.

'No, they won't,' said Mum.

Aunty Brenda looked shocked. 'You're never going to let your Dottie live in sin are you?'

'I don't care if she lives in Eastbourne as long as she's happy, Brenda.'

Which made us all fall about laughing.

Dad poked his head around the kitchen door. 'What's the joke?'

'We were just talking about your Dottie living in sin,' said Aunty Brenda.

'Over my dead body,' said Dad.

'It can be arranged,' said Mum, wiping her eyes.

'Don't I have any say in what happens in this family?' asked Dad.

'Probably not,' said Mum, winking at me.

'Well as long as I know,' said Dad, going back into the kitchen.

'Would you really not mind, Mum?'

'Marriage isn't something you rush into, Dottie. I know you love Ralph, but you have to sort this Peggy thing out first, and if that means living together, then that's what you must do. We never had the option in my day, did we, Brenda?'

'Heavens no, we just had to take a chance and hope it worked out.'

With that I burst out crying.

'Brenda, cup of tea, best china, plenty of sugar,' said Mum.

Aunty Brenda rushed into the kitchen and started rattling cups and saucers.

'Your Aunty Brenda never changes,' said Mum.

'I'm glad,' I said, smiling at her.

We sat and held hands and Mum dried my tears just as she had when I was a child.

Aunty Brenda put the tea down on the table.

'I've put four sugars in, Maureen.'

'That should do it,' said Mum.

Mum and Aunty Brenda swore by the medicinal effects of sweet tea for shock. I didn't have the heart to remind Mum that I had given up, and so I sipped the syrupy concoction and tried not to make a face.

Aunty Brenda was leaning forward in her chair, intent on hearing every word I had to say.

I looked at those two, strong, funny, wise women, who had lived through a war and lost people they had loved and who rarely complained about anything. Would they have got in a twist because a five-year-old child scowled at them? No, they were too busy making the best of what life had given them. I smiled at them both. 'Have I ever told you how much you both mean to me?' I asked.

Aunty Brenda's eyes filled with tears and Mum started searching for her bag of knitting.

CHAPTER TWENTY-SEVEN

I set about trying to find somewhere for us to live. Ralph was working during the day, so I was going to have to do it on my own, but I didn't mind – in fact I was quite excited. If we could find the right place, then maybe Peggy could get excited about it too.

Dad got the *Evening Argus* newspaper so every day I scoured the 'flats to let' listings. I wanted to find somewhere close to my job, so I circled any flats that were near to Kemp Town.

Mum and Dad still didn't have a phone, so I had to go down to the phone box every time I found one that I liked the sound of, but they were either too expensive or they didn't want children. I did see a couple that sounded okay but they turned out to be awful. I liked the look of a flat in Hove, the next town along, and although it was a bit far away, there were plenty of buses that could get me to work. It was described as a two-bedroomed flat with facilities, whatever that meant. I got the train to Portslade station. Halliburton Road was a two-minute walk away. It was a semi-detached thirties house with a beautiful bay window, but that was the only beautiful thing about it. The wooden gate was hanging off its hinges, and the front garden was so overgrown that I could barely walk up the path. The net curtains hanging at the windows looked grubby.

I couldn't see a bell so I knocked on the door. Immediately a dog began to bark and a woman started yelling at it. I was beginning to regret being there and actually started to walk back down the path when the door opened. The smell that wafted from the house nearly knocked me over – I certainly wasn't going inside. The woman was grubby and so was the dog. She was hanging onto its lead, and it was straining to get to me.

'Tell me what you want and be quick about it. Get down!' she screamed at the dog.

I said the first thing that came into my head. 'I'm sorry to disturb you, but I was wondering if you were going to vote Labour this year?'

'Piss off!' she screamed and slammed the door, nearly decapitating the poor dog in the process.

I hurried away from the house as fast as I could, still wondering what 'with facilities' meant.

I thought flat hunting would be fun, but it was turning out to be a nightmare. I wasn't going to give up though – there had to be somewhere out there that was right for us.

I got off the bus close to the estate and began to walk home. I was just about to pass our local shop when I noticed that there was a board in the window advertising stuff for sale. The shop was run by Mr Orme, who had known me all my life – Mary and I used to get our penny sweets there. There were a few adverts for jobs, a couple of cars for sale and there, between 'blue baby's cot' – which made me smile, because blue babies are pretty rare – and 'large rabbit hutch', was a flat to let. I went into the shop.

'I heard you were home, Dottie,' said Mr Orme, smiling at me. 'Had enough of London have you?'

'Something like that, Mr Orme.'

'Still, it must be nice being back with your mum and dad.'

'It is, but I'm looking for a flat to move into. I noticed there's a flat to let in your window.'

'Is there?'

'Yes,' I said.

'Let's have a look,' he said, coming out from behind the counter and going outside.

'I'd forgotten that was there. I should have taken it out.'

I must have looked disappointed.

'Well I suppose it might still be available. It was ages ago that I put it in there. Hang on and I'll get the card out for you.'

I looked at the postcard. 'Where's Oriental Place?' I asked.

Mr Orme shook his head. 'Well, it's not round here for a start.'

'Can I take it?'

'I don't see why not.'

'Thanks,' I said.

'Take care now, Dottie, lovely to see you home again.'

'Nice to see you too, Mr Orme.'

I usually avoided going past Mary's house, but I must have been preoccupied about the flat, and I was suddenly outside it. Oh how I wished I could turn back the clock. How I longed to open the door and run up those stairs and into Mary's bedroom. I looked up at her window. 'I miss you, Mary,' I whispered.

When I got round to my house, Mum was weeding the front garden. 'Any good, love?'

'Worst one yet,' I said, making a face. 'It was like *The Blob* meets *Hound of the Baskervilles*.'

'Who would have thought it was going to be so difficult to find somewhere to live,' she said, standing up and rubbing the small of her back.

'Are you all right?' I asked, concerned.

'Old age, Dottie, it comes to us all.'

It scared me when Mum said things like that. I didn't like to think that she was getting old.

'Don't look like that,' she said. 'I'm fine really, just a few aches and pains, nothing for you to get worried about.'

'You will tell me, won't you? If you're not feeling well?'

'I promise.'

'I found a flat to let, advertised in Mr Orme's window.'

'Round here?'

'I don't think so. I've never heard of the place.' I handed her the card.

'Fifty-five Oriental Place,' she said. 'No, it's definitely not round here, I would have heard of it. Clark's indoors. Maybe he knows where it is.'

I followed Mum into the kitchen. Clark was eating toast, a newspaper spread out on the table in front of him. I showed him the advertisement.

'It's down on the seafront, near the Palace Pier,' he said, looking at the card. 'There was a fire there a few months ago. I was sent out to take a few photos.'

'Well I hope the fire wasn't at number fifty-five.'

'I can't remember.'

'Is it all right though?'

'Not bad, beautiful houses, gone to seed a bit but still pretty impressive, and the sea is just across the road.'

'Will you look at it then, love?'

'Well it's worth a go. It can't be any worse than I've already seen.'

'Are you going to give them a ring?' asked Mum.

I looked at the card again. 'There's no phone number. I'll just have to take a chance that there's someone in.'

Mr Orme had said that the card had been in the window a long time, so the odds were that it had already gone, but I had a good feeling about it. It was too late now, but I would go tomorrow. I definitely would.

CHAPTER TWENTY-EIGHT

Oriental Place was just off the seafront, like Clark had said. Tall Regency houses flanked both sides of the street. They all looked to be about four storeys high, with stones steps leading up to the front doors. The houses must have been beautiful once, but now they looked sad and neglected. Number fifty-five was no better. Black paint was peeling off the door and an old pushbike was leaning against the railings that led down into the basement. I guessed that long ago this would have been the servants' quarters.

I walked up the steps and rang the doorbell. Nothing happened. I could hear it echo in the hallway, but no one came, and I could hear no movement from inside. Suddenly a window right beside me opened and a woman's head appeared. The head was topped with a frizzy mass of bright orange hair. She peered at me through large round glasses.

'Yes?' she said.

'I've come about the flat.'

'What flat?'

'The one that was advertised in the newsagents. I've got the card here.' I pulled the card out of my pocket and held it up for her to see.

'That was ages ago, dear, forgot it was still there.'

'So you don't have a flat then?'

'I never said that, did I, dear?'

'So you *have* got a flat?'

She pushed her glasses further down her nose and stared at me.

'I might have, dear.'

I didn't know what to say except well either you've got a flat or you haven't, but I didn't want to get off on the wrong foot.

'Just for you is it, dear?' she asked.

'No, there's three of us.'

'Not all girls, dear?'

'Well no.'

'Good. I find that girls are very unreliable.'

'Do you?'

'So who is it for then, dear? You and a gentleman friend?'

'We *are* getting married.'

'Are you, dear? Well that's nice, but to tell you the truth, as long as I get my rent on time, I am of the opinion that a person's living arrangements are their own business.'

'And there's a child.'

'Not a baby, is it, dear? Because I don't want my other residents being disturbed by a crying baby.'

'Oh no, she's five, she doesn't cry... much.' Except when I'm around, I thought.

She stared at me a bit more then said, 'Would you like to view the flat?'

Before I could answer, she had closed the window and reappeared at the front door.

'It's at the top of the house, dear. Will that be a problem?'

'No, no, I think that will be fine.'

Now that I could see more than her head, she was quite a vision really. She wasn't exactly fat but she was sort of wide and solid looking. My Aunty Brenda would have described her as thickset. My Aunty Brenda described a lot of people as thickset.

She was wearing an unusual assortment of clothes, which were, in their own way, quite spectacular. In fact it was hard to tell exactly what she *was* wearing. She had on a long patchwork skirt that came down to her feet, but over the top of that there seemed to be another skirt, red this time, with green flowers on it. Her blouse was bright yellow, and she had a belt around her middle with a bunch of keys hanging off it. The whole outfit was topped off with a long purple scarf.

'The name's Mrs Toshimo, dear,' she said, starting to climb the stairs. 'Rose Toshimo. My oriental gentleman passed on some time ago.

'I'm sorry.'

'Oh, he's fine. I talk to him every evening.'

I didn't quite know what to say to that, but thankfully Mrs Toshimo didn't seem to need a response.

'People found it quite amusing, dear, that I was married to an oriental gentleman and we lived in Oriental Place.'

'My name's Perks,' I said. 'Dottie Perks.'

'That's nice, dear.'

It was taking ages to get up to the flat, because Mrs Toshimo had to keep sitting down on the stairs. She was going so slowly I was frightened that I was going to tread on her skirt and send her toppling down on top of me.

'It's the rheumatics, dear,' she said. 'I'm a martyr to them. Not far now.'

Even though it was a sunny day, it was dark inside the house. On every landing, Mrs Toshimo pushed a light switch on the wall. I worked out that the light was supposed to last long enough to reach the next landing, but because of her rheumatics, we kept getting plunged into darkness.

We eventually made it to the top of the house and, after much fiddling with the keys, she opened the flat door.

The first thing that hit me was the mess. Dirty crockery filled the tiny sink and overflowed onto a grubby draining board. What you could see of the carpet, under all the rubbish, was threadbare.

'There's two bedrooms, dear, will that do you? And a nice little bathroom with your own private convenience. All mod cons, dear.'

I walked gingerly across the floor towards the window. It felt sticky underfoot.

We couldn't live here. Well that's what I had decided until I lifted the dirty net curtain and saw the sea. There it was, beyond the roofs and chimneys of the buildings on the other side of the street, all green and grey, its surface ruffled by white-tipped waves that raced and jumped beneath the wind. I knew that if I opened the grimy window I would be able to smell it. I thought about how, if I lived here, I would be able to look out of the window and see this every day. I imagined holding Peggy in my arms and showing her the sea. We would be able to watch the ships together. I imagined telling her stories about who was on the ships and where they were going. And that thought reminded me of Mary and all the places she had wanted to go, all the things she had wanted to do with her life.

I looked back into the room. It was a good size and with the two bedrooms it would suit us fine. It needed a good clean and a bit of paint, but if you could look beyond the mess, it could be nice. Together we could make it nice.

'How much is the rent?' I asked.

'Two pounds fifteen shillings a week, dear,' she said and then added. 'In advance.'

I chewed my lip. We only had Ralph's wages until I started getting paid. 'We can afford two pounds ten,' I said hopefully.

Mrs Toshimo stared up at the ceiling as if she was expecting spiritual guidance from her oriental gentleman, then she smiled. 'Well as it's not girls, dear, I will make an exception. Two pounds ten shillings it is, and I'll have it looking like a little palace. Will you be wanting the furniture, dear, or have you got your own?'

'My boyfriend has a council flat, so we have our own.'

'Ahh, I see. You've decided to go upmarket have you, dear? I like to see young people trying to better themselves.'

I had to stop myself from laughing out loud. If she thought this place was upmarket then God help her.

'I bettered myself when I met Mr Toshimo. He was very exotic, dear.'

'Was he?'

'Oh yes, dear, he was a cut above the rest.'

She chattered away as we went back downstairs.

'When do you want to move in, dear? Because I will need some time to clean it up. The girls that lived here did a moonlight flit you see, dear. Left me in the lurch, so to speak. I shan't have girls again – unreliable and messy.'

'Could it be ready in about two weeks?'

'Two weeks will be fine, dear.'

As we got to the bottom of the stairs she said, 'This must have been your lucky day, dear. There's not a finer flat in the whole of Brighton. All mod cons, dear. All mod cons.'

I was smiling as I walked across the road and onto the seafront. The tide was out and the sun glistened on the rivulets of water running down to the shore.

Mary and I used to love to run barefoot across the sand, our feet sinking into the cold wetness of it. I wondered what she'd think about the flat. I wondered if she'd be happy that Ralph and Peggy and I would be together as a family. I hoped so.

CHAPTER TWENTY-NINE

Peggy's face was bright red and sweaty as she stood in the middle of the front room glaring at us.

'I don't like it here,' she screamed.

'We'll make it nice, Peggy,' I said. 'Once it's painted and you've got all your own things around you, you'll love it, I promise.' I looked at Ralph for support.

He knelt down so that he was on Peggy's level, took a handkerchief out of his pocket and gently dried her eyes. 'You'll have your own room, sweetheart, and you can choose your own wallpaper and curtains. You and Dottie can have a girls' day out and choose everything.'

'Of course we can,' I said, smiling at her.

She scrunched up her face. 'I've got my own room at home, and I don't want new curtains.'

'*This* is going to be your new home, Peggy.' Ralph lifted her up into his arms and carried her across to the window then pulled aside the old net curtain. 'Look, Peggy you can see the sea, imagine that. You will be able to see the sea every day.'

'I don't like the sea.'

Ralph shook his head in despair as he put the little girl down. 'Now you know that's not true.'

Tears were now streaming down Peggy's face. 'Well it *is* true, it is. I don't like the sea, and I don't like it here.'

Yesterday I had brought Ralph to see the flat. 'Don't expect too much and you won't be disappointed,' I'd said.

We had taken the bus into town and then walked down West Street and onto the seafront. It was a blustery day, and the sea was kicking up white foam and splashing over onto the prom. 'Mary and I used to love it when the sea was like this,' I'd said.

Ralph put his arm around my shoulders as we stared out over the grey choppy water. 'We'll always be together, my love. Nothing can come between us now.'

I desperately wanted Ralph to like the flat, but as we'd turned into Oriental Place my heart had sunk. If anything, it had looked worse than the day I'd first seen it. We'd walked up the steps of number fifty-five and rung the bell. As before, the window had opened and Mrs Toshimo had stuck her head out.

'Yes?' she'd said, as if she'd never seen me before.

'It's me, Mrs Toshimo. Dottie Perks.'

'Of course it is, dear.'

'This is Ralph,' I'd said. 'I've come to show him the flat, if that's all right.'

'Now, it's not quite ready, dear, but two of my gentleman friends have moved all the furniture out, and they've cleaned it up a bit.'

I wondered how many gentleman friends she had.

'They are theatrical men, dear. They live in the flat below yours, lovely men. Very cultured, dear.'

Without saying another word she'd shut the window and opened the front door. She'd fiddled with keys around her waist while we stood in the dark hallway. Today she was wearing a long purple dress with silver embroidery around the neck. Silver and glass earrings hung from her ears, and a matching silver comb was holding back her red frizzy hair.

'Here's the key, dear,' she'd said, smiling. 'You don't mind seeing yourselves upstairs, do you? It's the rheumatics, they're giving me gip today.'

'We'll be fine,' I'd said, taking the key from her.

'Just knock on my door, dear, when you've finished.'

We'd walked up the dark stairway, pushing the light switch on every landing. Every time we pushed it, I'd said, 'Run,' and we'd giggled as we raced up to the next floor.

'You'll need a lot of imagination,' I'd said as I turned the key in the lock.

Ralph had turned me round so that I faced him and put his hands on my shoulders. 'Stop worrying, woman,' he'd said. 'I don't care what it looks like, okay? As long as I'm with you, I don't care where we live.'

'You haven't seen it yet.'

I'd opened the door and was pleased to notice that the smell had gone. Then we'd stepped into the room. It looked a lot bigger without the furniture, and I'd started to relax.

Ralph had smiled at me as he'd looked around the room. 'It's positively palatial.'

'Hardly,' I'd said, grinning.

'Really, it's fine.'

We'd walked around the rest of the flat. When we'd got to the bedroom, he'd taken my face in his hands and kissed me. 'No memories here, Dottie, just you and me and Peggy. I'll make everything up to you. I promise I will.'

I'd leaned against him and felt that I had at last come home.

'You haven't seen the best bit,' I'd said, taking his hand and leading him back into the front room.

'It gets better?' he'd asked, grinning.

I'd pulled back the net curtain. Ralph had stood behind me with his arms around my waist, and I'd leaned into him as we gazed out over the sea.

'Perfect,' he'd said.

We'd run down the stairs and knocked on Mrs Toshimo's door.

The room we'd entered had been bathed in light and as colourful as Mrs Toshimo herself. She had some good pieces of furniture, but they'd been laden down with papers, magazines and clothes. A faded pink chaise longue had stood against one wall with two green velvet chairs either side of a beautiful marble fireplace. The wallpaper had been old-fashioned, with a busy pattern of roses and green trailing ivy, and the curtains at the long windows had been grey velvet, held back by ornate gold tassels. On every available surface she'd had photographs, in mismatched frames. An old upright piano had stood in the bay, piled high with sheet music, some of which had slid onto the floor. The light that had streamed through the window had showed up the layers of dust on the old wood. She'd had a number of what looked like theatre posters on the wall, and I'd walked over to them.

'Those were my days in the theatre, dear,' she'd said.

'You were on the stage?'

One poster had been pretty faded, but I'd just about been able to make out the words. 'Madame Rose. The girl with the magic fingers.' 'Was that you?'

'That was in my glory days, dear.'

'How wonderful,' Ralph had said.

'I could have been a concert pianist, dear, but it never happened. You needed to come from money to pursue a career like that. But I played the halls and the theatres, and that's where I met my oriental gentleman.'

'Was he on the stage as well?'

'He was, dear. He was what was called an illusionist. Very exotic he was. This house was full of musicians and artistes when he was alive.'

Mrs Toshimo had closed her eyes as if she was remembering happier times.

'It's a lovely room,' I'd said.

'It is isn't it, dear?' She'd opened her eyes and smiled at us, saying, 'I like your young gentleman, dear, he's got the same colour hair as me.'

That was yesterday. Now we were staring at a little girl whose whole body was shaking with anger. How could one little body hold so much anger?

She glared at me. 'And I don't like you,' she said, sticking out her tongue.

'Say sorry to Dottie. That was a very unkind thing to say.'

'Well I don't like her. I want Fiona,' and she flung herself on the floor.

As I stared at the writhing little heap with sadness, Ralph's words came back to me. 'Nothing can come between us now,' he had said. He obviously hadn't reckoned on Peggy. I hoped that he was right.

CHAPTER THIRTY

Clark and Ralph struggled into the bedroom with the double bed.

'You could have told me it was three floors up,' said Clark.

'Now why would I tell you that?' I said, grinning.

Emma and I were putting plates, saucepans and cutlery into drawers and cupboards.

'Have you seen the view out of this window, Clark?' said Emma.

'I haven't had time to breathe yet, Em.'

'I think it's a great flat, Dottie.'

'You really like it?'

'I wouldn't mind living here – it's quirky.'

Emma had a liking for all things quirky. I really liked her and you could tell that she and Clark were totally in love. My little brother was a lucky guy.

Ralph had wanted Peggy to be part of the move, but she had dug her heels in where the flat was concerned. Part of me thought that he should have insisted she came, but the other part of me was glad that she wasn't here. I wanted Ralph and I to sort out the flat on our own. We'd made her bedroom as pretty as we could. Ralph had rigged up some shelves and I'd filled them with her books. I'd bought her a big soft brown teddy bear, and it was sitting on her bed. I wanted Peggy to be happy here, for us to be a family.

'I fancy an ice cream,' said Emma. 'Anyone else up for one?'

'Great idea,' said Clark. 'I wouldn't mind a break. That okay with you guys?'

'Of course,' I said. 'But I won't join you. I want to make the bed up.'

'You go on,' said Ralph. 'We'll find you on the seafront in a while.'

Once they were gone Ralph put his arms around me. 'I can't believe that this is actually happening. I can't believe that we are going to live together, under the same roof. How long has it taken?'

'I think maybe all our lives.'

I took his hand and led him across to the window. We stood together, looking out over the rooftops and chimneys to the sea beyond, and I whispered, 'We made it.'

'And tonight it will just be you and me,' he said, kissing the back of my neck.

We still hadn't actually made love. Peggy was always at the flat, and we couldn't do it at my house. I wished that I was a virgin, and I wished that Ralph was too. That's the way it should have been – that's the way it was meant to be, discovering each other, discovering sex for the first time. both of us together.

Ralph was talking, but I hadn't caught what he'd said. 'What?'

'I told Mum that we'll collect Peggy tomorrow.'

I turned to face him. 'That's wonderful. I can't wait for her to see her room. I hope she likes it.'

'You've done a great job. Thank you, my love.'

'I enjoyed doing it. I just want her to be happy here, Ralph.'

'I know you do. None of this is your fault, you know. It should be me she's angry with, not you. I sold her this whole new life, this whole new wonderful life, in Australia. I told her that she would swim in the ocean, that we would have barbeques outside in the sunshine. I even took her to the library and showed her picture books full of kangaroos and wallabies and koala bears. I told her that Fiona was going to be her new mummy and that we would all be happy together. She was so excited, Dottie. She was so happy she practically slept in that bridesmaid's dress. Then I took it all away. I didn't even take the time to sit down with her and explain why none of this was going to happen. I left my mum to do that, and I ran away to you. She should be blaming me, not you.'

Ralph had never explained all that to me before. No wonder she was so unhappy and angry – she had every right to be. Well I was going to make it up to her. I may not be able to give her Australia, but I could fill her life with love and I could make her feel safe.

'I'm going to do everything I can to make her happy again.'

Ralph held my face in his hands. 'You don't know how happy it makes me to hear you say that.'

We held each other close in this little flat that overlooked the sea, this little flat that was going to be our new home, and I thought that I would burst with happiness.' Shall we join the others?' I asked. The bed can wait.

'I'll race you down the stairs,' said Ralph, grinning.

As we were running down the stairs we almost bumped into a man coming up them. He held out his hand. 'Tristan Blake,' he said, smiling. 'Flat below yours.'

We both shook his hand.

'How's the move going?'

'Slowly,' said Ralph. 'But we're getting there.'

'Any help with the heavy stuff, just come and knock on the door.'

'Was it you that cleaned it?' I asked.

'Guilty as charged, but I didn't do it on my own. Stephen helped as well.'

'Well thank you,' I said. 'You even managed to get rid of the smell.'

'It was an old bag of potatoes under the couch. Can you believe that? Under the couch? It made poor Stephen retch. He's got a weak stomach, poor boy. I'm glad you are pleased with it. I'm surprised Rose managed to rent it out in the state it was in.'

'I nearly said no, but then I looked out of the window, and I was sold.'

'Oh, the view, that's the best thing about the flat. Stephen and I are very envious. We even considered moving up there ourselves, but poor Stephen's got wonky knees. Well I hope you will be very happy here. Darling Rose is an absolute sweetie. Now, once you've settled in, you must come and have drinks with us. Stephen is dying to meet you. He will be so jealous that I've met you first.'

'We'd love to,' said Ralph, 'but it might be a bit difficult once my daughter is with us.'

'Rose told us all about your little girl. Stephen and I adore children, so you can just bring her with you.'

'Thanks,' said Ralph. 'We will.'

We bought two strawberry cones and walked down to the beach to meet Clark and Emma.

They were sitting on the pebbles right at the edge of the sea.

'Isn't this glorious?' said Emma, smiling. 'I could stay here forever, I absolutely could.'

Clark leaned over and kissed her. 'You are so sweet,' he said.

'Be careful where you sit,' said Emma. 'There's lots of tar around.'

'Always has been,' I said. 'Mum used to get so mad at us when we came home covered in the stuff.'

'I remember that,' said Clark, laughing.

The four of us lay down side by side. I looked up at the clear blue sky and listened to the sea rattling the pebbles on the beach. I'll make Peggy happy if it's the last thing I do. Can you hear me Mary? I'll make Peggy happy. I promise I will.

That first night in the flat was wonderful. We sat on packing cases eating fish and chips out of the paper. We opened the little window and let the sounds and smells of the sea drift into the room. The joy of being on our own at last was overwhelming.

We kept smiling and feeding chips into each other's mouths and giving each other salt and vinegar kisses. A place of our own, the start of a new life together – it seemed that we had waited for this moment the whole of our lives.

As darkness fell over Brighton we made love. We explored each other's bodies; we tasted each other's skin. There was no taking, only giving and more giving, until I was taken to a place I hadn't known existed. We slept in each other's arms until the sun, streaming through the bare window, woke us up. We smiled at each other, remembering last night.

'Do we have to get up?' I groaned, snuggling down the bed so that my head rested on Ralph's chest.

'Nope,' said Ralph. 'We can stay here forever, until Mrs Toshimo sends Tristan and Stephen up here to investigate the smell. Only it won't be a bag of potatoes this time.'

'And we've still got loads of unpacking to do,' I said, yawning.

'Looks like it's going to be a lovely day. We can take Peggy down the beach later.'

'What time are you collecting her?' I asked.

'After breakfast. I thought we could take a picnic onto the beach, or we could cook if you like.'

I liked the thought of cooking our first meal together in the flat. 'What's Peggy's favourite food?'

'Shepherd's pie,' said Ralph. 'Definitely shepherd's pie.'

'In this weather?'

'In any weather.'

'Okay, you fetch Peggy and I'll shop.'

There was an open-all-hours shop opposite the West Pier called Raji's. It was about the only grocer's open on a Sunday for miles. The only other shops that were trading were the rock shops and places selling postcards, so we were lucky.

It was a beautiful day. There were children riding scooters and bikes along the seafront, followed by mums and dads carrying buckets and spades and blankets. What was there not to love about this place? I felt sure that in time Peggy was going to love it too.

I carried the food up the three floors to the flat. There was no chance of getting unfit living here. For the next hour I busied myself cooking and hanging clothes in wardrobes. I found Ralph's Dansette record player, then dug around in the boxes until I found his records. I chose 'Penny Lane' by the Beatles. I was happily singing along to it when I heard footsteps on the stairs. Ralph came into the room. I looked behind him expecting to see Peggy, but he was alone.

I stared at Ralph, confused. 'Where is she?'

'She wouldn't come.'

'Why?'

He shrugged his shoulders. He looked so sad. 'She just wouldn't budge. I told her about the shepherd's pie that you were making for her. I told her about the new room that was waiting for her. I tried everything but she just wouldn't have it. Mum even said that she would come with us, but nothing worked. The more I tried to persuade her, the more upset she became. In the end I had to leave her behind.'

We sat together on the couch, both of us lost in our own thoughts and neither of us knowing what to do.

CHAPTER THIRTY-ONE

I'd spent the morning cleaning the kitchen and now I'd had enough, so I decided to call on Mum. When I got there, Mum and Rita were pinning up some material that was spread out on the kitchen table. Mum couldn't say hello, because her mouth was full of pins, and Rita couldn't say hello in case her face cracked.

'So what are you making?'

'Curtains for Miranda Louise's bedroom,' said Rita.

The curtains were cream and covered with pink letters of the alphabet. 'They're really pretty,' I said.

'Yes, we think so,' said Rita. 'We thought it was time to introduce something educational into the nursery.'

'Bit young for that, isn't she?'

'No, she's not. If you surround a child with educational toys from an early age they will find it easier to learn later on. They're like sponges at this age.'

'Where did you learn that pearl of wisdom?'

'It's common knowledge in the world of education. You need to bear that in mind with Peggy, although she might be a bit old to benefit from it now.'

'Too old at five?'

'I don't know why I bother talking to you.'

Mum spat the pins out of her mouth.

'Mind the material, Mum!' shouted Rita.

'Sorry, love.'

I smiled at Mum.

'I didn't expect you round. I thought you'd still be up to your eyes in boxes.'

'Nope, we're all unpacked.'

'So how are you settling in?'

'I love it there, Mum, and I love being so close to the sea.'

'And Peggy? I bet she loves having the beach on her doorstep.'

'She's not with us.'

'Where is she?'

'At Ralph's mother's.'

'But why?'

'Because we can't get her to move into the flat.'

Mum looked really concerned. 'Oh dear.'

And then of course Rita had to put her two pennerth in.

'What on earth do you mean you *can't* get her to move into the flat?'

'Just like I said, Rita, she won't move in.'

'And you're going to indulge her in this, are you?'

'What would you suggest we do? Drag her there kicking and screaming?'

'Now, Dottie,' said Mum.

'Well, she seems to have the answer to everything. I'm surprised Nigel bothers buying a newspaper. All he has to do is ask Rita, font of all knowledge.'

'I'll ignore that remark, Dottie Perks, and just remind you that I am a mother, I have a child, so I am in a better position to have an opinion about bringing up a child than you are, and if you want my opinion—'

Which I didn't.

'It seems to me,' she carried on, 'that she is just being a spoilt little brat, and she needs to be reminded that she is a child who needs to do as she is told.'

I hated hearing these words coming out of Rita's mouth. It made me want to stand up for Peggy, to be on her side. It made me love her more.

'You're being too harsh on the child,' said Mum. 'She's had a lot of changes lately. You can't just expect her to do as she's told. She's not a robot, Rita. She has feelings, you know.'

'Well I won't stand any of that nonsense from Miranda Louise, I can tell you that.'

'Let's hope you won't have to,' I said.

'How long are you going to let it go on, love?'

'I'm leaving it to Ralph.'

'Is there anything I can do?'

'It's all such a mess, Mum. We just want to get her home with us.'

'Well that's the trouble, isn't it?' said Rita. 'She thinks she *is* home.'

I had never thought about it like that. 'I think you're right, Rita.'

Rita looked completely stunned that I'd actually agreed with her for once.

'Yes well…'

'Now come on, Rita, your Aunty Brenda will be here soon.'

'Aunty Brenda's calling in?'

'She's doing the sewing. We were doing the pinning, to give her a hand.'

'Good, I need to talk to her about going to London with Carol.'

'Why are you going to London with Carol?' said Rita.

'She's been spotted,' said Mum.

'What do you mean she's been spotted?'

'For modelling.'

'Carol?'

'She was approached in the butcher's,' said Mum.

'Carol was approached in the butcher's for modelling?'

If Mary had been here now we would have been making faces at each other. Mary found Rita hilarious. We could never keep straight faces when she started going on.

'Dottie said she'd go with her to London in case he was a white slave trader.'

'Oh for heaven sakes. What would a white slave trader be doing in the butcher's?'

'Well I suppose even white slave traders have to eat,' I said innocently.

Just then Aunty Brenda came through the back door.

'Dottie,' she said. 'Just the person I want to see. Lovely material, Rita.'

'We think so,' said Rita, looking pleased.

'Our Carol wants to go up to London Friday or Saturday. Would that be okay?'

'Saturday would be best, then I can see Polly.'

'There's just one thing that I don't really understand about all this,' said Aunty Brenda.

'What's that?' asked Mum.

'Why would a scout be interested in taking pictures of girls?'

'What are you on about?'

'Carol said that the chap who approached her in the butcher's was a scout. I thought scouts were all about dib, dib and dub, dub.'

It was at moments like this that I missed Mary the most. We would have giggled about this for weeks.

'Rita, cup of tea for Aunty Brenda. Four sugars.'

CHAPTER THIRTY-TWO

Everything should have been wonderful, but it wasn't. I loved my job, I loved my new home and I loved waking up beside Ralph every day, but both of us were at a loss as to how to resolve the situation with Peggy. Every morning we kissed each other goodbye, then I didn't see him again until at least 8 p.m. Sometimes it was even later, because he went straight from the bakery to his mum's to take care of Peggy. I went with him a couple of times, but it was obvious that I made everything worse, and I felt like an idiot in front of his mum. Peggy ignored me as if I wasn't there, and it made us all uncomfortable. His mum started cooking him tea, which made sense but saddened me. This was something that I had wanted to do for the three of us. I was coming home to an empty flat every night, and I was lonely. There was almost a desperation to our love-making. Were we trying to convince ourselves that everything was normal? We stopped talking about Peggy, or maybe it was me that stopped talking about her. I was beginning to feel something that I wasn't proud of. I was resenting the time that Peggy took away from us. I was starting to feel jealous of the little girl, but I kept those feelings to myself because I was ashamed of them.

I couldn't wait to see Polly. I couldn't wait to get away from the flat. I'd phoned and told her that I was coming and she'd screamed down the phone. Just hearing her voice made me happy.

Saturday morning arrived and Carol and I got an early train to London.

'What will you do while I'm away?' I'd said to Ralph that morning in bed.

'I thought it might be a good idea to bring Peggy here for the day, let her get used to it.'

'I think that's a great idea. Wouldn't it be wonderful if she wanted to stay?'

'Yes, that would be wonderful,' said Ralph.

As the train pulled slowly out of Brighton station, I felt the same relief that I'd always felt when leaving Brighton and that frightened me. It should have been different this time.

I was sitting opposite Carol, who looked half asleep. She was wearing the shortest purple hot pants that I had ever seen, making her long legs look even longer.

'I hate mornings,' she said, yawning.

'Well you're going to have to get used to them if you want to be a model.'

'Am I?'

'Successful models travel all over the world. I doubt very much that they get to lie in bed.'

'Oh I definitely want to be successful. That chap in the butcher's said I had a look of Jean Shrimpton, and she's really successful. Well, her and Twiggy.'

'I hope it works out for you, Carol.'

'I just want to get away from See-saw Lane, Dottie. I'm sick of living with my mum. She never stops nagging. *You* got away, why the bloody hell did you come back?'

Carol and I were first cousins and though we'd been thrown together over the years, at Christmases and birthdays and the like, we had never been close. I'd never shared anything personal with her, and I wasn't about to start now. 'Life,' I said.

'Well I'm not going to let life stand in the way of what I want to do. I'm not about to get some boring job, get married and have a string of kids. I'd rather bloody die, thanks very much.'

'I think you should have a go,' I said, smiling at her.

'Blimey,' she said, looking shocked. 'I don't think you've ever smiled at me before.'

'Really?'

'Yes, really. I always got the feeling that you and that Mary Pickles thought I was a bit of a joke.'

I felt awful that we had made her feel like that. 'I'm sorry.'

'It's okay, I got used to it.'

'Well I wish you hadn't had to.'

'There were times when I needed someone to talk to.'

'When?'

'When Mum and Dad were arguing. I used to shut myself in my room and put a pillow over my head, but I could have done with someone to talk to. I wanted to talk to you, Dottie. You may not want to hear this, but your Rita felt the same.'

'Rita!'

'We talked sometimes. I think she was jealous of Mary. I think a lot of people were.'

I was finding it hard to take all this in.

'It was like you were one person in two bodies and you didn't need anyone else.'

'It wasn't like that.'

'Well, that's what it felt like, Dottie.'

'Then I'm really sorry.'

I hadn't expected to have *any* conversation with Carol on the train journey, and I certainly hadn't expected to have one this deep. I think it was the most that either of us had said to the other for our entire lives.

'Let me see that business card again,' I said, changing the subject.

Carol dug around in her bag and handed it to me.

I stared at the name on the top of the card. 'Greg Palmer. Photographer. I think I might know this guy.'

CHAPTER THIRTY-THREE

Greg Palmer lived in Little Venice, which was a short walk from Paddington station. The area was green and lush, running alongside the canal, and it was hard to believe that you were in the middle of London. I looked at the card again. Greg Palmer, 'The Shenandoah', Little Venice.

'This doesn't tell us much. There's no street name.'

'Let's ask,' said Carol.

There was an elderly man walking towards us with a little white dog on a lead. We showed him the card.

'It's a couple of hundred yards along there,' he said, pointing back down the towpath.

We must have looked confused.

'It's a boat, big, blue and white. You can't miss it.'

We thanked him and walked in the direction he had pointed. We passed a row of canal boats, some of them beautifully decorated with intricate patterns of roses and castles in brilliant greens and blues and reds. It was alive with people. Some were washing down the boats while others were sitting in chairs on the small decks enjoying the sunshine. Kids were running around everywhere, and we saw a couple of boys stretched out on the roof of a boat called 'The Black Pig'. They waved to us as we passed.

This was just the sort of place that I could see Clark and Emma living. I must tell them about it, and I would bring Polly here. She'd love it.

'He lives on a boat?' said Carol, looking disappointed. 'I thought he'd have a studio.'

'The studio might be somewhere else.'

'I think that's it,' she said, pointing to a very large boat just up ahead.

As we got closer we could see 'Shenandoah' written on its side.

There was a small window open and strains of 'Like a Rolling Stone' by Bob Dylan were coming from inside.

'How do we get in?' asked Carol.

The poor girl looked terrified. I took hold of her hand.

'It'll be fine, and I'll be with you.'

'Thanks, Dottie.'

Just then a door swung open and a man emerged from inside the boat.

We stared at him with our mouths open.

'Bloody hell,' whispered Carol. 'He's gorgeous.'

'He's an Adonis,' I whispered back.

'But he's not the guy I met in the butcher's,' she whispered.

'Tony Rotchfort.' The man jumped down onto the towpath and held out his hand. This guy wasn't handsome – he was quite beautiful. His features were delicate, almost like that of a girl, and yet there was no mistaking that he was all man. He was wearing a white vest and his muscles rippled beneath his tanned skin. His hair was fair and it flopped over his eyes. He kept sweeping it back and my God those eyes – they were the darkest blue I'd ever seen. You could lose yourself in them.

I smiled. 'We're looking for Greg Palmer.'

'Carol?' he said, looking at me.

Well I was flattered that he thought I was the would-be model. 'No, I'm Dottie. Carol's cousin.'

Carol smiled her best smile and said, '*I'm* Carol.'

'Greg told me you were coming. He's had to pop out. I have been instructed to look after you. Tea?'

'Thanks.'

'Climb aboard then, girls.'

We had to duck down as we entered the cabin. The interior of the boat was stunning. The panelled walls were painted in the palest blue and the ceiling in a soft shade of lemon. It reminded me of the beach huts on Brighton seafront. Everything had a place – bookshelves lined one wall and canvases and frames were stacked against another. There was a table with a bench either side of it. A comfy looking sofa in the same yellow as the ceiling was positioned under the window, and pale blue cushions completed the look. It really was beautiful.

'Welcome to our little home.'

'It's lovely,' I said.

Carol hadn't moved since we'd stepped onto the boat. She looked like she was in a state of shock. 'Are you a model?' she asked, staring at him.

'Good God no,' he said. 'I'm a poor artist, struggling to put food on the table.' He was grinning at us. 'I am an undiscovered talent just waiting to be thrust upon an unsuspecting world.'

'Do you and Greg both live here?' I asked.

'We do. It's cheaper than a flat, and we like the community of the boat people.'

'I wouldn't mind living here,' said Carol, smiling at him.

'Boats come up for sale now and then. I'll keep a lookout for you.'

Tony was talking to Carol as if she was a grown-up, independent woman who might just decide to live on a boat in the middle of London, instead of the naïve little girl from See-saw Lane who lived with her mother. I looked at her face. It was glowing. Maybe she *could* be the woman that Tony was seeing. I kind of hoped so.

Tony made us tea in the little galley kitchen while Carol and I sat on the yellow sofa. The boat rocked gently beneath us. I could have stayed there forever – it was so peaceful.

Just then someone jumped down onto the boat, making the tea slop into the saucers.

'The man himself,' said Tony.

'Sorry,' said Greg, ducking as he came into the room. 'I had to deliver a couple of pictures. Glad to see that Tony's been looking after you.'

Tony grinned at him. 'Of course. Greg, this is Carol's cousin Dottie.'

'Hi, Dottie. You found us all right then? I thought afterwards that I should have explained that we lived on a boat.'

'I think they want to move in,' said Tony.

'We love it here,' said Greg, smiling at him.

'Tea?' asked Tony.

'Always. Now first of all thanks for coming all this way. Let me tell you a little about myself,' he said, sitting on the floor. 'I'm a freelance photographer, I sell my photos to newspapers and magazines but I also scout for model agencies based here in London.'

'Where would you be taking the pictures?' I asked.

Okay, I rent a studio from an elderly couple who run a tobacconist's shop a few streets away. They are very definite about what sort of photos we photographers take. They've given a couple of them their marching orders already. They insist on seeing the girls' birth certificates before they let them across the threshold. You *have* got yours, Carol?'

'Yes.'

'Good, so you see she is in the very safe hands of myself and Mrs Kovak.'

There was something very familiar about Greg. 'Have you ever sold any photos to *Trend*?' I asked.

'I covered the McCartney–Eastman wedding for them. Why?'

'I used to work there. I thought I recognised your name.'

'There you are then,' said Tony, coming into the room with Greg's tea. You're friends already.'

'So you know Peter?' I said.

'Nice bloke. He's kept the wolf from this little boat's porthole plenty of times.'

I felt happier about leaving Carol, knowing that he knew Peter.

'I want to visit a friend while I am in London.'

'Then off you go,' said Tony. 'We will take good care of Carol until you return.'

'Carol?'

'You go. I'll be fine.'

'Okay.'

I walked back to Paddington station and got the Tube to Islington, then cut across Highbury Fields and ran up the steps of 59 Victoria Terrace. I felt happy to be back, and I couldn't wait to see Polly. I rang the doorbell and waited. I could hear someone thundering down the stairs and then the door opened and there she was. We fell into each other's arms screaming. Mrs P poked her head out of her flat door.

'Hello, Miss Perks.'

'Hello, Mrs P.'

'Just visiting?'

'Yes, I have to go back to Brighton later.'

'Have a nice visit,' she said and shut her door.

'Nosy old cow,' said Polly.

'God, I called her Mrs P.'

'Don't worry about that.' She caught hold of my hand and we ran up the stairs.

'Oh, Dottie, I've missed you so much,' said Polly, pulling me down onto the couch.

'I've missed you too.'

'A mouse has moved into your room.'

'A what?'

'A mouse, a little brown mouse.'

'Are we talking about an actual mouse here, or a girl that looks like a mouse?'

'She scuttles.'

'That sounds more spiderish than mouseish.'

'No, she's definitely a mouse. She even squeaks like a mouse and she wears a lot of brown.'

'Not your new best friend then?'

'No, she's bloody not. Oh, Dottie, why did you have to go?'

'I'm beginning to wonder.'

'You're *not*, are you?' said Polly, suddenly looking concerned.

'No, no, of course I'm not,' I said quickly. 'Take no notice.'

'Too late, you'll have to tell me now.'

'Just stuff we've got to work through.'

'What about the flat?'

'It's lovely.'

'And Ralph?'

'Also lovely.'

'So what's left?'

'Peggy.'

'Ah, the child.'

'The child.'

'You look as if you need to talk but first tea? Coffee? Flat lemonade? Leftover sherry from last Christmas?'

'So much choice and so little time. I'm swaying towards the sherry, but I think I'll plump for coffee.'

'If I've got any. I always used yours, didn't I?'

'You did.'

I followed her into the kitchen. She rummaged around in the cupboard. 'We'll have to nick the mouse's coffee. I'll pay it back.'

'Never knew mice drank coffee.'

'Oh they do, gallons of it.'

'And cheese?'

'Pounds of the stuff.'

This was what I had missed, this daft, silly banter. It made me feel young again. My God what was I thinking? That I wanted this back?

We took our coffees into the front room, kicked off our shoes and cosied up on the couch.

'So what is it with Miss Peggy then?'

'She doesn't like me.'

'Of course she likes you, you're adorable and lovable.'

'Not according to Peggy I'm not. I'm the evil interloper. I've stolen her daddy away from her. I've sent Fiona away, and I've even managed to get rid of Australia.'

'Gosh, you've been busy.'

'I don't know how I can fix it, Polly.'

'And I had you doing cartwheels along Brighton seafront.'

'Just goes to show doesn't it?'

'So what exactly is wrong?'

'She refuses to move into the flat and until she does Ralph is miserable, and I feel as if everyone is blaming me.'

'I don't suppose they are though.'

'Maybe not, but that's how it feels.'

'I wish I could help.'

'Just being here and talking to you is helping.'

'I wish you were staying longer.'

'So do I, but I've got to get Carol back.'

'Maybe I could come and stay with you one weekend.'

'Of course you can.' Just the thought of Polly in Brighton made me happy.

'Would Ralph mind?'

'He's hardly ever there. He spends most of his time at his mum's.'

Polly and I whiled away the afternoon chatting and drinking coffee. I told her about Aunty Brenda thinking the photographer was a boy scout, and she thought it was hilarious. At one point during the afternoon I saw the mouse scuttle past.

'See, I told you, she scuttles.'

'I've missed this.'

'Me too.'

Leaving Polly was hard. I had been more relaxed in those couple of hours than I had been for weeks.

'Write and tell me when you can visit. I'd love to show you the flat and take you round Brighton.'

'I will.'

We hugged on the doorstep and I waved to her until she was out of sight. I walked across the field towards the station then got the Tube back to Paddington.

The sky was clouding over as I walked along the towpath; it looked as if it was about to pour with rain. As I neared the 'Shenandoah' I could hear music and laughter coming from inside. I tapped on the window. Tony came out and helped me onto the boat.

Carol looked happy. She was sitting on the lemon couch with her feet curled under her. I sat next to her. 'Take Five' was playing in the background. Greg turned the music down.

I smiled at Carol. 'So did you have a good time?'

'I had an amazing time.'

'The girl did good,' said Greg. 'I was right, she's a natural.'

'So what happens now?' I asked.

'I do the rounds of the model agencies and try to drum up some interest, but I'm quietly optimistic. Carol photographs well. Some girls have got the height, but the camera doesn't love them.' Greg smiled. 'The camera loves you, Carol.'

Carol blushed, which I thought was sweet. 'It was great,' she said.

I smiled at her. I was glad that she'd had such a nice time. 'So you'd like to do it again then?'

'I'd love to do it again.'

'And I'm sure you will,' said Greg.

Carol grinned at him. 'Really?'

'Like I said, the camera loves you.'

I wished we could have stayed longer. It felt so calm and peaceful sitting there with Dave Brubeck playing in the background and the boat moving gently beneath us. I could have quite happily curled up and fallen asleep.

Reluctantly I stood up. 'I'm afraid we have to catch a train,' I said.

Both men kissed our cheeks, and we waved goodbye to them as we walked back along the towpath.

A soft rain had started to come down and a mist was settling over the canal. It had an eerie feel about it. It reminded me of the TV series *Dixon of Dock Green* that Mary and I used to watch on a Saturday night when we were kids. In almost every episode London seemed to be shrouded in mist.

We got the Tube over to Victoria and settled down in the carriage as the train took us home to Brighton.

'I think I'm in love,' said Carol dreamily.

'With Greg?'

'No, Tony.'

'Oh.'

'What do you mean oh?'

'I'm pretty sure he's taken.'

'Taken with who?'

'Greg.'

Carol laughed. 'Greg?'

'I think they're a couple. In fact I'm sure they are.'

'Really?'

'Really.'

'What a bloody waste.'

'Shouldn't think Greg would agree with you.'

'Lucky git,' said Carol, grinning at me.

I was beginning to warm to the girl. She'd been good company. Maybe we could be friends after all.

'Thanks for today, Dottie.'

'I'm glad you enjoyed it.'

'I did, I really did.'

Carol stared out of the window; she seemed lost in thought. Then she turned to me and said, 'Do you really think that I could be a model?'

'Well Greg seems to think you can.'

'I hope so, because I think it's time to leave See-saw Lane.'

'Let's just see what your mum has to say about that first,' I said, grinning at her.

'Oh, don't,' she said, giggling.

As the train picked up speed I looked out of the window. The face staring back at me was not the face of someone wanting to go home.

CHAPTER THIRTY-FOUR

I had been working at Tom Brown's for two weeks now, and I loved it. I hadn't found the next Daphne du Maurier yet, but every manuscript that I picked up filled me with excitement. This could be the one, the diamond in the rough, the undiscovered talent that Tom was looking for.

'It won't last,' said Millie, smiling across from her desk.

'What won't?'

'Hope. I was like you in the beginning, but just wait till you've ploughed through the amount of garbage that I have. I told Tom that if he didn't get someone to help me I was leaving.'

'Really?'

'Well that's what I told him, but he didn't believe me. He knows I love it here. Something must have gone in though, because he took you on.'

'This job is a godsend. I don't know what I would have done if I hadn't got it.'

'You were in the right place at the right time, girl, and I'm afraid you have to stay forever. It's in the contract.'

I loved working with Millie. We got on so well. She was single and living at home with her parents.

'The perfect man just hasn't arrived yet, and I will settle for no less than perfect,' she said one morning.

'And what's perfect?'

'Kind, caring, handsome, oh, and of course loaded.'

'You don't want much do you?'

'I've kissed too many frogs, Dottie. I'm looking for my prince.'

'Even princes have their frog days.'

'So says the voice of experience. How many frogs have you kissed then?'

'Not that many as it happens.'

'At least you're married. I'm still living at home.'

'Who told you that I was married?'

'Well aren't you?'

'No, we live together.'

'Blimey, does Tom know?'

'Do you think he'd mind?'

'I don't know. No, I'm sure he wouldn't, he's pretty open-minded. Don't your parents mind?'

'My sister took the moral high ground, but then I wouldn't have expected anything less. We *will* get married, but we can't afford it just yet.'

'Well I think you're very brave. My parents would disown me. Nothing short of a personal appearance from the Pope himself will satisfy them.'

'Catholic?'

'Through and through, like a stick of Brighton rock.'

'Well I haven't got that to worry about.'

'You're the first person I've ever met who's living in sin,' said Millie, grinning at me.

I started giggling.

'What?'

'Well, it sounds like a place, doesn't it? Oh yes I'm living in Sin. It's a lovely little village just outside Lewes.'

Millie started laughing.

Tom came into the room. 'What's the joke?' he asked, smiling.

'We were just talking about living in sin,' said Millie.

'You should be so lucky,' he said, putting a manuscript on my desk.

'Is Tom married?' I asked after he'd gone back into his office.

'No, the only thing he's married to is the job. Why, do you fancy him?'

'Don't be daft.'

'Well, he's not a bad-looking bloke.'

'Do *you* fancy him then?'

'No, he's not my type.'

'And what's your type, Miss Millie?'

'Dark and moody,' she said, grinning.

Yes I loved my job, but home and Ralph were a different matter.

According to Ralph, Peggy had had a great time while I was in London. They'd taken a picnic down onto the beach, and she'd paddled in the water. Then Ralph had taken her to Peter Pan's Playground. I had hoped this might have changed her mind but she was still living with Ralph's mum.'

'Perhaps she can come again next weekend, and we can all be together. Would you like that, Dottie?'

'I'd love it. Ralph, if I thought that was what Peggy wanted.'

'Why do you have to be so pessimistic?' he'd said, frowning at me.

'Do *you* think she wants to be with me? Honestly, Ralph, do you think that's what Peggy wants?'

'I don't know what she wants any more. I just know that somehow or other we've got to make this work.'

I suddenly felt tired of the whole thing. 'Don't you think I've tried?'

'I'm sorry, yes, of course you've tried.'

The only person Peggy wanted to be with apart from her daddy was Fiona. She'd flung that at me the last time I'd seen her, and it had really hurt.

'She wants Fiona, Ralph, not me.'

Ralph had put his arms around me. 'But *I* don't want to be with Fiona, I want to be with you, and I would like Peggy to be part of us. This will get better – we have to believe that.'

'I want to, Ralph, I really do.'

But it didn't get better. Ralph was still going round to his mum's every evening and most weekends, and I was stuck on my own. I might as well have been living at home. At least there I would have had some company. I decided to take things into my own hands.

I looked through the phone directory and found a primary school ten minutes from work. I decided to go there in my lunch hour. If it was a good school then maybe Ralph could see the logic in it. Peggy would have to leave his mum's house and live with us.

The school was called Our Lady Star of the Sea, which I thought was a lovely name. It was in an old Victorian building, but it was quite small, and it didn't look scary. I didn't want Peggy to be scared. I wanted her to be happy, but she couldn't keep living with Ralph's mum. It wasn't fair on her, and it wasn't fair on us – something had to change. There were two doors. One said 'BOYS' and one said 'GIRLS', something leftover from Victorian times when, God forbid, the two sexes might actually mix. I don't know why but I went through the door marked BOYS. I was in that sort of a mood. The whole place smelt of fish and then I remembered that it was Friday. I couldn't see anyone that I could speak to, but I could hear the sound of children. I guessed they were eating lunch. Just then a woman walked through the hallway.

'Can I help you?' she asked.

'I'd like to speak to someone about putting a child's name down for the winter term.'

'They are all in the dining room. I'll try to find the head for you. Just wait here, I won't be long.'

I sat down on a bench and waited. I liked the feel of the place. It was scrupulously clean, the smell of polish mixing in with the smell of fish. The light coming through the long stained-glass window cast rainbow prisms across highly polished floorboards.

A lady was coming towards me. 'Mrs Doyle,' she said, smiling. I stood up and shook her outstretched hand.

'Dorothy Perks,' I said.

'Come into my office.'

I followed her down a corridor, between walls decorated with children's paintings.

Mrs Doyle's office was chaotic. Her desk, what you could see of it, was beautiful, as were the panelled walls that ran from floor to ceiling. The old bookcases were filled to overflowing with books of all sizes, and the light streaming through the arched window was amazing.

'How old is your little girl, Mrs Perks?' she said, smiling at me.

I wasn't sure what to say so I plumped for avoidance.

'She will be five in August.'

'And you would like her to come here?'

'We have recently moved to Oriental Place, which is near the Palace Pier, and I have just started working in Kemp Town so we would like a school close by.'

'Now most parents want their children to come here because we are a Catholic school. I presume you are of the faith.'

I hadn't realised that this was a Catholic school. The head must have seen the look on my face.

'You're *not* Catholic, are you?'

Not only am I not Catholic I thought, but I'm also living in sin.

'No, I'm afraid we're not. Would that be a problem?'

'Not necessarily, but religion is a big part of the ethos of this school, and we would want your little girl to be part of that. You would need to speak to your husband about it.'

'Yes,' I said. 'I think that would be the best thing.'

I felt so stupid as I walked back up the drive and out the school gates. The school was called Our Lady Star of the Sea for heaven's sake. Why hadn't I made the connection? Still, the head hadn't said she wouldn't take her. I would have to speak to Ralph.

Ralph was home by 6.30 p.m., which was early for him. I was cooking tea when he came in. I wiped my hands on a tea towel and put my arms around him.

'Well this is a nice surprise.'

'Peggy's gone to the park with her friend and her friend's mum so I was able to come straight home.'

'We can eat together,' I said, kissing him on the cheek.

'That's what I thought,' he said, smiling and producing a bottle of wine out of a carrier bag.

Ralph poured the wine while I dished up the sausage and chips. I cooked for both of us every night, but I usually ended up throwing Ralph's dinner in the bin. This was lovely and it gave me a chance to tell him about the school that I had visited.

'I really liked it, Ralph, and it's just up the road from work. It means I could drop her off in the mornings. She could start in September.'

'And who's going to pick her up?'

This was something I had been thinking about. Before Ralph married Mary he had begun an apprenticeship to become a plumber. He had loved it but had to give it up because Mary was pregnant. He was working at the bakery, and although he rarely complained, I knew he hated it.

'I wondered if you could take up your apprenticeship again.'

'Plumbing?'

'You enjoyed it, didn't you?'

'Very much.'

'I'm getting a good wage now, and once I've been there a while and proved myself, Tom said that he would give me a raise. I remembered you saying that your days were a lot shorter, so perhaps you could pick Peggy up.'

Ralph didn't answer right away. 'Well, I guess it's something to think about,' he said eventually.

'Would they take you back?'

'I'd have to look into it.'

'But it could work, couldn't it?'

'If they take me back.'

I wanted him to be a bit more enthusiastic about it. I hoped he'd be excited and that he could see the possibilities.

'Well?'

'I wished you'd talked to me about it first. I can't be rushed on this. I need to think about it, and I need to see what Peggy thinks.'

I could feel that familiar churning in my stomach. 'What is there to think about?'

'There's a lot to think about.'

'Such as?'

'Such as persuading Peggy to go to a different school than her friends.'

'This is ridiculous, Ralph.'

'It might seem ridiculous to you, Dottie, but I want my child to be happy.'

'And you think I don't?'

'I'm beginning to think that you don't want to consider Peggy's needs at all.'

We glared at each other. This was awful. I did want Peggy to be happy, and I felt hurt that Ralph could say that to me. Aunty Brenda was right. Peggy was coming between us, and it scared me.

CHAPTER THIRTY-FIVE

I never mentioned the school again. In fact I never mentioned Peggy again. I felt defeated by the whole thing. Ralph and I moved around each other. We were polite; we were kind. We left for work in the morning and kissed as we went our separate ways. I ate alone every evening. He came home later and later – sometimes I was already in bed. We stopped making love. I didn't know what to do, and I felt too ashamed to talk about it, even to Mum.

Thank God for Tom Brown and Millie. I threw myself into my work and eventually found that elusive diamond in the rough. I'd read the first couple of pages and then taken it home with me. The book was written by someone called Matthew Smith. The title of the book was *A Place Beyond the Mountain.*

It told the story of a young boy called Simmi who wanted to leave his small village in Africa to travel to a place of learning, a place where he could discover the world. A place beyond the mountain. It was so beautifully written that I couldn't put it down. His description of the little village was so real that I could almost feel the searing heat and relentless dust. I could smell the white and yellow acacia trees that grew in the garden. I was there beside the boy as he climbed the baobab tree and looked out towards the mountain. It was a story of hope, inspiration and eventual victory against all the odds. I was still reading it when later that evening Ralph came home.

I looked up from the book and smiled at him.

'You look happy,' he said, sitting down beside me.

I showed him the book. 'It's wonderful.'

Ralph nodded. 'It's nice to see you smiling, my love.'

And suddenly I felt the tears on my cheek. I'd missed this gentleness between us. I'd missed Ralph.

He held me in his arms. We didn't speak – there was no need. That night we made love, and I fell asleep dreaming of a boy who had a dream, just like Mary.

There was a bounce in my step the next day as I negotiated the wonky wooden stairs to the office. Perhaps this was the start of a new understanding between Ralph and I. Perhaps we could begin to work things out – be happy again.

Millie burst through the door. 'I've just laddered my new nylons on those bloody stairs. They cost me one and eleven. Has one of us got to break our neck before something's done? How come you look so happy?'

'Well for a start I haven't laddered my nylons and secondly...' I held up the book.

'You haven't?'

'I jolly well have.'

'You really think it's good?'

'It's amazing.'

'Have you told Tom?'

'He's not in yet.'

'What's it called?'

'*A Place Beyond the Mountain.*'

'Good title.'

'Good book.'

'Bloody stairs,' said Tom, launching himself through the door.

'You too?' said Millie.

'Why, what happened to you?'

'New nylons that cost me one and eleven.'

'Take it out of petty cash.'

'Oh, thanks, Tom. What happened to you?'

'The same, new nylons.'

I loved Tom's sense of humour.

'Dottie's got something for you.'

Tom raised an eyebrow. I held out the book.

'Now that's worth laddering my nylons for. My little diamond?'

I nodded. 'I think so.'

'Have you read it all?'

'Enough to know it's pretty special.'

'Then I hope that I will find it just as special.'

'I think you will. I really think you will.'

'Bravo,' said Tom, going into his office clutching the book. 'Where's my coffee, woman?' he shouted, winking at Millie as he went into his office.

'Coming right up, sir,' said Millie, laughing.

'No phone calls, Millie, just lots of caffeine and doughnuts. I am going to bury myself in Dottie's little find.'

'Your wish is my command.'

'Gosh, I hope I'm right,' I said, suddenly doubting myself.

'Have faith. Anyway Tom will soon tell you if you're not. He can sniff out a bestseller a mile off.'

I ran down to the little bakery on the corner for the doughnuts, the smell of baking made my tummy growl. I gave the doughnuts to Millie and settled down at my desk and thought about last night. There was a warm feeling in my tummy, which made a change from the anxious feeling I had been carrying around with me for weeks.

At four o'clock Tom emerged from his office. Millie and I stopped what we were doing and stared at him. It was hard to tell from his face what he was thinking. Then he gave a huge smile. 'Bingo!' he said.

I got up from my desk. 'Really? You liked it? You really liked it?'

Then Millie got up and we did a silly dance round the office.

'Do we have such a thing as alcohol in this place?' said Tom.

'I don't think so,' said Millie.

'I think I saw some bottles of Babycham under the sink,' I said, walking towards the little kitchen.

'God only knows how long they've been there,' said Millie.

Tom found a bottle opener and filled three plastic cups with something that tasted like toilet cleaner and we toasted out newest client-to-be. 'To Matthew Smith,' we said in unison and then almost reverently, '*A Place Beyond the Mountain.*'

'Dottie, do we have a number we can ring Mr Smith on?'

'Wasn't it with the manuscript?'

'No.'

'Sorry, Tom, I must have left it at home.'

'No problem. Bring it in tomorrow and we'll go from there. I think you should give him the good news, as you are the very clever girl that found him.'

'I'd love to.'

'Good. Now why don't we all have an early night and go home and celebrate.'

I smiled at him, but it was a hollow smile. I doubted that there would be anyone at home to celebrate *with*.

As I walked along the seafront, I found myself thinking about Matthew Smith, wondering what sort of guy he was and how he would react to the news that an agent liked his book. It had been a good day, one of the nicest days I'd had in weeks. I was so lucky to have such a great job. How different my life would be if I'd had to go back to Woolworths with all its memories.

I walked up to my flat and nearly fell over Tristan, who was sitting on the stairs outside his door. I was horrified to see that he was crying. I sat down beside him and put my arm around his shoulder.

'Can I help?' I said.

'It's Stephen – he's in the hospital.'

'What's wrong?'

'The silly boy decided to go for a run along the seafront. I don't know what he was thinking! He can barely walk, let alone run.'

'What happened?'

'His wonky knee gave out. He was lying on the ground for ages. People were stepping over him, Dottie, and I wasn't there for him. I wasn't there when he needed me.'

'How did you find out?'

'Someone eventually decided to call an ambulance and the dear boy had the presence of mind, through all that pain, Dottie, to tell them where he lived. Rose came up and broke the news to me. I nearly fainted.'

'I'm so sorry. When did it happen?'

'This morning. I thought he'd gone to get a jar of peanut but-ter as we'd run out – Stephen loves peanut butter on his toast – and all the time he was lying flat out on the seafront with people walking over him. I feel sick thinking about it.'

'Where is he now?'

'He's in the Royal Sussex County. They operated on his knee this morning. I've been there all day. They sent me home and told me to come back tomorrow.'

'But why are you sitting on the stairs?' I asked as gently as I could.

'I can't bear to go in the flat.'

'Would it help if I went in with you?'

'Yes, I think it would.'

'Come on then,' I said, helping him up.

'What must you think of me?' he said, sitting down on the couch.

'I think you're upset because your dear friend is hurt. That's what I think of you.'

'Now stop being nice or you'll start me off again.'

'There's nothing wrong with crying. My Aunty Brenda says it's the body's way of cleansing the soul.'

'I like the sound of your Aunty Brenda.'

I busied myself making tea then sat down on the couch next to Tristan.

'What makes it worse is that we had a bit of a spat this morning,' he said, taking a mouthful of tea.

'A serious spat?'

'Far from it. It was all about a bloody cat.'

'A cat?'

'Stephen wants a cat. I said how was it going to get out to do its business? Stephen said that it would be an indoor cat, and we could have a dirt tray, and I said I didn't want to live in a flat that smells of… well, you know…'

I smiled. 'Oh dear.'

'When I asked him how the wretched thing was supposed to get any exercise, Stephen said he would put it on a lead and walk it along the bloody seafront. Have you ever heard anything so ridiculous in your entire life?'

That's when we started laughing. We actually howled. In fact we made so much noise that Mrs Toshimo came up to see what was the matter.

'Is it bad news, dear?' she said, putting her head round the door.

'No,' said Tristan wiping his eyes, 'we were laughing about Stephen wanting a cat.'

'My oriental gentleman and I had a cat once. We called it Lillie after Lillie Langtry. Turned out to be a boy, dear, but there you are. We used to take him for walks along the seafront on a lead.'

At which point Tristan and I dissolved into more laughter. This wasn't the celebration I'd wanted, but it beat sitting on my own in an empty flat.

CHAPTER THIRTY-SIX

There was no telephone number for Matthew Smith, just an address. I was going to have to write to him. I asked him to call into the agency, or to phone if he was able to. I imagined him opening my letter and his excitement at learning that we liked his book. I felt so privileged that I had been the one to find him. It made trawling through all the rubbish worthwhile.

Ralph and I still hadn't talked about Peggy's new school, but I was determined to find the right time to bring it up again. Ralph had said that I didn't care about Peggy's feelings and that had hit a nerve. Maybe he was right, but it was hard to care about someone when they so obviously disliked you. You'd have to be a saint, and I was no saint. But I *was* the adult here, and it was up to me, not Peggy, to make this work.

I decided to surprise Ralph after work and meet him at his mum's house. Maybe the three of us could go for a walk, or to the park. I knew that's what they did sometimes. I hadn't made any effort to support Ralph. I had only joined him a couple of times at his mum's. How was Peggy going to accept me if she never saw me? If I was never part of her daily life? It was time for me to put Peggy's needs before my own. Okay, maybe she would still reject me, but I had to try.

Having made up my mind, I fairly skipped home along the seafront. Tonight I wouldn't be spending all evening on my own, waiting for Ralph. Tonight I would support Ralph and maybe, just maybe, Peggy would grow to like me a little. I wasn't expecting miracles, but a small truce would be a start.

I opened the front door of Oriental Place and was just about to go upstairs when Tristan came out of Mrs Toshimo's flat.

I smiled at him. 'How's Stephen?'

'He's moaning a lot, so I guess that means he's feeling better.'

'When can he come home?'

'He wants to come home now, today, but they won't let him go because of all these stairs. He reckons he can get up on his bum, but what if he falls? I'd never forgive myself.'

'Oh dear.'

'I've just been talking to Rose about it and bless her heart she says we can move in with her until he gets better.'

'Have you told Stephen?'

'Not yet. He's being so obnoxious I've a good mind to make him suffer.'

'You won't though, will you?'

'Of course not. I shall give him the good news this evening when I visit. They won't let him out right away because he's still in a lot of pain, but at least when he does come home, we won't have to worry about the stairs.'

'She's very good, isn't she?'

'You don't know the half of it, Dottie. Stephen and I owe her a lot.'

Tristan didn't enlarge on that statement, so I didn't ask.

'Fancy a coffee?' he said, walking up the stairs behind me.

'No thanks. I'm meeting Ralph tonight at his mum's.'

'I'm glad. You seem to be spending an awful lot of time on your own. I'm not being nosy – I just couldn't help noticing.'

'Well hopefully that's going to change. That's what tonight's all about.'

'Well good for you, girl.'

I freshened up a bit, changed my clothes and at the last minute grabbed the brown teddy bear off Peggy's bed and put it under my arm.

I remembered happy times at Ralph's house. Christmases and bonfire nights, standing round the huge bonfire that Ralph's dad lit every year. Holding sparklers in gloved hands and eating burnt sausages, then walking to the end of the garden and wishing on a star and being in love. Now as I approached the house I started to feel nervous. I didn't even know if I would be welcome.

I knocked on the door, and his mum opened it. She looked really shocked. We'd always got on well, so I couldn't understand her reaction. I know I hadn't been round to see them much, but they knew that Ralph and I were living together, and Ralph had never said that they disapproved of it.

She looked really flustered. 'Dottie,' she said.

She didn't ask me in, she just stood there staring at me.

'Is Ralph here?' I asked, smiling at her.

'Erm, no.'

Ralph's dad came to the door. I'd always liked Ralph's dad. He'd always made me feel so welcome, and I got the feeling that he thought Peggy should be living with us and not them.

'Hello, Dottie. We haven't seen you in a long time! How are you, girl?'

'I'm fine, Mr Bennett.'

'Invite the girl in,' he said to his wife.

'She's looking for Ralph,' said Mrs Bennett.

'He's at the park isn't he?'

Mrs Bennett glared at him. 'I don't think so.'

I saw a look pass between him and his wife and he started to backtrack.

'Well I could be wrong,' he said.

'You are,' said Mrs Bennett.

'Do you want to come in and wait?' Mr Bennett asked.

'No, it's okay. I'll try the park.'

I could almost feel Mrs Bennett's eyes boring into my back as I walked back down the path.

Something was wrong, and I didn't know what it was.

I walked back across the green and made my way to the park.

All the houses on the estate looked exactly the same – the only difference between them was the colour of the doors. Every couple of years the council came round and painted them. The paint came in two colours, green and blue. All the kids wanted blue, but no one was given a choice. One year we got a blue door and when we ran round to Mary's house the painters were about to paint her door green. You would have thought that they were about to demolish the house the way Mary carried on. She begged, she pleaded, she cried and then she was sick, right there on the pavement.

Of course Mary being small and cute and by now very pale melted the council man's heart. He went back to his van and took out a pot of blue paint. That was why, in a row of green doors, Mary's door was blue. Mary had nearly always got her own way.

I'd always loved living here. It was all I had ever known and all I had ever wanted, unlike Mary, who couldn't wait to get away. But now as I walked through street after street of identical houses, I was finding it hard to breathe, and I felt that familiar tightening in my chest. I longed for the sea and the taste of salt on my lips. I longed for Oriental Place.

The park wasn't far away, and I was soon walking through the old iron gates. I saw them straight away. Peggy was on the climbing frame and Ralph was watching her. The little girl was laughing and Ralph was smiling up at her. They both looked so happy that my heart melted. I wanted so badly to be a part of that happiness. I was just about to go over to them when Peggy jumped down and ran across the park. That's when I saw her.

Fiona had her arms open and Peggy ran into them. Fiona swung her around, the sound of their laughter filled the air and then Peggy was dragging her back towards the climbing frame. Ralph draped his arm around Fiona's shoulder as they watched Peggy hanging upside down on the bars. Peggy was looking at the world from an upside-down sort of a place, just like her mother used to do.

CHAPTER THIRTY-SEVEN

I left the park before they saw me. My heart was beating out of my chest. Ralph's mother had known. That was way she had acted so oddly – she had known that Fiona would be there. I felt betrayed and oddly ashamed. I wondered how long it had been going on. I didn't kid myself that this was the first time they had met. All those evenings I had spent alone waiting for Ralph to come home, sometimes waiting until after ten. I'd been a fool. They had made a fool of me. I was all over the place. I didn't know how to feel or what to do. They had looked so happy, the three of them, like a family. They didn't need me. I felt so terribly alone and so dreadfully sad.

How many people knew? How many people had kept this from me? Did Rita know? Was she laughing behind my back? And Mary's mum – had she been in on it? I didn't know who I could trust any more.

I couldn't face going back to the flat. I couldn't face Ralph. At that moment I never wanted to see him again. I felt so betrayed, and like a child I wanted my mum.

I fell into her arms when she opened the front door. I was still clutching the brown teddy bear. What had made me think that a stupid bear was going to make Peggy love me? She loved Fiona. She was never going to love me.

Mum led me inside and sat me down on the couch. I couldn't speak, I just sobbed and sobbed till there were no tears left, and all the while Mum held me and stroked my hair.

'I'm here, my love, I'm here,' she whispered gently.

When I was eventually able to speak I told her what had happened.

'Did Rita know, Mum? Did she know?'

'She better not have known, or I will have something to say about it. But no, Dottie, she's your sister, she's family – she wouldn't do that to you.'

'But she blamed me for their break-up. She might be happy that they're seeing each other again.'

'I suppose she might but not at your expense.'

'Ralph's mum knew.

'All I can say love is that most people do what they think is right. They don't set out to cause pain. If Mrs Bennett knows that Fiona is spending time with Peggy she's probably turned a blind eye to it, because she wants the child to be happy.'

'But what about *my* happiness, Mum?'

'You have to talk to Ralph.'

I couldn't get the image of Ralph and Fiona out of my head. They looked so comfortable with each other; they looked so happy together. The three of them looked more like a family than we had ever done. 'I can't talk to him, Mum.'

'He will be wondering where you are.'

'No he won't. His mum will have told him that I was on my way to the park. He will have guessed that I saw them.'

'Then you had best stay here until you decide what you want to do.'

'Thanks, Mum.'

'What about work?'

'I'm not sure I can face it. I'll see how I feel in the morning.'

'Do what you think is best, love. Do what makes you happiest.'

'I don't think I'll ever be happy again.'

'You will, my darling girl, you will.'

I couldn't believe that I was back in my old bedroom. I lay in the new sheets staring up at the stain on the ceiling. The day's events were going round and round in my head like a broken record, a series of scenarios where I confronted them both, where

I slapped Ralph around the face, where I broke down in tears and Ralph begged my forgiveness right there in the park in front of Fiona. Round and round it went until I thought I was going mad.

After what seemed like hours of tossing and turning, I finally fell into a fitful sleep where I dreamed a load of stuff that didn't make any sense. When I woke up, all I could remember about it was that I was running away, and that is what I decided to do. I would run away. It was the only thing that made any sense to me right then.

The great thing about being at home was that there was no phone. He would have known that I was here. I had been on edge all morning waiting for the knock on the door, but it hadn't come. I guess he just couldn't face me either. That or he didn't care.

I went down the road and phoned Mrs P at Victoria Terrace. Luckily she was quite happy to let me stay with Polly for a few days. She informed me that the new lodger had left, owing her two weeks' rent, and that she would get my old room ready for me. Thank God for Mrs P. I also phoned Tom and told him that I was having some personal problems and needed to get away for a few days. He was fine about it and wished me luck. There were so many things rushing through my head that if I didn't get away, I was going to explode.

I took a chance and went back to Oriental Place to get some clothes. I tapped on Tristan's door on the way up.

'You just caught me,' he said, motioning me into the room. 'I was just about to visit poor Stephen.'

'How is he?'

'I went to see him last night and they've got him up and walking. I told them that we would be moving into the ground-floor flat and they said he could come home in a couple of days. I've missed him so much, Dottie, I can't tell you.'

'Do you know if Ralph's home?'

'Haven't heard a sound from up there.'

'Do you know if he came home last night?'

'Now that I can't say.'

'I'm going to London for a few days.'

'Without telling Ralph?'

'Without telling Ralph.'

'Can I help?'

'I'm not sure anyone can help.'

'Well Stephen and I will be here when you come home. Come and find us and we will give you copious amounts of tea and biscuits.'

'Can you lie to Ralph if he asks you where I am?'

'Absolutely. I shall cross my fingers behind my back.'

I smiled at him. He was such a dear man.

'There you see – you're smiling. That's a start, isn't it?'

'Yes, it's a start,' I said.

The flat was empty, then I saw the envelope propped up on the table. I ignored it. I was scared to open it. Was it a goodbye letter? Was it an I'm-sorry letter?

I didn't even know what I wanted it to say.

I walked across to the window. We'd long since got rid of the piece of net. Now the glass was gleaming, and I could look straight over the chimneys to the sea. The sea always intrigued me – it was always changing. Sometimes it was calm, sparkling like a precious jewel under the glare of the sun. Other times it was angry, spitting white foam onto the prom. Today it was grey and dull, as if it couldn't be bothered to be anything else. I went into the bedroom. The bed hadn't been slept in. I wondered if Ralph had stayed at his mum's last night. I couldn't even think that he might have stayed at Fiona's.

I threw a few things in a bag and left the flat. I was halfway down the stairs when I ran back, grabbed the letter and stuffed it in my pocket.

CHAPTER THIRTY-EIGHT

The journey to London seemed endless; I had too much time to think. The letter in my pocket felt like a ticking time bomb. I could have read it now, on the train, but I just wasn't ready.

Why had everything gone so wrong? Maybe I was expecting too much. After all that had happened between Ralph and I, moving back to Brighton and starting a life together had seemed like the easy bit, but it had proven to be anything but. I wondered how much of it had been my fault. Had I not supported Ralph enough where Peggy was concerned? Had I not tried enough with the little girl?

Mrs P almost hugged me at the door – well she didn't exactly hug me, but she definitely made body contact in a huggy sort of way – and I was feeling so emotional it made me want to cry.

'Now you just go upstairs and make yourself at home. I'm sure Miss Renson won't mind you using a tea bag.' And she giggled as if she'd just made a joke.

'Thank you Mrs P… I mean Mrs Pierce, I'll do that.'

I went into the kitchen and turned on the tap. The water spat as I filled the kettle, and it made me feel at home. I went over to the window and opened it wide. Polly was always cold; it was me who liked the fresh air. Polly said I should live in Siberia. Right now that didn't seem like such a bad idea. I watched the people on the green and waited for Polly to come home from work. It didn't feel so strange being back in the flat. I'd been happy here; everything was familiar. The spitting tap, Polly's nylons draped across the backs of chairs and her beauty magazines piled up on the coffee table. If I felt anything it was that I'd failed. I'd made this big gesture of leaving London and running back to Brighton, and I hadn't made it work.

Eventually I heard the front door slam and Polly's footsteps on the stairs. She screamed when she opened the kitchen door.

'Why didn't you tell me you were coming? I could have pulled a sickie. Why are you here? Is something wrong? Oh I don't care why you're here, I'm just glad you are. Give me a hug.'

We fell into each other's arms.

'I've missed you. I've missed you.'

'I've missed you too,' I said.

'Did you know that the mouse had run off? What a hoot. She looked so holier than thou but she scuttled off owing two weeks' rent and Mrs P swears blind that she took the telephone directory with her. I mean why would anyone nick a bloody phone directory? Oh I'm so glad you're here.'

This is what I needed. Uncomplicated, funny, loving Polly.

'How long can you stay?'

'I don't know, a few days maybe?'

'I'm really happy, Dottie, but I can see you're sad.'

'I am a bit, but being here with you is helping already.'

'I think that maybe a visit to Mrs Dickens might be on the cards. What do you think?'

'I think that would be perfect.'

'Good, now forget the tea. I've got some wine. I went to an office party the other night. We were asked to bring a bottle, but there was so much booze there that I brought it home again.'

'Wine it is then.'

'And you can tell me what's up or tell me to mind my own beeswax. And for God's sake shut the bloody window.'

I went over to the window and pulled it closed. 'Pour the wine and I'll tell you the whole sorry story.

'I'm all ears.'

We sat either end of the couch with our legs tucked under us. The wine had a bitter taste, but as it hit the back of my throat I felt its warmth run through my body, and I started to relax.

'Is it the Ralph and Peggy thing?'

'Worse. It's the Ralph, Peggy and Fiona thing now.'

'He's gone back to Fiona?'

'I don't know, but I saw them at the park. He had his arm around her shoulder.'

'Why? I mean really, why?'

'I don't know, but I'm betting it's not the first time they've met.'

'How could he do that to you after all that's happened? I mean it doesn't make any sense. And what about Fiona? He practically dumped her at the altar! What the bloody hell is she doing canoodling with him at the park?'

'I really don't know, Polly. All I *do* know is that if he has been meeting Fiona behind my back, I must have idiot printed across my forehead. If he hadn't had his arm around her I might just think that he'd met her accidentally. I mean that *is* possible, isn't it?'

'Anything's possible. He might have just been tired and needed something to lean on and lo and behold there was Fiona right beside him.'

I couldn't help grinning. I was so right to come to Polly.

'Repeat after me: I am gorgeous and fabulous. Eat your heart out, Paul McCartney.'

'What?'

'You heard me.'

I raised my eyes up to the ceiling but repeated, 'I am gorgeous and fabulous. Eat your heart out, Paul McCartney.'

'Better?'

'Better.'

We spent the evening catching up, bemoaning Polly's un-love life and getting tipsy, and that was just what I needed to do.

Polly and I squeezed into the same bed that night. It was comforting to have her beside me. I closed my eyes and wondered where Ralph was right now. Was he missing me? Or was he with Fiona? I eventually drifted off to sleep lulled by the sound of Polly's gentle snoring.

The next day we took the bus up to Highgate and headed for the cemetery. We stopped on the way to get bread and cheese, not forgetting flowers for Mrs Dickens. Summer was on its way out and autumn was beginning to show itself. You could see it in the changing of the trees and the undergrowth that surrounded the ancient graves. The fallen leaves were slippery under our feet.

As always we were the only ones at her graveside.

'Hello Mrs D,' said Polly, sitting down on the old gravestone.

I sat opposite her. It was too wet to sit on the grass as we usually did.

'Go on then, tell her your problems.'

'I'm thinking.'

'What about?'

'About which problem I should ask her about first.'

'Just tell it like it is.'

Polly was dressed up like an Eskimo, but I'd taken off my coat so that I could feel the late summer sun on my face and on my bare arms.

Something made me pick up my coat. I put my hand in the pocket and my fingers closed over the letter. Polly wandered off amongst the graves. She liked to read the names of the souls who had passed – that's how she described them anyway.

I had a sudden urge to read the letter. I took it out of my pocket and traced the outline of my name with my finger. It made me feel closer to Ralph knowing that he had written the word 'Dottie'. I tore open the envelope and started to read.

Dear Dottie,

There's not much that I can say, is there? I could say I'm sorry that you saw Fiona at the park. I could say that I'm sorry it hurt you, as I know it must have done, but that's not going to change anything. I could say sorry for not waiting for you at the flat, but we would have argued, and arguing is not going to help. You see, I made the decision to meet up with Fiona. I made that decision even though I knew it would hurt you. I did it for Peggy. I did it because it was the only thing that I could think of that would bring her some happiness and it has.

I have been torn between the two people that I love most in the world. The only thing between Fiona and I is a deep friendship and a love for Peggy. It's you that I love, but I hope you know that already.

I can never give you what you want, Dottie. I can never give you what either of us wants, because it's too late for that. I can't give you back those two young kids who fell in love and talked of a bright future together. I ruined that future by making one stupid mistake, but that stupid mistake gave me Peggy, and I can never regret that.

I am moving back to my mum's house. I don't have a choice. I can't expect my mum to be responsible for raising my daughter, and I can't expect Peggy to go on living without her daddy.

This is not a goodbye letter, just a truthful one. Living apart is all that I can offer you. If I lose you, then I lose you, and it will break my heart, but this is not about me – in fact this is not even about us. The bottom line is that I have to make Peggy my priority.

And yes, of course I am sorry for all these things. I am sorry that they have happened to us.

Love always,

Ralph x

I put the letter back in the envelope as tears streamed down my face. It was the saddest thing that I had ever read. It was full of despair – Ralph had given up. His honesty was heartbreaking. He had been brave enough to put down in writing something we both already knew. We had been pretending, playing house, going through the motions of being happy, kidding ourselves that this would all work out. But there was nowhere to go. He was right – he couldn't give me what I wanted, what both of us wanted. I had been chasing a dream that had died a long time ago, a dream that had died with Mary. The only thing that I could do for Ralph now was to let him go. It had to come from me. He was so full of guilt over Peggy that I couldn't and wouldn't add to that guilt by forcing him to finish things between us. I could have clung to the fact that he still loved me. I could have clung to his words, that to lose me would break his heart. In fact, I could have reread the letter and found hope in it. I could have brushed aside what he was saying, and what he was saying was goodbye. My darling boy was saying goodbye.

CHAPTER THIRTY-NINE

I felt lost. There were times when I just wanted to run to Ralph and tell him that I was willing to accept whatever he was offering, but in calmer moments I knew that I couldn't do that. I also knew that in the end it wouldn't make either of us happy. For so many years I had lived in hope – it had kept me going. Even when Ralph married Mary, a part of me hoped that the marriage wouldn't last, that he would come back to me, that we would raise Peggy together. There were times when I even convinced myself that Mary wouldn't mind. It was Elton she loved, not Ralph. It was hope that had got me through those dark days. Even after I left Brighton and moved to London there was a part of me that still believed we'd be together one day. Even poor Joe didn't have all of me – there was always that place in my heart that would forever belong to Ralph. Well it was over. All that hope and yearning was gone. I knew that if I pushed Ralph he would agree to try again. I suppose it could even have worked for a bit, but in the end we would have ended up resenting each other. Best to walk away now. I wrote to him and told him that what he was offering wasn't enough for me. I wished him well. I let him off the hook.

Polly had wanted me to stay in London, but I needed to be near my family, and I missed Oriental Place. The trouble was that I couldn't afford the rent on my own, so I had to start looking for another flat. I would have to let Mrs Toshimo know that I was leaving. I would be sad to go. Ralph and I had had some difficult times there, but we had also had some lovely ones. I could have lived there and been happy. Ralph still hadn't answered my letter.

I was sitting at my desk, going through the pile of manuscripts. I was glad to be busy – it took my mind off the million thoughts that were flying round my head. Millie was filling me in on all that had happened while I had been in London.

'I wish you'd been here when he walked through the door.'

'When *who* walked through the door?'

'Your Matthew Smith.'

'*My* Matthew Smith?'

'He'll always be *your* Mathew Smith, Dottie – you were the one that found him. Unfortunately bloody Celeste-up-her-own-rear-end Partington-bloody-Spencer will always be *my* Celeste-up-her-own-rear-end Partington-bloody-Spencer.'

I was grinning from ear to ear. Millie had a great way with words, and it just cracked me up.

'So what is *my* Matthew like?'

'He's beautiful – he's the most beautiful man I have ever seen in my life. I want to go out and buy the wedding dress immediately.

Millie could always bring a smile to my face.

'He's sort of old-fashioned, you know. Polite and softly spoken, and my God, his eyes – you could drown in them.'

'Gosh, he made quite an impression on you, didn't he?'

'Just wait till you meet him.'

'Was he excited about the book?'

'It was hard to tell. I took coffee into him and Tom twice. I would have tried a third time but that might have been a bit obvious, and you know I don't do obvious. I do cool.'

'Did he look excited?'

'He's very calm, so maybe he was calmly excited, and he's got this lovely accent. He doesn't speak, Dottie, he purrs.'

'What sort of accent? Is he from up north?'

'I'm not exactly sure where Africa is, but I suppose it could be up north.'

'He's African?'

'Looks like it. Anyway he's coming in sometime to meet you.'

'He's coming in to meet me?'

'And sign contracts. Don't get too excited – I've got first dibs on him.'

I grinned at her. 'I thought you said he was mine?'

'Only in the literary sense, not the biblical.' Millie grinned.

The flat didn't feel much different without Ralph there. I had practically been living on my own anyway. Ralph had moved his things out while I had been in London, and I was glad – it would have been sad to have been here when he left.

I couldn't put off giving Mrs Toshimo notice, so I went downstairs. Tristan opened the door.

'Come in, come in! Stephen needs some diversion, and you are just the girl to give it to him. Stephen,' he shouted, 'you have a visitor.'

Stephen was lying on the pink chaise longue. He smiled as I came into the room.

'Amuse me, dear girl,' he said.

I grinned. 'I'm not sure that I can amuse you, Stephen. In fact I've got some bad news.'

'Darling girl, what's wrong?' asked Tristan, immediately looking concerned.

'I need to speak to Mrs Toshimo. Is she here?'

'She's taking Colin for a walk.'

'Who's Colin?'

'My cat,' said Stephen. 'Tristan gave in and bought me a cat. We called him Colin. He's adorable.'

'And there's more hair on the carpet than there is on the cat,' said Tristan.

'Admit it,' said Stephen. 'You love him.'

'He's growing on me.'

Stephen winked at me. 'He loves him.'

'So what's wrong?' said Tristan.

'Ralph and I have split up.'

'Oh, you poor thing,' said Tristan. 'Sit down.'

I sat down on one of the green velvet armchairs and promptly burst into tears.

'Darling girl,' said Stephen. 'Tristan, give her one of my grapes.'

'I'm not sure I can eat a grape right now,' I gulped, 'but thank you.'

'A cup of tea then?' asked Tristan.

'She needs wine, Tristan, not bloody tea. The girl's heartbroken.'

'Of course she does.'

'Isn't it a bit early for wine?' I said.

'Depends what part of the world you're in, darling,' said Stephen, grinning.

The front door slammed and Mrs Toshimo came into the room. She was holding a pink sparkly lead, on the end of which was a small black and white cat. She bent down and undid the lead. The cat immediately jumped up on the sofa and started licking Stephen's face.

'Has Colin been a good boy for his Aunty Rose?' crooned Stephen.

'Good as gold, dear. He walks to heel – he thinks he's a dog!'

'Well we're all a bit confused around here,' said Stephen, gently stroking the little cat.

'Hello, dear. Visiting the sick are you?' asked Mrs Toshimo, noticing me.

'I need to talk to you as well.'

'That sounds a bit serious, dear. Are you in trouble?'

'I am a bit.'

'Not the baby sort?'

'No, not that.'

'Her heart's been broken,' said Stephen. 'She has come to us for comfort and solace.'

'Then we will provide some, dear.'

'Thank you, but I'm afraid it's a bit more than that.'

'Explain, dear.'

'The thing is, I can't afford to stay in the flat on my own.'

'You can't leave us,' said Stephen.

'We forbid it,' said Tristan.

The kindness of these two lovely men was making me want to cry again. 'I don't want to leave, but I have no choice.'

'Let's talk about it, Miss Perks, or maybe it's time I called you Dottie, dear.'

'Do you want us to leave?' said Tristan.

'If you don't mind, dear.'

'Come on, hop-a-long, let us adjourn to the bedroom.'

'Best offer I've had all day,' said Stephen, giggling.

Once they'd gone, Mrs Toshimo sat down on the pink chaise longue and patted the seat beside her.

'Come and sit next to me, dear, and tell me what has happened.'

I took a deep breath. I didn't want to cry again. 'Ralph and I have decided to go our separate ways.'

'Was it the little girl, dear? I couldn't help but notice that she never moved in with you.'

'Yes. Ralph needs to be with her. He wrote me a letter. He was being torn between the two of us, and none of us were happy.'

'Isn't he worth fighting for?'

'I might win the fight, but I think I would lose the war.'

'Then you are being wise, dear. Sometimes you have to set people free. If they come back it is because they want to and not because they think they have to. Our happiness does not come from another person. True happiness comes from within ourselves. You may feel sad and lonely and disappointed, but those things won't kill you – they will only make you stronger. People think that the hardest thing is to walk away from someone you love, but sometimes staying can be even harder.'

'You remind me so much of my mum,' I said.

'Do you like it here, dear? Do you like Oriental Place?'

'I've grown to love it. I feel happy here, and I feel safe.'

'Then you will stay, dear.'

'I don't understand.'

'You will stay here in Oriental Place where you feel happy and safe.'

'But I can't afford…'

'We will halve the rent, dear. Will that suit?'

I looked at this woman who hardly knew me but who was offering me a lifeline, and I wanted to hug her.

'Can I give you a hug, Mrs Toshimo?'

'Of course you can, dear, and please call me Rose.'

CHAPTER FORTY

Ralph and I were sitting on our favourite bench looking out over the boating lake. Summer was behind us and autumn was making its glorious entrance. The leaves on the trees were slowly changing from green to brown and from brown to orange, falling like snow and drifting across the park. A breeze rippled the water and flopped over onto the path. It was all so familiar this place. We had played here as children, and we had walked here as teenagers. It was here, during those autumn days, that we had grown to love each other. Now it was autumn again, and we were saying goodbye. Ralph had eventually written and asked if we could meet. I had wanted to say no, I had wanted to bury my head in the sand and never think about us again, but of course I couldn't – we both deserved more than that. Our love deserved more than that.

We were easy with each other; we were familiar with each other's bodies. It seemed natural for Ralph to put his arm around my shoulder and for me to lean into him. Passers-by could easily mistake us for two young people in love.

We didn't speak for ages. I didn't want to speak. I didn't want Ralph to speak. Words caused pain, and I didn't think that I could take any more. It was Ralph who eventually broke the silence.

'Peggy started school,' he said.

'Does she like it?'

He nodded. 'I nearly cried when I saw her in her uniform. I don't know where the time has gone, Dottie. One minute she was my baby and the next she was walking away from me, without so much as a backwards glance. I managed to hold it together but Mum cried all morning.'

'I'm glad that she's happy.'

'She is. She's going to be all right. She's happy now that I'm with her again.'

'That's why we're doing this,' I said.

Ralph reached across and took my hand. 'I thought we could make it this time. I really thought that we could.'

There was a mist coming off the sea and a soft rain was beginning to fall. I pulled my coat closer around me. People were hurrying across the park, seeking shelter in the café. They must have thought that we were mad, sitting there in the rain, but I could have stayed there forever. I remembered the day that I took Ralph to see Oriental Place. We were leaning on the railings, staring out at the sea, and I remembered Ralph saying, 'We'll always be together, my love. Nothing can come between us now.' How full of hope we had been that day and how terribly naïve.

That last meeting with Ralph's mum was still niggling at me. 'You're mum knew, didn't she? About Fiona.'

'Yes, she knew.'

'I left the park that day thinking the whole world knew.'

'Not the whole world, Dottie, and God, I am so sorry that you had to find out like that. I am so sorry that I hurt you. I never meant to. I did a lousy thing to you, but I honestly believed that I was doing it for the best of reasons. Peggy kept on and on about seeing Fiona. It seemed the least I could do for her. I wanted her to be happy again, but that's all there was in it. You have to believe that.'

I lifted my head from his shoulder and looked at him. 'I know.'

He touched my cheek so tenderly. 'You understand?'

'I do, I understand.'

Ralph brushed my hair out of my eyes and kissed my forehead. This was torture.

He put his hand in his pocket and handed me a photograph. 'I thought you might like this. I found it amongst Mary's things.'

I looked down at the photo of Mary sitting up in the hospital bed with Peggy in her arms. 'I remember taking this,' I said.

I had gone to visit Mary just after she'd had the baby. I was dreading going – it was my mum that said I had to. I didn't want to see the baby that Ralph and Mary had made. But as soon as I looked into the cot at the end of the bed I was smitten. I thought she was the most beautiful thing I had ever seen. She was making little mewing noises like a kitten, and she was rubbing her eyes, then she looked up at me, and I fell totally in love with her. I couldn't be jealous– this lovely little girl was meant to be here. I remembered thinking, I might not be your mummy, but I will always be there for you. How ironic that seemed now.

'It seems a long time ago, but it's not really, is it?' I said, tucking the photo into my bag.

'There are times when I feel as if I've lived two different lives. A life that belongs to Peggy and a life that belonged to you and me,' said Ralph sadly.

'I wish it could have happened for us,' I said. 'Because I love you. I always will.'

'I want to say please don't forget me, but that would be selfish, because I want you to be happy.'

'I won't forget you,' I said. 'I couldn't ever do that.'

'You might, because there is something I have to tell you. I don't want you to find out from someone else.'

I stood up and walked towards the lake. Big fat drops of rain were plopping onto the water. It looked like an invisible hand was churning everything up. I could feel the rain trickling down the back of my neck and then Ralph's warm breath against my cold cheek and the weight of his hand on my shoulder as he stood behind me.

'We're going to Australia, Dottie. The three of us. We are going to try and make a go of it.'

I felt as though he'd punched me in the stomach. 'You're going with Fiona? You said there was nothing between you.'

'There's not.'

'So why then?'

'I want to make things up to Peggy. I want to give her back what I took from her.' He shook his head. 'I might be making one huge mistake here, but I've got to try. Fiona loves me, and she loves Peggy as if she was her own.'

That hurt. That really hurt. When Peggy was a baby I had loved her as if she were my own, and I knew by the way her eyes lit up when I walked into a room that she had loved me too. I should never have left Brighton. I should never have let my feelings for Ralph get in the way of my love for her. I should have been braver, but when I lost Mary I lost a part of myself too, and I had to get away from the town that had held too many memories.

I wanted sunsets and happy-ever-afters, not goodbyes. I took his hand in mine and held it against my cheek. If we had to part then we would part in love. I would let him go. We sat quietly, both wrapped in our own thoughts. Eventually I said something that had been on my mind for a while.

'Have you ever taken Peggy to see her mother's grave?'

'I've thought about it, but no, I've never taken her.'

'Would you mind if I did? If I took her to see Mary's grave before you go?'

'I wouldn't mind, Dottie.'

There was so much that I wanted to say. My heart and my head were full of words, but none of them would sit on my tongue, none of them would fall out of my mouth, and so I walked away from him. I walked away from the love of my life as my tears mingled with the falling rain, and I didn't look back.

CHAPTER FORTY-ONE

I don't know how Ralph had persuaded Peggy to spend the day with me but I was so happy that she was here. I held her little hand in mine as we knelt beside the grave. The last of the yellow roses were beginning to fade. Soon they would be gone, just as she and Ralph would be gone.

'What does it say?' asked Peggy, pointing to the gravestone.

I tentatively put my arm around her shoulder, and she leaned into me. The warmth of her little body filled me with a longing for the life we might have had.

'It says Mary Bennett, née Pickles…'

'What does *née* mean?'

'It means that she used to be called Mary Pickles, before she married your daddy.'

'Like Nanny and Granddad Pickles?

'*Just* like Nanny and Granddad Pickles.'

She stared at the grave as I continued to read.

'1946 to 1965. Beloved wife, daughter, sister and mother…'

'*My* mother?'

'Yes, *your* mother.'

'What else does it say?'

'It says loved and remembered always.'

'I don't remember her.'

'I know, and I'm sorry, because she loved you very much, and you would have loved her.'

I felt so sad sitting there beside Mary's grave. This was the first time I had come here since she'd died. I could feel my eyes filling with tears. I still missed her so much.

'Was my mummy your friend?' asked Peggy, breaking into my thoughts.

I wiped my eyes. 'She was my best friend in the whole world. We were just little girls when we met. Not much older than you. She was hanging upside down on some railings.'

'I can do that.'

'I know you can,' I said, holding her close. I kissed the top of her head. 'Your mummy was funny and clever and brave and very, very pretty.'

'I wish she wasn't in heaven.'

'So do I, my darling. So do I.'

We stood up. 'Do you know what I think we should do now?'

Peggy looked up at me. 'Mmm, go to the park?'

'Well we *could* go to the park, but *I* think that we should go shopping.'

So that's what we did. We strolled along the street hand in hand. Something had changed between us. She wasn't angry with me – I wasn't a threat any more. She would be going to Australia, and Fiona would be her new mummy.

We went into Forte's ice-cream parlour on the seafront and Peggy ordered a knickerbocker glory that was almost as big as her, and although it was chilly we sat outside looking over the sea, and we listened to the seagulls screech and squawk as they circled the Palace Pier. She grinned at me over the ice cream, her mouth smeared with chocolate.

'This is yummy,' she said.

I smiled at her. 'So are you.'

After she'd eaten as much as she could, we walked into town and made our way to Hannington's clothes shop. We took the lift up to the children's department.

'Shall we choose a dress for you, Peggy? Would you like that?'

'Okay,' she said, skipping ahead of me through the racks of clothes.

We chose a selection of dresses and took them into the changing room. We had such fun trying stuff on. I smiled as she posed in front of the mirror. This was how things should have been. This is what I imagined our lives would be like. The reality was that this would be the last time that it was going to happen.

We eventually found a beautiful yellow sundress that she loved. Yellow had been her mother's favourite colour. If Mary had been looking down on her little girl, I think she would have been happy.

'Dottie?'

'Yes, my love?'

'Do I look pretty?'

I brushed her beautiful red hair out of her eyes. 'You look fab,' I said.

I stumbled through those early days, barely noticing my surroundings. I went to work and buried myself in the pile of manuscripts sent in by hopeful writers. I must have eaten, but I couldn't recall what, though I did sleep, going to bed earlier and earlier. Sleep became my drug of choice, those hours between night and day when I could forget. Waking was the hardest part. I wanted to close my eyes again and not face the day.

I knew that I should go and see Mum and tell her about Ralph and me. I hadn't been ready to do that, but one Saturday morning I decided to go and see her. I caught the bus up to the estate and walked the familiar route to the house. I went round the back. Mum was hanging out some washing. She put the basket down and gave me a hug that lasted a fraction longer than usual. I could tell right away that she had spoken to Rita and that, because of Nigel, she knew what had happened.

'I don't know why I'm bothering to hang it out. It's bound to rain, but I live in hope.' She handed me the peg basket. This had always been my job when I was a child.

'Now let's go and have a cup of tea.'

I followed her into the kitchen. She washed her hands at the sink then put the kettle on.

I sat down at the table.

'So how are you, my love?' she asked.

'I'm okay, Mum.'

'I've been worried about you. Rita told me the news. I didn't want to interfere, but I was thinking about going to find that flat of yours today.'

'I'm sorry you've been worried, Mum, but I needed to sort things out on my own.'

Mum sat down opposite me. You must be very disappointed, after leaving everything in London to come home.'

'I'm glad I came home.'

'So you'll stay?'

'Apart from things not working out with Ralph, I'm really happy here. I love the flat, and I love my job, so no, I won't be going back to London.'

'Is there no hope at all for you and Ralph?'

'He had to make a choice between me and Peggy, and of course he chose Peggy.'

'Stop me if I'm interfering, love, but what I can't understand is where Fiona comes into all this? I mean I can understand him living back with his mum because of Peggy, but why are all three of them going to Australia? That's what I don't understand, and I said as much to your Aunty Brenda.'

'What did Aunty Brenda say?'

'Well let's just say that she wasn't impressed.'

'I can kind of understand it, Mum.'

'Well you're a better person than me, girl. Because I can't get my head round it at all.'

'I'm not a better person. I just think that we both gave up. We couldn't make Peggy happy together, and so he decided to give her what she wanted, what he had promised her, and that was being with Fiona.'

'Somehow I doubt that he's made the right decision for any of them.'

'It's out of my hands now, Mum. I have to let it go.'

'I suppose you'll have to leave the flat now that Ralph's gone?'

'That's the amazing part. My landlady has halved the rent, so I can stay there.'

'Well that was good of her, but why did she do that? I mean she hasn't known you that long.'

'I think she likes me, Mum.'

'And why wouldn't she? I shall write a letter and thank her. That's a very generous thing that she's done for you.'

'I know, I couldn't quite take it in myself.'

'The kindness of strangers, eh?'

'She's so nice, Mum, you'd like her.'

'She's been kind to my girl – I already like her.'

'She's kind of quirky, but I think you two would get on like a house on fire.'

'I'm sure that we would. Now I usually go to Rita's on a Saturday. Do you want to come with me, or are you busy?'

'As long as she doesn't go on about how happy they both are for Fiona. I couldn't take that, Mum, but I haven't seen her for ages, so I might as well come with you. I haven't see much of Clark either for that matter. How is he?'

'Who knows, Dottie. Times have changed. Your poor father can't get his head round it. Clark seems to spend all his time at Emma's house. Your dad keeps going on about sleeping arrangements.'

'Has he talked to Clark about it?'

'That'll be the day when your father talks about anything that might even vaguely refer to sex.'

I grinned. 'Poor Dad. He's got a daughter, who, until recently, was living in sin and a son whose sleeping arrangements he can only guess at.'

'Sad isn't it?' said Mum, giggling.

'How do you feel about it all, Mum?'

'Me? Oh I go with the times, Dottie. As long as people are happy and they're not hurting anyone, I can't see any reason to get hot and bothered about it. The trouble with your dad is that he thinks he's supposed to make a stand, when the truth of it is that he doesn't really know what he's supposed to be making a stand about, God love him.'

'Well at least Rita did it the right way.'

'Rita was always going to do it the right way, bless her. Now shall we skip the tea and get going? I'm sure Rita will give us one. I'm just going to give myself a lick and a promise, and I'll be ready. Will you be okay here?'

'I'll sit in the garden for a bit.'

Mum bent down and kissed the top of my head. 'I *am* sorry, love.'

'I know you are, Mum.'

'Okay, I won't be long.'

I went into the garden and sat on the old wooden bench. Dad and Clark had made it one year for Mum's birthday. I don't remember Dad ever making anything again.

I closed my eyes and lifted my face to the sun.

'Trying to get a suntan are you?'

I opened my eyes to see Carol coming through the garden gate. I smiled at her.

'I came round to ask Aunty Maureen for your address.'

'You just caught me. We're going to see Rita.'

Carol sat down on the bench. 'Guess what?'

'You've heard from Greg?'

She handed me a letter. 'I got it this morning. Oh, Dottie, I'm so excited. I haven't even told Mum yet, I just ran round here.

Greg says there's a small fashion house that likes my look and would like to see me in person.'

'That's wonderful, Carol.'

'It's more than wonderful, Dottie, it's bloody amazing.'

I grinned. 'Yes, it's bloody amazing.'

'I want to go now, right now, this very minute!'

'Well why don't you?'

'Not on my own. That's why I was going to see you at your flat, to beg you to take me again.'

'Of course I will but not today. Ring Greg and ask if we can come up to London next weekend.'

'How am I going to wait that long?'

'You'll manage.'

'I suppose I'll have to,' she said, pulling a poor-me face.

'Go home and tell your mum, then go to the phone box and call Greg.'

'Okay,' she said in a resigned sort of voice.

She started walking back down the garden.

'I'm really pleased for you, Carol,' I said.

'Thanks, Dottie, and by the way, I'm sorry things didn't work out with that feller of yours.'

'You know about me and Ralph?'

'It's been the main, boring topic of conversation for bloody weeks.'

'Sorry.'

'At least it's kept everyone off my back.'

'Happy to oblige, cousin dear.'

'And I'll tell you something else. I'm changing my name, and I don't care what Mum says.

I'm not going to get very far in my modelling career with a name like Carol Pratt.'

I had to agree with her on that one.

I smiled as I sat there thinking about her. I'd never really given her a chance, but to my surprise I found her really good company, and crikey – she actually had a fashion house interested in her. Good for her!

'Who were you talking to?' asked Mum, coming out into the garden.

'Carol was here.'

'On her own?'

'Yes.'

'That's got to be a first. What did she want?'

'She came round to ask you for my address.'

'Why does she want that?'

'She wants me to take her to London again. There's a fashion house interested in her.'

'Well would you believe it!'

'I'm happy for her, Mum.'

'So am I, love, and between you and me, I think it's high time that young lady left home and started spreading her wings.'

We took the bus round to Rita's and walked through the new estate. Of course it wasn't new any more, but that was still how people referred to it. Rita looked pleased to see me, which made a change. Miranda Louise was sitting in the middle of the floor surrounded by toys.

Mum went straight over and picked her up. 'How's my special girl?' she asked, holding her close.

'She's started pulling herself up on the furniture, Mum,' said Rita, smiling proudly.

'Who's a clever girl?' said Mum. 'Who's the cleverest girl in the world?'

'Where's Nigel?' I asked.

Rita ignored that and said, 'Can you keep an eye on her, Mum? I just want a word with Dottie.'

'Of course I will. Nanny likes nothing better that to look after her little girl, doesn't she, my angel, doesn't she?'

I couldn't help thinking that Mum got quite strange around the baby.

'We'll go in the garden shall we?' said Rita, looking at me.

I couldn't imagine why Rita wanted to go out to the garden with me. I guess I was just about to find out.

We sat down on the white plastic chairs. Rita looked uncomfortable.

'What is it?' I asked.

'Look, I'm just going to say it, okay? It's best if I just say it.'

'Say what?'

'They left this morning. Nigel took them to the station.' Rita reached across and took my hand. 'I'm really sorry, Dottie.'

I didn't have to ask who she was talking about.

CHAPTER FORTY-TWO

My heart was broken, but it hadn't informed the rest of my body. I still needed food, my lungs needed air and my heart still pumped blood around my body. From the outside I must have looked the same; it was the inside that was damaged. There were times when I didn't think I could survive another minute without being held by Ralph. I could read terrible stories in the newspaper about children dying, volcanoes erupting, houses burning down, but somehow all those tragedies barely touched me. My pain was mine alone, and it was all consuming.

I thought about Peggy often. I hoped that she was happy and that Australia was as wonderful as she was told it would be. I was so glad that we had been able to spend some positive time together. It may only have been one day, but it meant the world to me. Now when she came into my mind I saw a sweet, funny little girl with an infectious giggle rather than the angry little girl that she had been.

One evening I was walking home from work along the seafront. There was a cold breeze coming in from the sea. I saw Rose just ahead of me. It was difficult to miss her, with that shock of orange hair and her mismatched clothes. She was walking slowly, because she had Colin on the sparkly pink lead. I caught up with her and we walked home together.

'Come and have tea with me,' she said. 'Tristan and Stephen are at the hospital.'

'There isn't a problem is there?'

'No, just a check-up, dear. I think Stephen is doing well.'

Once we were inside the flat, Rose released Colin from his lead and the little cat jumped up onto the pink chaise longue and snuggled down, purring loudly.

I stood at the window. Daylight was fading. Soon the tall lamps along the seafront would light up the darkness, and the pier would come alive. I'd asked Tom about the time difference between here and southern Australia, so I knew that as I stood here in Rose's front room, Ralph would be sleeping and that Fiona would be by his side.

I hadn't noticed Rose coming back into the room. Sit down, dear,' she said, putting a tray of tea on the coffee table.

I turned away from the window, took off my coat and sat down in the green velvet chair. Rose sat opposite me. The autumn days had turned chilly and Rose had lit a fire in the beautiful marble fireplace. 'I do like a fire, dear. I find it very cheery.'

Rose poured the tea and pushed the cup towards me. 'I can feel your sadness, dear,' she said.

'I'm sorry.'

'Don't be sorry, dear. No one can see your broken heart. The sadness is in your eyes.'

'I miss him, Rose. I miss them both.'

'Of course you do, but the only way to avoid heartache is never to love, and that would be even sadder wouldn't it, dear?'

'I just want the pain to go away. It hurts. It really hurts.' I touched the place just below my ribs. 'Here,' I said. 'It hurts here.'

'Only time can do that, but it will get better. The body can't sustain that kind of sadness forever. It may surprise you to find that when it does go you will miss it.'

'I can't imagine it ever going.'

'But it will, dear, and once the pain has gone so is the hope. Pain is something that you can hang on to. It becomes who you are. Without the pain you don't know who you are any more, but it's only then that the healing can begin.'

'You know what that pain is like, don't you, Rose? I can tell.'

'I am like you, dear. When I love, I love with every part of me, so yes, I have been hurt too.'

'I wasn't prying, you don't have to tell me.'

Rose picked up the poker and rattled the coals, and a blast of warm air curled around my legs. It was comforting and homely. Rose settled back into her chair and smiled at me.

'I noticed that when we were walking home together you were looking down a lot,' she said.

'Was I?'

'Yes, you were, dear, so I would like to share something with you. Some wise words that were given to me by a very wise man, a long time ago.'

The room was warm and cosy, and the heat from the glowing coals seeped into my body, comforting me. I rested my head against the back of the chair, closed my eyes and listened as Rose told her story.

'We had a child once, dear, a little girl. We called her Selina. She was the most beautiful thing that we had ever seen. We counted her fingers and toes, we marvelled at her soft dark hair, we kissed her little cheek. To us, she was perfect, but they told us that she wasn't, dear. They said that those beautiful eyes were the wrong shape, that her sweet little hands weren't those of a normal baby. They said that our perfect baby wasn't perfect at all. They told us to put her away, forget about her, try again. But we brought our baby home, and we loved and cherished her until she was taken from us. If love could have mended her broken heart, she would be with us today.'

I didn't speak, but I could feel my eyes filling with tears. I listened as she continued.

'When my baby's heart stopped so did mine. I didn't know how to live. I didn't know how to breathe. I didn't know how to be. I wore my sorrow like a crown of thorns, like Miss Havisham in her wedding dress. I was a woman in mourning, and I didn't know how to be anything else.'

I opened my eyes and looked at her. 'I'm so sorry.'

'It was a sad time, dear.'

She gazed into the fire. Maybe she was remembering her little girl's face. I waited. She started to speak again.

'My oriental gentleman did all he could for me. He filled the bath every day and added the oils of his homeland. The house would fill with the fragrant aromas of white lotus and jasmine, and he helped me to dress as though I were a baby. I didn't want to leave the house. My sadness was too heavy a burden to take with me, but he persuaded me to accompany him on his daily walk along the seafront. I clung on to him as if I was disabled, and I suppose I was in a way. One day as we walked he said, "I want you to look up, Rose. There is a sky above you that is clear and blue. Lift your eyes and look up. Start counting chimneys, my Rose," and so I say to you, Dottie, what that dear man said to me. Look up and start counting chimneys.'

CHAPTER FORTY-THREE

There was no way that I could go to London, and I felt bad about letting Carol down, but Clark and Emma were able to go with her instead. Emma fell in love with Little Venice, just like I knew she would. Clark began looking into jobs in London with a view to them living there, and Greg was going to let them know as soon a boat became vacant. The fashion house liked Carol a lot and wanted to use her. It was run by a young new designer called Florence. The House of Florence. I thought it sounded lovely. It looked like the time had come for Carol to fly the nest and for my little brother and his sweet Emma to move away. The times they were a-changing.

There were still moments when a song could send me back to that dark place, but I was finding it easier to climb out again. I was able to laugh at Tristan's jokes and Stephen's gentle teasing. Rose tempted me with her delicious Chinese dough balls and Manju cake filled with sweet red bean. If I ate everything she put in front me I would go back to being the fat girl again. I loved my home and my family, and I knew that I would be made welcome there, but they worried about me, and I didn't want to burden them with my sadness. Somehow it was easier at Oriental Place. No one asked questions; they just let me be. It had become my sanctuary.

I started going down to Rose's flat almost every evening. Stephen and his knee were still the centre of attention, and he continued to hold court on the pink chaise longue. Sometimes Rose played for us, melodies she remembered from her glory days in the theatre. Stephen had a beautiful voice. He sang numbers like 'Stormy Weather', 'These Foolish Things' and 'Tea for Two'.

Tristan would join in with harmonies, their voices blending together perfectly. I loved those evenings. They helped me forget, if only for a while.

'We like the Beatles as well,' said Tristan. 'But we have yet to convince darling Rose that "Hey Jude" is just as worthy as "Little Brown Jug".'

'I prefer the old songs,' said Rose. 'I find them easier on the ear.'

'We'll convince her yet,' said Stephen, smiling at her.

I had never asked Stephen and Tristan their ages, or Rose for that matter, but I guessed that Rose was about sixty and the boys were in their early forties. I wasn't even sure what they lived on, because neither of them seemed to have jobs. When Rose had first shown me the flat, she had mentioned that they were in the theatre, but there didn't seem to be any evidence of that.

The hospital said that when Stephen was able to climb twenty stairs without pain, then he could move back to his flat. Every evening after work I helped. Rose and I walked behind him, and Tristan went in front. It was so comical that we nearly always ended up in hysterics, mostly because Rose would get an attack of the rheumatics, then all four of us would be stuck on the stairs in complete darkness, crying with laughter.

Work was my saviour, and I threw myself into it. Millie knew there was something wrong, but she hadn't asked what. I told her over lunch in a little café in Kemp Town.

'So you're not living in sin any more then?'

'No, I've decided that sin isn't all it's cracked up to be.'

'So you live on your own now?'

'I do.'

'Don't you mind? I'd be scared to death.'

'I suppose I might if I didn't like my flat, but I love it there, so I'm quite happy on my own. In fact I don't feel as if I am on my own.'

I told her about my friends in Oriental Place. 'Why don't you come round one evening? Come home with me after work and stay the night.'

'I'd love that.'

'Have you managed to get through your life without having your heart broken, Millie?'

'I don't think I've ever been in love,' she said. 'I mean, I really thought I was once. I had all the symptoms you know – heart palpations, weight loss, sleepless nights. Turned out I had diabetes.'

'You've got diabetes?'

'Yep, it's a right pain, because I love sweet things. Now and again I give into temptation and have some chocolate, but mostly I'm pretty good.'

'I'm really sorry.'

'The thing with a broken heart is that it eventually heals, but bloody diabetes is for life. I'd go for the broken heart any time.'

Our discussion turned to Matthew Smith, who we'd left in Tom's office before heading out to lunch. Millie had been right about him – he was indeed beautiful. She had raved about his eyes, but his lips were something else again. I noticed that Millie had gone to town on her make-up, and wasn't her skirt just a little shorter than usual?

'Was I right about Matthew or was I right?' she asked, biting into a bacon roll.

'You were more than right.'

'Do you think he's got a girlfriend?'

'How would I know?'

'Perhaps you could say something like "your girlfriend must be delighted about your book".'

'Why can't *you* say it?'

'If I say it he'll think I fancy him.'

'And if I say it he'll think *I* fancy him.'

I grinned.

'What?' Millie asked.

I could remember an almost exact conversation I'd had one day with Mary about Elton.

'Just remembering something.'

We wandered back to the office.

'Is my skirt too short?' Millie asked, staring at herself in the shop windows.

'Let's put it like this – if it was much shorter it would be a blouse.'

'Trying too hard?'

'Not cool.'

We went up the rickety steps one at a time. We couldn't trust going up them together.

Matthew was sitting at my desk. Well not exactly sitting. His body was long, and the chair seemed too small for him; he was more draped than sat.

I had seen him briefly earlier on, but we hadn't yet spoken. He got up and held out his hand.

'Dottie,' he said. 'Please allow me to introduce myself. My name is Matthew, and I am in your debt. You discovered my little book, yes?'

I sat there with my mouth open – it was like I'd been struck dumb. Not only was he beautiful to look at, his voice was like warm syrup. Everything about him was mesmerising.

Millie came to my rescue. She gave him her best smile and said, 'Yes, you have Dottie to thank for that. You should have heard her raving about it. She had you up there with Shakespeare.'

Matthew turned his attention back to me. 'You compare me to Mr Shakespeare? I am humbled, Dottie.'

I found my voice. 'Someone else would have seen what I saw. You are a wonderful writer.'

'But it was you that liked it, and I am very grateful.'

'I more than liked it. It's my diamond in the rough.'

Matthew looked puzzled.

'It's my job, you see, to find the little gem amongst all the dross. I was beginning to think that it would never happen. It's me that's grateful to you.'

He smiled his lazy smile. 'Then we shall both be grateful. And now I must go – I have a lecture to attend.'

'You're at college?'

'I am training to be a teacher.' He held out his hand. 'But we will see each other again, yes?'

'Of course,' I said.

As he left the office we both shouted, 'Mind the steps.'

' "Of course"?' said Millie, making a face. 'You should have asked when!'

'I'm not looking for a new man.' I haven't got over the old one yet, I thought.

'Well I don't wish to encourage you, because I'd quite like to make a move on him myself, but they do say that the best way to get over a broken heart is to find someone else.'

'That's just sticking a plaster over it.'

'I shouldn't think it matters what you stick over it as long as it helps.'

'He is lovely though,' I said, smiling. I guess I just appreciated Matthew's beauty as much as I appreciated the beauty of his book.

CHAPTER FORTY-FOUR

Tom was still trying to find a publisher for Matthew's book. A couple had been interested but not enough to make an offer. I couldn't understand why it hadn't been snapped up immediately.

'It goes like that sometimes,' said Tom. 'The books you don't think have a hope in hell take off and the brilliant literary masterpieces fall flat. It depends what's popular at the time, but it will happen. The right publisher will come along, and they will love it as much as we do.'

Matthew had come into the office one morning and asked if he could take me out to lunch. Millie was frantically nodding her head in encouragement behind him. I glared at her but accepted Matthew's invitation. There was a certain calmness about him that I liked. I had loved his book, and I wanted to know more about him. Millie was acting as if it was a date, but I knew that it was his way of saying thank you.

At noon he was waiting for me at the bottom of the steps. Millie stood at the top waving us off

'I worry for your safety on these stairs,' he said.

'You get used to them,' I said, smiling.

We chose a little café down on the seafront. It was a lovely warm day so we sat outside, eating sandwiches and drinking tea.

'So where are you from?' I asked.

'I come from a small village in Tanzania.'

'Are your parents still there?'

'Sadly my parents died when I was twelve.'

'I'm sorry.'

'I was left to look after my two younger sisters.'

'And you were only twelve?'

'Yes, just a boy. I didn't know how I was going to take care of them. I was scared, and I was alone.'

'It must have been terrible for you.'

'It was, but I had my two sisters to look after. It was not a time to feel sorry for myself.'

'I can't imagine how hard that must have been.'

'It was very hard.'

'I don't know anything about African names, but Matthew Smith isn't what I would imagine.'

'My African name is Oscu Kimbali.'

'Now that sounds more like it, but why change it?'

'I feared that I wouldn't be taken seriously with such a name.'

'I would have picked your book up whatever you were called.'

'Not everyone is like you and Tom and Millie. This world of ours is full of ignorance. There are many who fear what they don't understand. They see only the colour of your skin.'

I sipped the hot tea and wondered how anyone could fail to see what a lovely man he was, whatever the colour of his skin.

'How did you end up in Brighton? It's a long way from Africa.'

'I could barely make enough money to take care of my sisters.'

'Didn't anyone in the village help you?'

'No, and I understood why. They could hardly look after their own families without taking us on. They weren't unkind – they just couldn't help. In my country you are a man at twelve, but I didn't feel like a man, Dottie. I still felt like a child.'

I couldn't imagine what Matthew had gone through at such a young age.

'What did you do?'

'I tried to make a living from the small piece of land that we had. It was hard work, but I just about managed to feed us. Before my parents died I had been able to go to school. My parents knew the value of education, and in that they were unusual. I walked ten miles every day to get there and ten miles home, and I was glad to do it. All that changed when they died.'

I felt ashamed as I listened to Matthew's story. I had gone to the local school just around the corner and didn't think that I was lucky to go there. I'd taken it for granted.

'But how did you end up here?'

'I guess life would have continued the way it was, but one day a man from the next village asked to buy my sister. Kami was only nine years old. The man was in his fifties.'

'Oh Matthew.'

'I was terrified. I was just a boy; I couldn't protect them. I knew that from then on neither of my sisters were safe. I knew that I had to get them to a place of safety.'

I couldn't believe what I was hearing.

'I went to an elder of the village and begged for his help. He took pity on me and contacted a pastor in another town. The man took me and my sisters to live with him and his wife. He educated me and raised money to send me to England, and here I am.'

'What about your sisters?'

'Kami and Zina are well taken care of. They will stay with the pastor until I have finished my training as a teacher. I am in my final year. I will then return to Africa and take care of them myself.'

'So you are the boy in the book?'

'I think there is a part of me that is Simmi. I always wanted more than I had. I wanted to learn. Education is everything, Dottie. Without education you have nothing – you remain in ignorance.'

I felt humbled by Matthew's story. No child should have to go through what Matthew had. But he had survived, and I was in complete awe of him.

'So we have just one year to be friends, Dottie. Will you be my friend for one year?'

A friend for one year. A beginning and an end. No ties, no expectations, no forevers.

'Yes, Matthew, I will be your friend for a year.'

We smiled at each other and suddenly I felt at peace. I reached across the table and touched his hand. Mary and I should have been friends forever. Ralph and I should have been friends forever. I didn't believe in forevers any more. Matthew would leave me in one year, but that was okay, because he wasn't offering anything else, and I wasn't asking.

Winter arrived with a vengeance. Leaves leftover from autumn were ripped from the trees as gales buffeted the country. The seafront was almost a no-go area. The water tore into the shore, bashing against the sea wall and flooding the prom and the main road. My journeys home became a nightmare. I had to take to the backstreets where it was more sheltered. I had bought a second-hand bike that I loved, but Tristan and Stephen forbade me to ride it until the weather improved. It was like having two older brothers who looked out for me. Even worse were the wooden steps leading up to the office. I could actually feel the old structure swaying beneath my feet. My strategy was to take a deep breath and run up them as fast as I could. Millie on the other hand took forever to get up them, with me and Tom shouting encouragement from the top.

I woke up one morning to find that the wind had died down, so I decided it would be okay to ride my bike. It made the journey to work so much easier. I wrapped up warm and dragged the bike up the basement steps. The next thing I remembered was waking up in the Royal Sussex County hospital with Stephen sitting beside my bed staring at me.

He reached across and held my hand. 'Oh, Dottie, you gave us such a fright,' he said. I was surprised to see tears welling up in his eyes.

'What happened?'

'Don't you remember?'

I shook my head. 'The last thing I can remember is getting my bike up from the basement. How did I end up here?'

'We're not exactly sure, but we think that your bike hit the kerb, and you were thrown into the path of a van. Luckily the guy swerved and didn't hit you. You could have been killed, Dottie. We've all been worried sick.'

'Was that this morning?'

'No, my darling girl, it was two days ago.'

I couldn't believe what I was hearing. 'Two days?'

Stephen nodded. 'The doctors wanted you to rest. They gave you something to keep you asleep.'

'Do my parents know?'

'We didn't know where they lived. The hospital wanted the name of your next of kin, but all we could say was that it was Mr and Mrs Perks.'

'Please let them know, Stephen, but play it down a bit. I don't want my mum to worry and get ill again.'

'Don't worry, we'll go and see them as soon as we leave here.'

'Where's Tristan?'

'Talking to the doctor.'

'Am I hurt then?'

'You banged your head, but they say it isn't a dangerous injury.'

I put my hand up to my head and felt the bandage. Just then Tristan walked into the room.

'She's awake,' said Stephen, grinning.

Tristan sat down beside me and held my hand. 'How are you feeling, darling?'

'I'm not sure,' I said. I gingerly moved my head and winced. 'A bit sore.'

'What did we tell you about riding that bloody bike?' he said.

'The wind had died down,' said Stephen, jumping to my defence.

'You gave us an awful fright, girl.'

'I'm sorry. But how did you know about it?'

'Because it happened practically outside the door. Luckily for us Rose was taking Colin for a walk and saw the van driver sitting on the pavement and a crowd of people. She nearly fainted when she saw that it was you lying in the middle of the road.'

'Is the driver okay?'

'He wasn't hurt, just shocked. Rose took him home and gave him tea. He's been in, asking how you are.'

'That was nice of him. I wish I could remember what happened.'

'Maybe it's best that you don't,' said Stephen.

'What about my job?'

'We went there and told them what happened,' said Tristan.

'You've been very good, thank you.'

'I thought your Tom was lovely, and Millie is a sweetie,' said Stephen. 'And oh my God there was an Adonis there, skin like melted chocolate. He could have posed for Michelangelo.'

'I think that must have been Matthew.'

'Well all I can say is that he was very concerned about you. Didn't you think so, Tristan?'

'Very. He was all for coming straight to the hospital. We had to put him off. I shouldn't be surprised if he makes an appearance sometime soon.'

'Should we bring in a bit of slap, Dottie, just in case?'

'What's slap?'

'You know,' said Stephen, 'a bit of the old razzmatazz.'

'Make-up, darling,' said Tristan.

I giggled, which made my head hurt. 'You're a couple of old romantics.'

'Less of the old,' said Stephen.

'But you're right,' said Tristan, 'give us a sloppy love song, *Brief Encounter* on the silver screen, lovers walking off into the sunset, and we lap it up.'

Stephen smiled lovingly at Tristan. 'That's us, suckers for love.'

It wasn't hard to see how much these two loved each other, and I bet it hadn't been an easy road for them, yet they had come through it; they were still together. Maybe Ralph and I should have tried harder. It seemed now that we had let each other go too easily.

'Can I go home?'

'I've just been talking to the doctors,' said Tristan. 'They want to keep you in for another couple of days, just to be on the safe side.'

'Rose is getting a room ready for you downstairs. She wants to keep an eye on you,' said Stephen.

The kindness of these people never ceased to amaze me.

CHAPTER FORTY-FIVE

I had to stay in the hospital for another three days. Mum and Aunty Brenda arrived with bags of food, magazines and socks. Aunty Brenda always said that if your feet were warm the heat spread up to the rest of your body. They unloaded it all into the little cupboard beside my bed.

Mum reached across and took my hand in hers. It was as cold as ice. I rubbed it gently and noticed how wrinkly it was, with fat blue veins standing out against the white skin. The gold band that she always wore seemed thinner than I remembered. She had worn that ring for almost the whole of her life. Now it was embedded in the creases of her finger as if it had grown into the folds of flesh. The whole thing made me sad.

'You *are* all right, aren't you? Did the doctor say that you are all right?'

'I'm fine, Mum, really I am. I just bumped my head.'

'I got a terrible fright when I saw those two men at the door. I thought at first that they were from the Sally Army. But then they told me that you were in the hospital, and I couldn't understand it, because I didn't know them from Adam, and none of it made any sense.'

'She went the colour of chalk, Dottie! Thank God I was there at the time or goodness knows what would have happened.'

'Lovely men though, weren't they, Brenda?'

'A cut above.'

'They live in the flat below mine, Mum.'

'Well all I can say is that it was very nice of them to come all that way to let me know what had happened to you.'

Mum was clutching her old brown handbag tightly to her chest like some beloved teddy bear. She kept worrying at the catch.

'I'm okay, Mum. You don't need to worry.'

Mum dabbed at her eyes with a hankie. 'Just got a bit of a fright, love.'

'Your mother will always worry about you, Dottie. You might be all grown up, but you will always be your mum's baby.'

'Some baby,' I said, smiling.

'One of those men said that you fell off your bike.'

'I shouldn't have ridden it that morning, but I thought the wind had dropped. Stephen told me not to ride it, but I thought I knew better.'

'Which one is Stephen?' said Aunty Brenda.

'The shorter one with the fair hair. The other one is Tristan.'

'Tristan? You don't hear that name very often, do you?'

'It's an upper-class name,' said Aunty Brenda. 'It's only the upper classes that can get away with names like that. He would have had the mick taken out of him something rotten if he'd lived on the estate. I don't know how your Nelson got away with it, Maureen.'

Mum smiled at her. 'Yes, you do, Brenda. His best friend was Jack Forrest.'

Aunty Brenda smiled. 'Jack Forrest, of course.'

The two sisters were looking at each other with such sweetness, remembering a time long past. Aunty Brenda put her hand on Mum's arm and smiled at her. 'How could I forget Jack?'

Mum rummaged in her bag and pulled out a bar of chocolate.

'This is from your dad, Dottie. He went to the shops specially and bought it for you. You know he doesn't like hospitals, but he sends all his love.'

'Please thank him for me, Mum, and tell him that I'm all right.'

'I will, love.'

Just then the door opened and Rose came into the room.

'Oh, Dottie, you have visitors, dear. I won't come in.'

'Of course you can. Quick, close the door before someone sees you.' They were pretty strict about the two-visitors-to-a-bed rule. 'This is my mum and my Aunty Brenda.'

Mum and Aunty Brenda were staring at Rose with their mouths open, which wasn't surprising given what she was wearing. She had really surpassed herself with a green velvet coat that came down to her ankles and was lavishly embroidered with pink roses. Over the top of that was a cream lace shawl smothered in multicoloured sequins. Various pieces of jewellery hung from her neck, making a kind of tinkly sound as she moved. She looked like a colourful peacock against the stark whiteness of the room.

'You're looking much better, dear,' she said, leaning across the bed and kissing my cheek. She smelt of Oriental Place and the sea.

'I'm feeling much better, thank you. Mum, this is my landlady, Rose Toshimo.'

Mum let go of her handbag, stood up and shook Rose's hand. 'It's lovely to meet you, Mrs Toshimo. Thank you for what you've done for my girl.'

'I did very little, dear.'

'I think you did a lot. You helped Dottie at a difficult time in her life.'

'I smoothed her path a little, dear, that is all. If we can't bestow a little kindness as we travel along life's highway then it's a poor show, isn't it?'

'It is indeed,' said Mum, smiling.

Aunty Brenda stood up, smoothed down her skirt and smiled at Rose. I thought for one awful minute that she was going to curtsy. 'Pleased to meet you I'm sure,' she said, smiling.

'And I can see that you are sisters, dear,' said Rose, looking from one to the other. 'You look very alike.'

'We've grown to look alike over the years. We were very different when we were children.'

'People say that my oriental gentleman and I grew to look alike, dear.'

Mum and Aunty Brenda looked totally bemused and just smiled weakly at her. I don't think they had ever seen anyone quite like Rose in the whole of their lives. I would explain about the oriental gentleman later.

Rose was staring at Aunty Brenda very intently. Aunty Brenda was staring back at her as if mesmerised. Eventually Rose said, 'You have the gift, dear.'

'Do I?' asked Aunty Brenda.'

'What gift?' asked Mum.

'She has the seeing eye, dear.'

Mum stared at her sister as if she'd never seen her before. 'Really?' she said.

'I always thought I had,' said Aunty Brenda, looking pleased as punch.

'You never told *me*,' said Mum.

'Don't you remember when our cat Fluffy died and three days afterwards I saw him in our front room?'

'Vaguely,' said Mum.

'Everyone laughed at me.'

'Well you were always a bit on the fanciful side, Brenda. Are you sure she's got what you said she's got?'

'The seeing eye, dear, and yes I could sense her aura as soon as I walked into the room.'

'Imagine that,' said Mum. 'Imagine *you* having an aura all these years, and I never even knew.'

'Wait till I tell our Carol,' said Aunty Brenda. 'I bet she wouldn't know an aura if it bit her on the nose.'

'You must visit me at Oriental Place, and I will help you to develop your abilities.'

'Oh I will, Mrs Toshimo, I will.'

'Now, dear,' said Rose, 'I have told Dottie that she can move into my flat when she comes out of hospital. I am there all day, and I can take care of her, but I don't want to tread on any toes, dear. I'm sure you want her with you.'

I didn't know what to say. The truth was that I wanted to go back to Oriental Place, but I didn't want to hurt my mum's feelings. I hadn't reckoned on how well my mum knew me.

'I think my Dottie would like to go home, and I think Oriental Place is her home now, Mrs Toshimo. Is that right, my love?' she said, smiling at me.

'If you don't mind, Mum.'

'Not a bit. All that sea air will help you get better quicker.'

'That's settled then,' said Rose. 'She will come home with me, and you will all visit, yes?'

'We'd love to,' said Aunty Brenda.

A nurse came into the room. 'You are a popular girl, Dottie Perks,' she said, grinning. 'You have two more visitors.'

'I'll go then, dear,' said Rose. 'I was only popping in.'

Mum stood up. 'Your Aunty Brenda and I will get going as well, Dottie. I have to get your dad's tea, but we will be back tomorrow.'

'Don't forget to wear those socks,' said Aunty Brenda, kissing my cheek.

'I will get everything ready for when you come home,' said Rose.

Mum was leaning across the bed kissing me goodbye when Millie and Matthew came into the room. Aunty Brenda's face was a picture. Rose Toshimo was one thing but the beautiful Matthew was quite another.

CHAPTER FORTY-SIX

I was back home in Oriental Place, being fussed over by Rose and the boys. I was feeling much better but still surprisingly weak. I also had a black eye and a puffy cheek. Every day the bruising changed colour. It was now a rather autumnal shade of orangey yellow. Stephen said it was very fetching.

I had a lot of time to think as I recovered in Rose's flat. I thought about Ralph a lot. I wondered what he was doing and if they had all settled in Australia. I hoped that Peggy was happy now. She had to be, because that was why Ralph and I had parted. It had to have been worth it.

Lately when I thought about Ralph, I thought about us as children, before all the bad stuff happened. It was easier to think about those times. Remembering those carefree days made me feel happy because Mary was part of them too. I remembered how Ralph and I used to sit on the school field under the lilac tree. We didn't say much – both of us were kind of shy – but it was an easy silence. We liked being together. Sometimes Mary and Elton would run across the field and plonk themselves down beside us, and we would listen to them giggling and laughing about something or someone. Mary and Elton drew people to them in a way that we never would but we didn't mind – we didn't mind one little bit – and so as I recovered I would find myself going back to those times and remembering the way we were. What was it about Ralph that I loved so much? What had kept me going back to him time and time again? The truth is that I didn't know. I spoke to Rose about it.

I was lying on the pink chaise longue with one of Rose's colourful throws over my legs. It was late afternoon, and darkness was beginning to fall outside the window. Rose had lit the lamps, and they cast soft shadows against the walls. I felt relaxed and at peace.

'How did you know that Mr Toshimo was the right man for you, Rose? That you would love him forever?'

Rose sat down at the end of the chaise longue and smiled.

'I don't think that anyone can be sure that love will last forever, dear, but you see something in a person that draws you to them. It has to be more than looks; looks aren't enough. It's what's inside that is beautiful. I've bought books, dear, that have lovely covers only to find that the story has no substance, so I've given up on them. I never gave up on my oriental gentleman. He was my soul mate. He still is; death hasn't changed my love for him, and no one will ever replace him. Are you thinking about your Ralph, dear?'

I nodded. 'I don't seem to be able to give my heart to anyone else. I really hurt a boy called Joe, and he was lovely, and I think that maybe Matthew feels more for me than friendship, but I can't get Ralph out of my head, and I don't know why.'

'And you probably never will, dear, but you are young, and you deserve to be loved. I don't like to think of you being alone for the rest of your life. You have a big heart. Open it up, dear, and you might find that love will sneak in when you least expect it to.'

Could that happen? Maybe one day. Maybe one day I would be able to tuck Ralph away and allow myself to love again. I wondered what Mrs Dickens would say.

As I began to recover I started joining Rose on her daily walks along the sea front. It was chilly but the winds had died down. One day there was a weak sun filtering through the clouds so we decided to take a picnic down onto the beach. We leaned back against the old stone wall and let the sun warm our faces, Colin curled up on Rose's lap. After we'd eaten our sandwiches Rose closed her eyes and I walked down to the edge of the sea. The water was so calm, it looked like glass gently lapping the shore. I looked towards the horizon and thought of Ralph, so many miles away, so many oceans away. I had a lump in my throat as I walked back up the pebbles towards Rose.

Friday evenings became quite an event at Oriental Place. Mum and Aunty Brenda would arrive with sandwiches and home-made scones. Matthew and Millie would turn up with flowers for Rose, and Stephen and Tristan would come downstairs with bottles of wine. Sometimes Tom would come too. I loved those evenings. Rose would light a fire in the big marble grate and lighted candles were dotted about the room. She would wind up the old gramophone and play music. The old songs that she loved were the songs that Mum and Aunty Brenda loved as well. Sometimes Rose would play the piano, and we would all sing along. Those evenings were magical.

One evening I sat quietly watching everyone. Rose and Aunty Brenda were sitting at a little table beside the fireplace, both of them looking very serious as Rose introduced Aunty Brenda to Tarot cards. Their faces glowed in the light of the burning coals. Mum was happily chatting to Stephen and Tristan, and Millie was lying on her tummy on the floor playing with Colin. Matthew was standing by the fireplace. Sometimes I found it hard to believe how lucky I was to have found this place and these people. After Mary died I never dreamed that I could ever be happy again. In fact I can remember thinking that it would be some kind of betrayal to Mary if I let myself. As it happened life had other plans for me. I'd met Polly and Joe and allowed myself to smile again, and of course I would always have my lovely mad family, but somehow this was different. It was a feeling of belonging. Oriental Place had wrapped its arms around me and given me a new home and strangers that had become another kind of family. I wondered whether Ralph had found the same peace that

I had. The mirror above the fireplace reflected the faces of these dear people, some of their features blurred by the candlelight. I caught Matthew's eye, and he smiled at me.

I found myself thinking about Matthew a lot. I liked everything about him. I knew by the way he looked at me sometimes that perhaps he was falling a little in love with me, and that was okay – his gentle flirting made me feel wanted and cherished. I think he knew that I would never feel the same way, but we didn't talk about it, and I was glad. I wondered what my one year with Matthew would bring, but there was one thing I knew for certain: it wouldn't bring me pain.

CHAPTER FORTY-SEVEN

It was hard returning to work. The mornings were getting darker, and I had a job dragging myself out of bed. Rose and the boys had spoiled me, and now it was time to get back to reality. Once there though I loved it, even though my pile of manuscripts almost covered my desk.

'I've been trying to do some of them for you,' said Millie, 'but we seem to be getting more and more every day. It looks like everyone in Brighton wants to be a writer.'

'Don't worry, I'm back now, and I'm beginning to realise that you only have to read a few pages to know whether it's going to be any good or not. I knew Matthew's book was a winner after the first few lines.'

'Are Friday evenings going to stop now that you're better?'

'I hope not. I've really enjoyed them, and I think Rose has too, but I can't just presume that we can go on meeting at her flat.'

'I hope she says we can. Everyone is so lovely. I even like all the old songs. Your mum and your aunty are really cool, and I love Rose and Stephen and Tristan. Are they... you know?'

'No one has ever said as much, but yes, I believe that they are.'

'Well I think they're lovely.'

'So do I. There's a bit of a mystery there though.'

'Oh I love a good mystery! Tell me all.'

'When I first visited Oriental Place, Rose said that Stephen and Tristan were theatrical people, but they don't seem to work, or even go to the theatre for that matter. They go to the pictures but only during the day.'

'Why don't you ask them?'

'I have a feeling it's not to be talked about. I don't know why – it's just a feeling I've got.'

'And how about the lovely Matthew?'

'How about him?'

'Don't tell me you haven't noticed that he can't take his eyes off you.'

'We're just friends, Millie.'

'You might be *his* friend, but I get the feeling that he's got more than friendship on his mind.'

'I know.'

'And you're okay with that?'

'As long as Matthew is, then so am I. I really like him, but that's all.'

I passed the morning happily going through my pile of manuscripts. There was much sighing coming from Millie's desk.

'This is bloody mind-numbing.'

'Worse than usual?'

'*I* could do better and I have trouble writing a birthday card. I mean who told these people that they could write? They must have shown the stuff to someone.'

'Their mums I expect.'

'Well all I can say is that their mums aren't doing them any favours.'

'Who has been your best find?'

'Who do you think? Celeste-up-her-own-rear-end Partington-bloody-Spencer.'

'Whoops,'

'I found a Malcolm once.'

'What was the book about?'

'Bathing huts, you know the old-fashioned ones on wheels that used to be on Brighton beach.'

'Odd subject to write about.'

'Odd bloke – not like your Matthew.'

Just then Tom came out of his office looking very pleased with himself. 'Go fetch copious amounts of doughnuts, Millie.'

'What have you sold?' asked Millie, getting up from her desk.

'You will be delighted to hear that I have just sold *A Place Beyond the Mountain*.'

'You've sold Matthew's book?' I said, smiling.

'I have indeed. Small publisher, small advance, but they love it as much as we do. I really think that your wonderful find will be in the right hands.'

'That's brilliant news,' I said.

'When are you seeing him, Dottie?'

'Probably not till Friday, and I'm not really sure about that.'

'That's a week away,' said Millie. 'He has to be told sooner than that.'

'A letter's not going to be that much quicker,' said Tom.

'I suppose I could go up to the college, if I knew where it was.'

'Good idea, go, go, go. Leave now.'

'Really?'

'Take some bus fare out of the petty cash.'

Millie got the petty-cash tin out of the drawer. 'Go by train, Dottie – it's only two stops.'

'Where do I get off?'

'Moulsecoomb, then ask.'

'Bring him back with you if you can,' said Tom. 'We'll take him round the pub.'

I grabbed my coat and headed towards Brighton station. I got there just as the train pulled in. I settled myself into a seat and imagined Matthew's reaction when he heard the news. I couldn't have been more pleased for my friend. What if he wasn't there? Well at least I could leave a note – it would still be quicker than sending one. I stared out of the window as the train gathered speed. In no time at all we were pulling into the village of Moulsecoomb. I asked the man behind the ticket desk for directions and was pleased to find it was only a short distance from the station. Once outside I could actually see the college buildings.

I walked up the drive towards the main entrance. There were lots of young people milling around carrying books and bags. Everyone seemed to have a purpose, hurrying here and there. I had never considered going to college; it was never something that was talked about in our house. Seeing it now though, I think I would have liked it. I think it could have been fun, but I'd always thought that college and university weren't for the likes of me, which Mary said was bonkers – I could be whatever I wanted to be.

It was a big red building with steps leading up to the entrance. I had just started walking up them when I heard my name being called. I turned around and there, sitting on a wall, was Matthew. I couldn't believe my luck! I wouldn't have to go looking for him. He jumped down from the wall and walked towards me, grinning.

'What on earth are you doing here?' he asked.

I was just about to answer him when he was joined by a young girl.

'This is Danica,' he said.

The girl was tiny and very pretty. She was dark like Matthew with beautiful brown eyes. So Matthew had a girlfriend. I don't know why I was so surprised. He was a good-looking man – of course he had a girlfriend. I wondered why he had never mentioned her. Just then another boy joined us. 'And this,' said Matthew, 'is my good friend Taji.'

'My fiancé,' said Danica, smiling.

So it wasn't Matthew's girlfriend at all.

Taji smiled. 'Is this your Dottie?' he said.

Matthew put his arm around my shoulder. 'Yes, Taji, this is my Dottie.'

'We've heard so much about you,' said Danica. 'You are the very clever girl who found his book. He sings your praises day and night.'

'Someone would have found it – it's wonderful.'

'Come and meet the rest of my friends, Dottie.'

I wanted to be alone with him when I told him the good news about his book, but he was happy and smiling. and I could see that he wanted me to meet them.

We walked towards the wall where I'd seen Matthew sitting. A group of young people smiled at us as we apprached. 'These are my good friends, Dottie. Ekine, Talib, Nala, Ada and Akira.' They were all dark-skinned just like Matthew.

They were so chatty and welcoming. I was happy that Matthew had such nice friends. Then I noticed people staring at us and whispering.

'What are they staring at, Matthew?'

'I'm afraid, darling girl, that they are staring at you.'

'But why? Aren't I allowed here?'

The girl called Ada smiled at me. 'It's not you, Dottie – not you personally anyway.'

'What then?' I didn't have a clue what she was on about.

'They're all idiots,' said Talib angrily.

'Not idiots, Talib,' said Ada softly. 'Just ignorant.'

I didn't understand. Then I looked around the group and realised that mine was the only white face amongst them. 'Oh, I see.'

'Idiots,' said Talib again. 'I've a good mind to go over to them.'

Ada put her hand on his arm. 'And what good will that do, Talib? It will only make it worse for us.'

'You can leave us if you like, Dottie,' she said.

'I didn't come all this way to get intimidated by a bunch of small-minded people.'

'Good for you,' said Talib.

'Why *did* you come?' said Matthew.

I grinned at him. 'Tom has found a publisher for your book. You're going to be a published author, Matthew. A proper published author.'

Everyone started screaming and patting his back and shaking my hand – it was brilliant. Matthew stood up and walked a little way away from the group. I followed him. He was looking out across the green.

'Are you happy, Matthew?' I asked, standing beside him.

'Oh, my Dottie. I can't put into words just how happy.' He looked down at me, his eyes full of tears. 'Thank you.'

'Don't thank me, Matthew – you're the clever boy that wrote it.'

'And you're the clever girl that found it.'

'Well aren't we the clever ones then?'

'I'm sorry about those people.'

'Well I'm not. They mean nothing to me.'

'Do you still want to be my friend? Because there will be plenty of that.'

'Of course I want to be your friend. Who wouldn't want to be friends with a soon-to-be-famous author? Even that lot of idiots will be queuing up for your autograph.'

'I like you very much, Dottie Perks.'

'And I like you, Matthew Smith.'

And so began the year of Matthew and I. Sweet times with this sweet man. There was no future for us beyond a wonderful friendship and therefore no expectations.

It wasn't always easy. Matthew pretended not to notice the looks and the whispers. I didn't mind so much for myself, but I got really angry for him. I couldn't see why people had such strong opinions about seeing us together. I mean we weren't do-ing anyone any harm; we weren't hurting anyone, were we? I was proud to be seen with this beautiful man, and I was determined that we shouldn't hide away. What frightened me most was that someone might take the name calling further and actually hurt us, hurt Matthew. That really scared me.

One evening on my way home from work I stopped off at the open-all-hours to get some milk. I paid for it and was leaving the shop when a young girl came in. I stepped aside to let her pass when she said, or at least I thought she said, 'Slag.'

I stared at her retreating back as she went up to the counter. 'Did you just say what I thought you said?'

She didn't even turn round to face me. 'If the cap fits.'

Mr Raji the shopkeeper came flying round the counter and confronted the girl. 'Well, *I* heard what you said, and you can get out of my shop, and don't bother to come back!'

'Hold yer hair on, old man. I don't come into your shop out of bloody choice you know – in fact you're lucky I come in at all.'

Poor Mr Raji had gone bright red in the face. 'Out, out, out! Get out of my shop!'

Mrs Raji must have heard the rumpus and came running out from the back.

'What is happening? What is all this noise?'

'It was a customer, Mrs Raji,' I said. 'She was saying bad things about me. Your husband got angry.'

'Bloody girl,' he said, wiping his forehead.

'Come, Basu,' said Mrs Raji, helping her husband to sit down. 'How many times have I told you to ignore these things? You can think what you like but laugh with the customer as if you think that what they are saying is the funniest thing you have ever heard.'

'There was nothing funny about what she called this young lady, and I would like to remind you, Mrs Raji, that this young lady is one of our regulars.'

'You think that I don't know that, Basu? But you must think of your health. You are no good to me or this young lady when your ashes are floating down the Ganges river. Now go and sit down in the back, and I will take over.'

'Thank you, Mr Raji,' I said. 'I'm really sorry.'

'You have nothing to be sorry about. Girls like that one are not worth your spit.'

'Mr Raji!' exclaimed his wife.

I ran up the stairs to my flat, put the bottle of milk in a bowl of cold water to keep from going sour and put the kettle on for a cup of tea. I stood waiting for it to boil and thought about what the girl had said. She must have seen me with Matthew. There could be no other reason for her to call me that awful name – she was a complete stranger to me. Why did people have to be like that? I felt quite shaken up by the incident. The kettle boiled, I unscrewed the lid of the tea caddy and found that it was empty – something else I had meant to get at the shop.

I left the door on the latch and ran downstairs. I tapped on the door and Tristan answered.

'I've come begging.'

'Sugar? Milk?'

'Tea.'

'Tea I can do. In fact I have just this minute made one. Join me, darling, and we shall sup together. I don't like drinking on my own.'

'Where's Stephen?'

'Downstairs with Rose, visiting Colin.'

'Does Colin live downstairs now?'

'It makes more sense. Stephen retains visiting rights.'

Tristan poured my tea, and we sat side by side on the couch.

He stared at me and then said, 'Something is bothering you, am I right?'

'Well it shouldn't bother me. It's just something someone said.'

'Biscuits, we need biscuits,' said Tristan, jumping up.

Tristan opened the cupboard, took out a packet of custard creams and brought them back to the table. 'Now tell me all.'

'A complete stranger just called me the S word.'

'Sweet?'

'No,' I said, grinning.

'Sugar lips?'

Now I was starting to giggle. 'No.'

'Sensitive soul?'

'Is that what I am?'

'Isn't that what we all are?' said Tristan, reaching across the table and holding my hand.

'She called me a slag. I don't understand why people think they can judge me when they don't even know me.'

'Because they are idiots with very small brains.'

'But they're not all idiots, are they? The students and even some of the tutors at Matthew's college give us funny looks, and they're educated.'

'I don't know, my darling. Sometimes I question myself. Do I judge people because they don't think like I do? I hope not, but I fear I might. Now have a custard cream and forget about her. Dunk, darling, dunk.'

I dipped my biscuit into the hot tea. The cream melted on my tongue, and the sweetness filled my mouth.'

'Better?'

I nodded, took a deep breath and said, 'Tell me to mind my own business, but you and Stephen intrigue me.'

'What, boring old us?'

'You're far from that, and you jolly well know it.'

'I think that Stephen would like the idea of being called intriguing.'

'It's just that when I first came here Rose said that you were both in the theatre, but you don't seem to be.'

'Our theatre days are behind us.'

'You retired?'

'We ran away.'

'From the theatre?'

'From the world, darling. We ran away from the world.'

'Someone must have hurt you very badly. I'm sorry.'

Tristan stood up and walked across to the window. He was silent for a moment then he said,

'They didn't hurt me, not really. I wish they had. It was Stephen those bastards hurt.'

I didn't know what to say. I had never heard Tristan talk like that. I was used to his wit and banter; I had never heard him sound so bitter.

'I shouldn't have said anything.'

Tristan turned round and shook his head as if trying to shake away the memory. 'When I think what they did to that dear sweet boy I am as angry as if it was yesterday.'

'Dunk, Tristan, dunk.'

Tristan smiled and sat down beside me again. 'I think that is what everyone should do when faced with ignorance and small-mindedness. They should just bloody well dunk.'

'Amen to that,' I said, and we clinked cups.

CHAPTER FORTY-EIGHT

It was the run-up to Christmas. The nights had drawn in, and it was dark by 4 p.m. Matthew and I loved to walk along the seafront in the evenings, looking at the glittering lights strung between the old lamp posts. I had been looking at these lights since childhood, but I never failed to see the magic in them. Both piers were lit up and the dark water underneath was ablaze with the reflected lights from the carousel and the arcade. I watched Matthew as he leaned on the railings and looked out over the sea. I was making memories, tucking them away to take out again and look at when he was gone. Some nights we were joined by Tristan and Stephen. The four of us would wrap up warm and sit on the cold pebbles eating fish and chips out of the newspaper. Now and again other winter evenings would suddenly slip into my mind. Little snapshots of me and Ralph, Mary and Elton leaning over these same railings, looking at the same Christmas lights. This is where the ghosts were. This is where they would always be.

Matthew and I were still no more than loving friends. We held hands, we cuddled, but that was as far as it went. And yet I knew he wanted more. I just hoped that he wouldn't get hurt. I sometimes found myself questioning whether I had used him to fill the space left by Ralph and Peggy, because there was no doubt in my mind that meeting Matthew couldn't have come along at a better time.

Rose, Tristan and Stephen were going to spend Christmas Day in Rose's flat, and they'd asked me and Matthew if we would like to join them, but I wanted to be with my family. It was where I always wanted to be at Christmas. Much as I loved Oriental Place, Christmas to me meant being at home. Clark was spending the day with Emma's parents. This would be the first time that he wouldn't be home for Christmas, so there was no way I couldn't be there. Mum said that Matthew would be very welcome, and I was looking forward to us all being together. The only thing bothering me was Rita. We always had Christmas tea at her house, and I wasn't sure what her opinion of Matthew was going to be, but the one thing I could definitely be sure of was that my darling sister *would* have an opinion. I needed to run it past Mum.

I met her in the café on the top floor of Wades department store on Western Road. Wades was just about the poshest shop in Brighton. Mum had been bringing me, Rita and Clark here since we were kids. She used to say, 'We might not be able to buy any of the stuff in here, but we can afford a cup of tea and a bun.' I can remember as children how fascinated all three of us were by the brass containers that used to whiz above our heads carrying money from the desk to the girl in the office and how it would come whizzing back again with the change. The other thing about Wades was that they knew how to do Christmas. They always had a huge tableau in the window that would be covered in sheets till the great unveiling. Sometimes it would be a nativity scene and sometimes a Toyland scene. Wades was the best place for a kid to come at Christmas. I wished that I could have brought Peggy here – she would have loved it.

Mum was already sitting down when I got there. Aunty Brenda was sitting next to her, which was nice, as I hadn't seen her for a few weeks. She waved as I walked towards the table.

'Now let me look at you,' she said.

Aunty Brenda had been saying this to me for as long as I could remember but these days when she said it she winked. It had become a bit of a standing joke.

I kissed them both on the cheek and sat down.

'I ordered tea and toast for you,' said Mum. 'I know you like your toast.'

'Perfect,' I said, taking off my coat and hanging it on the back of the chair.

'How are Mrs Toshimo and the boys?' said Mum.

'They're all fine, and they send their love to you both.'

'We miss our Fridays,' said Aunty Brenda. 'But we don't like coming out on these dark nights do we, Maureen?'

'Your dad doesn't like me going out in the dark.'

'You could always visit in the daytime.'

'Not without you there,' said Mum. 'It wouldn't seem right.'

The waitress arrived with tea, toast for me and scones for Mum and Aunty Brenda.

'I wanted to ask you about Christmas, Mum,' I said.

'You *are* still coming?'

'Of course I am.'

'And Matthew?'

'He's really looking forward to it. It's just that Rita hasn't met him yet, and I'm worried.'

'You don't want to be worrying about Rita,' said Mum.

'Have you told her about Matthew?'

'Of course I have.'

'And?'

'Well you know Rita.'

'That's what's worrying me. I don't want Matthew to feel awkward. People stare at us, Mum. People stare at us all the time. Matthew behaves like it doesn't bother him, and I don't think it does for himself, but I know he feels bad for me. If I bring him home for Christmas I want him to feel as if he's wanted there.'

'Of course he's wanted,' said Aunty Brenda.

'I know all of you want him, but what about Rita? Is she going to make him feel welcome?'

'If she knows what's good for her she will,' said Mum, slapping butter on her scone as if she was plastering a wall.

'I just want Matthew to have the best Christmas he can have, because it's the only Christmas we'll spend together. I want it to be special. I don't want Rita spoiling it.'

'I do hear what you're saying, love. I can't speak for Rita. She has her views on things, but she's not unkind.'

'No, she's not unkind, Dottie,' said Aunty Brenda.

'She might not be unkind, Aunty Brenda, but she can make her feelings known without even opening her mouth.'

'Why don't you go and see her then?' asked Mum.

'I don't find Rita very easy.'

'Nobody does,' said Aunty Brenda. 'But she's your sister, and she loves you.'

'She's got a funny way of showing it sometimes.'

'I know, dear, but we all have our crosses to bear. Mine is called Carol, and she'd test the patience of a saint.'

'How is she?'

'She seems to be doing all right. She says this Florence person loves her.'

'Well that's good, isn't it?'

'I suppose so, but modelling isn't exactly a secure job, is it? It's not exactly a career.'

'Well that Twiggy girl's done all right for herself,' said Mum. 'I saw a picture of her on the side of the number fourteen bus last week.'

'I can't see our Carol on the side of a bus,' said Aunty Brenda. 'Can you, Dottie?'

'Well I think if a fashion house in London wants to use her, she should give it a go.'

'Really?'

'Why not? She won't know if she doesn't try.'

'But she wants to live in London. Am I supposed to let her?'

'I think I would, Aunty Brenda, and I think it would be better if she had your blessing.'

'You are getting very wise, Dottie. You get that from your mum.'

'I'll tell you what. I'll phone my friend Polly and see if Mrs Pierce has let my room yet.'

'She must have let it by now,' said Mum.

'Oh she did, but the girl left owing her rent and stole the telephone directory.'

'That is exactly what's worrying me, Dottie.'

'What?'

'My Carol mixing with people that steal telephone directories.'

'For heaven's sake, Brenda,' said Mum, laughing. 'It's hardly in the same league as the great train robbers.'

'Theft is theft, Maureen, and how do you know that the great train robbers didn't start their criminal careers pinching telephone directories.'

That's when Mum and I burst into fits of giggles, joined almost immediately by Aunty Brenda.

'So I'll ask Polly, shall I?' I said, wiping my eyes.

'I suppose so,' said Aunty Brenda 'At least it's someone you know.'

'Did your Mrs Pierce have to get another telephone directory, Dottie?'

'I haven't got a clue, Mum,' I said, biting into my toast.

CHAPTER FORTY-NINE

Two weeks to Christmas and Brighton was buzzing. The shops along Western Road were ablaze with fairy lights, spilling pools of liquid rainbows onto the wet pavements and brightening up the gloomy winter evenings. There were Father Christmases on every corner, rattling their tins. Dads were dragging Christmas trees along the pavements, the counters in the shops were laden with gifts and everywhere there were people, excited kids, harassed women and reluctant men, carrying bags bulging with presents. Everything was just as it should be.

I still didn't know what to do about Rita, so I decided to go and visit her. I wasn't exactly relishing the thought. The first thing she said when she opened the door was...

'I wondered when you were going to show your face.'

'You could always visit *me* you know.'

'I might one day.'

I followed her into the front room. Miranda Louise was sitting on the floor surrounded by toys. I couldn't believe how much she'd grown.

'This is your Aunty Dottie, Miranda Louise,' said Rita. 'Now don't be frightened. She's family. In fact, believe it or not, she's your godmother.'

'You've made your point, Rita.'

'Well she doesn't know you, does she? You could be anyone.'

Actually I did feel pretty guilty. I couldn't remember when I'd last seen her.

I knelt down and smiled at her. She was such a contented baby. She always had been, which I always thought was a bit of a miracle given who her mother was. 'I'm sorry I've been such a rotten aunty,' I said, stroking her little hand. 'I'll try and do better.'

She gave me a gummy smile.

'Well you couldn't do much worse,' said Rita.

'Okay, truce?'

We both sat down on the couch and watched the baby playing. She was babbling away to herself in baby talk. She really was very sweet. She was even growing into her ears.

'So what do we owe the pleasure of this visit? I very much doubt it was to see Miranda Louise.'

'It's about Matthew actually.'

'Oh, is it actually?'

'I wondered if you would have any objections to him coming here for tea on Christmas Day.'

'I might.'

This was exactly what I expected would happen. 'I knew you'd be like this.'

'Did you now? Has your landlady been teaching *you* how to predict the future as well?'

'Don't try and be clever, Rita.'

'I'll be anything I want to be in my own house, and I'll think whatever I like.'

'And we all know what that's going to be.'

'And that, my small-minded little sister is where you are wrong. I'm not sure whether I want Matthew here, because I don't know him. I might not like him, and it won't be because of the colour of his skin. I presume that is what you are getting at. If I decide that I don't like him then I wouldn't care if he was red, white and blue – I still wouldn't like him. In fact I think it's you that's got the problem, not me.'

'I don't have a problem with it.'

'Are you sure? Because it's you that's been banging on about it to Mum. How do you know why people are staring at you? You don't, do you? You've decided for them, just like you've decided for me. They might be staring at you because they can't believe that someone as gormless as you has actually managed to get a boyfriend.

'He's not my boyfriend.'

'Well whatever he is. You were wrong about me, so how do you know that you're not wrong about them?'

I didn't know what to think. Was Rita right? Was I being paranoid? I was certainly wrong about Rita, and I felt bad about that.

'And anyway you don't know those people. They're not your friends, are they? They're not your family, so why should you care what they think? The world is full of idiots, but they're not *your* idiots, are they? They're someone else's. And I'll tell you something else. I never really liked that Ralph Bennett of yours. I always thought that he was a bit lame.'

'Lame?'

'He never fought for you, did he? He got your best friend pregnant and married her but kept you dangling on a string. Then he practically left poor Fiona at the altar and went running back to you. Then he dumped *you* because a spoiled five-year-old had a tantrum, which sent him scurrying back to Fiona, who was daft enough to take him back. I didn't like Ralph Bennett, and it wasn't because he had ginger hair – it was because he always played the victim.'

I was a bit stunned actually. Rita had never expressed an opinion about Ralph before. Put like that I suppose he did sound a bit lame, but Rita didn't know him like I did. There wasn't a bad bone in his body. If he was guilty of anything, it was being too kind, and in being too kind he ended up hurting people. He hurt me because Mary probably came onto him, and he didn't like to say no. He hurt Fiona because he wanted to make Peggy happy, so he asked her to marry him, then couldn't go through with it, and he hurt me again by putting Peggy's happiness before ours. Yes, he hurt people, but he didn't mean to. Did that make him lame? Not in my eyes, it didn't. I decided not to pursue it. Instead I said, 'Rita, I owe you a huge apology.'

'It doesn't have to be huge but apology accepted.'

'So can I bring Matthew round on Christmas Day or not?'

'Of course you can.'

Right at that moment Miranda started clapping her hands.

'My sentiments exactly,' I said, smiling.

Millie and I had decorated the little office with paper chains and baubles. Tom had gone out and got a tree, which he dragged up the rickety stairs. We draped it with fairy lights and hung glass ornaments and tinsel from the branches. It was lovely, and when we came in in the mornings, the office smelt of pine and reminded me of my childhood.

One evening we had a bit of a party in the office. Celeste-up-her-own-rear-end Partington-bloody-Spencer came, and so did Malcolm the bathing-hut man. A lovely young Chinese girl who had written a cookery book was there, as was a children's author called Caroline, who was actually a man called Raymond, who for some reason didn't want anyone to know that he wrote children's books. Anyway it was all very Christmassy and jolly. There was mulled wine and mince pies and cassette tapes playing Christmas songs. Harry Belafonte singing 'Mary's Boy Child' was playing just as Matthew came in the door. He looked so handsome it took my breath away. He was wearing a long black coat and he had a red woollen scarf wrapped around his neck. He smiled his gorgeous smile at everyone and he lit up the room.

Matthew kissed me on the cheek. His lips were cold and soft, and he smelt of peppermints. I introduced him to Malcolm and went to get him a drink.

Millie was filling her glass with mulled wine, which smelt of cinnamon and nutmeg and Christmas.

She was looking across the room at Matthew. 'You *are* lucky, Dottie. It's Christmas, and I haven't had so much as a sniff of a boyfriend, and you didn't even have to leave the bloody office to get yours.'

'We're just friends you know, Millie.'

'Still?'

I laughed. 'Yes, still.'

'You must be bonkers.'

'Probably. Now what about Malcolm?'

'I'm not that desperate.'

'Just kidding, sorry. But I know there'll be someone rich and handsome out there for you.'

'Right now I'd settle for nice. I mean I'm not opposed to handsome, and rich would be a bonus, but someone nice to spend Christmas with would be lovely.'

I put my arm around her shoulder. 'It will happen, Millie, probably when you least expect it.'

'Perhaps your Aunty Brenda could practise the Tarot cards on me and see what my future holds.'

'I expect she'd love to. She's done the rest of us. Apparently my dad's going to travel to foreign parts, which is highly unlikely given that he has trouble venturing out of the estate and he needs medical back-up to get him round to Rita's.'

Millie laughed.

We looked across at Matthew. He was deep in conversation with Malcolm.

'Won't you be sad when he leaves?'

'Of course I will, but I'm not sorry that I met him.'

'But won't you be heartbroken again?'

'No. I have a theory that your heart can only truly break once. You can be really, really sad, and you can tell yourself that your heart is broken, but it's not, and you get over it, but true heart-break is something you never quite get over. That's my theory anyway.'

'That's a hell of a theory.'

'It's what keeps me going when I think of saying goodbye to Matthew. I'll be sad, but my heart won't break. Meeting him helped me through one of the toughest times in my life, and I'll always be grateful to him for that.'

We spent the next couple of hours singing Christmas songs off-key, except for Malcolm of the bathing huts, who surprised us all with the voice of an angel. We all cheered and clapped him, and he went very red and pulled at his collar as if he was choking, but he looked chuffed to bits. I winked at Millie, who mouthed back, 'No way.'

I think that we were all slightly tipsy by the time we left the office, and to add to the Christmas spirit it had started to snow.

Matthew put his arm around my shoulder as we walked along the seafront towards Oriental Place. 'Who would have thought that huts for changing your clothes in could be so fascinating?'

'Were you bored?'

'Of course not. The man has a passion, and anyone with a passion deserves respect.'

'I never thought about it like that.'

'And he didn't keep that passion to himself – he told the world about it.'

'And apparently the book sold really well.'

'So there you are. Malcolm is a trailblazer for all those like-minded people. He has set them free; he has glamorised the humble bathing hut.'

I giggled. 'You're funny.'

'You're lovely.'

The snow was falling around us in soft white flakes. It settled on the railings and drifted across the dark expanse of sea. We stood looking out over the water. Matthew took off his red scarf and wrapped it around my neck. Maybe it was the wine, or the snow, but everything felt magical. It was another special Matthew moment that I would hold on to and treasure. His coat felt soft and damp against my cheek, as he held me tightly against him. I felt loved, I felt safe and there wasn't a ghost in sight. Would I regret not giving him more? No, because however much I had moved on with my life, my heart still belonged to Ralph. Maybe it always would, and Matthew was too lovely a man to hurt. We crept up the stairs to my flat and let ourselves in as quietly as we could. We slept all night in each other's arms as the snow fell outside the window and turned Brighton into a winter wonderland.

CHAPTER FIFTY

I was at Brighton station waiting for the London train to come in. Polly was coming for the weekend, and I couldn't wait to see her. I'd written to her about Carol and she wanted to meet her, but mostly she wanted to see me and Oriental Place and Rose and the boys. I'd told her all about Ralph leaving, but I hadn't told her about Matthew. I was looking forward to the pair of them meeting. After my rather surprising conversation with Rita I had stopped caring so much about what people thought about us, and anyway I knew that Polly wouldn't judge him by the colour of his skin.

I sat down on a bench by the gates and watched the trains coming in, heaving and groaning and then lurching forward as they came to a stop. I watched the people leaning out of the windows to reach down and open the doors. I watched them stepping down, pulling their bags behind them, holding tightly onto the hands of their children. I watched as they hurried towards the gate to where I was sitting, where the guard was waiting to take the used tickets out of their hands. They didn't care about the guard. They didn't even see him. They were completely focussed on the people who had come to meet them.

I watched as the people who were waiting – not so many, but a few – stood on tiptoe to scan the faces of the people coming off the trains. I watched their expressions change from anxious to relieved. I watched the smiles break out and their hands shoot into the air as they waved and waved. 'Here, I'm over here,' and the matching response from the loved ones they had come to meet.

I remembered how it was for me, the day I had arrived from London to be with Ralph.

I remembered how nervous I was as the train pulled into Brighton station, how I wished time would stop, because I was afraid. I'd been afraid that he wouldn't be there, that fate would have intervened again and found a way to keep us apart. I'd thought of what I would do if he wasn't there, of how I would be alone again – how all I had given up would be for nothing.

But there he'd been, and we had run towards each other, and it had been like he was the earth, and I was the moon; we were separate, but we were drawn together – always separate but inseparable.

.The London train was due in any minute, so I got up from the bench and went to wait by the gate. There was a woman standing in front of me with a baby in her arms. The baby was staring at me over her mum's shoulder. Her eyes were grey – the same colour as mine. I kept smiling at her, but she just stared back at me with a very serious look on her face. She was wearing a red woolly siren suit, with wispy strands of fair hair escaping from the hood, and she looked cosy and snug. I tried making funny faces at her, but she was having none of it, and I began to feel like an idiot. I was wearing Matthew's red scarf; it made me feel closer to him somehow. I pushed it up my face so that it covered my eyes then I pulled it down, playing peek-a-boo. I did this a few more times until eventually the beginnings of a smile appeared on the baby's face.

At last the train arrived. I could feel my stomach clench with excitement at the thought of seeing Polly. Doors were opening, spilling their cargo of passengers onto the platform. I was straining to see Polly amongst the crowds of people heading towards the gate. Suddenly there she was, dodging in and out of the crowd as she ran towards me.

We fell into each other's arms. 'Welcome to Brighton,' I said, hugging her.

'You look fab,' she said.

'So do you,' I replied, taking in her gorgeous green corduroy maxi coat and long white boots. 'You look very London. I think my wardrobe has gone downhill a bit since I left.'

'Nonsense, you look just like a model.'

'A model for what though?'

'Don't start that again.'

I gave Polly another hug. 'Oh I'm so glad you're here. Do you want some lunch before we go home?'

'As long as it's by the sea, I would love some lunch.'

'Let's go then. It's straight down the road.'

'All roads lead to the sea eh?'

'Pretty much.'

We walked down West Street and onto the promenade. The snow had gone, leaving everywhere wet and slushy. There was a cold wind blowing off the sea that almost took my breath away.

'Quick, let's find somewhere warm,' I said.

'Not yet,' said Polly.

'Really? It's freezing.'

'You'll live,' said Polly, grinning. 'I want to walk on the pebbles and stand by the shore. You've talked about this place so much that I want to experience every single bit of it.'

'Come on then,' I said, wrapping Matthew's scarf over my mouth. We walked down the steps and jumped onto the pebbles.

'Race you to the water,' said Polly, taking off down the beach. She was like an excited child, and just for a minute she reminded me of Mary. I grinned and ran after her.

Even though it was so cold the sea was calm, rolling gently over the stones and rattling them back as the tide went out. Polly was standing transfixed, gazing out over the grey water. I was beginning to wonder if she had ever actually been on a beach before. 'This isn't your first time on a beach, is it?' I asked her.

'No,' said Polly smiling at me, 'but it's my first time on *your* beach.'

I had my hands stuffed in my pockets, but I thought my nose was going to fall off from the cold.

'Take me home, woman,' said Polly at last.

'I thought you wanted some lunch.'

'Could we grab some fish and chips and eat them at yours?'

'Of course we can. This is Brighton. Fish and chips we can do.'

We bought the fish and chips in a great chippy opposite the Palace Pier then hurried along the seafront towards home.

'It's exactly how I thought it would be,' said Polly as we turned into Oriental Place. 'I'm so glad.'

We ran up the steps of number fifty-five, clutching the hot bundles to our chests. I'd already told her about the light switches, and she found it hilarious.

Just as we passed the boys' door, Tristan appeared. 'I smell fish and chips,' he said. 'Stephen, they have fish and chips,' he shouted. He held out his hand. 'And who is this?' he asked, smiling at Polly.

'You know exactly who this is, Tristan. I told you my friend Polly was coming to stay.'

'But you didn't tell me what a vision of chic she was going to be,' he said, shaking her hand. 'Stephen, come and see this beautiful creature out here on the landing.'

Stephen put his head round the door. 'Oh my God, I want that coat. Take it off at once! I shall wear it to the party.'

Polly had been grinning throughout this conversation, looking as if she was thoroughly enjoying the whole thing. 'What party?' she said.

'We're having a Christmas party down in Rose's flat tomorrow evening,' I said.

'Isn't it exciting?' said Stephen. 'Everyone's coming. It's in your honour, darling, but we have to get a tree. You will come with us, won't you?'

I looked at Polly.

'We'd love to,' she said. 'And thank you for the party.'

'Think nothing of it, darling girl,' said Stephen. 'It was a good excuse for a knees-up, wasn't it, Tristan?'

'It was, dear boy,' said Tristan, smiling at him.

'These chips are getting cold. We'll see you later, boys.'

I let us into my flat and immediately turned on the two-bar electric fire. 'Best keep your coat on till it warms up.'

'Oh it's lovely,' said Polly, walking round. 'And you've got your own door. I'd love my own door.'

I knew what she meant. There was no real privacy at Victoria Terrace. Mrs P could walk in any time she liked, and she did. Rose wasn't like that.

'How can you afford to keep it on now Ralph has left?'

'My landlady, Rose, halved my rent.'

'Blimey, why would she do that?'

'I guess because she likes me, and she wanted me to stay.'

'Well that was jolly decent of her. I can't imagine Mrs P doing that in a million years.'

'Neither can I.'

'Oh, Dottie, it's so lovely to be here. I've missed you so much. In fact it's getting worse not better.'

'I've missed you too. Fancy living in Brighton?'

'I wouldn't rule it out.'

'Really? Wouldn't you miss London?'

'Do you?'

'No, but Brighton's my home. It's been easy to settle back down here. The only thing I've missed about London is you.'

'And Mrs Dickens?'

'Of course. Have you been to see her lately?'

'No, that place gives me the creeps on my own.' She shivered.

'And Mrs P still hasn't let my room?'

'I think the mouse pinching her telephone directory has put her off. I told her about Carol, and she's all for it.' Polly put on a funny voice. ' "If Miss Perks can recommend her then I'm sure she will be a perfectly respectable young lady." Now you've gone she seems to think you're wonderful.'

'That will be because I *am* wonderful.'

We unwrapped the fish and chips and ate them straight out of the newspaper. Polly closed her eyes.

'These are the best fish and chips I've ever tasted.'

'Brighton's good at fish and chips.'

'I'd be as fat as a house if I lived here.'

'Moderation in all things, that's how I deal with it. Any sign of a boyfriend yet?' I asked.

'I've stopped looking. There's only so many frogs you can kiss before you can't be bothered any more. How about you?'

'Well,' I said smiling. 'I've found a friend.'

'What sort of friend?' said Polly looking confused.

I popped a chip into my mouth.

'Well?' Polly asked. 'Male? female? Not that you need another female friend because you've got me.'

I laughed. 'His name's Matthew.'

Polly's eyes widened. 'Could he be more than a friend?'

I finished the fish and chips and put the paper on the coffee table. 'I hope not,' I said. 'He's going back to Africa in July.'

Polly stood up and put both lots of chip paper in the bin. She licked her fingers carefully one by one. 'I should have known it wasn't going to be simple. Your love life never is,' she said.

'It's a like life, Polly, not a love life.' I said

'As long as you're not heading for another broken heart.'

'Not this time.'

'Sure?' she said, looking concerned.

'As sure as I can be.'

'So come on, how did you meet?'

'Actually I discovered him. Or to be more precise I discovered his book.'

'Now you've lost me,' she said, coming back to the sofa and tucking her feet up under her.

'He wrote a book. I discovered the manuscript.' I said.

'He's a writer?'

I smiled. 'He's an amazing writer and a pretty amazing guy.'

'And Ralph?' she asked. 'How are you dealing with that?'

'By not thinking about it too much. He's gone, and there's nothing I can do.'

'And it was all because of Peggy?'

'I think that maybe there was more to it than that.'

'Really?'

I nodded 'Rita thinks he's weak; she thinks he enjoys playing the victim.'

'It's what you think that counts, love.' said Polly.

'I know.'

'I guess he has messed you about a bit.'

'But it never seemed like that at the time,' I said. 'Life just always got in the way. Anyway perhaps it's all been my fault.'

'And perhaps it hasn't, my friend,' said Polly, smiling gently.

CHAPTER FIFTY-ONE

Polly and I slept together in the double bed. It was lovely having her there beside me. We chatted well into the night and probably fell asleep mid sentence. We woke up to the sun streaming through the window.

Polly stretched. 'That's the best night's sleep I've had in ages.'

'What there was of it.'

'Were we that late?'

'I think so.'

'What are we up to today?'

'I think Stephen and Tristan are planning on taking us Christmas-tree shopping.'

'I've never bought a Christmas tree before. It should be fun.'

'I'm sure the boys will make it fun.'

'I really like them,' said Polly, getting out of bed.

'So do I. They feel like family.'

'What do they do?'

'From what I can gather, they used to be in the theatre, but something bad happened to Stephen. I don't know exactly what, but I think that perhaps he was attacked.'

'Oh my God, really?'

'I think so. Tristan never said in so many words but he got so upset when he was talking about it, saying that someone hurt Stephen. They don't go out in the evenings – not on their own anyway. I think Stephen might be scared to.'

'That's so sad. It makes me really angry that some low life can make them feel like that. Bloody people.'

'I know, but I think they're really happy, and they feel safe here in Oriental Place.'

'I can see why. There's something special about this house.'

'I really believe that's what got me through those first few weeks. I had Oriental Place and Rose and the boys. I was looked after. It would have been a lot harder if I hadn't had them.'

'Well I'm glad that you did.'

'I was sad for a while, but I had quite a few shoulders to cry on.'

Just then there was a tap on the door. Polly put her maxi coat around her shoulders and answered it. It was Tristan.

'Fry-up, ours, ten minutes. Shake a leg, girls.'

'Yummy,' said Polly.

When we got downstairs Stephen was dishing up sausages, bacon, eggs and beans onto four plates. He looked resplendent in a blue striped pinny. 'Tea everyone?' he asked, smiling.

'This is wonderful,' said Polly. 'What a treat.'

'Don't be fooled,' said Tristan. 'He's just after your coat.'

'You can borrow my coat any time you like, Stephen.'

'Divine girl,' said Stephen, pouring the tea into four beautiful china cups.

'Where are we going for the tree?' I asked.

'Not sure,' said Tristan.

'Woolworths always has plenty of trees. They stack them against the wall outside – or at least they used to,' I said, biting into a sausage.

'God forbid,' said Stephen. 'Woolworths won't do at all.'

'He wants the American-movies experience,' said Tristan, grinning. 'You know? That film where James Stewart is running through the snow.'

'*It's a Wonderful Life*,' said Polly. 'I love that film.'

'What's all that got to do with buying a Christmas tree?' I asked.

'Well,' said Stephen, 'there's always snow.'

'Which there's not,' I said, grinning.

'Okay,' said Stephen. 'We'll just have to imagine the snow bit, but there's always a forest of trees and sweet ruddy-faced children with sparkling eyes, frolicking about, shouting, "This one, Mama, this one, Papa," and when the guy hauls it into the station wagon those sweet children say, "Thank you, sir, have a wonderful holiday," or, "That man looks poor, Papa, shall we invite him to spend Christmas with us? I don't mind sharing my dinner."'

'Crikey,' I said, laughing. 'We might find the forest, but where do we get the kids? Especially kids like that.'

'Easy,' said Stephen. 'You and Polly will be the kids and me and Tristan will be your proud parents.'

'This is getting seriously bizarre,' said Polly.

'Oh, we love bizarre, don't we, Tristan?'

'The more bizarre the better, dear boy.'

It was decided that we would go up onto the Downs in the hope that we might stumble across a forest of Christmas trees and a man with a station wagon.

'Okay,' I said, 'just say we *do* find the perfect tree – how are we going to get it back?'

'Carry it, I suppose,' said Tristan.

'What, all the way from the Downs?'

'Bus?' said Polly.

'Do you think we'd be allowed on a bus with a Christmas tree?' I asked.

'I suppose it depends on the size of the tree,' said Tristan.

'Oh, huge,' said Stephen. 'It has to be huge.'

'If that's what you want, darling, then it will be huge,' Tristan replied, smiling at him.

'It's not going to happen, is it?' said Stephen sadly.

'It jolly well is,' said Tristan. 'If I have to drag it back branch by branch.'

'My hero,' said Stephen, smiling.

'Always,' said Tristan softly.

We took a bus to the top of the Devil's Dyke. It was so wild up there we could hardly stand up. A few brave sheep were snuffling around and even they were having a job keeping upright. The excitement I had felt on the way there had gone. This was mine and Ralph's special place. This was where he told me he loved me, and this was where he asked me to marry him. I walked away from the others and looked out over the Downs. I breathed in the freezing cold air; it stung my lungs and made my eyes water. I missed him. I just missed him. I felt a hand on my shoulder.

'Ghosts?' said Tristan.

I nodded.

'Tell them that they've got the wrong girl. Tell them that, just for today, you are a child buying a Christmas tree.'

I smiled and rested my head on his shoulder. 'Sometimes I wish I was a child.'

'We all do, my darling. We all do.'

I took a deep breath.

'Better?'

I nodded. He put his arm around my shoulder and we walked back to the others.

'I'm frozen', said Stephen, 'and there's not a forest in sight.'

'Let's go in the café,' said Polly. 'At least it will be warm.'

'Well it couldn't be much colder,' said Stephen, shivering.

We ordered four steaming mugs of hot chocolate and sat by the window, looking out over the hills.

'It's beautiful up here,' said Polly, cradling the hot mug in her hands.

'This is where Ralph proposed to me,' I said.

'I thought you looked a bit sad,' said Stephen. 'Oh dear, this is all my fault. Shall we get back on the bus and go to Woolworths? I'm sure the trees there will be perfectly fine. I mean they must have *come* from a forest.'

'I'll be okay,' I said. 'We'll jolly well find our own forest.'

'Bravo,' said Tristan.

Polly asked the girl behind the counter if anyone was selling Christmas trees nearby.

'There's a farm at the bottom of the hill. Tony,' she shouted. 'What's that farm down the hill called?'

'Didn't know there was one,' came the response.

'Yes, you do. It's run by that weird bloke. He comes in here sometimes with that smelly black dog.'

'Oh yeah. Sorry haven't got a clue.'

'It's at the bottom of the hill,' said the girl, turning back to Polly. 'I think it's called Toppings or Toppers or something like that, but I *do* know he sells Christmas trees. He's a bit weird though.'

'You've been very helpful,' said Polly.

We finished our hot chocolates and started walking down the hill. The wind was bitingly cold, and we were freezing. We were seriously thinking about giving up when we saw a white house through the trees. We ran down the last bit of the hill to try and warm up. On the gate was a sign that said Tappers Farm.

'Thank God for that,' said Polly. 'Now all we need is a forest.'

Tristan knocked on the door. There was a lot of yelling and dog barking before it was opened by a very hairy man – like *really* hairy. Like you could hardly see him for hair. He peered at Tristan but didn't speak.

'You must be Mr Tappers,' said Tristan.

'Must I?' said the hairy man, glaring at him.

'The sign on the gate?'

'What about the sign on the gate?'

'Well, it says Tappers Farm. I just presumed.'

'Well, you presumed wrong. What do you want? I ain't got no eggs. Bloody rooster's gay.'

I could see Tristan struggling not to laugh, and the rest of us had to turn away. He cleared his throat. 'We don't want any eggs, sir but we were wondering…' he said in his oh so refined voice.

'Wonderin' what?' the man barked.

'If you had any Christmas trees for sale.'

'How many do you want?'

'Just the one,' said Tristan.

'Round the back. Give me a shout when you find the one you want, and I'll come and chop it down.'

'Splendid,' said Tristan.

Polly smiled her best smile at the hairy man. 'Do you mind if we frolic a bit?'

'You can levitate for all I care,' said the man, going inside and slamming the door.

We walked around the side of the house and there, stretching out in front of us, were hundreds of trees.

'It's a forest,' shouted Stephen. 'It's a bloody forest.'

We had the best time running through the trees trying to find the perfect one.

'This one, Papa,' I shouted.

'This one, Mama,' shouted Polly.

'Frolic and sparkle, girls,' shouted Stephen. 'Frolic and sparkle.'

It was fun being so silly. I smiled, thinking how much Mary would have loved it. At last we all decided on the tree we liked, and Tristan went back to the farmhouse.

The man sawed through the tree with ease. 'Where have you parked?' he said.

'We haven't,' said Polly.

'We walked,' I said.

'Where do you live then?' asked the man.

'Just off the seafront,' I said.

'So how the hell are you going to get it home?'

'We're going to drag it,' said Polly.

He stared at us and then he said, 'I've met some odd people in my time, but you beat the lot of them. You'll be wantin' a lift then?'

'Well if you wouldn't mind,' said Polly. 'We would be very obliged, and we will of course reimburse you for your trouble.'

'You'll do what?' he asked, peering at her through bushy eyebrows.

'Reimburse you, sir, for your trouble.'

'We'll give you some money,' said Stephen.

'Don't want no money – just the five shillings for the tree. I'll have to bring my dog. He don't like being left on his own, and I have to warn you he smells bloody awful.'

We all crammed into a dirty old truck with the very hairy man, who for all his gruffness had a kind heart and a dog that smelt like a dead body.

CHAPTER FIFTY-TWO

When we dragged the Christmas tree into Rose's flat she immediately produced a cardboard box full of ancient decorations. 'They're at least thirty years old,' she said. 'But still good as new.' The fact that they must have been brought out year after year made them all the more special. I wondered if perhaps, one Christmas long ago, little Selina had been entranced by the shiny baubles and sparkling tinsel.

There was a roaring fire blazing away in the grate. We'd turned the main light off, and the room was gently glowing with the flickering of as many candles as we could find. Polly and I had worked all day in Rose's kitchen churning out sausage rolls, sandwiches and prawn vol-au-vents, then we'd gone upstairs and dressed up to the nines. Polly looked amazing in a scarlet catsuit, and I wore a black and white Mary Quant-type dress.

Stephen and Tristan looked wonderful in matching black velvet jackets and colourful cravats. They looked as if they had stepped out of another age, but it was Rose who had outdone us all. She was wearing a floor-length dress of the palest blue chiffon that swished as she moved. Diamond earrings hung from her ears, and silver bracelets circled her wrists. I thought that she looked beautiful. Like the young girl in the poster. I felt privileged to know her, and Polly was mesmerised by her. 'She's fabulous,' she whispered.

'Isn't she though?' I said.

People began to arrive, muffled up in warm coats, fur boots and scarves. I couldn't believe it when I saw my dad walk through the door. I flung my arms around him. 'I'm so glad you're here, Dad. How did Mum manage that?'

'She didn't have to. I've felt a bit on the outside of my kids' lives lately. Clark is always with Emma, Rita is busy with Nigel and the baby, and you've made a new life for yourself. I wanted to see where you lived and meet your new friends.'

'Thanks, Dad,' I said, kissing his cheek. 'You've just made my Christmas.'

'Then I'm glad I came, love.'

Mum and Aunty Brenda made straight for the fire, warming their hands and stamping their feet to get some warmth back into them. It was wonderful to have so many friends and family gathered together in one room. I felt blessed. As I looked around it struck me how different they all were. In age, in life experience and personalities, and yet they were all getting on as if they had known each other forever. I just felt so proud of them all.

This time last year I could never have imagined this. I could never have imagined Mum, Dad and Aunty Brenda here in Oriental Place with Rose and the boys. I could never have imagined Carol and Polly giggling and chatting away, or Tom and Millie playing waiter and waitress to perfection. And then there was Matthew – *my* Matthew.

Polly walked over to me. She was staring at Matthew with her mouth open. 'Are you really telling me that you're just friends? He's gorgeous.'

'I know he is,' I said, making a face at her. 'But he's still just my friend.'

'If you say so,' she said, grinning.

Rose played the piano and we sang all the old familiar carols at the tops of our voices. Matthew and I cuddled up on the pink chaise longue, drinking sweet wine and watching the lights from the candles and the tree reflected in the window. I lay my head on his shoulder and listened as Rose played the most beautiful melodies. Tom had his arm around Polly's waist, and they were swaying gently to the music, and Mum and Dad were dancing cheek to cheek under the mistletoe.

At the end of the evening Matthew and I stood on the front steps looking up at an ink-black sky, heavy with stars, twinkling above our heads. It was so still that you could hear the sound of the waves as they broke on the shore. I kissed Matthew goodbye and watched him walk down the road. I hadn't been looking forward to this festive season. It should have been our first Christmas together – Ralph, Peggy and me – but as I stood there alone on this oh so silent of nights, I felt at peace, and I knew that I was going to be okay.

That night Polly and I shared the bed.

'I'm a bit squiffy,' she said, snuggling down under the blankets, 'but I had a great time.'

'Did you like Carol?'

'She's a really nice girl. I think we'll get on fine.'

'I'm glad. Night night, Polly.'

'Night,' she said, yawning.

I was just starting to drift off when she said…

'Dottie?'

'Mmm.'

'Is Tom married?'

'Tom?' I said.

'Yes, is he married?'

'He's as free as a bird,' I said, smiling into the darkness. 'Why?'

'Just wondered.'

Well I never saw that coming, and yet why not? Polly and Tom eh?

The next day I waved a rather hungover Polly off on the train.

'Have a lovely Christmas,' I said, hugging her.

'You too, Dottie. I'm so glad I came for a visit, because I can see how many people care for you, and I can stop worrying that you're sitting all alone in your flat, sobbing your little heart out.'

'Not any more,' I said. smiling.

I waved until the train was out of sight and walked home. It had been lovely having her here. I'd miss her.

On Christmas morning Matthew came round to Oriental Place, then together we took the bus up to Mum and Dad's. I gave Matthew a small watercolour of the Palace Pier that I'd found in a little shop in the Lanes, and he gave me a beautiful silver bracelet. I loved spending Christmas at home, surrounded by all the familiar things I'd grown up with. Paper chains were strung from wall to wall, and paper lanterns and bells hung from the ceiling. These were the same decorations that Mum brought out year after year. After dinner we watched the Queen's speech on the telly and then caught the bus to Rita's. Dad spent the whole journey moaning about having to take his shoes off in the house and having to go outside to smoke.

He twisted round in his seat. 'She's got a shag carpet, Matthew,' he said. '*You'll* have to take your shoes off as well.'

'I don't mind, Mr Perks,' said Matthew, squeezing my hand.

'Well I bloody do,' said Dad.

'Think yourself lucky you've got shoes to take off,' said Mum. 'When we were kids there were plenty who didn't.'

'You're right, Maureen,' said Dad. 'I forget sometimes.'

'And as for smoking outside, I don't blame our Rita. She wants Miranda Louise to smell like a baby, not a roll-up in a nappy.'

As it turned out we had a really lovely evening. Rita was charming to Matthew, so I could stop worrying about what might come out of her mouth next. Mum was in her element playing with Miranda Louise – who looked as pretty as a picture in a little red velvet dress – and Dad didn't moan once about going outside for a fag. It was the most relaxed I'd ever felt in Rita's company.

The most surprising thing was how well Nigel and Matthew got on.

After Mum and Dad had gone home, Rita and I were in the kitchen washing up, and we could hear Nigel and Matthew chatting away. We made coffees for all of us and took them into the front room.

'Rita, did you know that Matthew is going to be a teacher?' said Nigel.

'Yes, Dottie told me.'

'I always fancied myself as a teacher.'

'You never told me,' said Rita.

'I never told anyone.'

'So why didn't you do it?' I asked.

'My dad had it all mapped out, and he'd decided that I was going to go into insurance the same as him.'

'And you just went along with it?' said Rita.

'I know, not very brave, but I had never questioned my parents' decisions. I was told that that was what I was going to do, and I did it.'

'That is very sad,' said Matthew. 'Having a passion is a wonderful thing, and no one should take it away from you.'

'Well it's too late now, unless our numbers come up on the Premium Bonds.'

Rita smiled at Nigel. 'I think you would have made a great teacher.'

'Really?' said Nigel, looking surprised.

'Yes.'

'Well there's nothing I can do about it now. I suppose I should have fought for it.'

'It's not too late. What about night school?' said Rita.

'Wouldn't you mind?'

'Of course I wouldn't mind. Not if that's what you really want to do. Let's look into it.'

We said goodbye on the doorstep and just as we were going Rita whispered in my ear, 'I think Matthew is lovely,' then she actually kissed my cheek. 'Happy Christmas, Dottie,' she said.

Blimey. Wonders will never cease, I thought.

CHAPTER FIFTY-THREE

Matthew and I saw the new year in quietly, on our own. This was the only new year that we would see in together, and we didn't want to share it with anyone else. As the clocks struck midnight we opened the little window and listened to the eerie sounds of the foghorns from all the boats on the water and the sirens from the power station along the coast at Shoreham. Then the bells from all the churches in Brighton starting ringing out into the night, welcoming in 1970. The sixties were behind us, the decade that had held so many memories, of me and Mary, Ralph and Elton. It had been a time of growing up and a time of saying goodbye, and now it was gone. There was a finality about it that made me sad. Everything about the past made me sad; I couldn't seem to make my peace with it. I didn't want to live in the past, but it felt like it kept dragging me back. I would never forget Mary, and I would always love Ralph, but I had to stop wanting what was gone.

I had been kidding myself when I thought that a year with Matthew would be enough. He'd brought me to life; he'd made me believe in myself. When I was with him I felt safe and cared for. I was going to miss this gentle man. We were just friends, no one would get hurt – that's what I'd told myself. I should have realised that true friendship is every bit as wonderful and precious as a love affair. In fact true friendship is probably the nearest thing to love that you can get.

Our meetings became melancholy, our laughter tinged with sadness as the year crept onwards towards its inevitable end. We packed as much as we could into that final summer together. A small publishing house in Scotland published Matthew's book, and we took a trip up there to see them. They were lovely, and they loved the book. The editor was a tiny bird-like woman called Fiona Morris.

'I have been looking forward to meeting you for so long, Matthew,' she said, smiling up at him. 'We think your book will do very well.' She frowned. 'I hope you don't mind me asking this but is your name really Matthew Smith?'

'My African name is Oscu Kimbali.'

'Why not use it?'

Matthew smoothed back his hair. 'I thought people would take me more seriously with an English name.'

'Well thank you for your honesty, but I think this book deserves to have your real name on it. If I'd written a book as good as this, I would be proud to have my name on the cover.' She shrugged. 'That is only my opinion, but it's not too late to change it.'

Matthew looked at me. 'What do you think, Dottie?'

'I think you should be proud of your heritage, and your African name is part of who you are. You shouldn't be afraid of what others think.'

'Well then,' said Matthew, 'I would like that very much. Very much indeed.'

'Would you like to see the cover?'

Matthew nodded, and Fiona opened her desk drawer and handed him a folder. The picture was breathtaking. It showed the boy Simmi in the baobab tree, gazing into the distance at an orange sun setting behind a mountain. Matthew had tears in his eyes as he thanked her.

We walked hand in hand round Edinburgh. We climbed to the top of the castle and looked down over the beautiful city. It was easier to make memories here, because there were no ghosts. I knew that when I thought about this place it would rest easily on my mind, and I wouldn't be sharing the memory with anyone else – it would belong to Matthew and I alone.

Matthew graduated from college with flying colours, just like I knew he would. We all went to the graduation ceremony. Even Polly came down from London to be with us and, of course, for the chance of being with Tom. It was lovely to see the start of something special happening between my two dear friends.

I didn't know exactly when Matthew was leaving. But now that he had finished college, I realised it was going to be soon, and I was beginning to panic. I had been so sure that I would be strong enough to handle it. If I could say goodbye to Ralph and still survive then saying goodbye to Matthew should be easy. But I knew it wasn't going to be easy at all.

I was cuddled up by the fire in Rose's flat. 'Why am I feeling so bad, Rose?' I said.

'You love him, dear, and when you lose someone you love you mourn that love. Of course you do.'

'It's Ralph that I love.'

'There are different kinds of love, dear.'

'My mum said that to me once.'

'Your mother is a very wise woman.'

'I know.'

'I just thought that it would be easier than this.'

'That would make you foolish, dear, and I know that you are far from that.'

'So I just let him go?'

'He will go home to his sisters, which is what he must do, and you will stay here. Let him go with a smile, dear, because he will be hurting every bit as much as you are. When you truly love someone, you want the best for them, and the best thing that you can do for Matthew is to set him free. Don't make him feel guilty for leaving you.'

Suddenly it seemed so clear. Rose had made sense of it all.

I smiled at her. 'I can do that.'

'I always knew that you could, dear.'

When the time came, Matthew wouldn't let me go to the station. We said goodbye on the beach. We held hands and walked down to the water's edge.

'If you miss me, Dottie, come here and look out across the sea and know that I will be thinking of you on the edge of another ocean.'

'I will always miss you, Matthew, but I'll be okay. We'll both be okay.'

'That is what I needed to hear, my Dottie, and so we can say goodbye, yes?'

'Yes.'

We walked across the road and collected his case from Oriental Place. He said goodbye to Rose and the boys, and I stood on the steps and watched him walk away from me without a backwards glance. I wasn't sorry that I had met this special man. I wasn't sorry that I had walked beside him for this one year. Matthew was gone, but he'd given me new memories and perhaps even taken away some of the ghosts.

I went back inside the house. Rose and the boys were standing in the hallway looking anxious.

'Tea?' said Stephen tentatively.

'Dunking biscuits?' said Tristan.

'That would be perfect,' I said,

Tristan gently wiped away the tears that were running down my cheeks. Stephen hugged me, and Rose took my hand and led me into the front room. I knew that I was going to be all right.

CHAPTER FIFTY-FOUR

Aunty Brenda was sitting at our kitchen table bawling her eyes out.

'I can't believe she's gone, Maureen. The house is so tidy it's doing my head in. I went into her room this morning and found Katie Bunny down the back of the bed. She's never slept a night without Katie Bunny since the day she was born.'

'I suppose that's what growing up is all about, Brenda.'

'To tell you the truth I never thought she'd amount to much. I know that's a terrible thing to say about your own daughter, but you know what she was like. She was a waste of space on a good day. And to top it all, she's decided not to be a Pratt any more.'

'I know, Brenda, and we're all very proud of her.'

'What are you talking about, Maureen?'

Mum looked puzzled.

'She's changing her name, Mum. She doesn't think that Pratt is a good name for a model,' I said, giggling.

'Oh,' said Mum, looking sheepish. 'I thought you meant…'

'We know what you *thought* I meant, Maureen!'

'Sorry, Brenda.'

'Well I think she's going to surprise us all,' I said quickly. 'Living in London, being a model. Who would have thought it? And she's with Polly, not a stranger. Polly will keep an eye on her, and if she's concerned about her she'll let us know.'

'I've got so much to thank you for, Dottie. You've been a good friend to her.'

'I wish we could have been better friends growing up.'

'Well you are now, and that's all that matters.'

'I'm going up to London at the weekend to see them. I can take Katie bunny with me if you like.'

Aunty Brenda smiled at me. 'You're a good girl, Dottie. Are you okay now that Matthew is gone? You must still miss him sometimes.'

'I felt really sad when he first went away, but it's been a few months now, and I'm feeling better about it.'

'It's true, Dottie, about time healing all wounds,' said Aunty Brenda, who had a saying for all occasions.

Maybe not all wounds, I thought.

'He was a lovely man,' said Aunty Brenda. 'Such a gentleman. I really thought that you two might have made a go of it.'

'Just friends.'

'I wish some of your sense would rub off on my Carol.'

'I think Carol is going to be fine.'

'I hope so.'

Aunty Brenda finished her tea and put the cup and saucer in the sink. 'I'll pop home and get Katie Bunny,' she said. 'Give you two some time on your own.'

I knew that there was something on Mum's mind. I could tell as soon as I'd walked in, and Aunty Brenda's hasty departure was suspect. It was confirmed when Mum reached across the table and held my hand.

'What is it, Mum?'

'I haven't known whether to tell you or not, but I didn't want you bumping into him and getting a fright.'

'Bumping into who?' I said, but I knew who she meant. Ralph. I suddenly felt as if I'd eaten a huge meal that hadn't digested properly. Or maybe it was longing that was filling up my whole body. A longing to run round to his house, to hammer on his door, to be wherever he was.

'Oh dear, I shouldn't have said anything. You've gone white as a sheet,' said Mum, standing up. 'I'll get you a cup of sweet tea.'

I couldn't speak. I watched her put the kettle on and stand with her back to the sink waiting for it to boil. I could feel my heart thumping out of my chest. Why did it always have to be like this? It wasn't fair. I was doing all right; I was coping. Having him on the other side of the world was less painful than bumping into him on my doorstep, and now he was here, and all the old feelings of love and loss came rushing back. I felt helpless.

'Are they *all* here?' I said.

'I know Peggy is with him, and I imagine Fiona must be too.'

'They're not back for good, are they?' I felt sick; I couldn't bear it if they were back for good.

Mum poured the tea and sat back down at the table.

'Just a holiday. I bumped into Mrs Pickles. She's so happy to be seeing Peggy.'

'Do you know when they're going back?'

'I didn't like to ask,' said Mum, shovelling sugar into my cup. 'It seemed a strange thing to ask. Was I wrong to tell you?'

'No, Mum. At least if I *do* bump into them I won't make a fool of myself.'

'That's what I thought.'

Well at least I was going away at the weekend, and I wouldn't have to worry about bumping into them in London. If only I could hide away in London until they went back.

I was sitting on the couch in 59 Victoria Terrace, watching Polly pouring two glasses of wine and putting them on the coffee table. 'Why couldn't he just stay in bloody Australia?' she said. 'Why does he have to come back and upset you again?'

'I suppose he wants to see his parents and let Peggy visit with her grandparents. They were bound to come back to visit some-time. I'm just finding it hard to get my head around.'

I took a sip of the wine. It was cold and sharp – it was lovely. I leaned back against the cushions. 'I just wish it didn't affect me so badly. I think I've made my peace with it, then Mum mentions he's in Brighton and I go to pieces. Why do I do that, Polly?'

'I think you know the answer to that one, my friend.'

Of course I knew the answer. Time and distance hadn't changed the fact that I loved him.

'Do you know how long they're staying?'

'Mum didn't like to ask.'

I picked up my glass of wine and walked across to the window. I felt empty inside. Polly had Tom, Carol was starting a whole new exciting life as a model and what did I have? A lifetime of memories but no one to love.

'You won't always feel like this, Dottie, you won't.'

I turned around and looked at her. 'Well I have for most of my life.'

'But you haven't been *sad* for most of your life, have you?'

I smiled at her. 'No, I haven't. I'm just feeling a bit sorry for myself.'

'You're allowed to do that. Just not for too long.' She stood up and went across to the record player. She selected an LP and put it on. The sound of Paul McCartney singing 'Yesterday' filled the room.

'Why did you choose that one? It's one of the saddest songs on the record.'

'I thought you could have a good old cry, get it all out and then we can talk about *my* love life for a change.'

Polly always helped me to laugh at myself. 'I'm a selfish cow, aren't I?'

'Totally. I don't know why I love you so much.'

'So tell me – how is it going? I really *do* want to know,' I said.

Polly seemed to light up from the inside. 'I can't tell you how perfectly happy I am, Dottie,' she said, smiling.

'I'm so glad, but I would never have put you and Tom together in a million years.'

'Why not?'

'Because you're my best friend, and Tom's my boss. Two different parts of my life. But I couldn't be happier for you both.'

'He's changed my life, Dottie. I can't wait to hear his voice on the phone. I can't wait for his visits. Victoria station has become my favourite place to be.'

Polly's happiness was infectious. I reached across the couch and put my arms around her.

We were still like that when Carol came flying up the stairs and burst into the room.

'What's wrong?' I asked, jumping up.

'Oh hello, Dottie. Get me a drink quick. I've just met the Beatles.'

'You've just met who?' I screamed.

'The Beatles – all four of them! They spoke – they actually spoke!'

'To you?'

'They said hello in that funny accent.'

'Did you say hello back?' asked Polly.

'I couldn't speak.'

'You just met the Beatles and you didn't speak to them?' I said.

'Not a squeak,' said Carol, giggling. 'Not a bloody squeak.'

So not only was Carol becoming a model she'd actually met the Beatles. She's been in the same room, breathing the same air as Paul McCartney – *my* Paul McCartney, as my dad once said. My life was going down faster than the Titanic. Not that I was bloody jealous or anything.

CHAPTER FIFTY-FIVE

On the train back to Brighton my tummy was in knots. I was expecting that, but what I wasn't expecting was this overwhelming sensation of coming alive, of feeling the blood pumping through my veins, filling my body. I had forgotten how that felt, and I wanted to hold onto it, hug it to my chest. Ralph was going to be there, in the town where I lived, around the next corner, passing on the other side of the road, walking on the beach. We would be breathing the same air – no oceans between us, only a distance that was of our own making.

I saw the letter as soon as I came through the door. It was propped up on the dresser in the hall where Rose put all our mail. I knew from the handwriting that it was from Ralph. I ran up the stairs to the flat. I couldn't wait to open it, yet I was scared stiff at what it was going to say. I sat on the bed and turned it over and over in my hand. There was no stamp on it, so I guessed Ralph must have delivered it by hand. I took it out of the envelope. It was just one page. I began to read.

Dear Dottie,

I have started to write this letter so many times, but today I am going to finish it. I've wanted to see you ever since we returned to Brighton but didn't know whether you wanted to hear from me. We are going back to Australia on Wednesday, and I would love to see you before I go. I will wait for you on our bench in the Lagoon every evening between six and eight. I don't want to cause you any pain, and I realise that I am probably being totally selfish, but it would mean so much to see you. Please try and come, Dottie.

Love,

Ralph x

I must have read it a thousand times and changed my mind a thousand times. It was Sunday, so I had three days to make a decision. Was I strong enough for another goodbye? Could I go through all that again? I didn't know. I decided to run it past the boys.

Tristan read the letter. 'Dilemma, darling. Dilemma,' he said, passing it to Stephen.

'He does seem to make a habit of pulling you back in, doesn't he?' said Stephen.

Tristan took hold of my hand. 'What is your heart telling you to do, dear girl?'

'Run as fast as I can to the Lagoon.'

'And your head?'

'Get drunk and go to bed.'

'My heart wins every time,' said Stephen.

'It does, doesn't it,' said Tristan, smiling at him.

The three of us sat quietly, mulling it over.

'What about a dummy run?' said Stephen suddenly.

'What do you mean?' I said.

'Well let's go the Lagoon and see if he's there.'

'What if he sees us?'

'We'll wear a disguise.'

'What sort of disguise?' I said, giggling. Only these wonderful men could make me laugh about it all.

'Sunglasses.'

'And you don't think we might look a bit suspicious. Three of us lurking behind a bush wearing sunglasses?'

'Where's this bench he's on about?' said Tristan.

'Just inside the entrance to the Lagoon.'

'Then we could approach from the seafront and hide behind the café. Can you see the bench from there?'

'I think so.'

'We can pretend we're in a James Bond film,' said Stephen.

'Are you up for it, Dottie?' said Tristan.

'Okay, we'll do it,' I said, grinning.

'Dark coats,' said Stephen.

Tristan smiled at him. 'Absolutely.'

It was almost a quarter to seven by the time we reached the Lagoon. I was feeling excited and nervous at the thought of seeing Ralph.

'It's bloody freezing,' said Stephen, pulling his coat around him.

'James Bond never lets the weather get in the way of an important mission,' said Tristan.

'But James Bond isn't as delicate as me,' said Stephen, pulling a pathetic face.

'Well you'll just have to man up, darling.'

We slid down the grassy bank at the back of the café and peered round the side of it. The bench was further away than I had thought, and it was dark.

'Can you see him?' asked Stephen. 'Is he there?'

I peered into the darkness. It was hard to tell from this distance.

'I'll get closer,' said Tristan.

'He'll see you.'

'I'll be careful,' said Tristan in a weird kind of Sean Connery voice.

'That accent's making me go all shivery,' said Stephen.

Tristan grinned. 'Calm yourself, dear boy. Okay cover me – I'm going in!'

'Be careful,' said Stephen. 'And return to us safely.'

'If anything happens to me, remember that I love you both very much.'

Stephen started giggling, which started me off, which started Tristan off, so that he couldn't go anywhere till we'd all calmed down.

'Oh this is such fun,' said Stephen, wiping his eyes on his coat sleeve.

I hadn't laughed so much in ages. The love of my life was probably only yards away, and here I was playing at being a spy. The whole thing was becoming quite bizarre.

We watched Tristan walk across the children's playground towards the bench.

There was a bitter wind blowing in from the sea, and we were getting colder by the minute.

'What we do for love, eh?' said Stephen, stamping his feet, trying to get some warmth into them.

After what seemed like forever Tristan slid down the bank and joined us.

'Well?' I said.

'Yes, it's definitely your Ralph.'

What had felt like a silly game a minute ago now felt real. Ralph was a couple of hundred feet away. I felt sick.

Stephen put his arm around my shoulder. 'Shall we see you back home then?'

'I thought this was just a dummy run,' I said, panicking.

'Well you're here now, girl, so you might as well put the poor boy out of his misery.'

'Do you want to see him, darling?' asked Tristan gently.

I took a deep breath. 'Yes,' I said.

'Well go on then, and like Stephen said we'll see you at home.'

I gave them both a hug and began to walk across the park. Ralph was standing by the lake, looking out over the water. I watched him for a few moments, drinking him in, unable to deny my feelings for him.

'Ralph?' I said. He turned around and his face lit up. He was only a few steps away. Just a few steps and I could hold him in my arms. Every part of my body was screaming to hold him.

'I didn't think you were coming.'

'I wasn't sure myself, but I'm here.'

'Yes, you are,' he said, smiling.

We stood there staring at each other, not knowing what to say, but it didn't matter. We were here, we were together, and that was all that mattered. And then I was in his arms. Touching him, breathing him in. I couldn't get enough of him.

'You're cold,' he said, touching my face.

'It doesn't matter.'

'I've missed you so much Dottie. I've missed you so much.'

I looked into his lovely green eyes, my heart was full of him. I shivered.

'Let's get you into the warm,' he said. 'There's a pub up on the main road. Shall we go there?'

I nodded.

There weren't many people in the pub, so we had our choice of tables. We chose one close to a lovely open fire. I took off my coat, and Ralph went to get us a drink. I watched him as he stood at the bar. He was so familiar to me – the way he stood, the width of his shoulders, the way his hair curled over his collar. Time fell away. It was as if I had only seen him yesterday – that's how it had always been between us. My tummy was making little rumbling noises. I didn't know whether it was nerves or the fact that I hadn't eaten. I just wished it would stop.

'Warming up?' he said, coming back with the drinks.

'Mmm.'

Ralph sat down opposite me and sipped his drink. 'I don't know what to say to you now you're here except thank you for coming.'

'I wasn't sure that I should, but I wanted to see you. I knew I would regret it if I didn't.'

He looked down at his hands. 'I just couldn't go back without at least trying.'

He was as nervous as me, and somehow that made me feel calmer. This was Ralph, the boy I loved. Maybe seeing him again wasn't the greatest idea in the world, but if I was really honest with myself I knew that I would see him before I'd even opened the envelope. I smiled at him. I took a sip of my drink. 'So how is Australia?'

I could see him visibly relax. 'Different, very different. It's a lovely country.'

'And how are you?'

'I managed to get another apprenticeship.'

'Plumbing?'

'Yes, plumbing.'

'And you're happy?'

He started messing with his hair, the way he always did when he was nervous. There was a sadness in his eyes as he looked at me.

' I'm doing the best I can,' he said.

He reached across the table and held my hand. 'Oh, Dottie.'

My heart was so full of love for this boy, but he was going to leave me again. I was going to have to say goodbye again. I shook my head. 'What do you want me to say, Ralph? I don't know what to say.'

'I know, and I'm sorry. I just wanted to see you again. I didn't mean to upset you.' He stared into the fire as if searching for the right thing to say then looked back at me. 'I have so many regrets. Some days I feel as though I'm living someone else's life. I miss you."

'I miss you too,' I said softly.

The drink and the warmth from the fire were making me feel calmer. I loved seeing Ralph's face across the table. I could have stayed there forever, but it made me feel sad, because for us there had never been a forever.

'We never really fought for us, did we?' I said sadly. 'Not really. Maybe we could have made it work if we had been a bit braver.'

'And now it's too late. Is it too late, Dottie?'

'You can't keep running away. You have Peggy to look after, and you can't let Fiona down again.' I hadn't realised that I was crying until Ralph wiped away the tears that were running down my face.

'This isn't what I wanted. I didn't want to hurt you. I don't know what I thought. That maybe we could just talk.'

'About what, Ralph?'

'I've got it wrong again, haven't I?'

'Not wrong. I didn't have to come, and Ralph?'

'Yes, my love?'

'I'm glad I came.'

'Really?'

'Really.'

After that we just sat quietly gazing into the fire, both of us lost in our own thoughts. There was nothing left to say. As we got up to leave, Ralph took a letter out of his pocket and handed it to me.

'From Peggy,' he said. 'She did a drawing for you.'

I took the letter. I was touched that she had wanted to write to me. 'How is she?'

'She's happy. She's made some friends. She's even getting a bit of an Aussie accent.'

'Thank her for me, won't you?'

'You can thank her yourself. I've put our address on the back.'

We walked home along the seafront. The sea was choppy and dark, bashing against the old stone wall. The lights from the two piers further along the coast looked welcoming in comparison.

We said goodbye on the steps of 55 Oriental Place. I clung on to him as if I was drowning. I couldn't believe that we were saying goodbye again.

He held my face in his hands. 'I love you,' he said. 'I always will.'

I watched him walk down the road. I watched him until he was nothing more than a shadow. He was alive, he was well and every night we slept under the same sky. For now that was enough. For now that would have to be enough.

CHAPTER FIFTY-SIX

Six months have passed since that day. It was hard at first, and I struggled through the days. I became withdrawn, and I knew that my friends and family were worried about me. One morning I woke up, looked in the mirror and said, 'Okay, Dottie Perks, enough is enough. You have a life to live. It might not be the one you wanted but it's *your* life, and it's up to you to make something of it.

I had a whole week off, because – hallelujah – the landlord of the building we worked in was at last going to replace the rickety steps. All the mail was being delivered to the bookmaker's downstairs, so all I had to do was walk to work every morning, collect the manuscripts and work at home. It was like being on holiday.

Being at home every day, I noticed that Rose had stopped going for her daily walk with Colin. In fact she seemed to have stopped going out altogether.

'I'm just a bit under the weather, dear,' she said when I asked her about it.

The boys took turns going downstairs to sit with her. Sometimes it would be lunchtime and she would still be in her dressing gown. She was adamant that there was nothing wrong with her, and however much we nagged, she refused to see a doctor. We were all worried.

The new stairs were installed, and I went back to work. Every evening I had a quick bite to eat and then took over from the boys and sat with Rose. Mostly she slept. When she wasn't sleeping she would talk about the past. She talked about her days in the theatre, telling me about the people she had worked with and the beautiful dresses she had worn. She talked about her oriental gentleman, and she talked about Selina, her perfect little girl. Then she'd close her eyes, and I would lose her for a while.

None of us knew what to do. Even Colin sensed there was something wrong and rarely left her side.

'Well I think we should just get a doctor in whatever she says. The woman's ill – we can all see that,' said Tristan.

'But she doesn't want a doctor,' said Stephen. 'Shouldn't we respect that?'

'No, I don't think we should. She's not eating enough to keep a bird alive.'

'She doesn't seem to be in any pain though, does she,' I said.

'Well we've got to do something,' said Tristan.

'What if I moved downstairs so she's not on her own?' I said.

Tristan nodded. 'I think that would be good.'

'Do you think she'll mind?'

Stephen smiled. 'Tell her it's that or the doctor.'

I moved into Rose's flat, and I slept in the little box room next to her bedroom. I think she liked me being there, and we all felt better knowing that she wasn't on her own.

One evening we were listening to some old records on the gramophone. The man that was singing had the most amazing voice. 'Who's this singing?' I asked.

'It's the great Mario Lanza,' said Rose, smiling. 'In my day he was every girl's dream – a heart-throb, dear, like your Paul McCartney.'

'Was he as good-looking as Paul?'

'He was Italian, dear, dark and handsome.'

'And tall?'

'Not so tall, dear. Italian men very often come up short, but he made up for it in looks. He was a film star as well. His most famous film was *The Student Prince*; I went to the pictures every night it was on.'

'Does he still sing?'

'He died young, dear. It was very sad – he was only thirty-eight.'

'What did he die of?'

'Too much drink, too much food – too much of everything, dear.'

'That's really sad. My Paul's not like that.'

'I'm glad, dear. Mario Lanza was a great loss to the world of music, but he was his own worst enemy.'

Suddenly she started coughing. I jumped up from the chair. 'Can I get you something, Rose? A cup of tea?'

'Not just now, dear. Maybe later.'

'We're all worried about you, you know.'

'I know you are, dear, and I'm sorry to cause you worry.'

'Don't you think it would be better if you knew what was wrong?'

'I know what's wrong, dear.'

'You *know* what's wrong?'

'Yes, dear.'

I didn't understand.

'I'm dying, dear.'

I stared at her. I couldn't take in what she was saying. 'No, you're not,' I shouted.

'Don't be upset, dear. I've known for a long time. I'm at peace with it.'

'Well I'm bloody well not. You're talking as if there's nothing that can be done. There must be something they can do. Some treatment – there *must* be.'

'That's not what I want, dear, and I need you and Stephen and Tristan to help me with this decision.'

'But why don't you want any treatment? You can't want to die.'

'Of course I don't want to die, dear, but I'm *going* to die, and I want to do it my way. I don't want to be stuck in a hospital bed getting pumped full of poison just for a few more months of life. I want to die here in Oriental Place. This is where all my memories are, dear, and this is where I want to end my days.'

I knelt down on the floor beside her chair and took her hands in mine. I had grown to love this woman, and I couldn't bear to lose her, but this wasn't about me. Tears were running down my face. 'If that's what you want, Rose, then that's the way it's going to be.'

'And the boys?'

'Will feel the same. We'll look after you the way you've looked after us.'

'Thank you, dear,' she said and closed her eyes.

The three of us stayed with her until the end. Most of the time she slept, but we played her music on the old radiogram and hoped that she would hear it. She died early one morning as the sun was coming up over the sea. She looked so peaceful, and I was so glad that she had been able to die in the house where she had been so happy. Our hearts were broken. Oriental Place seemed to die a little too.

Stephen and Tristan took the pale blue chiffon dress to the undertaker. We wanted her to look as fabulous in death as she had in life.

One night we all sat together in Rose's front room. This was where we felt closest to her.

'Did Rose ever mention any family?' I asked.

Tristan shook his head. 'I think a niece may have visited once, but that was a long time ago, and I don't remember Rose mentioning anyone else.'

'How do we find out?'

'I really don't know.'

'If she *has* got family somewhere then shouldn't they be planning her funeral? And wouldn't the house be theirs?'

'Perhaps we should put a notice in the paper. Someone might know something.'

So that's what we decided to do. I called in at the open-all-hours and spoke to Mr Raji. He called his wife and told her that Rose had died. Mrs Raji broke down in tears.

'Lovely lady,' she said. 'And so brave. Her husband was a lovely man too, a true gentleman. I am very sorry for your loss.'

'Thank you. We want to put an advertisement in the paper, to see if Rose had any relatives. Can you do that?'

'Yes, of course. Just write down what you want to say and I will telephone it through.'

I took a piece of paper out of my pocket. 'We already have,' I said, handing it to him.

'Do you know if she had any family, Mrs Raji?'

She shook her head. 'They were always on their own, always together. Do you remember anyone, Basu?'

'No, there was only the two boys she took in. Terrible business that was.'

'What do you mean?'

'I don't think that is for the young lady's ears, Basu.'

'I'd like to know,' I said. 'If you don't mind telling me.'

'If you're sure,' he said.

'You *are* talking about Stephen and Tristan, aren't you?'

'Yes, yes. Stephen and Tristan.'

Mr Raji went to the shop door and changed the sign from open to closed.

'Please come through to the back,' said Mrs Raji.

I followed her into the back of the shop.

'Please sit down,' she said gently, 'and Mr Raji will explain.'

I sat down and so did Mrs Raji, but her husband remained standing.

'It was a gang of hoodlums,' he said. 'They attacked them one night, right here on the seafront. Mrs Toshimo heard them screaming. When she got to them, one of them was naked, tied to a lamp post and covered in paint, poor boy. They had the other one pinned to the ground. Mrs Toshimo went right in there, right in the middle of them, and she saved those boys.'

I could feel my eyes filling with tears. I knew something bad had happened but nothing like this.

'Then she took both of them into her home, and they never left. It was all over the papers.'

'Did they find the people that did it?'

'Oh yes, they found them, but they got no more than a slap on the wrist.'

The tears that had been threatening to engulf me spilled from my eyes, and I was sobbing.

'Yes, you cry dear girl,' said Mrs Raji. 'Tears will ease the pain.'

I tried to control myself. 'It's just so sad.'

'It got even sadder,' said Mr Raji. 'Those sweet young men had to go to court to prove that they were not homosexual. Their pictures were in all the papers. They suffered more than that gang of thugs.'

'Basu, get the young lady a glass of water.'

'It's so hard to take in,' I said.

Mr Raji came back with the water. I sipped at it.

'Better?' asked Mrs Raji.

I nodded. 'We would like you to come to the funeral,' I said.

'It would be an honour,' said Mr Raji. 'Just let us know when it is and we will shut the shop.'

We waited as long as we could, but no one came forward from the inquiry in the *Evening Argus*. And so Rose was buried. The little church was packed. Polly came down from London. Tom and Millie were there. Local shopkeepers, friends from her days in the theatre and of course all of my family.

Stephen, Tristan, Tom and Nigel carried the coffin into the church to the voice of Mario Lanza singing 'Only a Rose'. We had a small gathering afterwards at Oriental Place and we played all Rose's favourite songs. Rita sat beside me on the pink chaise longue and held my hand. Miranda Louise made everyone laugh with her baby giggles and smiles, but there was no Rose, and it was a sad little affair.

The three of us continued living at Oriental Place, but we weren't sure whether we actually had any right to be there. None of us wanted to live anywhere else. This was our home, and it was Stephen's place of safety – I understood that now.

'I wish we were rich,' said Tristan. 'We could buy the place.'

'But who would we be buying it from?'

'I suppose if there's no relatives then it reverts back to the state. I think that's how it works.'

About a week after the funeral we got a letter from a solicitor. His name was Miles Granger, and his offices were in North Street. He asked to see all of us.

'I can only think of one reason he wants to see us and that's to ask us to vacate the house,' said Tristan.

We were all feeling pretty miserable as we trudged up the hill to North Street. It was bad enough losing Rose, but it looked as though we were about to lose our home as well.

A young girl ushered us into Miles Granger's office. He came round his desk and shook each of our hands. He must have been in his early fifties. He was just as you would imagine a solicitor called Miles Granger would look. He was impeccably dressed in a dark blue suit, white shirt and red tie, and he had a lovely kind face. At least if we were going to be given bad news it helped that he looked friendly.

'Now,' he said, sitting back behind his desk. 'Have you brought your birth certificates as I asked?'

'I have them here,' said Tristan, handing him all three birth certificates.

We hadn't a clue why he wanted them. I guess we were about to find out.

It was very quiet in the room as Miles Granger shuffled through some papers. We waited. He smiled at us.

'Maud Roberts came to see me three months ago. She knew that she was dying, and she wanted to settle her affairs. I have here her last will and testament. It is very simple and straightforward. She has bequeathed her house, known as 55 Oriental Place, and all monies in bank accounts and shares equally to Mr Tristan James Blake, Mr Stephen Clive Palmer, Miss Dorothy Ava Perks and Colin. I don't have a surname for Colin.'

'Colin's a cat,' said Stephen. 'But who's Maud Roberts?'

The solicitor looked down at some papers on his desk.

'Oh I'm terribly sorry. Mrs Roberts did tell me that you knew her as Rose Toshimo.'

You could have heard a pin drop in the room. The three of us stared at Miles Granger as if he had three heads.

'Are you quite sure?' said Tristan eventually.

'Quite sure,' said the solicitor, smiling at us.

'So we don't have to move?' said Stephen.

'Not if you don't want to. What you do with the house now is up to you.'

Stephen burst into tears. Tristan and I were close to it.

'Can I offer you a drink? You look as if you need one.'

'I think we'd like to go home,' I said. I looked at the others and they nodded.

'Well if I can't interest you in a drink then perhaps you would like to have a little celebration later,' he said, opening a cabinet and handing Tristan a bottle of what looked like champagne.

'I will be in touch,' he said, seeing us to the door.

We all shook his hand and thanked him.

'Don't thank me,' he said. 'Thank the lovely Maud.'

'Rose,' said Stephen. 'She's Rose to us.'

'Of course,' said the solicitor, smiling.

We didn't speak all the way home. We were in total shock. Tristan opened the front door, and we went inside. We stood in the middle of Rose's front room and looked at each other.

'So Rose was really Maud,' said Tristan. 'And she was never married to Mr Toshimo.'

'She never lied to us though, did she?' I said. 'I mean I never once heard her refer to him as her husband. She always called him her oriental gentleman.'

'I think our Rose was a bit of a dark horse,' said Tristan, smiling.

'Do we really own this house?' asked Stephen, looking around the room.

Tristan smiled at him. 'We do, my love.'

I walked over to Rose's cabinet and got out three of her best crystal glasses. 'I think this is what she would have wanted,' I said.

Tristan poured the champagne and we raised our glasses to the poster of 'Madame Rose. The girl with the magic fingers.'

'To Rose,' we said in unison.

CHAPTER FIFTY-SEVEN

It had been Tristan's idea to turn Oriental Place into a theatrical boarding house, and although I wasn't that sure to begin with, it was proving to be a huge success. It had taken about six months before we were ready to open it to guests. Rose had never used the basement, and when the three of us had first stood in the gloomy damp space beneath the house I understood why.

'Okay,' Tristan had said. 'It doesn't look much now...'

'You can say that again,' I'd said. 'It's awful. It smells like something's died down here.'

Stephen had done a bit of a twirl. 'Imagine pink carpets and chandeliers, darling.'

Tristan had smiled at him. 'We were thinking of a B&B, dearest, not a ballroom.'

'Just trying to bring a positive note to the proceedings.' Stephen had looked around. 'Okay, maybe not a ballroom, but wouldn't it make a wonderful kitchen-diner?'

I hadn't been convinced. 'Really?'

Stephen had put his arm around my shoulder. 'Think outside the box, Dottie. French dressers, wooden floorboards, onions hanging off the ceiling.'

'Onions hanging off the ceiling?'

'Work with me, Dottie.'

'Believe me, Stephen, I'm trying.

'And me and Tristan looking fabulous in matching aprons, cooking up a storm.'

'If you say so,' I'd said, giggling.

And that's where we standing now, in our beautiful kitchen, minus the onions, admiring the sparkling white dishwasher that had just been delivered.

'Imagine,' said Stephen, examining his hands. 'No more washing-up. Bliss.'

The boys had been running the boarding house for five years, and although it was hard work they loved every second. I'd moved back to my flat on the top floor, and we'd turned Rose's sitting room into the residents' lounge. The hallway was now a reception area, complete with a beautiful mahogany desk we'd bought from a little antique shop in the Lanes. We had had such fun in those early days, kitting the place out and renovating the basement. We had kept Rose's sitting room almost exactly as it had been when Rose was alive, complete with the faded pink chaise longue and the green velvet chairs. The posters were still on the wall, and the piano still had pride of place in front of the window. At first Tristan and I had wanted to put new furniture in there, but as Stephen pointed out, 'It's perfect as it is. It looks like a stage set for *The Importance of Being Earnest*. They'll love it.'

He'd been right – no one who stayed in Oriental Place felt intimidated. They loved the old-world charm. They felt at home there and came back year after year. It was like having old friends to stay. Various actors and performers would sit in the lounge, reminiscing about plays and musicals they'd been in. Someone was always tinkling on the piano or playing the old radiogram. The house had come alive again, with Stephen and Tristan taking centre stage as the magnificently flamboyant hosts. They had found their place; they weren't scared any more. If Rose was looking down, I think she would have approved.

When Miranda Louise turned five she started school, and Rita joined us at Oriental Place. We had become so busy that we welcomed her with open arms. She helped the boys in the kitchen and served at the tables. The most surprising thing of all was how well the three of them got on. I would often hear shrieks of laughter coming from the kitchen. She stopped taking herself so seriously – Tristan and Stephen wouldn't let her. These days when she tried to take the moral high ground it was easier to bat her down without her taking offence, and she and I became friends at last. This made me very happy; I really felt that I had my sister back – the sister I remembered from when we were children. I didn't kid myself that we wouldn't still have the odd spat, but something had changed, and I knew that we would be okay.

Mum and Dad didn't say much about it, but I could tell how pleased they were.

As for Carol, well we didn't see much of her these days, but when she did come home she was driving a flashy new car. Aunty Brenda told anyone who would listen about her famous daughter, the model.

The annual summer show was playing at the end of the West Pier so all our rooms were full. We had twin sisters staying who were contortionists and did very bendy things with their bodies. They looked perfectly normal at breakfast, but I went to see the show with my mum and my Aunty Brenda, and we were totally shocked. As Aunty Brenda said, 'There's nothing natural about that, Dottie. Legs aren't supposed to go round the back of your neck.'

'Well the way I see it,' said Mum, 'if they can make money out of having a bendy body then good luck to them. I wish mine was more bendy.'

I had decided to stay at the agency and let the boys run the boarding house. I loved my job, and I hadn't been ready to give it up. Between us, Millie and I had found a lot of new authors. I was good at my job, and I was getting better at discovering those diamonds in the rough that Tom was looking for. Every day was exciting – every manuscript I took off the pile could be the next big thing. Millie and I arranged book launches. We dressed up and swanned around, feeling glamorous and just a little bit important. I was never going to be a writer, but I loved being around them. I was in awe of them. I was a round peg in a round hole and I loved it.

Tristan said, 'That's all very well, darling, but you can't make your job your life. I'm not saying that you should go out with any old Tom, Dick or Harry that happens to be passing the front door, but there must be someone out there for you, and you won't find them slaving away all day and staying in all evening.'

'My heart is already taken,' I said, making a face at him.

'I don't know why you don't take the "No Vacancy" sign out of the window and hang it round your neck.'

'I might just do that,' I said, grinning.

Polly moved to Brighton, and she and Tom got married in a lovely little church overlooking the Downs. After the ceremony we all piled onto the Palace Pier and rode the carousel and the ghost train, screaming like teenagers as cobwebs brushed our faces and ghostly images jumped out of the darkness. At the end of the day we all went back to Oriental Place for drinks and a knees-up. Polly and Tom were a perfect match, and we were all delighted with the arrival of their twins Kate and Charlie. Polly and I laughed ourselves silly when we realised the significance of their names. We took to calling them Mr and Mrs Dickens.

Millie was the biggest surprise of all, having shacked up with Malcolm the bathing-hut man, who adored her and turned out to be quite the knight in shining armour. I'd never seen her look so happy.

And as for me I'd resigned myself to the fact that I was destined to be alone, and I was happy with that – well most of the time I was. In bed at night when the house had settled down and everyone was asleep I thought about Ralph. I wondered if he and Fiona had had a child of their own. As far as I knew they had never come back to England again. I wondered if he was happy, and I wondered if he ever thought about me. I had kept in touch with Peggy. I sent cards for birthdays and Christmases. I sent little gifts. She wrote little notes back to me. Ralph always added something at the bottom of the page. Nothing momentous, just thanking me for Peggy's present or telling me how she was doing at school. He always asked how I was and always ended it with a kiss. I kept all the letters in a little box under my bed, and I would often take them out and read them. It was a connection; it made me feel closer to them. As Peggy got older she was able to tell me more about her life and her friends. She even told me about a boy in her class that she liked. I cherished every one of those letters.

And so life went on, and it was a good life, a full life. I loved my job, I had great friends and family, and I told myself that I didn't need anything else. That was until the day I went to visit my mum.

'You're looking well, Dottie,' she said, smiling at me as I kissed her cheek.

'So are you, Mum. You've done something to your hair. It looks nice.'

'Your Aunty Brenda gave me one of those home perms. You know, the ones that come in a box.'

'Mary and I used to sell those at Woolworths.'

'Your dad says I look like Rita Hayworth. I've made him an appointment at the opticians.'

I laughed. 'I'm sure Dad's eyes are perfectly fine.'

'I've just made some tea.'

I laughed. 'You've always just made some tea.'

'It's the Irish in me, Dottie. The Irish live on tea. I think my mother gave it to me in my bottle instead of milk.'

'You never talk much about your parents, Mum.'

'I suppose I've been too busy bringing you children up to think about my own childhood.'

'You were happy though?'

'Oh yes, love. Mum was a bit strict, but she had to be, because my dad was soft as butter. I wish you could have known him, Dottie. He was a wonderful man, and he would have loved you.'

'I wish I could have known him.'

'My heart broke the day he died, but life goes on, doesn't it? We learn to go on. And you, my love, are you happy?'

'I'm fine, Mum. Busy but fine.'

'I'm glad, Dottie.'

Mum started to pour the tea. I think I knew what she was going to say before she said it.

'They're back you see, love. For good this time. They're back for good.'

After leaving Mum's I didn't want to go back to Oriental Place – there were too many people there, and I really needed to be on my own to sort my stupid head out. I walked all the way along the seafront to the Lagoon. This was where Ralph and I had said goodbye. This was where he had told me that he was going to Australia. I can remember feeling so empty as I walked away from him that day, but I can also remember a sense of relief knowing that I wasn't going to bump into him, knowing that I wouldn't have to keep looking over my shoulder all the time. It was final – he was going away for good. I could, at last, find some peace. As it turned out I *had* seen him again. He'd turned my life upside down again, and I'd had to get over him again. This was beginning to feel like a recurring nightmare. Why couldn't they stay in bloody Australia? Why come back to Brighton? Wasn't this world big enough to find somewhere else to live? There were hundreds of cities and towns to choose from. Brighton was a small town – I was bound to see them, and I didn't know how I was going to handle it.

I sat on our bench overlooking the lake. The bench where Ralph and I had sat and dreamed our dreams of a future to-gether. Two seventeen-year-olds, little more that kids really, but we knew what we wanted and didn't doubt for one second that we'd get it.

I could hear the sound of children playing in the playground on the other side of the green and the clanging of a bell on the little railway behind me. Dad used to take Rita and me here when we were kids. Each carriage had a bell in it with a rope hanging down that we'd ring as we travelled round and round. That's how I felt about me and Ralph – that we just went round and round, not going anywhere but not able to get off.

I had to get over this. I was thirty-one now. I had loved Ralph almost all my life. I had given him my childhood and my youth. I had cried so many tears over him that it was a wonder I had any tears left. I had given him my heart, and I had loved him, and I had trusted him. I had said goodbye to him over and over again. Well I wasn't about to run away this time. I had Oriental Place, I had friends, I had a life, and I was determined to live it the best way that I could.

I hurried back along the seafront. I couldn't wait to get home. Oriental Place was real – it was solid. It didn't break my heart; it didn't let me down. I was holding my head up high as I opened the front door.

I didn't recognise her at first, the girl with the red hair sitting next to Tristan on the pink chaise longue. Then I looked into her eyes and it was as if Mary was looking back at me. She stood up. Peggy at twelve was taller than Mary had ever been.

She looked unsure as she said, 'Dottie?'

I put my arms around her, and she started to cry. I looked at Tristan over her shoulder.

He stood up. I nodded as he went towards the door, and he looked back at me and smiled.

I eased Peggy back onto the couch and sat down beside her. 'Don't cry,' I said.

'I'm so sorry! Oh, Dottie, I'm so sorry.'

'What do you have to be sorry for?'

'Everything! I spoiled everything, didn't I? Dad said I hadn't, but I knew I had. I knew that it was all my fault.'

I took a hankie out of my pocket and gently wiped away her tears. 'You were just a child. What happened between me and your dad was *our* fault not yours.'

'But you would have been together if it wasn't for me being such a spoiled brat.'

I smiled at her and shook my head. 'That's what I thought once, but I know better now.'

Peggy frowned. 'What do you mean?'

'Do you really think that you were the only reason things didn't work out between me and your dad?'

'Yes.'

'Love is a funny old thing, Peggy. You'll find out yourself one day. Do you know what I really think happened?'

'What?'

'I think that we wanted to hurt each other. Me because he married your mum and him because I ran away to London and left him to look after you. I think that in the end we didn't know how to be happy together. You were just an excuse, because we couldn't face up to the truth. We couldn't tell each other how we really felt. I wasn't angry enough and your dad? Well he wasn't strong enough. We pretended everything was all right when it wasn't.'

'You're not just saying that to make me feel better, are you?'

'No, I think I could have knocked one crabby little girl into shape if I'd put my mind to it.'

Peggy grinned and took hold of my hand. 'So it's okay?'

'Of course it's okay, and I'm sorry that you've been feeling like this.'

'I was a pain though, wasn't I?'

'You were an unhappy little girl.'

She nodded.

'And now you've all come home.'

'Just me and Dad.'

My heart was pounding out of my chest. 'And Fiona?'

'She's staying in Australia. She likes it there; she didn't want to leave.'

'I don't understand.'

'I never wore my dress.'

'They never got married?'

She stared at me with Mary's eyes and said, 'My dad loves *you*, Dottie.'

I didn't answer. I didn't know what to say.

'He doesn't know I'm here. I'm supposed to be getting chips. I left him on the pier. He'll be waiting for me.'

'I'm glad you came to see me, Peggy.'

'So am I.'

We hugged on the doorstep and I watched her run down the road. So Fiona wasn't with them. Something stirred inside me. Was it hope?

'Go after her.'

I turned round to see Tristan standing in the hallway behind me. 'What?'

'Go after her, my love.'

I didn't move.

'What are you waiting for? '

'I don't know.'

'The only man who is ever going to make you truly happy is the father of that girl that just went out the door.'

I looked into the face of this dear man, and I knew that what he was saying was true. I turned towards the door then looked back. 'Here goes,' I said.

I hurried down Oriental Place and turned left towards the Palace Pier. Peggy was standing outside the chip shop. 'I waited,' she said, smiling. 'Just in case.'

I gave her a hug, and she handed me one of the bags of chips and a sixpence.

'You'll need it to get onto the Pier,' she said, grinning.

I crossed over the road, put the coin in the slot and squeezed through the turnstile. The pier was packed. It was the end of the summer holidays, and it seemed as if everyone had come to the coast to make the most of the fine weather. I squeezed my way through the crowds, past families, little children in sunhats, men with sunburned shoulders and women who were hanging on to their arms and laughing.

'Excuse me,' I said. 'Excuse me.' And then I saw him. He was about halfway along the pier, leaning over the railings and gazing out across the sea. He was wearing a black jacket, like the one he used to wear, and his hair was still that beautiful red-gold colour that I'd always adored. Even from here I could see that he looked older, a bit heavier, but it was still Ralph. When I saw him I still felt exactly the same as I always had; it was no different now to how it had been when we were teenagers. I wanted to run to him. I wanted to make mad passionate love to him right there in the middle of the Palace Pier with the whole of Brighton looking on. I wanted to hold him in my arms and never let him go, but I didn't, because I didn't have to. I knew that at last we had all the time in the world.

EPILOGUE

It's autumn now, and the leaves on the trees are turning from green to gold, and the days are pulling themselves in, preparing for winter. It's too early yet to think about Christmas, but I've got a feeling inside me similar to the one I used to feel when Christmas was approaching. I feel excited. I feel like I can hardly wait for the next moment of my life to come. I feel happy. At last I know what it's like to really be alive.

I've always liked autumn. It's always been one of my favourite times of year.

'Are you warm enough?' he asks and I smile and say: 'Yes,' and I am, even though the air is so cold that I can see my breath, and the river down below is silvered, as if it might be about to turn to ice.

We are standing close together, our bodies touching all the way down from our shoulders to our feet, and that feels right; it feels how it should be.

We are *so* high up. We gaze out over the city. The sun is low in the sky, and it's sending out a gorgeous light that colours all the west-facing windows on all the buildings, and all the cars and all the trees and all the boulevards, the same shade of red.

'So this was your dream?'

I hesitate a moment. Should I tell him that coming to Paris and standing on top of the Eiffel Tower with the man I loved was never my dream, it was Mary's? She gave me her dream, passed it on to me, and I looked after it for her, carried it with me, held it safe all this time, just as I've held onto my memories of her; my love for her.

I can feel Ralph looking at me. I know he's wondering why I'm so quiet, and the truth is that I'm quiet not just because of

Mary but because I want to remember every single detail of this day, from the moment Ralph and I woke up in bed and made love in that sleepy, delicious way that only happens when two people are completely at ease with one another. I want to remember the breakfast of steaming, sweet hot chocolate served in glass cups at the outside table overlooking the Seine, and the croissants we ate, warm and buttery and so different to the buns we have in England. I want to remember the walk along the Left Bank, looking at all the books in the stalls and the booksellers smoking and looking terribly French and glamorous and the posters and artwork tied to the park railings. I want to remember Ralph saying: 'Let's go into the park,' and how we walked for a while, following the path, and how lovely it was with the autumn trees and the colours of the sky reflecting in the lake. I want to remember the bench on which we sat, underneath the trees, fallen leaves, red and gold and brown, jewelling the grass around us and how Ralph took a box from his pocket and passed it to me and how I opened the box and inside was a ring. It was a simple ring – a gold band with a single small diamond.

'Peggy chose it,' he told me. 'She said you'd like it.'

'She's a very perceptive girl,' I said. Like her mother, I thought.

'It's up to you,' Ralph said, 'which finger you wear it on. I didn't want to presume, but…'

'Are you asking me to marry you?'

He nodded. 'Yes.'

And after that we kissed. We kissed rather a lot, and the breeze picked up the leaves, and they drifted about us like confetti, and in the distance music was playing, and Paris was going about its business being the City of Lights, the most romantic city in the world.

I want to remember how we bought a postcard with a picture of the Eiffel Tower and wrote 'We're going to be married' and posted it to Peggy, who was staying with my mum and dad, so that she'd know we were thinking of her, even though we would probably be back before the card.

I want to remember how we drank a brandy in a bar to warm us up and how the bar was bright and full of mirrors and brass and glass and things that sparkled and gleamed and how I caught sight of my face in the mirror and how my nose and cheeks were as red as the scarf around my neck but how I realised I had never looked more beautiful.

And after that I want to remember how we made our way to the Eiffel Tower and paid the woman in the kiosk for tickets to travel up in the rickety little lift and how closely we stood together as it rattled upwards, the city growing smaller and smaller beneath us. I want to remember how my heart was beating as we made our way out onto the viewing platform, into a sky that was wide and gorgeous with the glowing sunset and the city so breathtakingly lovely beneath and how I was so happy that Ralph and I were sharing this view – that it was something we would always have that was ours and ours alone.

I never want to forget a single second of this perfect day with the only man I have every truly loved.

So I don't say anything.

I simply take hold of Ralph's hand and we stand together at the top of the Eiffel Tower, gazing out over Paris, watching the smoke curl up from a thousand fires in a thousand apartments and counting chimneys.

LETTER FROM SANDY

Thank you for choosing to read my second book, *Counting Chimneys*.

For those of you who have read *The Girls from See Saw Lane*, I hope that you enjoy revisiting all those characters and travelling beside Dottie on her journey into the 1970s.

I would be very grateful if you could take the time to leave a short review, these are so helpful to a new writer and it has been a joy to read the wonderful reviews that you have already posted. Thank you for your support and for buying my book.

If you'd like to keep up-to-date with the latest news on my new releases, just sign up here:

www.bookouture.com/sandy-taylor

I do hope that you enjoyed my story.

Sandy x

ACKNOWLEDGMENTS

I would like to thank my amazing family: Kate, Bo, Iain, Kerry, Millie, Archie and Emma for all the joy you give. You mean the world to me.

For my brothers and sisters, nephews and nieces for always supporting my writing.

To Louise Douglas for your constant help and encouragement. To Louie and Wend with love always. To all my amazing friends. To Jade Craddock for giving me a headache with your edits but making this a better book.

To the wonderful team at Bookouture. Oliver Rhodes, my amazing publicist Kim Nash and my lovely editor Claire Bord, thank you all.

To my readers, thank you so much for buying my book, I hope that you enjoyed it.

And to my agent and friend Kate Hordern for always being there for me and calming me down when I have those little worries. You are wonderful.

I am so glad that I picked the phone up that day. Thank you.

CPSIA information can be obtained
at www.ICGtesting.com
Printed in the USA
LVOW12s0320190717
541842LV00009B/184/P